I0650182

A Perfect Night for Murder

by

Robin Jansen

Antoinette Postell The Lost

Copyright Notice
This is a work of fiction. Names, characters, places, and incidents are either the product of the author's imagination or are used fictitiously, and any resemblance to actual persons living or dead, business establishments, events, or locales, is entirely coincidental.

A Perfect Night for Murder

COPYRIGHT © 2025 by Robin Lee Jansen

All rights reserved. No part of this book may be used or reproduced in any manner whatsoever including the purpose of training artificial intelligence technologies in accordance with Article 4(3) of the Digital Single Market Directive 2019/790, The Wild Rose Press expressly reserves this work from the text and data mining exception. Only brief quotations embodied in critical articles or reviews may be allowed.
Contact Information: info@thewildrosepress.com

Cover Art by *Lea Schizas*

The Wild Rose Press, Inc.
PO Box 708
Adams Basin, NY 14410-0708
Visit us at www.thewildrosepress.com

Publishing History
First Edition, 2025
Trade Paperback ISBN 978-1-5092-6294-6
Digital ISBN 978-1-5092-6295-3

Antoinette Postell The Lost
Published in the United States of America

Dedication

For my Steven who often makes his opinions known.
For my Matthew who hears my stories.
For my Kim who encourages.
For my Kingston and Karter who are clever.
For my Kalen who loves us.
And special thanks to my editor Lea Schizas who has
endless patience and spot-on advice.

Chapter 1

"'She walks in beauty, like the night, Of cloudless climes and starry skies.' Always one of my favorite poems, but I got a better one for ya, Byron. How about: 'She walks in beauty, like the night, tip-toeing among corpses.'" I pose with the book in one hand while I tuck the other under my chin. "It has a bit more zing, huh? Do you approve of my amendment?"

With a violent thrust, I rip the poem from the page and fold it into fourths before slipping it into my rear pocket. Who'da thought I'd be reading British romance again? Ah, my newly discovered love brings it out in me. I return the leather-bound book to the shelf between Robert Frost and e.e. cummings.

A thought strikes. Wouldn't it be fun to know if Byron's love for his cousin's wife was ever satiated? I look at myself in the hall mirror. "If you could have dinner with anyone dead or alive, who would it be?" Playing both parts, I roll my eyes as though trying to decide. "Lord Byron, may I have the privilege of having dinner with you this evening?"

Love. Such a strange thing—one I never experienced—until now. The first time I saw her, she tramped through a park filling with snow, dressed in

1

stark black. The perfect dark silhouette being cloaked in white. Despite her stoic demeanor, her long hair fell down her back in currents as wild ocean waves. Her ridiculous laughter made me smile for the first time in months. Sadness reflected in her scarlet-colored eyes as she viewed the dead. Perfection, at long last.

I studied her while she adjusted her posture and lightly stroked her neck. Her eyes darted around the area as though looking for something or someone. Me? Visually I drew an invisible line down her spine with my eyes. It doesn't make sense that a person can actually feel someone watching them, but somehow, she did. That night our souls were destined. Could these possibly be the very same feelings Byron felt when he met Mary Chaworth of Annesley? ' And all that's best of dark and bright, Meet in her aspect and her eyes.' again Byron's words speak of her.

Though not a poet myself, I am the author of the crime scenes she visits. So far, four in all. Four in Lincoln Park, that is. Not counting the others. People come out of the woodwork like rats, crowding around the scene whenever there's a body. I watch them carefully. They mask their faces with a look of utter horror, but their eyes reveal their true nature as a tantalizing emission of electricity courses through their veins. Though I'm surrounded by the low buzz of people, I prefer to stand off by myself. I need a low profile to observe and study people. I take the opportunity to pick my next victim. Kinda of like grocery shopping in the meat department.

Presently, I'm no more important to her than a misplaced rock in her path. Or, a book without a bookmark. Though arm's length away many times, she has yet to see me. Our first face-to-face meeting needs to be perfect. Well planned. When the time is right, I'll reveal my true self. It will take her by surprise. I love surprises. Surely, she does too. I am her savior.

Living her life by the clock makes it easy to predict where she will be and when. Six a.m. the light in her bedroom switches on. The apartment lights are like her footprints from room to room. Eight a.m., she crosses the street to her VW Bus. Later in the day is trickier. It depends on how long she remains at the office and how many meetings she attends. I, on the other hand, also have responsibilities.

Sometimes, she grabs a quick bite at a particular diner. I sit at the back table while she eats on a stool at the front counter. When her feet hurt, she slowly removes her loafers, or snow boots, and rubs her feet against each other. The wait staff is treated kindly. She is a softer kind of woman and I take note of her frequent acts of charity, like leaving a large tip for the tired waitress with kids. Giving her sandwich to a homeless person. So far, she performs acts of benevolence. This marks her as easy prey. She can be tricked.

Droplets of perspiration form on my brow then drop on my shirt, creating a pattern. "Damn. It's hot in here." The temperature of the room is too warm for my liking. I open the window allowing in the sharp winter breeze. The floor-to-ceiling curtains gently sway, their glass button tassels tinkling against each other.

Turning around, I walk the length of the bookcase, running my fingers along spines. Some are smooth while others are cracked, decade, musty, and rough with age, like certain women. What is her skin like?

Soft? Calloused? Does she use lotion? If so, is it scented? Yes, I know her in part, but there is so much more to learn.

There's a line of mailboxes in the building's foyer. Not one of them bears my name. I stand in front of her windows which offer a clear view of the street from the third-floor apartment. The sound of air brakes draws my attention downward where a city bus pulls to a stop at the corner of Clark Street and Wellington Avenue. People exit as a new crop of late afternoon folks climb the steps hoping to find a seat in an already over-crowded bus. A woman attempts to enter at the same time and pushes against the passengers who are exiting. Women are predictable, vain to a fault, self-absorbed, and shallow.

I must plan and practice our first meeting, like a theatrical performance; a chance meeting at the diner or even on a city bus. This is my first time in her apartment, taking note of her stuff. Her passion is books—gag me, of the romantic genre, she likes stringing buttons for some lame reason; she is smart and analytical, and (a gray cat appears around the corner and stares at me) she has a cat. So unexpected. Something I hadn't calculated at all. I frown. That thing must go. I race toward him, but he quickly disappears.

Traffic pattern sounds change, signaling the change of the day. The afternoon draws to a close. With winter upon the city, it'll be dark soon. Already too much time had been spent here, fiddling about. I will get rid of that damn cat another time.

Before leaving, I need to see where she sleeps. I find her bed chambers, down the hall, second door on the left. To my horror, it's an absolute mess. A moment of disappointment surges, as I wonder if I've gotten it wrong to love her. The space is unexpectedly messy with an unmade bed, scattered clothes, piles of files with papers sticking out, stacked one on top of the other on the nightstand, along with even more on the floor making it hard to move through the room without tripping. The closet door is open, appearing to vomit out all the stuffed clothes inside of it, not to mention the pulled-out dresser drawers with a look of being ransacked. Several pairs of shoes were flung willy-nilly.

I sit at the edge of the bed, doing my best to get my heart palpitations under control. Breathing in and breathing out. Counting my heartbeats. I smile. Then laugh at myself. Obviously, I'd be the neat one in this relationship.

I gather the discarded clothes and put them into the laundry basket. The clothes draped over the back of a chair I hang in the closet. Gently, I shut the dresser drawers. No time to straighten that mess. Shoe mates are now paired together then lined up, toes touching the wall. I push the closet door closed with a click.

A silver frame of a little girl with red curls catches my eye. I pick up the photograph and stare into it. Carefully, I open the frame and turn over the picture. Just as I hoped, there was writing on the back. *Suzette, age 6. Dated twenty-four years ago.* "Suzette? Who the fuck is she? I need to understand her importance since this is the only photograph in the entire place. I hate not knowing this detail. I return the picture to the frame and set it back on the dresser in the exact position.

Arms spread wide, I drop backward into the double bed, making a crucifix with my body before rolling side to side, finding it too small. We need a new bed. A bigger one. One that was just right. "Though you don't see me, I am near. My hand is close. Oh, to be so close that I can smell your perfumed body. I ache." I press her pillow to my face. What if she rejects me? My fingers angrily dig into the blankets. Rejection was a tool of torture never to be tolerated. No, no. Impossible. She was much too kind. She was—Perfection.

It was exhilarating when I stood arms-length away from her, unnoticed. We were nearly shoulder to shoulder at the diner, paying a bill. Somehow, again, she sensed my presence. First, she rubbed the back of her neck. Then her breath caught. A spark slowly wormed its way down her spine, causing her to twist her upper torso, giving off a shiver. At last, she shifted her weight from one leg to the other. Another shiver followed. I stifled a groan. She was so hot.

Hours ago, she lay right here, in these tangled sheets. Impulsively, my hand slides into my pants to feel my erection. *Careful. You don't want to leave DNA just yet. Heavenly treasures. Death draws my beauty to me. Some say there is no god, but I say there is, and we work together. God creates people. I create the dead. She studies the dead. And together, we share the same hobby. TV psychiatrists agree this is an important element in making a relationship work.*

Bodies are merely trinkets I lay at her feet, like a riddle to be solved. Meanwhile, the cat-and-mouse game I play is a great way to begin our love affair.

Late afternoon turns to early evening and rush hour is in full swing. Scattered flakes fall and whirl like confetti. The bottom was falling out of the temps. Soon, conditions would deteriorate—so the channel 9 weatherman says. Religiously, I check the daily forecast. Zero conditions plus snarled traffic equals delay of rescue units. A perfect night for murder.

Ahead of the storm, I tighten the straps on my small backpack. Not much is needed—knife, zip ties, a protein bar. I keep it light to use my energy on other matters. The best weapon is terrified eyes and the muttering pleas for salvation. The quiver of lips. The mouth opens to a stalled scream without a sound emerging—sleep paralysis while awake.

Ah, tonight. Tonight. I revel in the sound of wind as the outside building door closes with a click behind. The cutting wind fuels my veins. The buzz of traffic saturates my body. Pure adrenaline makes striking so effortless. I'm strong, clear-headed…ready. Tonight, she'll appear. She'll feel me there but won't be able to see me, for I am invisible.

The drive across the city to the park is done with relative ease, even during rush hour. Knowing the side streets, the alleyways, the shortcuts are part of my job. Just as the sky turns black, I arrive. Hands in pockets, head down, I stroll the area despite the drop in temp, it's the dead of winter approaching the New Year.

I think of everything. To avoid wearing an accurate shoe size, I select boots two sizes smaller than mine, from a thrift store where the security cameras never work. Thanks to my skills, that is. Wearing clothes that make me appear larger, too. All this is done purely for the prey—the bear in the wood's thing. The bigger the appearance the more threatening. Adrenaline—my cocktail. Fear—their poison.

The snow comes harder, heavier. Wetter. Best not go too far into the park. It's a new unexpected element.

Don't want to get bogged in it.

The wind off Lake Michigan is beastly. I pull on my knit balaclava and search for tree shelter away from the wind. A dark place that is not only near the street but also has a nondescript area creating false safety. There it was. The fir stands approximately three yards from the jogging path. A sign. A miracle. Delighted to find it was easy to move around as I try it out. To enter, I break several smaller branches in the back that are close to the ground. This gives the perfect cover to crouch and wait but also room to work and subdue. To spend time with the victim.

My legs ache from the cold and the crouching position. I shift my body to lean back on my heels. Tree limbs, weighed down from fresh fallen snow, poke my face. I gaze around, giving thanks to god for perfect eyesight. What a pain it'd be for eyeglasses to be smeared with wet or even broken during a struggle.

A long, jittery breath draws unexpectedly. Location is most important, as realtors will tell you. I know that for a fact. Away from the street, toward the lake, is my favorite spot. My locations are never used twice. I need less traffic, zero witnesses, dark, blizzard-like conditions, and dumbass cops. But with all the murderous elements and talk of a serial killer, those crazy joggers have the tendency to run closer to the lighted street lately. And park lights are a definite hazard in the line of my business. It's my own fault. When joggers adjust habits to the threat, I too adjust.

And tonight, I will see her again with dead offerings at her feet. "Ready or not, here I come."

Chapter 2

City Park, Chicago
Toni

Traffic was jammed on Lake Shore Drive, streets were narrowly passable. To get around the snowy mess, Toni Postell made a hard right onto the unplowed side street, caked in ruts of ice. The conditions were too dire to safely drive in. Her headlights caught sight of a young child darting across the street. The surprised look on the young face sent shivers down Toni's spine. Where was the child's parent? Toni glanced about but saw no one else.

Toni quickly spun the wheel in the opposite direction, which sent the out-of-control vehicle careening down City Park's hill, heading directly for Lake Michigan. Pine trees stroked the sides of the vehicle. She gripped the steering wheel hard, her knuckles turning white. Tony panic-pumped the brakes, then pressed them to the floor to avoid hitting a row of conifers. Abruptly stopped, she lurched forward and banged her forehead on the steering wheel. Blood trickled down her face, onto her lips and settled into the folds of her neck. Already she felt the rise of a tender bump. She took a shaky breath and then another.

Dazed, she leaned against the headrest to regain focus. The scenery only seemed to tip and swirl in the headlights. Wipers continued to swipe back and forth—offing flakes. This space was eerily quiet. Dark. It'd be nearly impossible to survive these freezing temps. She had to find the child. Toni stared out the windshield at the frosty air moving around the trees. No silhouettes.

Toni jerked open the car door handle as frigid air rushed into the bus. "Hello?" she called out above the wind. An unexpected urge drew her attention toward the water. There stood the child, coatless, motionless, staring back at her. The child beckoned. Was she flesh and bone or another apparition?

"Are you okay?" Toni took several slow steps forward. Did the child just nod at her? Hard to tell in the flurry of weather. "Let me help you. Please, come with me."

No response.

"I'm a safe person. Come with me. I'll take you home." She held out a gloved hand.

Still no response. The specter melted into the tree line. The mist cleared as her heart picked up. Toni found herself alone, speaking to a sapling. For a moment, she nearly lost her equilibrium. "Seeing things again, eh?" she asked herself. Toni waved her arms, shooing away thoughts.

Moving forward, she nearly fell into steeper snow. Walking unsteadily through white drifts, Toni called Suzette's name, speaking to her in French at times. Was she chasing death or was death chasing her? Cold penetrated her thoughts causing her foggy mind to clear. Finally, she had to admit it was a figment of her imagination. She feared she would lose her way in the park right along with her mind. "Get your shit together," she scolded herself. "Or you'll be taken to the nuthouse, too."

Toni turned back in the direction of where she came. After stumbling around a bit, there were headlights, now dimmed by a dying battery. Easing into the vehicle and banging shut the door, she felt an immediate relief from the bitter cold. Trying the ignition once more she heard click, click. Pumping the accelerator didn't help. The scanner beside her blared: Northeast side of Cook County all units. Stabbing in Lincoln Park.

"Crap."

A squad flashed lights right behind her.

"Crap, crap, crap."

Toni grabbed her purse and checked the loaded gun. She slid it under her seat then buttoned her coat, breathing deeply, not wanting to cause alarm to the officer. Time to stop chasing phantoms and get her head on straight, attributing her muddled mind to bonking her head on the steering.

"I have an 11-54." Approaching the car, the officer spoke into his radio.

"Officer," she said a bit breathlessly while lowering the window. "Took a wrong turn, skidded on ice. Landed here. There was a little girl....I mean, a person. Was checking it out but didn't see anything once I got out. Must have been a dog."

"You mistook a dog for a child?" He seemed suspicious.

"In my defense," —she smiled, trying to sound silly enough the officer might believe her error as normal— "lots of blowing snow out here and it was a quick sighting."

The scanners sputtered and echoed: Cook County

20th precinct all units needed at 4500 North Shore Drive block at Lincoln Park.

"What are you doing with a police scanner?" The officer shined his flashlight on her face, then stepped back as he unsnapped his holster. "Is that blood on you?"

"Whoa. I think you misunderstand. No need for a weapon, officer. I hit my head when I came to a stop. Let me show you my ID. It's in my purse, okay?"

"Okay."

Toni withdrew her wallet ID and handed it to him.

"Excuse me for not recognizing you right away, Special Agent Postell, but are you in need of medical assistance? You seem confused. Let me call an ambulance, but I can also take you to emergency in my squad."

"No. I'm fine, but I need to get to that crime scene."

"Yes, ma'am." He dropped his guard. "Let's get that bus of yours running. You flooded the vehicle; I smelled it on my approach. Easy on the gas this time. By the way, I'm Officer Pirelli."

This time, the engine started. "I'll never hear the end of being rescued by a street cop," she muttered to herself as Pirelli walked away.

The snow let up, but the wind continued. Toni fishtailed a few times driving in the police car's tire tracks. She looked down at her hands gripping the steering wheel and drew in a shaky breath. She hated driving in this mess, especially at night.

Passing townhouses and apartments with a view of the lake, she noted silhouettes peering through windows to watch. Murder was a spectator's sport. Tomorrow the headlines again would be about the police's inability to catch a killer.

The only empty parking spot at the crime scene, which wasn't already taken up by cop cars and flashing lights of emergency vehicles, was next to a green dumpster. After easing into the space, Toni placed the Glock into her holster, then snapped it shut. Next, she checked the Bluetooth snowflake pin on the collar of her wool coat and the recorder in her pocket communicated. It was a handy tool when recalling information. What's remembered and what's said can often turn out to be two different conversations. It was invaluable in building her Murder Book.

Dressed in a long black coat, snow boots, knit hat and leather gloves, Toni pulled up the hood on her coat for added warmth. She slugged through the gusting snow toward the police spotlights illuminating the crime scene of unforgettable horrors.

Chapter 3

Lincoln Park—Crime scene
Jack

Lead Detective Chicago PD Jack Autry hunched over the recent kill. Drag marks in the snow led from the sidewalk along the ground to where the body now lay; in the open and a good twenty yards from the street. A pool of crimson blood spread around the body onto the white snow, crystalizing it.

Autry assessed the scene. All the other victims were hidden beneath firs, but not this time. Most likely Frosty decided carrying dead weight in this heavy snow was too difficult. It looked like after dropping the body, he pulled it for several yards more. The medical examiner just rolled up in his van and his forensic team suited up in hooded one pieces to not contaminate the crime scene. Lights were set around, illuminating the area.

"Autry." Brady, the medical examiner, was a recent hire. He was a surly middle-aged man with three failed marriages under his belt.

"Brady." Jack nodded back the greeting.

"Why couldn't we have gotten a killer who preferred summers?" Brady joked.

"We have plenty of those too. Steamy summers with humming buzz flies and maggots aren't my thing either," Jack retorted.

"I guess you're right." Brady was on his knees with his reading specs studying the body. "I'd say we've got another Frosty event."

"We'll probably be holding a press conference in another ten hours, conference at noon. I need as much information as possible by then." The lead detective was in his mid-forties. Dark hair curled at his collar. Laugh lines fanned out the corners of his mouth even when he frowned, like now. Stubble crowned his square jaw signaling he had put in a long day.

"Where's the sex object of the FBI," he asked, glancing around.

Jack gave a chuckle. "You can't say things like that these days. Special Agent Postell will be here at any moment. Treat her with respect."

"As always. I will." Brady winked. "Geez."

"Her uncle is the head of the Chicago FBI office. Plus, she's nice. Smart."

"Looks like she's charmed you as well as half the force."

"Let's just keep this business," Jack said, feeling wired.

"I hear you." Brady carefully removed snow from the victims face then cussed when the wind picked up to destroy his work, having to start again.

Autry noticed Special Agent Postell approach. As usual, she held her head high while taking long striding steps, looking sure of herself. Postell landed on the balls of her feet, giving her hips a roll. She was the bright spot at any crime scene.

Not delivering her usual greeting, Toni seemed paralyzed as she stared at the body. Then came the flash of horror at the condition. She turned to gag. Jack admired her quick recovery. He understood. Even seasoned cops weren't always able to hold their stomachs at gory death scenes.

"Agent Postell, glad to see you finally made it," Jack said, glancing up. "Are you okay?"

Chapter 4

Toni

Toni regarded Jack Autry with high regard for being the most honest and forthright detective she had ever worked with. He remained stoic and focused at these scenes. While she breathed slowly, trying not to faint—willing herself not to have a meltdown.

And there it was, the victim's face. The body lay on her back, staring up at them. Looking directly at her—or so it seemed. *I shouldn't be here. Others will follow to my death. Hurry.* Almost as if she was accusing Toni of not solving the case sooner. The empty, wide open blue eyes collected snowflakes on her lashes and hair. A frozen mannequin. Smeared mascara and eyeliner circled her eyes where it froze in place as drifts of white grew along her frame. Dried blood matted the long hair.

Toni's tears stung her cheeks while the wind rubbed them raw. Hailed as being the best at solving crimes, she knew she was losing control. Seeing bodies fresh like this had produced a nice sized ulcer in her gut. Peaceful dreams wore a thing of the past, while nightmares and sleepless nights overtook her psyche.

As always, Toni wondered what the anticipation of death was like for this jogger. Did the victim see it coming? Feel it coming? Did it occur during a frenzy of panic when she traded her life for death? Every cell of the body went far beyond mere terror. Thoughts got haywire. Muscles froze. It was a full fledge assault on the nervous system. If she became the victim of a cruel attack, how would she defend herself against an unknown creature who lay in wait, determined to end her life? *So, this is it? This is how I die.*

The blood and pine stench gave off a sweet tang that churned her insides. She gagged again, and turned away from the scene. Head down between her legs, a dog's bark drew her attention. Strays attracted to the scent began their approach. Toni stood and waved her arms. "Shoo! Go away, go!" They took off only to circle back again, this time growling and baring teeth. Packing snow into balls, Toni threw several hitting the animals in their noses and sides. Quickly they turned, disappearing into the landscape.

Jack pulled the police scanner from his pocket. "Someone, get animal control out here, pronto."

"Ten-four," someone responded.

"What've we got?" Not wanting to make a big deal out of her queasiness, she ignored his question.

"Fifth jogger murdered since the first snow."

"ID?" She thinly frowned, noticing the victims' jogging pants and unzipped quilted jacket.

"Nothing."

"He waits for joggers during a snowstorm to attack. Then deposits them under fir trees. Tucking them away," she said.

Brady gave his steel-rimmed glasses a push with the orb of his thumb. "Interesting, isn't it? He brutally murders, but still wants to protect them from the cold."

"I don't think he's protecting them from the cold.

He doesn't like them. He sees them as mere objects."

"Serials don't like an audience," Autry added. "And what statement is Frosty making tonight?"

"Frosty is unsure of himself so he practices dominion over the female gender. After each killing, he feels a certain amount of remorse, so he hides the bodies away. It's interesting because he has an inner struggle between good and evil."

"Murders are complicated," Brady said.

"Most murders are very simple. Especially with serials." Toni squared her back.

"You think it's simple because you're the profiler and know this stuff." Still on his knees, Max Brady's eyes wandered over the body like they were rest stops. "This time the killer finished her off immediately instead of allowing the elements."

"How can you tell?" Toni wanted to know.

"This time he drove the knife all the way into her temporal lobe then twisted causing immediate death. If that wasn't good enough, he sliced her neck. Just for good measure."

"'The night man cometh'," Toni said. "An opera by Charlie Kelly."

"Your cultural education is impressive."

Toni didn't like Jack's tone. It sounded monotone as if she wasn't being any help at all, at least that is how she took it.

"I'm puzzled by his actions tonight too." Toni cleared her tightening throat. Quickly, she wrapped her arms around herself, as body heat escaped in shimmering waves until she could barely breathe. Wholly queasy from the scene, she swallowed hard. "Was the body left out here more exposed to the elements than the others, or did you pull her out after you got here?"

"She was left here, next to the tree, not under it."

"Strange. Frosty's MO is to render the jogger helpless, sit with her till she dies, while hidden beneath the firs. It's his ritual."

"Ritual?" Brady's brows shifted.

"You know, a prayer. A fetish with a particular object. An act he performs which isn't sexual, which we already know from previous autopsies."

"Time of death puts it between ten p.m. to midnight. Okay. Let's bag her." Brady stood.

Toni and Autry stepped back to make room.

"Are you all right?" Jack's breath, scented with garlic and Dijon mustard from fast food, swirled around them. The top of his ears and tip of his nose were fire red from the cold. Toni noticed his all-weather coat didn't seem to work in this weather. For that matter, hers didn't either.

"Yes, of course." She covered.

"Why the shift? Is he evolving?"

"Not evolving. It's unexpected. Something is off about tonight." Toni looked around as though the answer might be out there. "The others were first incapacitated just enough so he could spend time with them. Then leave them to the elements as Brady pointed out. Tonight, he pushed the knife all the way into her temple. No need to hide her body—he was finished with her. No foreplay with death."

"Something happened that he hadn't foreseen?" Brady asked.

Autry stamped his feet to kick snow from his boots.

"Something interfered so he had to work fast. Perhaps she was out with a companion when they became separated, but her partner came up on the scene. Or Frosty was surprised by another person? Whatever or whoever it was, Frosty wasn't finished, and if he left her alive while chasing down the second person, she might escape. So, he quickly finished her off, then went after the other."

"If there were two, why aren't there signs of a struggle?" Brady asked.

"The snow and wind would have covered it. We may have even walked over it."

"A tandem murder." Jack stared at the body.

Toni looked from Brady to Autry. The wind gust made her pull the scarf around her ears and nose—holding warm breath against her face. "Then there's a second body."

Chapter 5

Jack unfurled his arms as he called out to police and CSI team members. "I want a radio blackout. News of a possible second victim is to be kept quiet. Everyone, turn off your radios. Remain at your stations. Do not allow anyone past the tape."

"With all these squads and lights with commotion out on the street, I bet the press from every station are already on their way," Toni said.

"No one gets on my crime scene. Hear me?" Jack hollered to the officers. "CSI team, start fanning out; set up grid markers. Look under trees, bushes, undergrowth…the public restrooms, under park benches, garbage cans, the playground; any place that a body could be stuffed. It's night and in this snow, things are easily missed."

"By trampling all over the park, we could destroy that evidence," Toni said.

"That concerns me too but right now my priority is checking for a second victim, alive or dead." Jack went fir to fir, pressing back the needle spiked branches, searching beneath the frozen undergrowth as limbs dumped snow onto his head and back of his neck.

Toni turned to one of the CSI team members. "Who's the first officer on the scene?"

"I am." A large officer within hearing distance stepped forward.

"Officer Pirelli?" Toni asked in surprise. "Who called it in?"

"A young couple. They were walking their Dobermans between storms when they spotted the body. My unit was the first to respond just a little after midnight. I took their statements. Afterward, when the area was being secured, I drove in a four-block square to see if I could spot anything, or anyone unusual."

"And did you?" Brady asked.

"Yes, I found Special Agent Postell stuck in snow." He glanced at her, seemingly proud of himself.

Jack and Brady chuckled.

"Officer, when you spoke to the couple, did they have anything to offer? Did they spot anyone? Maybe other joggers?" Toni asked as she melted with embarrassment.

He shook his head. "Nothing. No one. I took down their personal information."

"Good. Did you happen to ask what they were doing out in this weather?" She took their information, which he handed to her.

"Just walking their dogs who had been inside all day. If you excuse me, ma'am, I need to get to my post." Leaving hefty boot prints in the snow, Pirelli loped away, his thick frame vanishing in the darkness.

Jack returned, winded. His voice sounded like a dry murmur. "You're right. There's another body."

Toni stood over the second body. It hadn't been dumped, rather it had the appearance of being carefully placed near a park bench under a streetlight. Snow nearly covered the remains. Only a leg and right side of the head could be seen.

"I want lights set up here, and somebody get me

another makeshift tarp to work under." Brady hurried toward them with his medical examiner's bag. "Busy night. And I hate working out in this stuff, but I don't want to lose potential evidence. I want the snow bagged down to the ground in a ten-foot diameter like we did with the jogger."

Once the tent and lights were in place, Brady began the delicate task of brushing snow from the body. Purposefully, Brady turned the victim's head slightly until it faced directly up. Starting at the waist, Brady worked upward toward the shoulders; neck chin, cheeks, nose and when the snow was carefully brushed away from the lids, everyone gasped.

Horizontal pieces of glass were stuck as miniature daggers in the open opaque eyes. Blood slowly seeped into the mix, creating an eerie appearance of ruby colored diamonds glistening under the lights.

"Is that what I think it is?" Autry winced.

Brady gently removed a piece with tweezers. "Glass." Brady continued to brush snow away. "There's more glass in the hair."

"A fall out of a window?" As always, Toni became transfixed by the eyes. She couldn't stop staring at them. It was as though they held secrets they took with them into eternity.

"There are plenty of cuts to examine and measure, but how they got there is still to be determined. Glass in the hair and embedded in the face's skin and neck. Impact had to be hard." Brady began to vacuum the torso, revealing more. "And it's another female victim. But this one is wearing a nightgown and bathrobe. Coat is unbuttoned. She is wearing pink fluffy slippers. Okay, I'm done vacuuming. Let's bag her feet and hands. Get her out of here."

"What was she doing dressed like this in sub-zero weather?" Autry muttered.

"Let me guess—not jogging," Toni said.

"My wife always walks our dog in her bathrobe with a coat over it. Sometimes slippers, sometimes boots."

"Slippers, really? Hey, maybe one of the dogs in with the strays belongs to her?" Toni surmised. "Look, the coat is all jumbled up around her waist, Jack. It was put on her after she died. You can't dress a dead person and make it look right. Someone close to her put the coat on her."

"If someone was 'so close to her' how come she was killed?" Autry said.

"Either the murderer did this or someone who was in the room when she died. Obviously, they took great care to keep her warm. This isn't the murder scene either. She was left here."

Officer Pirelli approached again, stepping into the perimeter. "Got radio blackout, but a bit too late for police chatter. The news people are probably on their way. Whoa. What have we here?"

"Officer, what do you think you're doing!" Brady hollered.

"Sorry." His eyes widened with embarrassment as he glanced around as though wondering where to stand.

"You never step this close to a victim unless rendering aid or collecting evidence which I am now doing. It's not only disrespectful but I fear you might have also destroyed potential evidence. We're losing enough as it is in all this damn blowing snow. Now get away from me."

Pirelli held up his hands and backed away.

"Go stand out there and direct traffic!" Brady pointed to the street.

"Yes, sir." Pirelli stormed off.

The smallish man made the giant of the land obey him. For some reason, the visual amused her.

"What's so funny?" Brady snapped.

"Nothing, nothing at all." Toni waved him off. "Check her pockets for ID," she told Jack.

Jack silently searched. His wiry frame gave him a distinct advantage when working close to the ground, whereas her legs often cramped.

"I need to stretch a bit." Toni stood then walked holding a flashlight. By now, sleet pelted against her coat like big, old nasty spit wads. A large sheet of plastic was caught on a tree limb making a loud snapping sound when the wind caught it and spun about as a phantom. Toni skirted around the police tape and stopped at the outer edge near the pine and fir trees, near to where the first body previously lay. Toni started piecing together the night's events. Cocking her head slightly downward, she spoke quietly into the snowflake brooch.

"Victim two found face up. Glass in eyes and hair. Dressed in a leather coat over a bathrobe. Nightgown beneath. Satin, I think. Expensive. Gown rode up about her waist and skin exposed to the air. Slippers remain on feet. Blood pooled under skin. Frost bite? Or dead for hours before dropped? This crime scene is relatively small. Evidence being collected; snow shoveled into plastic bags. At lab, we'll see what we've got."

Toni took a moment to look around at the exquisite older homes, condos and apartment buildings—some with penthouses. All with spectacular views of the lake. Growing up, this was her neighborhood, along with the friends she attended private school with. How she loved living here with her parents and siblings. Sailing on the lake. Hide and seek in the park with friends during warm weather. It still felt oddly like home. Now she lived in what was known as 'Boys Town'. An interesting part of the city with vintage apartment buildings, small shops, and theaters.

Despite the frigid temp, a crowd remained with a mixed emotion of excitement and fear. Excitement with the activity that would be tomorrow's headlines. Fear of the killer who lunged out of a blizzard to sink a blade into flesh and watch as life drained.

The gentle moniker of Frosty was much too kind. Rather, she'd dub him Monster. However, there was another killer out tonight. A new one. She rubbed her arms. Jack watched her. Ah, he looked straight at her.

Humming, Autry suddenly removed his hands from his pockets, as though meeting his opponent on the ten-yard line. The streetlamp revealed his face had gathered in a mixture of a scowl and irritation. He walked closer. "We have Frosty's killing and now this homicide. Totally unrelated. But the two will be lumped together by the public."

"How can they be lumped together when they are poles apart? The woman is in her night attire with an overcoat for god's sake. And, Autry, just look at the location; it's within yards of the street under a streetlamp which is as good as a spotlight. It looks like she was taken from a car and tenderly laid out, while all the others were hidden deeper in the park under snow-covered brush—discarded. One body was regarded as trash while the other was cared for. Frosty didn't do the street side kill. It's totally wrong from start to finish. There is never ID on the joggers; whether they don't carry it, or whether Frosty takes it, we don't know. By the way, was there ID on the second victim?" The razor-sharp wind made her nose drip. She found a shredded tissue in her pocket along with a crinkled cellophane package of crackers.

"Are you going to eat those?"

"What?" Toni made a face. "These? You must be hungry."

"Missed lunch and dinner. And you're the one carrying them around in your pocket." He grabbed them from her and tore off the cellophane, pushing two at a time into his mouth. "We have to verify."

"Verify? Then there was identification on her."

"Driver's license in her robe pocket. Who carries their license in their pajamas?" He shrugged.

"Show me the driver's license."

"I don't take orders from the FBI." Jack quipped. "This is my crime scene. My city."

"And here I thought we were partners."

"We were partners till you took another job."

His words made her stumble. "Another job?"

Jack seemed angry, or perhaps disappointed. Hard to tell. "I don't know what you mean. We *are* partners. The one and only job I have is this one. Frosty's."

"Here are my conditions—"

"Conditions? Stop right there." Toni held up her hand. "Before you say another word, I want you to know that the FBI doesn't make deals with the Chicago PD."

Anger turned to electricity as they stared one

another down.

"Lower your voice. We don't want the team to think we're arguing." Toni glanced around, hoping no one was listening.

"We—do—this—my—way." Jack enunciated each word quietly.

Toni's smile sank into a smirk. She hated ultimatums and Jack was pushing her.

Swallowing the last of the crackers, Jack reached into his pocket and pressed the plastic into her hand. "Her name is Victoria Taylor."

"Taylor? Whoa, any relation to the Mayor of Chicago?" Toni stared at the photo.

"I also found her government clearance badge." He dangled it in front of Toni, who snatched it.

"His daughter?"

"We just need eyeball verification from a relative."

"Whoever left her wanted her found and identified quickly."

"Listen, Postell, give us a chance to talk to her parents first before this information goes to the Bureau. My department should deliver the news, not the suits."

"Absolutely." Toni softened as she handed back the license and badge. It was time to make nice, find a soft spot in Jack's demeanor. "I'll do it your way."

"Thanks. Just so you know, I hate it when you pull the FBI card." Jack's eyes narrowed.

"And I hate it when you pull the 'this is my city' card." Toni countered. "Look, we have to work together on this. We're one team. Not two."

"You're right. After all, we're partners, right—for a little while longer?" Jack slowly pulled the license and badge from between her fingers and walked with

Toni toward the curb.

"We withhold nothing from one another. From this day forward." She crossed her heart and held up her hand as if taking a pledge. "Complete transparency."

For a fleeting moment, Toni tried to imagine being with Jack somewhere other than at a crime scene. She liked the idea. He might open and tell her something personal about himself. The thought warmed her. She touched his arm.

Jack immediately reacted by smoothing the collar of her coat. "Your teeth are chattering." He smiled. "If this body does turn out to be the mayor's daughter, then this investigation is already in trouble."

"I agree. He has mob connections up to his hairpiece." Toni felt glad she had this conversation recorded so later she could analyze it. "Can you imagine being married to someone like the mayor?"

"Ah, not really." He paused for a moment, as if seeing her for the first time. His voice became low and soft, "You're cold. You need something warm to drink. Toni. A warm bed."

"Yes, Jack?" Her eyes took him in. Being around this cocky detective was both exhausting and exhilarating. The man was passionate, he was smart, and he never flaunted his obvious good looks to get his way.

"It's been quite the night. Two bodies." His voice trailed off.

"Two bodies," she echoed. "And yes, I could use something warm to drink. And sleep. I bet you could as well."

"Yes. I think we both deserve—"

"What?"

"I have this feeling about you." He cocked his head to the side and gave her a smirk.

"A feeling?" She wanted to say more but didn't. It was best to let Jack speak first.

"You're keeping something from me. What?" The inflection of his voice changed.

"Keeping something from you? Are you speaking professionally, or personally?"

"Professionally, of course."

"It's about the second murder. Taylor's killer didn't know the details of the real serial, thinking a dead body in the park would be enough to connect them but it's not. Then Frosty gets spooked by something in the park."

"A possible witness?"

"Make those two living witnesses. Frosty and Taylor's killer. I have a hunch they saw one another."

Chapter 6

Toni

The bodies were loaded. Lights and tarp were packed. Evidence bags were initialed and sealed. Only the yellow tape was left behind to snap in the wind.

Toni sat behind the wheel waiting for her bus engine to warm while watching Jack, who was always the last to leave. She pressed her recorder and listened to the elements of tonight's discovery. Then she fast forwarded to their conversation. Interesting. They nearly had a moment. But thanks to Jack's question about her new career move, the possibility passed. Lost at the crime scene. And how did he find out anyway about her job offer? She sizzled.

The offer still hung in the air, with the contract unsigned. Yea, she lied to him. It wasn't time to tell him, or anyone, about her plans. Besides, she was uncertain and didn't want the offer to get between them unless she took it. There was also another matter that Jack was totally unaware of. She withheld information about Frosty. Being FBI, she wasn't in the habit of blabbing all her information to the PD. Then again, the FBI was also unaware. Maybe she'd be long gone when Jack learned of her dishonesty. Still to be decided.

By now the engine had warmed and heat was blasting, defrosting the windshield and her body. She watched Jack walk toward his squad car. Staring at him from afar was so high school, so unlike her usual self. Normally, she shied away from personal attachments but with Jack everything was different. It couldn't be helped. Didn't want to help it. As far as Toni was concerned, Jack was the slayer of modern-day dragons, making him the hero of her story. Not even subzero wind could take her breath away like the sight of Lead Homicide Detective Jack Autry. Tonight, a murderer prowled Lincoln Park. And Jack Autry prowled her heart. He just didn't know it. And couldn't ever know it.

Mentally, she wasn't ready for a relationship. She'd ruin it and it'd become another black spot in her life.

Working together all these months, Toni came close to asking him out a dozen times, but at the last minute always pulled back. Her feelings remained hidden. Toni didn't want to chance being rebuffed. Instead, their relationship remained business. Dead people and DNA evidence kind of business. Toni felt sure the only way Jack would show interest in her was if she became a victim. He'd feel beholden to solve it. Not exactly her idea of a great romance. Yet, he managed to flood her neurons with emotions of unrequited hope. What was he about to say when he quickly changed the subject? She'd never know now, so she'd write her own ending—the way she wanted it to be. It would go something like: "Let's go on a stakeout. I'll bring hot coffee. You bring the donuts. Make them chocolate glazed."

"I'm leaving the scene of Jack Autry." Toni shifted gears. It was time to zoom back to her little flat where she lived alone with her cat. A treasure she picked up from another recent crime scene, aptly named Perp.

A city snowplow pushed right past. She'd follow in its tracks. Just as she put the bus into gear, lights flashed in her rearview mirror. Pirelli? No, the press arrived on site with the cables and trucks equipped with satellite dishes. All they'd get now was their anchor standing on the curb while pointing at a dark park in one hand and holding a mic in the other. There was a line of news trucks rolling up with their radar swirling about on van roofs. Blowing snow floated in the narrow sphere of headlights.

"The ground helicopters have landed, beware, Jack." That was one in a thousand things they had in common, disdain for news folk. They got in the way and to think she has been asked to become one of them. Even more so, she might even accept. How ironic. They always released information prematurely. Got facts wrong. Almost never cared—just print a retraction somewhere which no one ever read or even heard. Well, she would be different. Honest, forthright. Facts only.

Journalists popped out of their vehicles, slamming doors and yelling instructions as they scrambled for good positions to view the crime scene. Nothing to see here, people. Wind blew their hair while gloved hands wiped camera lens clear. "Damn them." Not wanting to be seen, Toni shoved her gear into park, then slunk down into her seat to watch.

Admittedly, show biz folk were handsome but masqueraded as seasoned journalists. Chosen more for their looks than their skills. Never learning their lesson, they shouted questions at tired lawmen, knowing they weren't at liberty to divulge information. "When are you going to catch Frosty?" The newswoman stamped her feet trying to keep warm.

Autry stiffened as he continued toward the squad car. The impatient expression on his face was priceless. It made her laugh.

The 1964 VW bus was like waving a red flag of information to reporters. She seemed to be the only crazy in a city where parking was at a premium to drive such a large beast. Really, she needed to trade this old bus in for a dark sedan of some sort, one that wasn't always breaking down on her.

Someone banged on Toni's windshield. With a jolt, she turned to see channel 5 reporter's face. Toni lowered the window and was pinged in the face by snowflakes now turning to sleet. It felt like pins. "Geez. Can't you simply knock politely?" Toni noted Miranda Styles' evening attire of a long gown, high heels, with a fur coat. Toni figured it was the real thing. Poor minks.

"I did but you didn't respond. Can you help me here, Agent Postell? I need the name of the dead girl." Miranda shivered.

"I see you've been out. Another evening ruined by another crime scene. By the way, street salt is a real doer on clothes and your rhinestone satin heels are loaded with it."

"Don't concern yourself. Just give me the name of the dead girl."

"Another jogger. No ID." She shrugged.

"I hear there was another body?"

"Two bodies? Is that what you heard?" Toni feigned surprise. "I had no idea. I should be going to you for my information from now on."

"Come on." Miranda's face was a frosted rose. Her false eyes lashes brushed the inside of her eyeglasses.

Toni glanced in the rearview mirror at the heated news truck. An awkward silence grew between them. Finally, Miranda spoke. "What's the preliminary?"

"You know I can't say." Toni pulled an invisible zipper across her lips.

"I hate how tightlipped you all are. Ugh! And I hate how my pen just ran out of ink!" Miranda pitched the pen across the street.

"Ah, that's not good for the environment." Her bus was toasty warm by now. Toni removed her knit hat. Long black tendrils spilled across her shoulders and down her back. "Gotta go now, bye." She waved her fingers once more shifting into first.

"Wait. Do you have an extra pen I can use? Please, at least help me out with some ink, okay?"

"Why not? It is Christmastime after all." Toni bent down to the floorboard and pulled her purse by the strap up into her lap. Raking through the contents, she finally found a pen.

"That purse is so big it could hold a head."

"And I probably have everything imaginable in it, even one of those. Ah, found one. A pen, not a head. Hope it works. Merry Christmas." Toni sat up straight and held it out, but now Miranda was halfway across the street heading for the tightly packed news crew.

Chapter 7

Wellington Ave—Chicago, Ill.
Toni

Twenty minutes later, she circled the block around her building. For the hundredth time, Toni considered using a city garage. Hard to swallow the extra expense, but at three hours past midnight, in sub-zero weather blizzard-like, nearly any price seemed reasonable. The restaurant across the street occasionally let her park in their lot after hours. And 4 a.m. was certainly considered after hours.

With keys in hand, she crossed Wellington Avenue and hurried toward the three-story Greystone apartment building with the curly numbers of 735 scrolled in deco style lettering. The building itself was an old Chicago landmark, built a hundred years earlier in the early nineteen twenties.

The heavy door behind her shut automatically, relocking with loud clicks. Tired, she rounded the newel post, then slowly walked up the carpeted steps till she reached the third-floor landing, with two apartments on opposite ends of the small hall. Once she unlocked the double bolts on her apartment, she stepped into her refuge where her blood pressure eased.

The kitchen to the right. Living room to the left. In between ran the narrow hall with a full bathroom and the only bedroom. Original features in the living room included the wood and multi-tonal tile mantel with molding running around the room. Floor to ceiling shelves were packed with books, files, and mementos. Throughout, the old, plastered walls were painted sage. By the looks of her furniture, a pristine chenille couch, a mahogany pie crust table, and fringed shade on the iron floor lamp, someone from the 1920's could have been transplanted into Toni's apartment and never would have guessed that one century had passed and another century was decades old, except when they turned around to see the state of art technology, which sat prominently against the long wall; top of the line computer system, fax machine, printer, scanner, stereo, DVD player, Wi-Fi, 500 TV channels.

The opposite side had three large bay windows with the view of the cross streets of Clark and Wellington, framed by heavy velvet drapes. In between each curtain panel were long strings layered with antique glass buttons which hung from the rod to the floor. At daylight, mini rainbows spun through the room. Collecting antique buttons was the one impractical dalliance she allowed herself.

Toni hung her coat, scarf, and hat on the hall tree, along with her purse and holster.

The Russian Blue cat circled her legs.

"Dinner is very late, huh? Or is breakfast quite early?" She lovingly scratched behind his ears. Perp followed Toni into the kitchen where a freshly opened can of cat food was placed on a highchair. Perp jumped up to eat off the tray.

Toni returned to the living room to check email. The envelope containing the invitation to her sister

Mallory's New Year's Eve party caught her eye. She tapped the invite against her cheek, wondering if she should ask Jack to accompany her. What would be his answer? If he said 'yes', what did they have to say to one another all evening? Awkward. If he said no, that would always be between them. Awkward-er. Dreams were safer than reality. No, she wouldn't ask Jack. In fact, she wouldn't even go. Toni tossed the invitation out and clicked on her electronic Murder Book documents; then opened the file named FROSTY. A new date and information needed to be added—todays. She read the dates in order.

Oct. 17th—first victim first snowfall

Nov. 10th—second victim, second snowfall

Nov.15th—third victim, third snowfall

December 19—fourth victim snowfall.

December 19—Victoria Taylor. Unrelated to Frosty. Fifth victim found in the park.

Not long ago, a monster came to the city of Chicago. He killed dental assistant Mary Perkins on Oct. 17th, librarian Helen Noosa on Nov. 10th, dance teacher Betsy Lopez on Nov. 15th, and a Jane Doe Dec. 19th.

From her case file, Toni pulled up pictures of the women searching for physical similarities. Hair color varied, as did their heights and weight. They were all between twenty-five and thirty to thirty-five. Obviously, he didn't have a physical type. There had to be something that either triggered him about each individual woman, perhaps a trait, or a connective thread of knowing Frosty, or tied to a particular place.

Men who prey on lonely, unsuspecting women to bilk them of their life savings only to disappear are bad enough. Blue collar crimes are usually the kind of cases she worked. Most of the investigations were done by computer to track the perps or in person interviews. Since October she worked the serial murder park case. Serial killers love the thrill of the hunt and just as the victim relaxes, in a familiar place, they jump, dumping their body. It put her in mind of her ex. "By the way, ex-fiancé William, being dumped is never a good feeling, even if it's just figuratively."

The landline rang. *Please not tonight, Frosty. I am so tired.* Frosty phoned after each kill to revel in his achievement. It was an umbilical cord he used to tie himself to Toni. Not only did it frighten her, but it changed her behavior. She hated him for altering her life. Hated herself even more for not telling Jack, or the FBI, but she had her own reasons. Try as she may not to answer, she always did. Not only to build her profile further but hoping to nail his ass sooner.

"It's late." She stifled a yawn when she answered.

"What no greeting of 'hello'?"

"Hello." She rolled her eyes. Her stomach growled, reminding her she hadn't eaten since yesterday's breakfast.

"It was a lovely evening for a jog in the park, don't you agree, Special Agent Postell?"

"Not such a lovely evening for everyone, Frosty."

"Frosty! There it is again. I love that name. Love that name. It sounds so delightful like a refreshing drink. What flavor should I be?"

"What flavor do you want to be?" She kept her voice steady, without emotion.

"Peach? Strawberry? Apple? Cranberry? I know, how about a bloody Frosty?"

She punched the button on the phone to record their conversation. Her hands shook but she forced her voice to remain even. "The name 'Frosty' is so misleading. It came from a newspaper reporter. I'd like to know your real name. The one you were given at birth?"

"Howdy Doody, Grace Kelly, Andy Williams—Marilyn—"

"Stop." She interrupted, rubbing her forehead, wondering if these calls would ever lead her anywhere.

Three stories up, he was like a phantom haunting the place: looking through walls, gazing in windows. There was a bay of them. Toni crossed the room with the phone and peered out to the street. The sky was clear. Morning colors of daybreak were minutes away. Strings of antique glass Czech beads and antique buttons clashed against each other, making a tinkling sound.

"By the way, Agent, you should be stern with Detective Autry."

"How so?"

"Don't let him push you around. He can be so misogynistic. You have every right to see evidence especially the ID."

"Ah, so you saw and heard all that. How?" He had to have been within earshot. Could she have reached out and touched him? If so, he had to have been part of the team. She felt a rush of panic. She closed her eyes and concentrated on breathing.

"You know I am accurate." His voice sizzled with delight. His voice sounded distorted with the synthesizer he spoke through. "It was a real circus at the park tonight with me as the ringleader. Even Autry had no clue till you sorted it out for him."

Toni's thoughts kept whirling. Maybe he wasn't part of the team, only dressed as one. It wouldn't be unusual for a murderer to stick around a crowded crime scene to watch. In all the commotion and blowing snow, it was perfect cover for someone who didn't belong.

"Grrrrr. Are you still there? You've gone silent on me."

"You didn't call to talk about Autry."

"Special Agent Postell, you are a very clever girl. But take heed. I am even more clever. You and me. We are a good match."

"We are nothing alike." Toni picked up a Ticonderoga pencil from the desk and threaded it through her long hair. Yet, it was an interesting concept that he thought so.

"No, Special Agent. You have no idea who I am. It's possible you saw me and didn't recognize me. Slipping much?"

"I may not know your face, or name—but you are predictable."

"Predictable?" he grizzled.

Now he was the one who seemed unnerved.

It felt good to push him off kilter. "All one needs to do is watch the weather report. Boom. You are out hunting joggers in Lincoln Park."

"You talk like a smartie pants. If you know where I am going to be, why aren't you there to stop me?"

"Tell you what; next time, let me know your exact time, day, location. I'll be there waiting." Her voice raised in irritation.

"You should jog in Lincoln Park some dark

evening in the snow. The summer solstice will be upon us in several months so there is only so much time left. I'll be like Frosty the Snowman and melt away come this spring. But let's not talk about that. Our time is limited."

"You don't plan to stop the killings until the snow stops?" The hair at the back of her neck rose. In Chicago, that could be early May.

"I didn't say that."

Toni remained silent.

"I think you'll like me when you know me better. It's always fun talking to you. You're exactly what every crime scene needs, a profiler with a wicked sense of humor. Tell me, do you ever think of me—sexually?"

Toni's breath caught. Another silence ensued. Seconds ticked. His insanity held captive, trapped in his game, to make her profile more detailed. Right now, she was the only one he openly spoke to as his true self. It was important to ferret him into the open to stop these murders. She held the receiver tightly, feeling her hands shake, willing her calm to return. "Yes, I do think about you. You are my job," she finally said.

"Do you dream of me?"

"I dream of getting you off the streets."

"In chains? Oh, some S&M? Ask me anything. Get personal."

"What drives you to kill?"

"Ah, come on. Play with me. I've watched you. You appear solemn, stiff, well put together. I'd like to undue you. Let down your hair, Agent, and fly with me."

"I do find you interesting in a psychological way.

How do you select the women? Or happen upon them? And why during blizzards?" She ignored his contempt. "It was a bad night for you."

"It was a de-light-ful night for me."

"Let's discuss your latest victim."

"Yes, let's."

"You hurried tonight. That interests me."

"Which victim are you referring to? The body in the park, or the one near the street?"

"The body near the street isn't yours." She knew the difference and now he couldn't take credit for it. Hopefully, he would snap, give himself away, lead her to him. With each dead girl, Toni felt more and more responsible. Guilt. She rode it like a storm that never dried. It began years ago with Suzette. That was her first failure. "The one near the street interests me more."

"The street? The street? Who the fuck cares?"

"I care."

"Since I had nothing to do with that one, therefore I won't discuss it."

"You saw who did." Toni kept her voice steady.

"You are darn toot'n I did. I am not talking about any other murder, do you hear me?" he shouted. "Mine is the important one. The one near the street is irrelevant. You need to take notice."

"I do take notice. The Chicago PD takes notice. All of Chicago takes notice. The FBI takes notice. We all want to help you." Toni's tone softened, hearing his rage. The last thing she wanted was to set him off that he commits another murder because of it. "I only need your help. Help me."

"I relieve their pain and suffering. The world is an

ugly place. Filled with starvation. Hatred. Cruelty. I rescue them from all that."

"You can't rescue them."

"I chose for them and for you."

"You chose for you." She stared off remembering the faces of the dead women.

"*Thus mellowed to that tender light which heaven to daudy day denies,*" Frosty replied.

Toni perked up. Where did she hear those words before? Thankfully they were on the recorded line to listen again. "Would you repeat what you just said?"

"Did you hear this might have been the coldest night of the year so far?" Frosty sang rhythmically as he cut her off.

"You saw the other killer and they saw you," she mimicked. Hair along her arms pricked. She pulled the pencil from her hair and tossed it across the room. "Frosty, you always control every aspect of the crime scene, but not tonight. Tonight, the crime scene controlled you and made you change your behavior. Because of it, you are running scared. This I know. I'm going to find you, Frosty, because you're nothing but a monster, and monsters mess up sooner or later. Now tell me. Tell me about the person who dropped the girl in murder scene two?"

The phone clicked. Poof. He was gone. *Damn, I pushed too hard.* Toni got up from her chair and walked the room. There was something odd. Something out of place that didn't fit. What was it? The air felt haunted. Toni remained centered in the space, her eyes searching for what she didn't know. Then she focused on the bookcase. There it was. All her books were set in a perfectly straight line, side to side, top to bottom.

Except for one. As though a snake might be hiding there, she carefully pulled Lord Byron's book from the shelf. The space was only slender enough to hold the volume. Nothing more. Maybe that was it? A poem of Lord Byron? She listened to the recording and then flipped to the index to get the page number, but the page was missing. All her college texts were bought second hand. Margin notes, highlighted sentences, missing pages were the norm. Toni slid the book back into place being sure the binding matched the edges of the others.

Chapter 8

Toni

By now, sunlight cruised over the tops of the buildings, sending rays through the buttons and beads, painting miniature rainbows on the wall. Breathing deeply to quiet herself, she began tapping at the top of her eyebrow's forehead, cheeks, down to her underarms to relieve anxiety, a trick she learned from watching an Instagram meditation. Hitting all seven meridian points, she felt better. In control.

It was then she felt a draft. Aware of traffic noises. The rumble of a garbage truck drew closer, making its way down the street. The everyday sounds made her feel normal.

Wait. Colors and sounds and a draft. No, that was wrong. Suddenly, it occurred to her she shouldn't be hearing the street. A clatter of buttons tinkled. Toni turned to see a breeze coming in through a slightly opened window, parting a draped panel that curled from the wind. The buttons kept clattering.

The windows should be closed. Not open. Tightly locked. Why hadn't she noticed this as soon as she walked in hours ago? She closed them the day before she left her apartment. Or had she forgotten? With so much on her mind, it was hard to keep up with the small everyday stuff she did automatically Stepping into the morning sunlight flooding the spot on the wood floor, Toni paused to listen for out-of-place noises in her apartment.

Had Frosty broken into her domain—her safe place? Had the call come from within her apartment? Panicked, she quickly moved to recheck both the front and back door.

Silently, she removed her Glock from the holster. Knowing all the squeaky points of the old wooden floor, she tried to avoid them. With her weapon pointed toward the floor, at her side, she slowly tiptoed down the hall, back against the wall.

At her bedroom door, she wasn't sure what or who was inside—if anyone. Glock now at waist level, she swung around the corner, turning on the light at the same time. Her eyes widened as she witnessed an orderly room, far from what it looked like just this morning. Toni got to her knees to peer beneath the bed. Next came the closet. Shoving aside hanging clothes from one side to the other, holding them up. Nothing.

The laundry basket was filled with the clothes she had worn all week, instead of on the floor where she dropped them. Or thought she dropped them. The clothes she put over the back of her old upholstered armchair were now hanging in the closet. Or was she doing things she couldn't remember simply due to stress? That's what looking for another less oppressive career was all about. Taking pressure off her that she could concentrate on living a more untethered, unstressful life.

Nothing seemed to be out of place on her dresser, and glad to note Suzette's picture was placed just as she had left it. One by one, she pulled out her dresser drawers. They appeared to be the same, rifled through, by her.

Toni began to question herself. Was she so tired at night that she cleaned up after herself and forgot about it? Perhaps she forgot to close the front window as well? She turned to see her bed was still unmade. Was she doing things like straightening her bedroom without being aware of it? As a child she slept walked. It was the talk of breakfast whenever it happened. Toni's mother never mentioned she cleaned in her sleep.

Stepping back out into the hallway, she looked behind the door in the small bathroom. No one. In the kitchen, she slowly opened the pantry door. Empty. Only extra paper towels, toilet paper, and unopened cat food sat on the shelves—the important things. Lastly, Toni checked the backdoor. Secured.

Now she made sure all the windows were locked. Turned on the security alarm. For several minutes, she stood in the hallway, unmoving, barely breathing, waiting for out-of-place sounds. It was quiet. Just to be safe, tomorrow she'd call the locksmith and have all new locks put on the doors.

Exhausted, Toni had just enough strength to crawl into bed, where Perp had already tucked himself into the fold of a pillow. Lying on her side, Toni kissed the top of the cat's head and listened to his sleepy purr. She stared at the window to a spot where ice had collected on the inside then melted, making the wallpaper peel away—yellow roses against a white background. She heard the grandfather's clock in the hallway strike eight times. Eight a.m. and all was well. Thoughts of Frosty behind prison walls filled her with happiness and determination. Just as she drifted off to sleep, a commotion of screams came from the apartment across the hall. She lurched out of bed, navigating the narrow gap between the end of her bed and stacks of Frosty files, and headed toward the door. She stopped long enough to pull on her coat and slip the Glock into the pocket.

Chapter 9

Frosty

Tonight's bodies were heavier than the others due to the deluge of snow that made it more difficult. My anger grew. How maddening to always shift plans, factoring in variables like body weight of the target and the moisture of snowfall. I was the player. It was part of the puzzle sweet Antoinette tried to put together. She played the game with me while acting all concerned over those dead women. Only I know the truth, she didn't fool me. Not for a moment. '*Of cloud filled skies meet in her aspect and her eyes'*. "Dead eyes are my goal. They don't see a thing and their tongues don't speak."

Maybe I need to be patient a bit longer. But if Sweet Antoinette rejects me, even once, there would be one choice—death. After all, I do this for her. It's about time she takes notice and quits gaming. The puzzle she plays will lead her to me. Only then will she understand the depth of my love. It will set her free.

After that, we'll skip on out of the city leaving all this death making behind. Find a place we can settle in as a happy couple, perhaps in a warmer climate. Near the ocean. I bet Toni looks great in a bikini, but she might prefer a one piece. Whatever she wears is my choice. The man of the house, namely me, will be the breadwinner and she, the stay-at-home wife. I'm sure she'd rather cater to me than traipse all over town hovering over dead bodies. No, I'll take her away from all that. All day, she'll dream of me coming home. First, we'll make love, then have dinner.

What new job can I get? I stroke my forehead in thought and settle on the couch thinking about it. Certainly not the one I now have. The only reason I still murder is to catch her attention. Romance. That's what she wants. That's what she will get. Okay, so I had a similar problem years ago. I was much younger. Who can blame a kid who just turned eighteen for finally trying out sex? And murder.

Mom and I vacationed at a ski resort in Wisconsin—a place called Lake Geneva. Skiing was new to me. I was signed up for lessons and then there she was. An expert ski instructress. Much older by ten years at least.

Everyone called her Stormy. Gorgeous girl with large blue eyes and hair so blonde that she stood out against the gray sky. After our lesson during the day, we started skiing together at night under the resort's spotlights. On top of the Majestic Hill, one could see the lights of the town sprawled out along the shore. It was my first intimacy. She seemed willing but I found it hard reading signals.

Naked in the snow from the waist down, pants around my ankles, I didn't even feel the cold. Flesh touching flesh electrified me. Stormy's skin was soft. I said 'I love you' just as I finished. That made her laugh. Stormy thanked me as she pulled up her snow suit. Once on her skis again, she gave herself a push down the hill with her poles. Still unsure of my ability to ski, especially in the dark, I went slowly. Yet, I was happy. In love for the first time. Mother was wrong. It was good to let someone into your life.

When I reached the lodge, I looked for Stormy, but she wasn't anywhere to be found. Someone told me she left for the night. The next day, she was back to instructing beginner skiers but refused to take me on again as a client. Said her class was too full. That day a monster emerged. I sat below the hill and watched as she laughed with an older man. Then touched his arm. Stormy was a slut.

If she hadn't been, she probably would be alive still.

Chapter 10

Toni

Christmas music blared from the opposite apartment. There were screams, which made Toni's heart hitch, but when it was followed by a bit of laughter, she realized it had to be a get-together, albeit an early morning one. There was even an aroma of sugar cookies in the air. Deeply sighing, she turned around to return to her place but then realized the commotion was so loud, she'd never be able to sleep.

Toni padded across the hall in bare feet, where she pounded on the door with her fist and then pressed the doorbell numerous times.

The door swung open. There stood pudgy red-headed Jo Kline with her cheerful pixie face. "How nice to see you! I'm positively thrilled you've finally decided to accept the invitation to my cooking class. This morning, we're making and decorating Christmas cookies. Attention everyone! Look, Toni Postell from across the hall is here," Jo chattered.

Cheers of welcome resounded from inside the apartment, echoing through the stairwell. There was so much applause, Toni nearly felt obliged to take a bow. But didn't.

"Don't just stand there. Come on in. Give me your coat." Jo stepped aside to welcome her into the apartment while Tony stepped back. No one was about to touch her.

"We have some lemonade and little finger sandwiches, pretzels, chips, salsa, brownies, and tons of festive Christmas cookies too. Homemade, not store-bought. The store-bought ones gag me—do they gag you, too? We're exchanging recipes and you don't want to miss. I'll give you my recipe so you don't feel left out."

Someone shoved a red paper plate into her hands piled with two layers of beautifully decorated cookies.

"No!" Toni remained at the doorframe, needing both hands to keep the plate from tipping its contents onto the floor. "I'm not here to join your 'festivity'. I'm here to complain about your noise level. Look, I was up all-night working."

"Oh, you must have the night shift at your job." Jo lifted her hand to her mouth.

"Yes, that's right, I do. Now I need to sleep." Toni's tone softened.

The cookie celebration and music suddenly ceased, the ensuing silence rushing toward her like a tsunami. The group stared at her finally aware she wasn't here to learn cookie making after all. Jo's eyes were huge, and her mouth hung open as a broken screen door with a missing hinge.

"I need to rest. So shh-h. And, ah, Merry Christmas to all and to me a 'goodnight.'" Toni smiled sweetly. She tried returning the plate, but Jo just sadly turned and shut the door in her face. "Well that wasn't neighborly."

Now someone pounded on the building's front door, downstairs. Someone buzzed the person in as she heard the door open and then shut.

"Postell! Where are you?"

"Jack? I'm up here!" Toni was elated Jack was here.

The unexpected visitor took two steps at a time coming closer and closer. The old floors creaked beneath his heavy feet. She smiled with anticipation and looked down at her nightgown sticking out from between her coat flaps. Her hair was a mess. She tried smoothing it out with one hand, wishing she had taken the time to shampoo it when she first got home.

"What are you pulling on me, Postell?" Jack never looked angrier. That was saying a lot.

This was not a social call. "What are you talking about?"

Jack shoved a newspaper in her face. Toni pushed it back and read the headline MAYORS NIECE FOUND MURDERED. Victoria Taylor's name was neatly printed in boldface just beneath her picture.

"Oh, so Victoria Taylor wasn't the mayor's daughter, but his niece. Interesting."

"I'll never trust you again, never," he growled. "You said you'd keep the name to yourself until the family had been informed."

"I did—so, how'd it end up in here?" Toni was puzzled.

Jack grabbed a red and white Santa cookie off her plate. It disappeared in two bites. He exchanged the newspaper for the entire plate. "Miranda Styles said she got the name from a female FBI agent. I saw you two talking at the park."

"I'm innocent."

"In fact, I'm on my way to the Bureau right now to

get you off this case."

"Good! You do that. And while you're there, be sure to ask to speak to the Director of Chicago's FBI, Charles Palmer. He's the one who put me on the Frosty case."

"FBI Charles Palmer, I know him, and I will!" Jack hurried back down the steps, the plate still in hand. The outside door fluttered shut.

With a swing of her hip, Toni slammed closed her apartment door then twisted the bolt locks.

Beyond exhaustion, Toni headed for bed when her coat on the hall tree caught her eye. The snowflake pin was still on the collar. Following the cord down into her pocket she discovered the recorder was gone. How did that happen? Someone had to have gotten close enough at the park to lift it from her pocket. And that could've been nearly anyone, only Miranda was her best bet. She could easily have snatched it when Toni reached for the pen in her vehicle. Angry, she dialed Miranda's office. It went to voicemail. "You can run but you can't hide. We need to talk. By the way, I need my recorder back."

Toni flopped into bed, angry at Miranda, angry with the neighbors, and angry with herself for being angry with the neighbors. But glad to be angry with Jack for his lack of trust. Anger felt better than heartache.

Snuggling down into her covers, Toni listened to the silence of her apartment noting it was also quiet next door. She might have hurt their feelings. Maybe even crying into their cookbooks? No, probably eating delicious food. No one ever talked when there was good food to be eaten.

Toni turned in her bed and faced the wall. Between

the bed and the wall was a side table. On it was the framed picture of four-year-old Suzette. "Oh, *ma petite* Suzette. *Je t'aime, je t'aime*."

"Bye, bye, Toni. See you later." Why did she remember those words with such clarity when other facts about that day were lost? Little Suzette with the red curls; the blue dress and Peter Pan collar. A big smile on her sister's face as she gazed back over her shoulder toward the camera.

Toni closed her eyes to hold back the tears that seeped between the lids. The numb feeling of the black hole began creeping closer; she tried to resist but the power of its pull was dreadfully strong. *Oh, Susanna, don't you cry for me.* Here came the nightmare which filled her bedroom and dominated her life. It was as if she were a restless soul wandering the graveyard with no plot to fall into. Christmas was near and anything, but sugarplums, danced in her head.

Chapter 11

Toni

Hours later, the call came from the mayor's office, directly from the horse's double chinned chops. Toni arrived at the city's administrative center early afternoon. Seated next to her was the FBI Director of the Chicago office, Special Agent Robert Palmer—her mother's brother and reason she chose the FBI as a career. Across from them sat the obese Mayor of Chicago. Cigar smoke rose above his head like smoke signals.

"I'm sorry to meet you, sir, under these circumstances." Toni offered her hand.

"Me too, Special Agent Postell. And thank you." The mayor reached across the desk to shake her hand. "Today is particularly hard for my family and me, so I'll get right to the point." Wearing grief on his face, she noted he hadn't gotten his hairpiece precisely on straight this morning; it was a tad askew, wishing she could tug it into place for him. "I hear you were at the park last night on the Frosty case when the body of my niece was found."

"Yes, sir, that's correct." Toni was dressed in a modest tweed skirt and lined blazer over a silk blouse. She pressed her legs together and looked down at her best pumps, noticing a thin line of dried street salt on the heel. She reminded herself only to answer the questions she'd be asked, offering nothing more. Unasked information may swing things in a direction she didn't need to go.

"What's your take on this crime."

"I assume you're referring to Miss Taylor, and not Frosty."

"I don't give a hang about this Frosty character. Only about my niece, unless…in your professional opinion, her death connected to the Lincoln Park murders?" His lowest chin jiggled when he spoke.

"No, sir, I don't." Toni cleared her throat and sat taller, squaring her shoulders. "But—we need further investigation."

Director Palmer nervously cleared his throat. Perhaps he was concerned she'd give away too much.

"I want to know everything you know so far."

"Everyone may not agree with me on this, but I believe they are two different cases. As I said moments ago, it's still early."

"Really?" he said with amazement. "Tell me why not."

"There are several reasons. First off, Frosty is brutal about the girls he leaves, the way we find them; shows no remorse, no emotional connection. He enjoys ambushing. A surprise attack throws them off balance, giving him the advantage. He sees women as disposable, and his assaults are well planned. On the other hand, Victoria's killer tried to make it look like the serial by discarding her in the park. Her death was unplanned, perhaps an accident."

"An accident?" The Mayor jumped in surprise. He squashed his cigar into the large ashtray. "Tell me more."

"Whoever did this cared enough to put her in a coat. Keep her warm. Protect her. Even her driver's license and security badge was on her for quick identification."

"Wait, you are saying, even though Victoria was dead, her killer still wanted to keep her warm."

Agent Palmer leaned forward. "I know this is hard for you to hear. Perhaps we should stop here."

"Quiet, Palmer. I'm talking." The mayor glared at Palmer, then smiled at Toni. "Go on."

The change in demeanor made her blanch. No one had ever spoken to her uncle in such a brisk manner.

"It's someone who knows her. Cares for her. Victoria's killer is unorganized in his thinking. He wasn't prepared at the time of her death, which makes me feel it wasn't premeditated, but rather a crime of passion—maybe even an accident, as I said."

"If it was an accident by someone she knows, why not call an ambulance." Tears gathered in his eyes.

"I don't know, sir, but I'll find out."

"Someone close to her did this." He repeated as his eyes trailed from her hands to her eyes.

"Yes, I believe so." Toni nodded. "Although she may not have even known them. But the person who left her at the park felt an attachment to her. Real or imagined."

"I see." He leaned back in his leather chair. "This morning I called the Chicago's branch of the FBI and spoke with your boss here. Special Agent Palmer tells me you're the best profiler. After speaking to you, I agree. It's going to take the best to catch the killer. At my request, you've been pulled off the Lincoln Park

murders and give this your full attention. Top priority."
He slammed his fist on top of the desk.

Displeased, Toni tried to hide her shock. Normally it'd be a plum case which she'd eagerly accept—no more Parkside bodies with eyes wide open in panic. There'd just be interviews, investigation, as her cases once were. But what would Frosty have to say about it? His reaction could be retaliation or escalation of the killings. Her stomach twisted.

Desk and pencil sort of investigation with endless leg work of interviews. The kind of stuff she relished. Yet, she was fully committed to the Lincoln Park murders. Having worked with the Chicago PD for months, she felt duty bound to see it through. Severed from this case, Toni felt betrayed by her uncle. She cleared her throat and moved slightly in the armchair. "I thank you for your confidence in me. However, I feel a particular loyalty to the Lincoln Park murders and prefer remaining with this case until the time my resignation takes effect."

"Your resignation?" Taylor shook his head. "What's this about?"

"I assure you there are many other profilers with more years of experience that are quite excellent." Toni smiled.

"Oh?" Mayor Taylor shot an annoyed look at Palmer. "You left this information out."

"Yes, I told you she was extremely faithful and committed. She knows people. And it's just those short of qualities we need on this most important case." Palmer tried to chuckle lightly before addressing Toni in a firm tone. "Agent Postell, this isn't a matter of what you'd rather do, or not do. As of this moment, you've been reassigned, and your resignation is terminated. You'll finish out your original contract."

Flabbergasted over the unexpected change of assignment, there was no use to plead her cause further. She was under orders. Buried. She glanced at her purse containing her unsigned contract.

Shifting gears mentally, furious, she held her temper. "In that case, I'll need a list of relatives and friends."

"I anticipated your request, so I had this readied for you." Taylor opened the top desk drawer and pulled out three sheets of names, addresses, and phone numbers, all neatly typed. These papers she would read in private. Toni folded the papers in half and slid them into her briefcase.

"Thank you. It'll make a good start." Toni felt disciplined. Overridden by men.

"Another good resource would be Beulah and Scott Collins."

"Friends?" She didn't smile.

"No, no, no. The Collins are the married pair that takes, rather took, care of my niece and her residence."

"Were they present the night of the murder?"

"No, it was their night out. I believe they were visiting with their children in Park Ridge."

They knew her daily routine, patterns, friends—secrets too? Toni wondered as she made a note. A great lead. "Anyone else?"

"My niece was employed here. She managed my outer office with utmost efficiency." He pressed the intercom button. "Celia, I need a list of all our office employees with their address and phone numbers."

"Right away, sir."

"Could we also get a list of everyone coming to this office in the last six months? Even for a lunch date with anyone? Type of business? How often they visited and who they visited with? Anyone who flirted with Victoria, or if she mentioned anyone who made her feel uneasy?"

Again, the mayor contacted Celia for the information.

"I'll need several days to complete this," she responded.

"As soon as you can. Set aside all your work in the meantime." He clicked off the intercom.

"In situations such as these, Mayor Taylor, the FBI first looks at family members. It's important we clear the members so we can start spreading our investigation out from there, eliminating possible suspects one by one. We do that with a polygraph test. I want to start with you. This will be an excellent way for the other family members to feel more compliant by your example."

"Of course. I don't mind being hooked up to a poly. I welcome it. It'll be a show of trust for the city as well. I don't want gossip hitting the papers that I refused the box."

"Would today be all right?" Toni pressed.

"No, it's not a good day. I'm helping with the service arrangements and we're expecting out of town family for the funeral. I'll be in right after the first of the year with my wife."

"January first?"

"All right, January first." His voice broke, tears filled his blood-shot eyes.

"Do you need a private moment?" Toni started to

rise from her chair.

"No." He waved her back down. "This is important. Continue with your questions. Please."

"All right." Toni cleared her throat then diverted her eyes from his for the moment. "Did your niece have a husband, fiancé, boyfriend, significant other?"

"No husband, but there were always boyfriends. They're included on the list. Um, Ms. Postell, I hope you understand there are details of her life we don't want released to anyone, least of all the media."

"I'll treat this with the outmost discretion. You have my word."

"Find the psychopath that did this to her."

"Excuse me, sir, but I don't think we are looking for a psychopath."

"Agent Postell, please, you don't need to school the mayor…"

"Shut up, Palmer. You said she's the best, now unleash her," the mayor growled as he rapped his knuckled on the wood desk.

Toni drew in a big gulp of air. "With no signs of forced entry, and Miss Taylor dressed the way she was, in her nightgown and bathrobe, I would suspect it was someone she knew quite well. I'm sorry. I'm not suggesting anything here. Although it would have been an unexpected visitor."

"Profile?" Taylor asked.

"It's premature to draw a conclusion. I must inform you that at this stage of inquiry, everyone is a suspect, including you and your wife, the Collins couple as well. I think that's all we need for now. Thank you for your assistance, mayor."

The mayor stood and walked them to the door. "I'd

like daily briefings."

"You have my uncle's and my condolences." Toni offered her hand, feeling slightly annoyed at her uncle for being so accommodating. She hated it when people were granted special privileges because of their station in life. Money too. It made the law look unfair.

Once they were out of earshot on the sidewalk, Palmer blasted his protégé. "What was that about in there? I just handed you a career making case and you balk? This is a great opportunity for you." He put his hand on Toni's shoulder to slow her pace.

Toni stopped. "You pushed me in a direction I didn't want to take. You blindsided me in there. How could you? I own the serial case and need to stay connected to it. Afterwards, I have other plans."

"Solve this one, and you're back on Lincoln Park. No one sweats the details like you. And leaving the agency is nothing but a foolish move on your part. Whatever nonsense is driving you to do so, stop it. Go talk to a shrink." He walked briskly ahead. Toni lagged as she trailed him into the parking garage.

"It's not unusual for a profiler to be working several cases. I can do both," Toni reasoned.

"The only reason I allow you to talk to me in this way is because you're my sister's daughter. If any other agent said the things you said to the mayor, or to me, you'd be canned." They kept walking to his sedan. "Normally working two cases, there'd be no problem. But this is high profile."

"So is Frosty."

"You just made my point. No agent can handle two high profile cases. I know it's a bit early to start building one on Victoria Taylor's killer but tell me your initial thoughts."

"It's probably someone no one would suspect. Someone educated, intelligent, this type of person is harder to find because he or she disappears in a crowd or part of the circle of family. Lives a normal and structured life. Your turn. Bring me up to speed. Has the crime scene been established yet?" Toni got in the passenger side.

"Yes, it's her home. I have the key. We're headed there now." Palmer wheeled the car onto Congress Avenue in the Loop.

"Mafia territory. Let's hope we don't bump into the Morelli crime family in that neighborhood."

"What makes you say that?"

"Not only are the members of that family close to the mayor's, but they also practically own and run Chicago's Gold Coast. If it wasn't for my mess up, Roman Morelli would be in prison right now." There, she said it; it was out in the open. She was singularly responsible for setting a criminal free.

"You did a good job on that case. Judges and prosecutors can be corrupt. Juries are tainted with their own preconceived ideas. Evidence is what speaks truth and that's what you used. Evidence." Palmer hit the steering wheel with the flat of his hand.

"Thanks to me, it spoke loudly enough at his trial for an acquittal which put him right back on the street. I'm not working with this scumbag again, even for the mayor."

"You're not." His sideways glance at her was sharp.

"If the mayor brings in his friends to help find the killer, we'll be up to our throats in retribution." Toni crossed her arms.

"Don't talk like that. It'll get you into nothing but deep trouble. Just keep building your case."

Chapter 12

Toni

They pulled in front of a three-story mansion, the front lined with stained glass windows. Tall gothic iron gates went all the way around the property. It appeared a veritable fortress.

"Wow, this is where Victoria Taylor lived?"

"And the mayor lives right next door."

"Impressive," she said, looking between the two residents. "There's barely twenty feet between the two residences. Why not a downtown condo in the heart of the city? She was young, attractive, and I imagine with plenty of suitors. Why live here in a residential district with the uncle right next door?"

Palmer let the question go unanswered and led them into the place.

"The Collins won't return until after the first of the year."

Toni stepped from the foyer into the reception area. Paneled wood circled the room while a huge copper chandelier hung over their heads. The winding staircase was reminiscent of a Gothic castle. Large rooms filled with antiques opened to the left and the right of the grand entrance.

"Wow, this is gorgeous. But you can't tell me this was her style of decorating."

"You're right. This was first her parents' residence. Later it was gifted to her. The crime scene is this way."

Toni frowned. Her method was to walk through each room alone and let the place speak to her, as she threaded together the events of the night. Palmer decidedly was in command here. His method seemed narrow. She looked his way with surprise.

The wooden floor created echoing sounds under the heels of their feet. Toni viewed the living room as warm and inviting. Elizabeth Ashley textiles were the mainstay from the curtains on the window to the fabric on each piece of furniture, which was in direct contrast to what she had seen so far. At least Victoria left a mark of her taste somewhere. Center of the room was the broken coffee table with the pulverized glass.

"So, this is why Victoria was covered in glass. She fell into it."

"Perhaps slammed into it."

That synopsis was perplexing. Jurors needed motive, Toni did too. She walked to the end of the room then took small steps back toward the table while trying to figure out where Victoria stood before the attack. She studied the rug for foot striations, or a turned-up corner. "There aren't signs of a struggle. And why would falling into a table, albeit glass, be enough to kill a young woman? With natural reflexes, she'd close her eyes, right? The cuts should be from the outside of her lids. There seems to be quite a bit of blood here on the rug. Maybe a carotid artery was sliced?"

"The forensic team will take it to the lab to measure for blood amounts for the coroner's report. Notice anything else in the room?"

"Like the two glasses on the bar alongside of the

open bottle of wine, behind me?"

He nodded.

"Why hasn't it been taken for evidence? It needs to be tested."

"I told forensics to hold off a few hours until you had a chance to see the scene in the raw form."

"I appreciate that. When they take pictures, I want a close-up of everything in the room and, of course, have everything dusted for prints—especially the glasses and wine bottle. Sorry, you know this better than I, and right now, I sound like I'm the one in charge."

"You are the one in charge. I'm here only to acquaint you with the crime scene, then it's all yours."

"Everything needs to be treated as evidence. The position of the furniture. The drag marks of the armchair across the room. We need not just collection of forensic evidence and fingerprints and determine what belongs and what doesn't belong. That is as important as DNA on a murder weapon. Time is a major factor," Toni said.

"First forty-eight hours technology catches up with evidence."

"La Commese." She bent over to read the wine label. "I think in translation its something like The Start. My dad drinks this brand. The wine is not sold in the United States. It must be specially ordered from France."

"Actually, it's a nonsensical French name."

"Odd."

"Ordering rare wines from all around the world isn't any big deal to people like the mayor. It's also a symbol of their wealth and standing in the community.

As you look around, what else do you see?"

"The room appears staged." Toni looked around at the tidy space. "Every crime scene is a story of its own, but I wonder if this one has been cleaned. Only the coffee table is broken and everything else remains perfectly untouched. No dust either. I need to speak to Ms. Collins to see when the room was last cleaned."

"Toni, I can't tell you how pleased I am that you're running this case now. I know you were upset about being taken off the Lincoln Park murders. But this one will help move you up in the agency."

"Moving up doesn't interest me. Solving cases does. But I just can't do it anymore."

"Sounds like it's getting to you."

"Yes. Floating faces. Blood. Death. It's all I see at night. Hard to sleep."

"I bet I can find you a nice desk job. Send you back to white collar crime but in administrative position. Nice salary bump goes with it."

"I'll think about it, although I may already have plans."

"I know your nerves are raw for being yanked from a case. By the way, Frosty is an appropriate name for a cold weather freak," Palmer commented. "Frozen bodies…"

A snort later, I say, "Well, I guess it's better than the heat of summer when you find bodies humming with maggots."

Toni walked back out to the foyer and opened the hallway closet. Counting ten women's coats and jackets and furs altogether, she then pushed them aside to look at the back of the closet and down to the dozen pairs of boots and extra shoes on the floor. Everything was the same size and had top designer labels. Lucky girl.

Next, Toni went into the kitchen. On the counter was take-out from Spaghetti Warehouse. She lifted the lid and stepped back from the smell of spoiled food.

"This should be bagged and checked too." Toni noticed there was more food than one person could eat. There were two wine glasses. "I want to make sure all evidence is taped, recorded, and preserved. I think we need to isolate this property longer than the usual period. Also, we must maintain the chain of custody so it cannot be challenged in court."

Both cell phones buzzed. "Looks like we're needed at the Bureau. Toni, you're needed in the decomposition room."

Chapter 13

Toni

It was a relief to see Jack at the Bureau. Her intent was to smooth things out between them after Miranda got between them. Yet, Toni carried a level of guilt due to the fact it was her recording that gave the name to the media.

Toni watched Jack from the corner of her eye, dissecting his gestures as to his mood. He looked at her as though seeing the bump on her forehead for the first time and pointed to it, mouthing the word 'ouch'. She nodded. They walked together through the forensics wing of the building, and stopped in the lab to read the prelim report on Victoria.

"Interesting. Victoria's slippers not only had carpet fibers from her house but also an unidentified carpet that has yet to be found," Toni commented on the report.

"I was present when the polarized light optical machine ran the slippers earlier." Director Palmer's area of specialty was forensics; having processing a hundred crime scenes for hair and fiber evidence before he was made chief over the Chicago office.

Palmer handed the colored graph back to Brady for explanation. "Infrared energy through fiber fetoscopy produces peaks and valleys. Some of the fiber matched the carpet from Victoria's house as one would expect, but there is also another unidentified carpet fabric her slippers picked up. It may have come from the trunk she was transported in. It's a wool blend with some calcite."

"Calcite? Isn't that used on roadways?" Jack asked.

"In road construction." Brady nodded.

"There's road construction all over the city, including the alleyway of her house."

"All this tells us is she could've worn her slippers taking out the garbage," Jack said.

"I doubt she takes out her own garbage." Toni arched a brow.

Jack rubbed his chin with the back of his hand while looking at her. Just as quickly he looked away. To ease the uncertain moment, Toni pretended sudden interest in removing a piece of fuzz from her coat as Palmer made copies of the report. The copy machine acted up, taking longer than usual, so Toni walked into the hall and watched as lab technicians sorted through mounds of city garbage taken from the night before. "Be sure to test all straws, plastic utensils, food, open cans of soda and anything else for DNA."

A chorus of moans was quickly followed by a thumbs-up.

"Last night, I noticed a large sheet of plastic hung up in a tree." Jack walked up behind her.

"That's it!" Toni said, twirling around.

"That's what?"

"That's how Victoria was transported to the scene without losing the slippers on her feet. She was wrapped in the plastic, taken curbside, then the wind took a hold of the plastic."

"I'll send someone out for it immediately." Brady picked up the office phone. After a brief conversation, he said, "Follow me into the decomp room. Let me show you what I've gotten so far from my prelim."

In the decomposition room, the ventilation system was hard at work, sucking out all the harmful odors and germs from dead bodies through the exhaust fan. No windows—just the harsh overhead lights that created headaches starting at the back of the head.

The focus of the room was Victoria Taylor herself, lying uncovered on the stainless steel table attached to the sink. It tilted slightly forward, draining away body fluids. The Y incision started at the clavicle and met at the sternum. From there, it traveled down around the navel then ended at the pubis. A small thread from being sutured stuck out a couple of inches. By now her skin had turned sickly pale with a green hue. Her lips were barely parted with deep lines from dehydration. Her long hair had been combed straight back and the end of it hung over the table. Her eyelids, closed.

Brady picked up the stats file and read. "Everything on Victoria Taylor is within normal limits." Looking up, he added, "But we're waiting for tissue, blood, fluid reports. I swabbed everything. Results should be back in seventy-two hours." Reading again, he concluded, "But her brain, liver, heart, and the rest of her organs are just what they should be for a healthy woman her age." He closed the file and handed it over to Toni who shuffled through the report until she got to the body diagram where the contusions had been circled. Then she passed it to Jack.

"Her eyes were in grim condition. I pulled out about twenty shards of glass." Holding it up, Brady rattled a lidded plastic container.

"You know about the coffee table?" Toni asked suspiciously only just now having seen it herself.

"Yes, of course." Brady shoved his glasses back up on his nose, an annoying habit he did when he was excited about his work.

Toni shot a dirty look at Palmer.

"Shouldn't there have been a reflex of shutting her eyes?" Jack asked.

"Exactly! Once all the labs have come in, we'll know more."

"Any marks she was held down, or beaten?" Toni asked.

"None."

"Was her neck broken?"

"No, I found nothing wrong with it. Oh, but the jogger's neck—now that was broken."

"Broken?" Toni repeated.

"It fits with our theory that Frosty was in a hurry not to be seen," Jack said.

"How much blood did Victoria have in her at the time of autopsy?" Palmer steered the conversation back.

"According to her weight and size, I estimate she'd have about four point seven liters of blood. We drained four liters." He held up his measure, now empty of the liquid. "Something else I found interesting." Grabbing a scalpel, he then made a linear incision in a couple of reddish areas on the skin. "The bruising came after death, when there was no more blood pressure. See? Blood in the underlying soft tissue hasn't spread."

"Cause of death?" Palmer asked.

"There are no indications here from my initial autopsy report that she should be dead, meaning, I can't determine why she died. Cause of death is yet unknown. The lab report should answer that when it comes back."

Call me the minute it comes in and have a copy faxed to me at home, please." Toni washed her hands in the sink.

"Will do." Brady went back to work. "But it can be weeks to have the full report. Be patient."

"Aren't you staying for the prelim autopsy report on the other girl?" Jack asked Toni.

"Take good notes." Frosty's recent phone call had her on edge. The change of assignment made her irritable. It wasn't time to tell Jack about it either. "Fill me in later."

"Hot date in the middle of two cases?"

"An afternoon of interviews."

"Jobs?"

"Suspects. Just let it go, Autry."

Chapter 14

Toni

It was after six in the evening when Toni walked into the precinct looking for Autry. Besides the case they had to discuss, there was also that little matter about her sister's New Year's Eve party that she decided to bring up after all. No sense in wondering what might have been. She needed facts. The issue before her was how to ask since it was more of a personal favor. Deep breaths. Nerves were jittery as she rubbed her sweaty palms on her jacket. Toni stood on a square of linoleum and scanned the chaotic room. She spotted Jack. He frowned at her. Not so great. But followed him into his office. The New Year's Eve was ticking down to the bewitching hour.

His office was smaller than most and suited him just fine. It kept the people who wanted to see him at any given time to a minimum. One large window overlooking the street was directly behind his chair, so anyone entering was distracted by traffic. No personal pictures or artifacts cluttered his desk or walls, just pictures of the dead girls and a map of the city. Just like her, he had no life. Most people never noticed his Chicago Bears football picture, framed in silver and sitting on the file cabinet. Toni heard he once had a promising career as a linebacker but blew out his knee on his first big play, first game, in the NFL pro's. Damn bad luck.

Time and again, Jack acted as though she was a neophyte agent who was more of a prima donna than a seasoned warrior in the field. For months they worked crime scenes together, shared information, had the same goal in mind to get the killer. They had history; albeit it was only about a half a year when they first met over a jumper she was trying to talk down off a bridge on the Illinois River just off Congress Street.

"I don't appreciate the accusations you made early this morning about the mayor's niece. Don't you want to hear my side of the story?"

"We made a deal, and you broke it." His piercing stare, like shards of ice, tore right through her.

Toni noticed his buttoned-down white shirt was a tad bit tight which emphasized his pugilist physique. Not wanting to be distracted, she looked up into his eyes and got that old feeling about the rug being pulled out from beneath her. Jack had a streak of hard headedness under a layer of easy charisma. At times, the thought of him tugged warmly at her heart. This wasn't one of those times.

"Tell me, why the attitude?" No matter how she personally felt, backing down just wasn't her style, but right about now, she could use a mouth full of antacids. Toni opened her purse and searched for Xanax.

"You don't see the importance of giving the bereft space without those news vultures tearing up their front lawns with their trucks and held microphones in their faces? Reporters ask such moronic questions. What assholes."

"Jack, I didn't leak the information. And as for

Mayor Taylor, he's used to dealing with the press. By the way, I need water." She cradled the pill in her hand.

Jack handed her his water bottle.

She wiped the top of the bottle on her sleeve.

"Oh, yeah? But is he used to his niece being dead? And what about Victoria's parents, who are private citizens? Next time I must break the news to a family that their loved one has been brutally murdered, I want you there right beside me." Getting up from his seat fast, the roller chair spun out, hitting the wall behind him. "City official or not."

"I think I know what happened. My recorder with the information was stolen."

"What? You mean our conversation was recorded? You actually recorded it?" He was incredulous. "You recorded what was said at a crime scene?"

Toni held his gaze, feeling like a child having a schoolyard stare down. Who'd give first? They both did when Chief of Police Saverino walked into the office.

"Okay, you two, pipe down. I can hear you all the way to my office! By the way, Agent Postell, congrats on your new case. We'll miss your insight into the serial."

"New case? You mean new job?" Jack looked from Saverino back to Toni.

Ah, oh. She had wanted to tell Jack in her own way about the change of assignment. She blanched.

"I have a new assignment."

"You haven't told him?"

"I was just about to." Toni flushed.

"Postell has been exclusively put on the Taylor case," Saverino answered for her. "Congratulations."

"Thanks." It was a plum case and it felt good to be

recognized as such.

"What about the Lincoln Park murders?" Jack demanded as his face flushed with fury. "The FBI is there officially to assist Chicago PD. We're working these together."

"Jack, I explained to the mayor that my first priority was to the Lincoln Park murders, but he didn't care, neither did the FBI Director. You know how bosses can be." Toni avoided Saverino eyes.

"So, what do we do now since we lost our profiler?" Jack directed his question to Saverino.

"Well, according to your own words, you were going to ask the Bureau to replace me," Toni blurted so the chief would know. "Replace me."

"You what, Autry?" Saverino shot back at Jack.

"I was joking."

"Hang on. I'll still work the park murder case," Toni butted back into the conversation.

"Is that a smart thing to do?" Saverino asked.

"What I do on my own time is my business." There was no way she'd let go of this one.

"It's been a long day for us all. Autry, go home, you've been working twenty-four hours, and never know how soon you'll be called back. Get some sleep. We need a fresh mind. Postell, there's no hard feelings about you being reassigned and we're grateful for any help you can continue to give us on this one. Now both of you leave. Go." Saverino walked out.

A map of Lincoln Park was thumb tacked to the wall. Toni walked closer to look at the marked circles where the bodies were found. "This is right across from the zoo. Jack, do you think Frosty is an employee? Or a former employee?"

"I've personally interviewed each person and have copies of their work logs," Jack answered, irritated.

"Mind if I take a look?" She spun around and placed her hands on her hips.

"Yea, I do. You're no longer on the case, remember?" The detective walked to the door and opened it, asking her to leave. Clearly, this was not the moment to ask for New Year's Eve favors.

Furiously, she grabbed her heavy coat and sailed through the door without a word. Toni was soon on the street with unbuttoned coat flapping in the cold wind. Frustrated, she headed toward the bus stop. Icicles smacked the pavement as she blazed past buildings. Just as she decided her working relationship with Jack was over, he drove up in his Honda. Noticing him out of the corner of her eye, she watched in surprise, and stifled a smile when he stopped and rolled down the passenger window. He laughed. At least it was nice to see him display a friendly face.

"Hey, where's that VW bus?" he asked.

"It's parked at my place. I took the CTA today." Toni held her nose in the air, keeping her city fast stride.

"I thought maybe you got another ticket and finally lost your license." Jack kept right on smiling.

"Wouldn't you love it if I had?" Toni fought against the smile tugging at the corners of her mouth. She slowed her clip. Only Jack Autry could warm her heart in freezing temps.

"Get in. I'll drop you at home."

Toni stopped to consider his offer. If this was his way of making up, then she'd take it. Jack leaned across the seat and opened the door for her. The passenger door was barely shut when he accelerated. Toni kept her eyes on the cars ahead. The loafers on her feet were icy and damp. Her teeth chattered.

"My car certainly isn't as unique as yours, but it'll do. At least the heater works. Where did you find your old relic?"

"Actually, 'relic' is the wrong word. It's retro and in pristine condition, thanks to my brother." Toni softened her mood.

"Mechanic?"

"No. Andre owns a used car lot in Libertyville. He employs a great mechanic who keeps it running like a top for me."

"Aren't you the lucky one."

"I am." Toni watched traffic.

"I thought your 'pristine condition' bus had broken down and Pirelli got it going for you?" He poked.

"It was merely flooded. It's just fine." She crossed her arms.

A veil of silence suddenly dropped between them. Toni busied herself by staring out the window at the storefronts and people shopping along the street going in and out of doors. "Jack, I'd never betray you or the department."

"Okay, apology accepted."

It was as close to an act of contrition as she'd get from Jack, but it was enough.

"I imagine talking to the Taylor family wasn't easy. It must be extremely hard dealing with relatives at a time as this." Unfortunately, firsthand experience always came in handy. "Tragedies like this can split them into pieces."

"I've seen it way too often."

"Then why put yourself through it time and again? Why not find a less stressful job in another division? Or a desk job?"

"You sound like Palmer."

"Come on, show biz isn't your thing, admit it."

"How'd you hear about the offer, Jack?" She turned in her seat to look at him.

"I'm a detective. Thus, I find out stuff." His smile was cock-eyed.

"Well, since you think you're such a great detective, then you must know that my contract is yet unsigned, plus my resignation, rescinded." Toni pulled the visor down to see the mirror, then tugged her long hair into a messy ponytail.

"Thought the deal was buttoned up." Jack glanced sideways.

"Profiling is my calling. The crime scenes are difficult for me, but satisfaction comes when the bad guys are off the streets. You hate breaking bad news to the family but sometimes they are responsible."

"That's worst of all. 'All happy families resemble one another, but each unhappy family is unhappy in its own way'."

"You've read Leo Tolstoy? I'm impressed."

"I read Tolstoy and grew up near Cabrini Green." Jack turned on the left blinker.

"I had no idea. That's a bad area. Drugs, gangs, violence."

"Crime is down since the projects were replaced with better housing. The area is making a comeback. But now we have the problem on the other side of the city where the poor want to find cheap housing again. Before the gangs had their own territory. No one is into sharing the streets."

"The streets will never be cleared of crime." Toni sighed.

"Not in this world and no one is ever safe. Even power and privilege are no guarantee of safety. Just ask Victoria Taylor. Oh yea, she's dead. Families don't always know what is going on with one another. But I imagine the Taylor's were close."

"What makes you think they were close?"

"Just how the mayor has reacted to his niece being murdered. She worked for him. Her parents gave her the big house to live in."

"Well, families can seem to be close yet are strangers to one another." Toni lifted her eyebrows.

"Are you trying to tell me something about yourself, Postit?" At the stoplight, he stared at her.

"Postit?" she asked in surprise.

"My new nickname for you. Thought it was time you had one."

"Okay. I'm not trying to tell you anything about me. There are just things I've picked up along the way. By the way, how's Victoria's parents?"

"Smooth move, changing the subject from personal back to professional. I respect that about you. Most women are open books. Open-boring-books. Not you. You're closed and that makes you interesting. Ah, Ms. Taylor's parents weren't doing well when we last spoke to them." Jack applied his brakes for a pedestrian who was jaywalking. The elderly lady with mousy hair worn like a curtain smiled at him and he gave her a short wave in return. "I just hope the right person is caught. Sometimes in the department's zeal to get the killer, we overlook somebody or something important. We don't want to jump to conclusions and make mistakes, especially not with this one. That's probably a big reason you were pulled in on it. They want it done right and done fast. Choosing you was smart."

"What a nice compliment. Thanks, Jack."

"Case in point," Jack continued, scratching the tip of his nose, "prosecutors withholding evidence to get a conviction. Cook County underwent mayhem in the last few years with new discovery that the court systems knowingly prosecuted and put on death row guiltless people. There've been plenty of wrongful conviction cases. It was my pleasure to personally arrest some of those judges and prosecutors, too. Crime looks bad on everyone, but ten times worse when the very people who are supposed to uphold our laws break our laws."

"Law school students ferret some of these cases out in their graduate courses. The governor wisely suspended all executions. Someone said their prayers."

"Prayers? Do you pray, Postit?" Jack seemed interested in her reply.

Not knowing which answer would win her most admiration in his eyes, she chose the truth. "I use it only as an expression."

"Well, have her put in a good word for us on this one. I want all my bases covered."

Seriously? Toni wrinkled up her nose at him. It was a surprising request coming from a hardened investigator. Perhaps he was being polite, or cute? Now was the moment to stop treading in virgin religious territory and she returned to the real problem at hand.

"Faith creates a soft mind, makes for easy prey. But they do serve a function and there is a place for them in society. People of passion are good for clothing the needy and running soup kitchens, but it takes realists, like you and me, to keep the streets safe. We need to maintain our focus or we're no good at our jobs."

"I need to ask a personal favor." Toni crossed her fingers.

"Let me guess. You know someone who'd be perfect for me and want to fix me up."

"My sister Mallory is having her annual New Year's Eve party." Toni ignored his comment. "There'll be lots of scrumptious food and live music."

"Pass."

"That answer came fast."

"Should I say it slower? P-a-s-s." A grin slid up the side of his face.

"State officials will be in attendance, too. Meeting them would be good for your career." Was there nothing she wouldn't say to get a date with Jack?

"My career is just fine. Besides, schmoozing is not my thing."

"You don't understand. I need someone to take me." Pity. That might work.

"You? Are you asking me out on a date, Postit?" His jaw slacked in jest.

"No, not like on a real date. It'd be more like an…appointment," Toni softly responded.

"Appointment?" He laughed, smacking the steering wheel with his hand.

"Forget it."

"New Year's Eve is the biggest night of the year. It's tomorrow night, and this is short notice. What makes you think I don't already have a date?" Jack's brown eyes sparkled. She loved what she saw.

"Do you have a date?" Toni asked mundanely.

"No."

"Great, then you'll come with me?" She held her breath in hope.

"No, not great. I have plans of sacking out on the couch in boxers while washing down a sausage and anchovy pizza with a cold beer."

"That's certainly not an evening a woman would enjoy." Toni pursed her lips.

"Well, it's the kind of evening I would enjoy. And the reason I remain single. I'm not a party type of guy. Home holds more interest. I have a years' worth of TV programming to catch up on."

"I'm willing to pay you."

"Sounds to me as if an old boyfriend will be there." He whistled.

"It's worse than that. My sister Mallory is engaged to my former fiancée."

"Ah-ha! I knew there was a reason." He honked the horn—twice. "Tell me how he broke it off with you."

"That's personal."

"Come on, we're partners, right? No secrets. Tell me."

Toni gave a sigh. "All right. It was a hurried relationship. Engaged too quickly. I think we were really on the skids for months when I was dumped."

"How'd he dump you?"

"What an insensitive question."

"How'd he dump you?" Jack repeated.

"Text."

Jack laughed so hard he choked. "Text?"

"This entire conversation is humiliating."

"I hope, at least, you kept the ring."

"I donated it."

"Good for you. What charity?"

"A homeless woman."

"Wow. Great move. By the way, how do you feel seeing your sister with the man you love?"

"Pardon *moi*, he's not the man I love."

"But you must have loved him once—you were engaged to the man."

"No. I love no man. Once I thought I loved Will but since I got over him so easily, I realized I never loved him. I was just lonely." Toni remembered the relief mixed with mortification.

"Then your sister really did you a favor. Listen, take my advice and don't put yourself through a party you do not want to go to. Say you're sick and stay home. Better yet, join me at my place. I'll put on pants."

"No!"

"Okay, then I won't wear pants." Jack smiled. Gosh, he did it well.

"That's not what I mean, and you know it." Toni pulled at his arm. "Do you know nothing about family dynamics? Please come with me."

"Oh, all right, I'll go—how much?" He grinned.

"What?"

"I'll go with you on this charade, but you said you'd pay me for my time. Now I'm asking how much." He stared at the heavy traffic moving on all sides of them along Lake Michigan that lay in frozen stillness beneath the glacial winter sky. He cut someone off in traffic and got a long honk from the other driver. Jack didn't react.

"But you'll have to dress nice too."

"I see high numbers." He tapped his fingers on the steering column.

Toni closed her eyes. "Just tell me your price. I'll dig around inside my piggy bank when I get home."

"Breaking open the bank for me? All right. I'm persuaded. What time will you pick me up?"

"What?" She turned in her seat.

"Teasing. No girl has ever picked me up for a date—or for an appointment. I'm not about to start. However, it is Christmastime and I'm feeling downright charitable. I forgot to contribute to my favorite charity this year so to make up for my oversight; there'll be no charge to you."

"I'm your charity this year?"

"You are."

They pulled in front of the brownstone apartment building. Jack put the car in park. "Call me with the particulars. Oh wait, I have a late Christmas gift for you." Reaching around to the back seat, Jack handed her a thick folder.

"What's this?"

"It's for the Lincoln Park case. Inside are the names of the Lincoln Park Zoo employees for the past year and their work logs."

"Thanks. Now I'm almost sorry I didn't get you anything. But why am I getting them just now?"

"It took a while for all the interviews and background checks."

Toni nodded, then climbed out of the car and over the mound of snow at the curb where it was deposited by a snowplow. When Jack's car disappeared down the street, she let herself into the building and ran up the steps to her apartment.

Chapter 15

Two months ago

The intial role with the FBI involved investigating white-collar and blue-collar crime. Needing a bit more excitement she put in for a transfer. Excitement came. The evening that Antoinette Postell was requested by the Chicago Police Department for field assistance marked a significant turning point.

It was the night of a late dinner in the West Loop after the symphony. From there she went onto drinks with friends where chatter and joking grew more irrational. By midnight she arrived at her apartment, removed her camelhair coat, and stepped from her heels that were damp from the fresh snow as the cell rang. That was months ago. From then to now, four joggers had been murdered. Whoever was committing these murders was in a frenzy.

Antoinette Postell settled onto a wobbly stool at the diner's counter and ordered a cup of potato soup along with a slice of sourdough bread. A winter coat draped her shoulders. Pinned to the collar was a Bluetooth mic disguised as a nondescript snowflake brooch. 'Toni' read down the plastic covered menu, which contained plops of dried ketchup, accompanied by a collection of fingerprints. Imagining unidentifiable germs, she dug through her purse for the small bottle of hand sanitizer.

It was then she noticed the contract, pulled it out, unfolded it, read through it once more, sighed, then folded it back into the side pocket.

From habit, Toni surveyed the room, noting each facial expression and scanned body language. The holstered Glock felt uncomfortable on her side, making her shift on the ragged vinyl of the stool. Just as she began to unholster it, her cell rang. The caller's name swept through her like a winter gale.

"Hey, Uncle Robert." *Please let it be a friendly call.*

"Special Agent Postell," he said, using her official title.

The timbre of his voice made her flinch with dread. "Director Palmer," she corrected.

"Another body in Lincoln Park, near the lake. Police are at the scene. They need you there. Now."

"Me? At the scene?"

"Yes. Second body this fall, and you're now assigned."

"They want me at the crime scene while the body is still present?" Her stomach lurched with dread. Up to this time, she was called in after the body had been removed from the crime scene and at the morgue. She found police reports and studying crime scene photos extremely helpful. Stress was not a problem at that time.

"You'll work the crime scenes alongside the PD. We'll touch base tomorrow."

Toni paid her bill while leaving her food on the counter, along with a ten-dollar tip.

By now it was dark. The onslaught of snow and wind brought hundreds of Chicago snowplows onto the city streets to combat growing drifts. Toni slowly shifted gears of her 1970 VW Bus. Tall business buildings loomed to the left, against the wet sky. Further down were townhomes and privately owned condos, as well as apartments. Facing another crime scene in the dead of night, she once again envied the families gathered snug in their beds. That's where she wanted to be right now, in her own home along with her cat, and soaking in a hot bubble bath. If her uncle realized how exhausted she felt after her twelve-hour day, he wouldn't care.

For two miles, she argued with herself: should she go home or continue to the crime scene? Exhaustion battled with her sense of duty. She decided that finding an available parking spot would be a sign to stay. If not, she'd report in she was too ill to be of assistance, go home, and just for tonight, leave crime fighting to someone else. It was difficult to look at the brutalized bodies even in the morgue. In the field she needed to be like the hardened cops who she stood shoulder to shoulder with. Respect was everything.

As bad luck would have it, there was one empty spot, seemingly just for her. Her mother referred to such things as 'serendipity' in her Southern way. Toni slid into the spot, across from a residential area. Lines of glossy painted doors framed by white stone porticos were flanked by early Christmas decorations. Usually, the windows gave nothing away of the treasures inside, only outlined curtains against the cold could be seen from the street. However, tonight was different. Sirens and swirling lights brought spectators to their windows.

Shifting the bus into park, Toni noted what a lovely spot in the city this was, with privately owned homes which looked out over Lincoln Park and Lake Michigan, acting as the gatekeepers of normalcy. Safety was a complete façade because a monster continued to terrorize the city.

That's how it started with the Chicago PD homicide department.

****

Present Day

Ever since, she worked late at night in freezing weather, taking Zinc and Vitamin C to ward off sickness, she quickly became the queen of stress. Tonight, she read through the zoo employee files Jack gave her. Despite the early morning hour, Toni found it hard to sleep. Agitated, she spread out the police files on the coffee table. It proved to be lengthy and she was glad the person who compiled it was thorough as well as organized. However, it'd take a week to look through all the details. For now, she set it aside to focus on the Murder Book she built.

All along, she figured Fosty's trigger was the snowstorm. How wrong she had been. That's when he exploded. His build up was hours, or days, or weeks before then. The murder in the park was the result. The target. Her mind raced with theories. Had a family member pushed too far? Or a female who made him feel inadequate? Did the female joggers remind him of someone who belittled him? Had he been losing jobs and took it out on women who he perceived as weak? Or was it just opportunity?

There were many possibilities and little time to focus. She leaned back against the couch, touching the bump on her forehead. It was smaller now, a bit discolored, leaving her with a trail of annoying headaches that aspirin couldn't touch. Toni closed her eyes. She imagined Frosty to be a white, educated male in a position of authority, yet he was someone who felt powerless. Most likely raised by a dominant, single mother with a continual history of extreme abuse toward her male children. This would cripple the child, resulting in unrestrained fury. Why did some act out their rage while others with similar backgrounds became meek and mild? The human psyche was fascinating. She loved analysis, figuring it out like a puzzle, not the reality of dead people.

Toni leaned forward and jotted in the Murder Book. Frosty is between the ages of 20 to 35. Poor female relationships, recently divorced or broken up with a girlfriend, perhaps just lost out on a job promotion, drives a flashy sports car, but the inside is filled with old newspapers, trash and spoiled food. He likes the flash of the car, but not the car itself. His mind is too focused on his job and the killings. It's used as a tool to attract women.

In the files, Jack had circled three names. Two divorced men, and one single man, employed by the park zoo during the first murder; all three terminated since then. There was no information on the type of cars they drove. Her replacement needed to go to the DMV for that information. Looking through the papers, she noticed everyone had been interviewed, just as Jack said. They seemed to have good alibis, but she still placed all three at the top to have them checked again. It'd be easy for a zoo employee to slip into the park while on duty to slay.

A talk with the ex-wives would be in order. They were just too good of leads to not follow with a second interview. Toni gathered up the papers and slid them together. Although she wanted to work on this case, she had to admit it would be difficult to give her full attention to both cases.

Hopefully, a new profiler would be assigned to the Frosty case soon. Of course, she'd hand over the Murder Book but after she made a copy.

If she could pick her successor, it'd be Agent Susan Hunter. The gal was more than capable. Toni remembered a rumor they dated for a time. Shifting gears, it made her want to know the particulars; how long they were together, if it was passionate, what was the cause of its demise. She tried to imagine them as a couple. A twinge of jealousy touched her heart. It was time to get that out of her head.

Chapter 16

New Year's Eve
Mallory's party

The special occasion needed to be emotionally
managed. Between excitement over spending an
evening with Jack in a social setting that was fraught
with situations that could go totally awry with her sister
involved, Toni decided she need something to calm her
nerves. That's when she remembered the bottle of wine
from two Christmases ago, cooling in the vegetable
drawer. A gift from her uncle.

Rarely did she drink—maybe two glasses a year.
Her general physician noted her as a 'non-drinker'.
Toni fished out the bottle, dug through a kitchen drawer
for a bottle opener. It was then she noticed the label. It
was the same wine that was at Victoria Taylor's home,
and the brand her father drank. She popped the cork and
slowly poured it into a water glass. She drank it in one
gulp, then had another, which she sipped.

It was eight p.m. Jack Autry would be at her flat to
pick her up soon.

She chose to wear her mother's vintage Vera Wang
gown, a black sleeveless cocktail dress with a V-
neckline, which fit her body like a glove. Brave enough
to wear since she had dropped a few pounds and started
eating healthily again. The sheer fabric in the backless

dress allowed her back to be seen without feeling exposed. It was chic and gave off a Audrey Hepburn stylish flair. She tugged her long hair into a swirl in the back of her head, leaving errant whisps of hair to soften her face. Her makeup started with a light base coat, followed by transluscent powder, rouge on each cheek, followed by mascara to emphasize her long lashes, and finished with red lipstick.

She watched the minutes tick away, waiting for Jack. When it was 8:30, she wondered where he was. At a crime scene? It'd be totally like him to forget to call.

Fifteen minutes later, the apartment buzzer sounded from the downstairs door. Toni hurried to press the button, allowing Jack into the building. In the hallway, she leaned over the stair railing. "Come on up, Jack."

The sound of his galloping heavy feet on the steps made her heart beat faster. Unexpectedly, her hands became cold and sweaty. Toni wobbled in her heels down the hallway and into the bedroom, where she tore her good camel hair coat out of a dry cleaner's bag and hurried back to the front door. There he stood.

Jack was inside her apartment for the first time.

His face opened into a huge smile. "Wow."

"It's vintage." She slowly turned around. "Don't you dare whistle."

"There is no breath left in me to whistle. You are gorgeous, Postit." His gaze absorbed her entire body. "And now it's time for our 'appointment'." Jack helped her into her coat, then guided her down to the car, where he opened her door.

"I'm returning your file to you." Toni placed the

folder on the backseat.

"You can keep it longer if you need more time," Jack said, sliding behind the wheel.

"No, I'm finished. On top are three names of interest warranting a closer look. You'll see my notes." Toni silently wished for a kiss at midnight. It was New Year's Eve. Kisses were mandatory.

"Thanks, Postit."

"We need to come up with a plan for this evening."

"I'm not following you."

"First of all, just for tonight, please don't call me 'Postit.' Call me by my first name, Antoinette. Toni is a nickname. I don't want my sister to think this is a sympathy date."

"Is that how you see it?" He scowled.

"Don't you?"

"I see two adults going out for a nice evening together." Jack's gaze returned to traffic.

"Okay. That's a very good beginning for our love story." Toni kicked off her heels and rubbed the bottom of her feet on the mat. "Pretend you like me."

He sighed. "I do like you."

"Pretend you like me as your—girlfriend." Toni felt ridiculous saying that word.

"What's your sister's address again?" Now he seemed aggravated.

"It's a penthouse downtown looking over the Illinois River." Toni handed him the address on a piece of paper. "I've only been there a few times."

Holding the paper up to the dome light, he whistled. "Swanky. Your sis has big bucks?"

"Yes." Toni shrugged, hoping this wouldn't be a big deal to him. Wasn't this how things started out last year at this time? She was on her way to Mallory's New Year's Eve party with her fiancé, Will. By midnight, Mallory was kissing Will and she was on her way home in a cab alone—and without Will—and without the ring. Neither of them would ever see that again, having dropped it into the hand of a homeless woman. "Happy New Year," Toni sang out through fresh tears.

The woman quickly slid the ring on her middle finger.

That was last year. This year was brand new. With a bit of luck, she'd return this time with the same guy she left with. "My twin brother Andre and his wife will be there. You'll like them. Andre is the one I mentioned before who fixed up the VW bus for me."

"I thought his 'mechanic' fixed up the bus for you." He chuckled.

"Touché! You got me back with my own words. Andre and Marie have been married for about four years and have two cute kids. Why am I telling you this?"

"Nerves. People tend to talk too much when they're jumpy. Slow down and take deep breaths while I tell you about my family. They're a dozy too. It'll be like trading battle stories." Jack laughed. "Want to hear?"

"There should be about a hundred people there at the party, like friends and business associates," Toni rattled.

"Guess not."

"What?"

"I asked you a question, but you didn't hear me."

"I'm so sorry. What's the question?" It was hard to focus on anything other than getting through the door, over the threshold and into the party, through the party and back home.

"Forget it."

"Give me the question again."

"No."

"Sorry, Jack. My mind is preoccupied." She rubbed her brow against an impending headache.

"Okay, if this is a real date and you're my girlfriend, we better figure out our love history." There came that big smile again.

It was nice to see Jack had a mischievous side to him. "Good!" She clapped her hands. "How long have we been dating?"

"Six months, isn't that about how long we've known one another?"

Yes, it is, but we can't tell her that. Mallory will know something is up because I haven't mentioned you. How about we dodge the question, so we don't have to lie. Say not long."

"Okay, translation; we've gone out for a little while then. We met over the jumper's body at the river that was just down from her place, too."

"No! We can't tell her the truth because it's not—"

"…it's not romantic enough? But it's the truth."

"It has to be romantic." Toni noticed a couple in the car next to them. The woman was playing with the driver's ear. She looked at Jack, suddenly wanting to touch his ear too. Kiss his cheek and snuggle into him.

"Something like, brag to your girlfriends kind of romantic?" His eyes sparkled in the headlights of the passing cars.

"Yes, that kind of romantic."

"You don't consider meeting over a body as

romantic?"

"I already said 'no', and if you do, you're warped." Toni folded one arm over the other.

"But we did meet that way. It was warmer out then, too. I remember you standing there in the shadows wearing a very short skirt, no panties."

"What? No!" Toni gasped.

"Your button-down blouse wasn't buttoned and I could see your cleavage."

"That's not true either! I wore faded, baggy jeans and an old t-shirt that said Chicago Cubs."

"I kept wondering who you were." Jack ignored her protests. "At first, I thought you might have been someone who egged him on to jump."

"You can't be serious." She covered her mouth trying not to laugh.

"Totally. Anyway, I think it's a nice way to meet. People meet on the job all the time." A grin hung on his face. "This story has a touch of drama and a pinch of sex."

"We need to come up with a new idea." She stared into space, wondering if she and Jack were ever going to connect on some level and if so, what level would it be? Professional respect? A bit of romance? Both? Neither? Two ships passing?

"We were introduced by a mutual friend, just won't mention the jumper's name."

Covering her ears, she answered, "Not over a dead person. Let's say I was investigating—a disreputable person and I…"

"…needed information…"

"…so I went to the precinct."

"…and saw me and I asked you if I could help

you."

"I said 'yes! Yes, you can help me!'" Toni looked at him and smiled. "Because you do help me."

"Like I'm helping you tonight, and you do come into the precinct asking questions."

"And you do answer them."

"Good, that's settled. When we go out, where do I take you?"

"Dinner, we eat dinner and go to the movies."

"I don't like romantic movies. What do we see?"

"Mysteries."

"Okay, that'll work, but what kind of restaurants do we like?"

"All kinds. Mexican, Italian, German."

"But not Sushi...I hate that." He stuck out his tongue.

"You should try it sometime, Jack, it's really good."

"Not sushi. No way."

"Okay, not sushi."

"Have we been to museums?"

"No, but we want to go."

"This sounds complicated. Let's keep them talking about themselves."

"Oh, look, here we are." Toni pointed at the building.

The valet parked the car, and the couple took the elevator to the tenth floor where they were greeted at the door by a butler dressed as Santa, who cheerily took their coats. "Who's he?" Jack asked under his breath.

Toni shrugged her shoulders. "Never seen him before. Maybe he's a rental for this evening. If it were my party, I'd have him in a clown suit."

"You do enjoy the element of surprise," Jack mused.

"And there's plenty of that waiting for us this evening."

Chapter 17

New Year's Eve Party

"Antoinette!" Mallory floated into the room and planted a quick kiss on her sister's cheek, noticing Jack a split second later. With gasps of approval, she swung her right hip toward him and asked, "And who are you?"

"Mallory, I'd like for you to meet Jack Autry, and Jack, this is my sister, Mallory Hughes."

"Half-sister," Mallory explained. "Hi, Jack."

Toni thought her sister looked achingly beautiful in the impeccably sleek red designer dress of clinging red fabric paired with a long diamond necklace and matching earrings.

Mallory crinkled her plucked pencil thin eyebrows at her younger sister and her big glossy smile dropped into a frown. With a hint of accusation, she said, "What do you have on? Augh! That isn't one of mother's dresses, is it? Oh no, Antoinette, it is! How funny! Macys has a bargain basement for people like you."

Jack was right. She should've called in sick.

Thunderclouds gathered along Jack's brow. In a dramatic gesture, he swept his hand over his heart, looked into Toni's violet eyes and said, "The dress you wear is stunning. You're a vision of loveliness tonight, my love, and I can't keep my eyes off you. Stay close by me. I don't want to lose you to another man." With surprising gentleness, he offered her his arm as a life preserver, and she grabbed a hold. Together they walked into the party.

"A vision of loveliness?" Toni nervously laughed. "I've never heard you talk like that."

"I heard it on TV once. The killer murmured it as he stabbed his girlfriend in her heart."

"Score one for streaming video. And next year I'll have the flu. I feel it coming on already." Toni nervously fanned herself with her black evening pearl clutch.

"Now I know why you don't have much to do with your sister, she's a shrew, but now you've got me hooked to know more about your family and your ex. Where is he? I want to meet him next. Is he as big a dope as Mallory?" Jack was filled with vinegar. Just the way she liked him.

"You can decide that for yourself soon enough." They walked toward the buffet table. "And just as I promised lots of food."

"I've looked forward to this moment all day." Jack started loading up a plate with rich foods and dessert. "I can see why your sister is jealous of you."

"What are you talking about? Mallory isn't jealous of me."

"You've not only got the brains in the family, but also all the beauty." Jack held a cream puff.

Toni reached for a baby carrot. "Oh, now you're teasing."

Jack turned to Toni. "Women like Mallory are a dime a dozen. You, on the other hand, are drop dead gorgeous. And tonight, I like how you're wearing your hair in a loose bun with some of it coming undone. Your complexion is soft with very little makeup. I like you this way. Toni, haven't you noticed all the guys ogling you whenever you walk in the precinct? You set our hearts racing." He stuffed the dessert in his mouth and in two swallows, it was gone.

His words were better than aspirin. "Ogling me? I thought it was my Glock that garnished all the attention."

Jack picked up a baby carrot from her plate. "What's the point of this? Do you know nothing of Holiday Spirit?" He dumped a few cream puffs onto her plate. "You and your sister look nothing alike."

"We have different dads. I take after mine, who's a French filmmaker."

"Will I meet him tonight?"

"Presently he's producing a film in Paris, so no, you won't meet him," Toni explained with an air of importance.

"Is your mom with him in France?"

"No, my mom isn't with him. She doesn't venture far." Toni sighed and changed the subject. "Oh, look, there's Mayor Taylor. Let's offer our condolences."

"No thanks. I've already done that at the precinct. Besides, I'm comfortable right here." He reached for fudge.

"Stop! All that sugar isn't good for you." Toni grabbed his hand.

"Neither is being stabbed. Loosen up, it's the holidays," he said. "Nights like these are the reason we even have New Year's Resolutions."

"Mallory's dad had the food catered. Have you heard of Daniel Hughes?"

"Daniel Hughes? Not *the* Daniel Hughes?" Jack swooned.

"Yes, that's him." Toni was delighted.

"Sorry. Never heard of him." He slid a piece of nutty white fudge into his mouth.

"You must have heard of him. Danny's Food chains are all over the Midwest."

Jack swallowed before he replied. "No, but I have heard of Kroger's. If you said 'Kroger's' I'd be impressed."

"Daniel Hughes is also a great philanthropist providing inner city kids scholarships to private schools of fine arts and makes other worthy contributions. Know that ice rink in Lincoln Park? He raised a few million to build it." She pointed at the smear of chocolate on the side of his mouth and handed him a linen napkin.

"Thanks." Jack wiped his mouth. "It sounds to me you like this Daniel Hughes."

"What's not to adore about him? But his life hasn't been an easy one. My mother divorced him after they had Mallory. Then Mom married my dad the day after the divorce was finalized."

"Interesting. An affair."

"Andre and I were born less than a year later. We're twins." Tears welled. Toni swallowed hard not wanting to mention little Suzette. "It's remained a mystery to me why Uncle Danny was good to Andre and me. He was there for us, as much as he was for Mallory. Although not related by blood, his devotion to us is like a second dad."

"You come from a large family?"

"It depends on perspective and definition of a

family. He's not here tonight, but you must meet my adopted Uncle Herschel. He has a shoe repair shop under the El. I guess some of us are a family of choice and biology."

"A very interesting family." Jack looked at her as though he saw her for the first time. Perhaps in a new way. He set down his plate and reached for her hand. After kissing the inside of her wrist, he entwined his fingers with hers. It became a perfect moment which translated into a feeling of floating.

Suddenly, Mallory was back and wasn't alone. Her fiancée—aka the ex-factor—was saddled up beside her. "Jack, I'd like for you to meet my fiancée."

"Congressman William Schofield. It's nice to meet you, sir." Jack dropped Toni's hand and vigorously shook the congressman's hand. "Toni, he's your ex?"

"And you are?" the congressman asked.

"My date."

"We know, Antoinette. It's Will I wanted Jack to meet." Mallory looked as though she wanted to devour Jack.

"Jack Autry. It's an honor to meet you, sir."

"He's a detective with the Chicago PD," Toni explained.

"I guess your professional careers caused your paths to cross. Did you meet on the job?"

"Jack and I recently reminisced about that, weren't we, honey?" Toni mischievously looked at Jack who grinned at her. By the look in his eyes, she could tell he formulated a plan. She couldn't wait to hear.

"It was romantic. Half a year ago we met on the Congress Street Bridge under a canopy of stars where she was cloaked in dark shadows. I wondered, 'who is this sensational gal?' but didn't have the courage to ask her out till recently."

"How lyrical of you to put it like that," Mallory said. "Tell me more."

"Jack's shy. But as he said, we met on the bridge, and found out I was a profiler—I found out he was a detective—and then he thought about me—right, Jack?" Toni nudged him.

"Yes, I certainly thought about you. And a few days later, you came into the precinct for information on that case." Jack rolled his eyes slightly and Toni could tell he was struggling to remember what to say.

"What case is that?" Mallory wanted to know.

"We aren't allowed to say. All cases are highly confidential," Toni quickly answered.

"That's right, you needed that important (cough) information about—that confidential case. And I helped you.'" Jack cleared his throat.

"And that was the first of many wonderful evenings together." *At crime scenes.*

"We don't like Sushi." He tossed a conspiratorial smile her way.

Toni giggled uncontrollably. "And we haven't made it to the museum yet either, have we, Jack? But we do watch mysteries on TV." By now she was quite tickled and could hardly stand still so she swatted him with her purse and stamped her feet causing another long strand of dark hair to pull loose, falling across her face. Jack smiled and gave the curl a tug.

"Under a canopy of stars, huh?" Mallory wistfully repeated.

Daniel Hughes arrived with a tray of glasses filled with eggnog. "Good evening, everyone. Antoinette, that dress couldn't be lovelier on you."

"Thanks Uncle Danny. The food is outstanding as usual." Did his compliment about the dress connect to a memory of her mother and their time together?

"Whatever is left will be taken to the homeless shelters in the morning."

"You're the most thoughtful man." Toni added, "I'd like for you to meet Detective Jack Autry. He's in charge of solving the Lincoln Park murders."

"A pleasure to meet you, detective. I applaud you for all your hours of devotion. I'm sure the mayor has a way of keeping everyone hopping down there."

"Yes, sir, but that's my job."

Danny handed everyone a glass. "Toni, did you get my Christmas present?"

"Yes, I did. And as usual, you're spoiling me." Toni raised her glass to him.

"Have a good time in the Bahamas. Hey, I'm sure the detective will love to use that extra ticket I included." Daniel winked at the young couple.

Toni blushed over the innuendo.

"We intend to, but we've got some dead bodies on our hands to take care of first."

"By the way, Mallory, when are Andre and Marie coming?" Toni asked.

"They're not. Andre called a little while ago. It's the flu." Then Mallory turned to her dad, "The governor and his wife are over by the piano. Let's greet them. By the way, Toni, my gift from dad was a trip to Europe."

Jack choked on his drink.

"Here, you got some nogg on your shirt." Toni grabbed a white Damask cloth napkin and dabbed at the spot. She looked up into his face and he was staring at her. His breath was on her lips. She licked her lips. He put his hand at the small of her back and pulled her into him. The man knew how to get her heart going. "Jack."

"Sometimes it's best to say nothing at all." Jack looked around and then pulled Toni into another room. They were alone. He closed the door. In the background, the song by Louis Armstrong played from the living room; *Give me a kiss...* Jack held Toni and slowly waltzed her around the room. Strong arms, surefooted, he knew where to step and steered her with ease.

"Where does this talent come from?" She laughed as he tipped her back and then twirled her around.

"My mother. She was a dance teacher. When I wasn't playing football, I was at her studio learning. The waltz is my forte. It really helped me on the field."

"Off the field too." She looked into his eyes and felt the first twinges of love.

Jack slowed their step to a halt. They stood toe to toe, still in the dance position, his left hand around her waist. Jack's eyes. His mouth. His breath on her face. Toni knew they were on the precipice of their first kiss. She took a deep breath and closed her eyes, locking in this memory. Jack pulled her closer to him. Yes, this moment was enough to build her dream on. Jack tipped her chin toward his mouth and kissed her on the lips, sweetly. She had a death grip around his shoulders and held on as the Ferris wheel of emotion carried her up into the night and back down to earth again.

"Let's say we leave?" Jack whispered into her ear. "We'll take a drive through the park. It's snowing. Maybe find Frosty tonight. Just you and me—how about it?"

"I'll grab my coat." Toni clapped her hands. What a great evening this was turning out to be.

"I'll wait for you by the rented Santa."

Toni hurried into the master bedroom. This was the perfect night with a perfect guy. It couldn't get any better. The whole professional vibe between them had evaporated and in its place was new excitement. Promises of love. Emotionally, Toni was still back at the scene of the kiss. Returning to the crime scene was her new favorite thing to do, and in this case, a necessity. A kiss. Strange how one kiss took them in another direction. Well, it was New Year's Eve. It was time for wishes to come true. Even big impossible desires had a chance this time of the year, such as Jack thinking she was gorgeous. If only she had her recorder on her, she'd play his words repeatedly. It'd be her preferred bedtime audible.

Now she needed to find her coat. There it was on the bed with a pile of furs. She folded hers over one arm and then something on Mallory's bureau caught her attention. It was a stunning black silk purse baguette with a gold cord drawstring at the top, with antique beads and European buttons, accented further with sterling silver chatelaines. The iridescent carnival glass buttons sewn into the fabric among the silk embroidery were all too familiar. Toni pulled opened the purse and read the inside label sewn into the deep pink satin fabric, Roberta Demere. Next to it was a receipt for five of these baguettes at four thousand dollars a pop. Toni shook her head at Mallory's constant extravagance. Or rather, Uncle Danny's generosity.

Toni hurried to meet Jack at the front door. Only the butler waited there. She left her coat on a nearby chair and glanced about the room. There he was, cornered by William and deep in conversation. Poor Jack. She'd save him. When she got closer, she heard her name mentioned.

"Antoinette never wholly recovered from her little sister's kidnapping—none of them did. In fact, it destroyed the entire family—except for Mallory. She's the strong one. Toni still holds herself personally responsible for Suzette. It's silly of her to do that because there wasn't anything a little girl could have done," William explained.

"So, 'Antoinette' has or had a younger sister?" Jack looked surprised.

"Yes. Didn't she tell you?" Mallory asked.

"Antoinette has a habit of emptying her heart to everyone who listens. I'm surprised she hasn't told you," Will said pointedly.

"I let Antoinette open to me in her own way, in her own time." Jack turned to see Toni. "Hey, ready to leave?"

His face displayed pity. Pity for her. Only a moment ago, the evening had wings and possibilities. Now he looked at her so differently. Adoration had melted into disappointment. She was no longer a strong, smart, beautiful woman, but a weak creature. Her face burned with anger as her shoulders drooped. A tug to the skirt of her dress, pulled her attention downward. She stared into the imaginary specter of dear, sweet Suzette. *Toni, are you okay? Is there something wrong?*

"Toni, are you okay?" It was Mallory tugging at her dress, calling her name.

It wasn't time for Jack to know her deepest hurt, her lifelong nightmare. "Time to go now, Jack." She pushed him hard with both hands and headed for the door as their phones buzzed. Another body was found. This time the woman was alive.

Chapter 18

Midnight—January 1

The city flew past on the other side of the car window as they drove in silence. Jack concentrated on traffic and focused on what lay ahead at the park. The red light and siren on top of his car helped to clear traffic. Toni watched fireworks pop and whistle in the dark abyss above Navy Pier.

In minutes, they arrived at Lincoln Park. On one side of the crime scene tape was police enforcement working in concentrated silence. On the other side were partyers hooting and blasting toy horns. It felt surreal.

Jack parked and bolted from the car. Toni did her best to keep up holding her gown above her knees, but her heels sank into the snow, covering her feet, impeding her ability to move quickly. The ice became painful on her skin.

Scanning the arc of the trail and the location of the trees, she couldn't help but wonder why the victim chose this spot with its sheer ice to run. The other paths were regularly cleared with salt pelts, this section hadn't. The fir trees were particularly thick here, blocking out the glow of streetlights. Most of the women in the city had stopped jogging here unless they ran with a male companion. Why jog tonight, New Year's Eve, of all nights?

Thank god this jogger was still alive when she was found. The crime scene looked like a mishmash of wet potatoes caused by the medics, now gone with the victim to the hospital. The blood spatter patterns were intriguing. It clung to the tips of the firs as red cranberries. It was impossible to tell the size of the teardrops of blood to get the precise angle of impact. What was under all those thick branches and heavy dormant brush where they couldn't see? Wondering the same thing, Jack crawled beneath into the undergrowth to have a look while half a dozen policemen trained their flashlights on him. It was hard not to go in with Jack but since she had been officially taken off the case, she didn't want to compromise the evidence. It was the very thing a defense lawyer would use to throw out in a trial.

Toni stood back. It was eerie being so close to where the woman jogger had been hauled into this secret compartment. A wild, sick animal carried his prey away into his den. Had he laid in wait for her, peering out for someone to happen by? He had to be in excellent shape in order to tangle with the women who religiously ran even in the cold of winter. Another sign of male dominance to prove his

Agent Susan Hunter arrived. A brown stocking cap covered most of her short brown hair, with a few lengths escaping.

"I thought you were taken off Frosty?"

"That's right."

"Well, I've been reassigned to this case now. Are you here on consult?"

"Jack and I were together when the call came in."

Hunter looked at Toni from the crown of her head

down to her feet. "Your heels are ruined, and you have got to be freezing."

"I am. Can't feel my legs anymore." Toni detected a look of resentment on the woman's face and hated the stab of unexpected jealousy.

"What do you have, Autry?" Hunter asked, freezing Toni out of the conversation.

"Just got here. Come and have a look for yourself." Jack stooped low to the ground, then got to his knees. He called out, "Get me a police photographer. It's like a cave in here. I'd say there is a good-sized space about seven feet by four between the lowest firs which hang to the ground and then the tree trunk. Looks the same all the way around it. I want the city called tonight and have them trim all these branches up to about five feet. These are giving our guy cover."

"Lincoln Park managers aren't going to like the trees be desecrated like that," Hunter said, peering under the trees.

"Well, I don't think parents like their daughters being desecrated and murdered either!" he snapped back.

"What's the victim's name?" Hunter seemed taken aback by his sudden annoyance.

"Lisa Foreman. She lives off Diversey," Officer Pirelli answered.

"That's my neighborhood. ID on her, then?" Toni asked.

"We found it in the snow," Pirelli said.

Agent Hunter looked hard at Toni. "Unless you have clearance, please get behind the tape with all the other 'ped-es-trian-s'."

Toni reluctantly left. Digging around in her pocket

she found a dry cleaner's ticket and a pen. Lisa Foreman, Diversey, she scribbled. Growing numbness in her hands and fingers made it difficult to write.

"Is Special Agent Postell still here?" Officer Pirelli yelled over the din of the crowd.

"Here." Toni held up her hand and waved it at him. Her eyeballs felt prickly, and her cheeks burned.

"Autry asked me to find you. He wants you."

Good. That made her an official invitee. She was legal. There wasn't much Hunter could say about it now, just scowl. And that she did well. It was Toni's turn to ignore her.

Toni crawled beneath the firs, catching her heel on the hem of the dress. "Thanks, Jack. I appreciate you letting me back in on this one," she said, untangling her dress.

"I can't do this without you. We started on this case together and that's the way we'll finish it." He held her gaze for a beat of her heart.

It was warmer under the bows of the fir trees. "Wow, look at this area," Toni said. "Frosty can really take his time in here. But notice how black it is without light. He comes prepared, even with a flashlight along with his knife. The kill bag must be small. Like a fanny pack."

"Well, he certainly wouldn't be hauling a full-size suitcase on rollers," Special Agent Hunter dryly said.

"After the attack, he must have thought she was incapacitated enough to remain here and freeze to death. He was wrong. She crawled out and made it as far as the street when someone driving past saw her and called 911." Toni ignored Hunter.

"Amazing. Usually, he cuts just enough to paralyze

the women, it leaves them fully conscious as they slowly freeze or bleed to death. We found her alive. We're going to get him. It's a good sign, Special Agent Postell."

Toni smiled.

Jack, shifting his weight, rose unsteadily, grabbing Toni's shoulder to prevent himself from falling. "Hey, you're soaking wet. I'll have Pirelli drive you home."

"No, I don't want to leave."

"I'll fill you in tomorrow. It'll be like you never left."

She wanted to stay, but wearing evening clothes in this weather wasn't ideal. "Okay, but I'd like to see the report in the morning—if you don't mind."

"I don't mind." Jack helped her out from the twist of branches.

Hunter waited. "I'll take it from here, Agent Postell."

Toni gave a weak smile before following the police officer to his vehicle.

"I want to get Frosty." Pirelli made small talk as he cranked up the patrol cars heat.

"We all want to get him." Toni shivered.

"No, I want to get him myself. No one else."

She looked at him quizzically. "Going after him alone isn't safe. Even after this one is caught, there's always another to take his place. By the way, you don't happen to have any precinct talk to pass along to me, about the mayor's case?" Toni removed her shoes and rubbed her feet to circulate the blood.

"No. Just that we're still waiting for the purse we found on her to come back from forensics."

"A purse? Are you certain?" Toni hadn't been

informed and now she wished she hadn't reacted so quickly in front of the officer. The last thing she wanted was to appear out of the loop—even though she obviously was.

"I'm certain. It was tucked beneath her, entwined with her clothing."

"Did you see it?"

He nodded.

"Describe it to me."

"From what I remember, it was one of those expensive designer purses."

"Brand name?"

"Roberta Demere."

"Roberta Demere," Toni repeated, thinking about Mallory's purse.

"The designer restores only antique purses and details them with different stuff."

"I must compliment you on being such an expert on women's purses."

"Not really an expert. I just know my sister loves them. Of course, she can't afford any, so she copies the style and sells it to her high school girlfriends. Makes a nice profit."

"A young entrepreneur."

"You have to go to Demere's studio to get one— she won't allow any outlet store handle them." Perilli took a right onto Broadway.

"So, they are exclusive; one-of-a-kind creations which makes them all the more desirable."

"Only the rich, or the stupid, buy from her." The officer rolled his eyes.

"Interesting. By the way, I live on Wellington and Clark Street across from the old Ivanhoe Restaurant."

"I know just where that is."

"Great." She blew on her hands, then kicked up her feet closer to the heater.

"I've been watching you for some time."

"Watching me?" Toni wasn't pleased.

"At the gym."

"I'm sorry, I never saw you there."

"I teach self-defense classes. I've watched you kick box. You're a dynamo," he said with admiration.

"I used to run in the park all year round, no matter the weather. I loved it. With the serial out there, I bought the gym membership."

"Smart lady." Jared Pirelli pulled up in front of her brownstone. "More women should follow your example. By the way, I haven't seen you there lately."

"I'll be back soon enough. Thanks for seeing me home." Climbing out of the police car, the irony of returning home the second New Year's Eve in a row without her date didn't escape her.

Following her nightly routine, she checked her doors and windows, fed Perp, took a long hot bath, and slipped into fresh flannels. Toni lay wide awake in bed staring up at the ceiling. Thinking. Running pieces of the case repeatedly through her mind. Jack had no right to withhold information from her. This is the second time that she knew about. Then again, she also withheld information from him. It was hard falling asleep. Not only because of the crime scene, but Frosty always calls her within an hour of his killing when she is home. Half dread, half expectation.

Toni turned over in bed and plumped up her pillow. Perp meowed as she readjusted herself among the blankets. Toni stroked the cat and thought about the antique beads and buttons hanging on long cords in her front windows. Over the course of several years, Toni purchased hundreds and hundreds of antique glass buttons with threads of pinks and purples swirling through them along with Czech glass. Old glass artisan beads caught her eye as well. They all were unique and quite expensive. A few months ago, she bought oodles and then wondered how she could afford to pay rent and eat the next month.

When Mallory stopped by, she noticed the new treasures from Europe. They were sorted out in small boxes. The iridescent swirling colors of some; the antique French Champlevé enamel AP and Cir Paris gilt button, the rare ceramic blueberry croton, the mirrored buttons, the more common Victorian silver black glass buttons from the 1800s and dozens more. Along with the antique Czech beads, she had to have them all; just like she had to have Will the moment she saw him. The buttons were unique, but Mallory pressed, "Name your price." So, Toni did name it, and it included three months' rent plus enough groceries to fill her pantry and freezer. A whooping price far exceeding her cost, but Mallory wrote out the check as though it was no big deal to her, which it really wasn't.

Toni turned in bed as her brain became numb with sleep. There was music and Jack. Buttons floating on string in the breeze. Kisses to build dreams. She was happy for one night at peace.

The landline rang.

Chapter 19

She woke up suddenly to a high pitch buzz. Groggily—head clearing from sleep—she identified the ring of the landline. *Oh god, not again.* By the time she drifted off her thoughts were of Jack but now her heart pounded in her chest as she tossed the covers over Perp and grabbed for the wool blanket to wrap around her shoulders. Her bare feet were cold on the floorboards as she hurried down the hall. *Maybe it's not Frosty. Maybe it's Jack calling to make sure I got home okay.*

"Hello?" she answered with a shaky breath.

The voice crawled up her spine and made a hole in her gut. "Happy New Year, Special Agent. Did you like my present?"

"I prefer chocolate creams," she answered wryly, trying a bit of humor to shake off the doom of death.

"I'm such a naughty boy. I give you gifts and all along I find that you are just a simple woman."

"Another therapy session?" She rubbed her forehead.

"For you or me?"

"You, of course."

"I know you're alone."

"I live alone. But you know that. I'm considering a roommate. A big burly man who screens my calls. Or a vicious pit bull who only loves me and hates everyone else."

"Such a crabby girl you are today. Thought you might like someone to talk to." His voice slid around the room.

"I'm just fine. You woke me up."

"The New Year's Eve gift I left didn't give you something to dream on?"

"Someone did a number on you. Was it your mother?"

"I have no mother. No father. No sister. No brother. I'm unworldly."

"Tell me, I really want to know. Why? Why do you murder these women?"

"To get your attention."

"You have it. What's next?"

"Want to meet?"

She rose slowly from the chair with expectation. "Yes."

"I can arrange that."

"How soon?"

"It is so gratifying that you want to meet me."

"It's about time, don't you think?"

"I'll call sometime with a time and place."

"How about today? Let's not waste time. There's so much to say in person." Toni hoped she wasn't pushing too hard.

"You're right, but I need to fit it in with my schedule."

"Do you work overtime?"

"We'll meet soon. One shade of night more, one ray of day less."

Click.

The tone of the conversation echoed in her mind. Frosty enjoyed playing games. She spent enough time deciphering cryptic messages in her career to recognize this might hold a deeper meaning. Again she reached for Lord Byrons poems remembering that particular poem was missing. "One shade of night more, one ray of day less," she murmured typing the words into the browser 'She Walks in Beauty, Like the Night' and there it was, a poem she was fond of during English lit, class years earlier. Was Frosty in her class? Studying the lines, she quickly discovered his recited words varied from the original. *He's adapting the poem to fit our situation.* At her desk, she pulled out her notes and started cross referencing the lines. It pulled her closer to a truth she had yet to grasp. Time passed as she immersed herself in the task, the world around her fading into the background.

She glanced at the clock. It was nearly time to head out. Packing away her materials, she couldn't help but feel a mix of anticipation and dread. This day was the beginning of a new year, and if Frosty's cryptic words were any indication, she was in for many more long nights.

Chapter 20

Toni

Frosty wasn't her case anymore, but with all the time and engery invested, to simply walk away would be problematic. He referred to the women he murdered as his gifts to her. A sick mind would only say that. Her responsiilty was to the dead and to the living. Not him. A tight knot formed in her gut, put there by worry, over his potential actions once she stops answering his calls. Stops interacting with him. How will he react when she's no longer at crime scenes? When he feels he's lost total control and can no longer toy with her? Will he come for her?

The Taylor murder was a huge weight to carry as well. All eyes were on the FBI, city officials put pressure on the department, the mayor was under fire, the family looked to them for justice. The life of a young promising woman was cut short by someone she knew.

The right course of action was to distance from Frosty immediately and focus entirely on solving Victoria Taylor's murder, the love child of Chicago's mayor. Keeping his real kinship a secret would be itself a challenge. Sooner or later, she won't be able to juggle both cases. Fortunately, Jack seemed to keep the park murder's door open to her, and she felt comfortable walking through it whenever she wanted—but how will he react when she steps away?

Last night's news wasn't all bad. It wasn't murder. It was attempted murder. Jack called with news that Lisa Foreman was still alive. The heaviness she carried seemed to lift a bit.

Toni drove to Memorial Hospital. But first she picked out a bouquet of spring flowers to brighten the room. She wouldn't question her about the attack or Frosty. She'd leave that to Hunter. For now, she'd sit with her and hold the hand that was still warm because Frosty at last had failed.

Toni showed her badge to the receptionist. "I'm here to see Lisa Foremen. Room number?"

The greeter tipped her head in acknowledgment and then accessed the computer for the information, which quickly flashed on the screen. A look of shock rushed her expression. "Hold on a minute. I'll be right back."

When the receptionist was out of sight, Toni spun around the computer and read the words 'Deceased.' Toni left the flowers. The ground seemed to drop out under her. Frosty did succeed again. How she hated him.

Pushing both the heavy glass front doors open, Toni was back out on the noisy city street with snowplows grinding down the streets and cars honking. Finding the first trash bin, she bent over to release her breakfast. In the short distant, a siren whined. The bright winter sun glared harshly down on the snow, piercing her eyes without mercy. Digging around the inside of her large purse, Toni couldn't find her sunglasses through the tears, and momentarily decided to focus on breathing. Once inside her vehicle, she began her anti-anxiety tapping, beginning at her forehead.

The first day of the year and the Taylors would be in for their polygraph at headquarters. There was just enough time to work some of her unharnessed anger out at the gym. Luckily, her gym bag was still at the back of her bus.

After changing clothes, Toni stood with feet planted firmly on the mat, face-to-face with the enemy, who just happened to be in the form of a red punching bag. Toni was merciless, relentless. With each punch of her curled up fist, it spun about on its metal chain, swayed to the side trying to ditch her, or barely moved depending on her strike. She imagined it to be Frosty. Dark, frozen figure with daggers for teeth.

Too many dead bodies, motionless as concrete, stared up at nothing. A cowardly human did this to another person. One just like him destroyed her family years back; the lone woman who took innocent little Suzette into the car as they walked to the corner store for their mama. What were they buying that day? Candy? How exasperated her mother had been with her. Desperate. "Can't you remember something, Antoinette? Please, Antoinette, remember. Anything?"

"No, Mama."

After Suzette was taken, her life's focus shifted to finding her. As a child, she did her own investigations, looking through tall grass, crossing streets to check alleyways, knocking on neighbors' doors to see if they remembered a car parked two doors down. The reason she entered the FBI was to find out what happened to Suzette. She applied for the Missing Persons

Department but Agent Palmer guided her into forensics instead. The sooner Frosty was caught and Victoria Taylor's case was solved, the sooner she could find out what happened to her sister.

Jack admonished her when he accused her of telling Miranda Styles the name of the murder victim. He mentioned she needed to see the faces of the family who learned of their daughter's murder. She knew how it felt all too well, because once upon a time, she was the face of the family. Daily she wondered if her sister was she dead. If not, what happened to her? Was she adopted into a family and lives a happy life? Or is she living her lifeout in a backyard shed held captive? Now the red punching bag turned into the woman who took Suzette. She hit it harder and harder. Fury seemed to fry her bones and the pain was endless.

"I'd hate to be the one you're mad at." Jared Pirelli caught the back of the bag and held it still. "Go ahead and hit it again."

"Oh, hi. I forgot you work here." Breathless, Toni took a few steps back.

"Forgot me?" He laughed. "I'm part owner. And a full-time cop. Are you okay? I drove you home last night, remember?"

"Of course." She blinked, confused he'd even mention that. "Sorry. I didn't recognize you without your uniform." She shot him with a despondent look as perspiration rolled down her body. She wanted to be left alone. No small talk. "I'm busy beating up a bad guy, if you'll excuse me."

"I'll let you get back to him. Make sure you kick his ribs," Pirelli teased.

An hour later, Toni tossed her coat over her

workout clothes and headed for home to change. The Taylors would be at the precinct soon and she needed to observe their body language.

Pirelli stopped her at the door by grabbing her elbow. She withdrew from his touch. In the field that would be considered inappropriate, but here in the gym it wasn't. She had to remind herself of that. "Glad I caught ya. Here, read this. I'm opening my own gym, but this time as a single owner. This time in the burbs. If it does as well as I think, I might just move there permanently."

"Giving up policing?" She raised her brows. He seemed out of place as a police officer, although he was nice enough. Just kind of displaced. Perhaps this new gym would fit him more?

"Maybe. I'm fully invested with the city so makes a good time for a new opportunity. I like the River Forest area. I'll give you a free lifetime membership if you want to be a client."

"Thanks. That's a bit of a drive for me, and this gym is in my neighborhood. So—"

"I understand. By the way, you still look tense." Not budging from the door, he seemed interested in her.

Was he about to ask her out? The thought gave her chills, and they weren't good. This person wasn't her type. She didn't care for bulked up men who seemed to put their energy and time into body building.

Flyer in hand, Toni averted her eyes to read the advertisement offering defense classes. "Impressive. The fitness industry must be good to you. I may just sign up for the classes, until you move, that is."

"We already have a waiting list, but I can get your name to the top. Just don't wait too long." He flexed his muscles more than needed against the weight of the glass and metal entrance. She wanted to laugh at his bravado, but held back.

"Thanks for the tip. Congrats again. And thank you again for seeing me home last night."

"My pleasure, ma'am."

Jared took a step back, then opened the door while taking a deep bow.

Turning from Clark onto Wellington Ave., she found a parking spot near the corner. Home again, home again, riggedy jig. The phone rang as soon as she closed the door to her apartment. "Hello?"

"Why hello there, Special Agent Postell, profiler extraordinaire."

"Wow, two calls in less than twenty-four hours. Ready for our meeting?" She wasn't pleased he called again so soon.

"I'm thinking of you." His breath was halting. It made her wonder if he was beating off.

"What's the hold up? You mentioned meeting. Let's get to it. Let's meet."

"Not yet." He paused.

"Aren't our therapy sessions helping? We have formed a kind of weird relationship, don't you agree?"

"Oh, is that what you call them?" Uproarious laughter. "I knew you enjoyed them as much as I do. I mean, you always answer your phone."

"That's easy enough to stop." Toni tested him.

"I doubt you will. You're as intrigued by me as I am with you."

"There's one way to find out. You call, I will not answer. What will you do then?" Again she played with the possibility.

"Tic-tac-toe. Don't play with me. It's not nice. I'll win this game."

"It's a one-man game because I don't play. Listen, uh, what did you say your name was?" Silence. "Okay, Mack the Knife, you call me because you need to fill a void in your life. Most serials never call the FBI. You do. You're in emotional pain and although you want to stop, and live a normal life, you can't. The killings are your muscle relaxants. But death and urge never really leave you. When you call me, it's a cry for help. I can get that for you. Let me help you, please. These women don't deserve this. You know this. Let me help you."

"You see, Special Agent Postell, I don't want to be helped. I like things just as they are. With you scared. And with your mind fully engaged on me. Expecting my phone calls. I don't like sharing. You belong to me." His voice died out somewhere between his mouth and his soul. The line went dead.

"What? No poem this time?" she sarcastically asked Perp as the cat circled the top of her desk.

She held the phone for a moment, then dropped it back on the cradle. Did he somehow know she had been moved to another case? Was there an announcement about the FBI taking on the Taylor murder? Wouldn't that be the normal? Toni flipped on the early evening news.

There was Miranda holding a mic, talking into the camera, full of confidence, discussing the jogger who died earlier this morning. "Lincoln Park used to be a safe place to take your family for picnics and swimming and games. Now it's turned to a place of horror."

A long ago memory resurfaced. It began with

sunlight and laughter. Her family was at Lincoln Park. They were having a picnic on a quilted blanket. All sorts of delicious deli food was spread out. She recalled egg salad sandwiches, potato chips, potato salad, assorted olives, three kinds of cheese, relish, fat sliced bread, and cookies. Chocolate chip, she thought. Maybe there was more food. Memories shredded with time, leaving bits and pieces that usually didn't fit. Her mother and father laughed. The kids laughed too, not really understanding what was funny. Their parents stopped to kiss. Toni smiled at them. Then she and Suzette and Andre laughed, but Mallory scowled, crossing her arms. Suzette called her oldest sister a baby. Mallory protested and gave her a shove.

Toni glanced at the clock and was shocked to see the time. The mayor and his wife would be at the FBI within thirty minutes for their polygraph test. It was important for her to be there. She quickly showered and dressed in wool slacks, a blouse, and cardigan. Not wanting to fight traffic, she ubered, and jotted out additional questions for the tester to ask.

Lucky for her, Toni arrived minutes before the Taylors and had time to go over the list. Toni stood behind a two-way mirror. The mayor was questioned first while his wife waited in another room.

"Do you have a cold?" the examiner asked.

"No, I do not."

"Just answer yes or no."

The examiner began measuring changes in heartbeat, blood pressure, and respiration. Nervousness, anger, sadness, embarrassment, and fear can all be causal factors in altering one's heart rate, blood pressure, or respiration rate.

"Was Victoria Taylor your niece?"

"Yes."

The examiner appeared calm, but Toni had observed enough of these that she knew that something was off.

"Did you kill or cause harm to Victoria Taylor?" the examiner asked.

"No."

"Do you know who did kill or cause harm to Victoria Taylor?"

"No."

"Did you help cover up the killing?"

"No."

Now the tester went on to ask Toni's questions.

"Did you wish to see harm done to Victoria Taylor?"

"Of course not!" he shot back.

"Answer yes or no."

"No."

"Did you get along with Victoria Taylor?"

"Always—yes."

"Were you aware of anyone plotting to hurt Victoria Taylor?"

"No."

"Do you like to swim?"

"Yes."

"Are you the Mayor of Chicago?"

"Yes."

"Are you aware of any unlawful dealings of the decedent?"

"No."

"Do you know Lisa Foreman?"

"Who?"

"Lisa Foreman. Please answer yes or no."

"No."

It was interesting to watch the questions flip flop between the ordinary and the important. The examiner was good at his job. He knew how to throw people off so they didn't get comfortable. Now it was Emily Taylor's shot. She was asked the same questions, rephrased. But her results were immediate and clear. They both passed with only one of the examiner's questions to the mayor was questionable. No hint of deception. Before they left the station, Mayor Taylor handed her a sealed envelope. "Here are the names and current addresses of all her known friends since childhood, the people I've had business within my office, with whom Victoria would have had contact. As you can surmise, these are highly confidential. Please don't release them to the press. The only reason I was so blatantly honest with all my dealings is, I want whoever did this taken care of, no matter who it is. I trust you to be discreet." He handed over the thick sealed brown envelope."

"You have my word," Toni promised.

At home, Toni took out the papers from her briefcase. She shivered at all the names connected to the mob, including Roman Morelli. She remembered as a teen they had gone on a few dates, not knowing his dad was the top mob boss. In fact, she innocently assumed he just was part of a nice Italian family who lived in a modest home near the Gold Coast of the city. It was that short-lived relationship. The district attorney said the defense would use our teenage crush to get him off. Even though it had been years, it was still referred to as 'tainted fruit'. Her personal vendetta because of the breakup. Hard to prove who broke it off over fifteen years ago.

Scanning further down to the end of the pages was the last name. Her eyes locked on it. This person had nothing to do with the mob but everything to do with her family.

Chapter 21

Toni

It was a beautiful funeral. How could it not be? The woman was well-loved. Hundreds of white roses, supposedly Victoria Taylor's favorite, adorned the church. A basket for donations "Against Women Violence' was set on a table at the back.

Jack and Toni stood together near the rear doorway. The church was a limestone cathedral just off Illinois Street. It was a bleak winter day in a line of drab days. Thanks to slightly above freezing temps, the white snow no longer filled the streets but plenty of sinking crusty mounds of dirty snow did.

Toni wore an all-black ensemble. Her woolen dress fell below her knees. Beneath, she wore black tights. Black pumps. She shrouded herself in a chic black overcoat borrowed from her mother's closet which completed her ensemble. Jack was in a dark blue business suit with a tie.

"I was hoping to get a few minutes at the funeral to talk," Jack whispered to Toni.

"Talk about?"

"Are you sure you can handle two cases?"

"Want me to be honest?"

"Of course."

"I'm dedicated to both. But it's not easy."

An elderly lady dressed in tones of grey with a veiled, round hat resting on her head, turned halfway about in her pew to frown at them. She held her finger to her lips just as sounds from the organs blasted through the cathedral as an eerie call to death.

During the funeral, people cried and clung to one another. There at the end of the long, narrow aisle was the open casket, center stage. Toni couldn't see from where she stood near the door. Not meeting her in life, she chose not to view her in death. A ten-foot cross hung at the front of the church above the pulpit.

"Are you doing okay, Postit?" Jack nudged her gently with his elbow, then placed his arm around her waist, tugging her into his side for only a moment. She felt safe. Protected. His touch was welcome. She wanted more from him. For so long, she had walled herself off from others and Jack seemed to be scaling that wall. If she were Rapunzel, she'd let down her hair.

"Jack, there's something I need to say." Was it the moment here in church that made her suddenly feel brave enough to pour out her heart to the man she admired and desired to be with? "There are things you need to know."

"Ssh!" A different mourner castigated them with dirty looks.

Jack nodded toward the door. Outside, they stood on the steps, under the eaves, away from the sharp wind. Toni's heart was so full of raw emotion that she wanted to tell Jack how she felt about him, but when she looked into his pensive eyes, she decided against it. It was time to remain professional. Unrequited love wasn't her forte. Toni did what she did best; she turned to a reliable subject, work. "I understand a designer purse was found under Taylor's body."

"Yes, it's in the evidence room at the precinct." He hunched his back against the sharp wind.

"I need to see it." The icy wind made her shiver.

"Sure, it's your case," he capitulated while watching her eyes.

"Yes. Since it's my case, I should've been informed of the purse. Why wasn't I?"

"It's a purse." He shrugged. "I thought you'd be at the precinct by now to go over what the police department has. Too much partying over the holidays?"

"It's out of the line of command for me to learn about major evidence from a patrol officer. I was caught by surprise and looked like a fool."

"Are you sure you can really handle both cases?" he repeated.

"Don't worry about me. I need support from the PD. That includes what was picked up at the crime scene. All that needs to be turned over to FBI headquarters to my attention." Toni accidentally snapped at him. It made the tenderness drain from his face.

"Yes, Special Agent." He rocked back on his heels.

"This can't happen again." Toni felt torn between her feelings for the man and doing her job.

Jack shifted his stance. "Pirelli?"

"Yes. It was rather humiliating to be brought up to speed by him."

Jack let out an angry sigh.

"Find anything of interest with the purse?" Toni asked.

"It's a fancy purse. A bit of money. Not much. Cell phone."

"Are you kidding me? A cell phone too? I need to see it all. Especially the calls and texts. Anything stand out?"

"We have a tech guy working to unlock it."

"I'll come to your office later today. The mayor gave me a list of names Victoria came in contact with daily both on and off the job. A few on the list you might be able to help me with."

"Who?" His interest seemed piqued.

"I'll tell you when I come in to look at the purse."

"Toni, about the other night at your sister's."

"I had a great time." She cut him off.

"I'm sorry I couldn't drive you home."

"Think nothing of it. I'm getting used to going home alone after New Year's Eve by now. I appreciate you helping me out with the date situation." Purposefully she became all business. Emotionless. It was a way to protect her heart.

"Date? I didn't think it was a date. I thought it was an appointment."

"One of these days we'll find out what it really was."

"I had a great time, too." Jack's smile returned and it was totally engaging.

"I see you're a man of many talents." Toni gave a lopsided smile. "There's something I need to get out into the open about New Year's Eve."

"Let me guess. After the party, Congressman William Schofield called you. He became wildly jealous seeing us together. The next morning, he arrived, his arms laden with flowers, candy, diamonds and promised to love you forever. He even threw in a summer home on Martha's Vineyard. Being confused, you have no idea what to do, so you need my guidance."

"If I didn't know you were teasing, I'd think you'd lost your mind for sure." She playfully nudged him, softening her emotions.

"Are you sure?" A sense of relief crossed his brow and his eyes sparkled mischievously in a way they had on New Year's Eve.

"You're right, there's a lingering feeling and it's called 'distaste' and 'disgust' toward Will. He had no business saying anything about me to you."

"I think he meant well when he told me about your sister, Sue."

"Suzette." Toni flared at this insensitivity of shortening her name.

"Suzette. I think that's what makes you tick now. Suzette's disappearance drives you forward to solve crimes. Trauma shapes us."

It was unnerving and tantalizing to have him understand her. He seemed to be stepping emotionally closer than a moment ago. She did her best to soften her voice but anger and hurt still bubbled about the purse. "I didn't realize you were both a philosopher and a detective who recites Tolstoy."

"With my job, it calls for anything I can manage."

"You might be right about Suzette as my driving force. Her kidnaping remains a mystery. I want to tell you about it but not here. Not today. And maybe someday, if I am lucky enough, I'll find out what happened to her."

"How will you start the search?"

"Who says I haven't already been searching?" Toni looked up at him.

"Tell me more."

"Not yet. The day of the kidnapping remains foggy in my head. I remember we were walking hand in hand to the corner store to get candy."

"What kind?"

"Not funny."

"Just trying to lighten the moment. Sorry. Continue."

"There was a lady who walked up to us. I think she got out of her car when she first saw us. I don't really remember much beyond, but the police came. I don't think I was any help."

"You were traumatized, that's normal. Was there a ransom demand?" He put his hand on the small of her back. It felt comforting.

"No, never. That was quite baffling since my parents were wealthy and would have willingly emptied their bank accounts to get our sweet Suzette back. My guilt never leaves." Toni's sadness overwhelmed and she gasped, choking back tears. "Sorry. I didn't think I'd become so emotional telling you."

"It's okay. It's the funeral. It's the dreary day. Makes us more suspectable to sorrows." It was as if Suzette was comforting her although it was Jack who spoke. He lifted her chin and peered into her face. "Schofield said you blamed yourself. How could you even begin to feel what happened to Suzette was your fault? And maybe instead of being a hot shot on TV, you should find your sister. It's time. Maybe I can help in some way."

Before Toni could respond, the funeral procession started out of the church. The top of the coffin was engulfed with hundreds of white roses and dozens of flailing satin ribbons. Wind picked up. A wide gulf of people spread from the door on to the icy ground. They walked mundanely toward their cars for the drive to the cemetery in the burbs.

Jack left her standing alone and followed along as his eyes swept the crowd. Toni trailed. But instead of following in Jack's footsteps, she worked the crowd in the opposite direction.

Would Victoria's killer be here? Sometimes an absence speaks louder. Reading expressions was nearly impossible. Bundled against the cold wind, everyone looked down, their heads shrouded in hats, scarves, hiding expressions. It was hard telling who came with whom. They appeared innocent. Normal. And there was Will walking along the side of the mayor. In minutes, the hearse moved at a snail's pace down the street with an entourage of cars following. Now, the only person left in front of the church was her. Even Jack disappeared into the lineup of cars.

Feeling frustrated and lonely, a time like this called for a visit to Uncle Hershel's. She hadn't seen him since the day he dropped off her gift, the week before Christmas. Toni drove her VW downtown and quickly found a parking space near his small shoe repair shop under the L. She smelled the odor of leather and polish a half block away and heard his brittle voice as she reached the door.

Chapter 22

"These are the best shoes in all Chicago Land!" Uncle Hershel Freeman informed his customer. "They don't make shoes like these anymore. You only need one pair for the rest of your life. And maybe a new sole, or two, just for extra measure." He yanked off his shoe and slammed it on the counter to show the elderly man, who seemed as if there were nothing more interesting in the world than that black sized 10 men's shoe. "I bought these back in 1965 and I've only had to put new heels on them. I wear them every day."

Toni waited for him to finish with the small cue of people dropping off their leather goods for repair. The store was a dying art in the ever-changing city. Daily, he extolled the importance of repairing and not replacing. He had been in this one location for nearly fifty years, and the cramped quarters suited his purposes just fine.

"My beautiful Antoinette!" Uncle Herschel looked up and held our his arms. "What do I owe this visit? Are you hungry? Need lunch? You look tired. The dead getting you down? What do you hear from your father, and have you visited with your mother recently?"

"Uncle Hershel, I've missed you so much." She wrapped her arms around him and hugged him tightly. For her, he was her real home; a dad when she needed one, a counselor when she needed advice, and a shoulder to cry on when she needed a safe place. Today she needed all those things.

He rubbed his large, wrinkled hands together. "Come into the back of my shop, I have a Babka, turkey kabanas and maamoul with dates."

"My mouth is watering."

"Great, come and we will enjoy." Uncle Hershel locked the store, flipping the cardboard sign from OPEN to CLOSED in an elderly lady's face.

"Open the door for me!" she demanded, turning the knob with her knotted fingers.

"Oy vey! Go away." He waved her off and then pulled the shade down in her face.

Behind the curtain that separated the front of the store with the back, Toni sat at the little wood table in the cramped storeroom. Herschel busied himself taking the food from the countertop refrigerator; meat, bread, kosher spread, and babka. "Come, help yourself." He sat in his chair with a thump; his bulky tummy rubbing the edge of the table.

Toni took a huge bite of a kosher sandwich, causing her cheeks to bulge out on either side like a hamster.

"Yahweh must have whispered in your ear to come see me today. I have another Hanukah present for you. I bought this one after I dropped off your mittens." Uncle Hershel got to his feet and stumbled around a bit moving aside boxes until he found it. "Ah-ha! Here it is."

Toni lit with anticipation. How she loved presents. Carefully, she opened the lid of the small blue box and inside were vintage buttons. "Oh, Uncle Hershel. They're gorgeous and so unusual. Even with all the collecting over the years, I've never seen better. Such sparkle and quality." Picking them up, she turned them over in one palm. One by one, she held them to the light.

"They come from the Holy Land. I'm glad you like them, but mittens are a better gift. How will buttons keep your hands warm?"

"Your love keeps my hands warm. I adore all your gifts. And I wear my mittens every day. They keep the cold off my hands. Here they are." Toni turned about and pulled them from her coat pockets and waved them at him before putting them back. "See?"

Satisfied, he smiled. "If you ever get tired of chasing the bad ones on the streets, you should come and sell shoes with me. We can eat like this each day. Shoes are much safer than guns." He stuffed a piece of rye bread in his mouth. "Listen to me, I have a large storage room on the second floor. Give me the word and I'll clean it out. You can have the space all your own. There's even a bathroom. I won't use it. Only you."

Toni put the lid back on the box and put them on the floor beside her purse. "I'd enjoy each day, being close to you. I love you, Uncle Hershey."

"I love you too, but enough, enough, try the Babka. You haven't had a bite of it." The plate was pushed closer. "Now I must ask you again. How long has it been since you've seen your mother?"

"It's been a while. I saw her right after Thanksgiving."

"Go see her again. You should put it on your calendar to see her each month. I know she misses you."

"Do you really think she sees me?"

"Antoinette, it doesn't matter. Do it for you."

"I'll think about it, Uncle Hershel."

"Aw, remember when you used to call me Uncle Hershey?"

"I still call you that at times. It's because you always had a Hershey bar in your pocket for me. I love you, Uncle Hershey, because you love shoes and people. And me."

"Ah!" Jumping to his feet, he took his suit jacket off the hook where it was hanging. From a pocket he pulled out a Hershey bar and held it up. "See? I am always prepared for one of your visits. How can Uncle Hershel forget his niece? Never!" He patted her back. "Toni, I want you to come to Temple with me this Saturday."

"Oh—I'm just not up to…"

"You need faith, Antoinette. I pray for you when I go to temple."

****

Toni was at the police station bright and early the following morning. Jack slapped down a thick folder on the desk between them. Toni quickly snatched it and flipped it open. "This is the forensics on Victoria Taylor. Are all the test results in?"

"Some are still out. Brady dropped these off this morning."

"Brady? But I'm—"

"Just hold on. I know what you are about to say. By the time you get back to your place you should have his emails too. So will the FBI."

Toni returned to the report. "It's all here; blood, tissue, fluids, the swabs. No seamen present, no strangulation. What? It says she died of a heart attack. A woman her age?" Toni held up the glossies of the murdered victim. Jack handed her a magnifying glass to look at the minute items. The victim appeared to be complacent as if it were her destiny. No shock of fear, no moment of surprise; only rest. That is except for the eyes. By now, Jack had repositioned himself on the front edge of the desk. Occasionally, he kicked out his leg and touched her leg with the toe of his shoe, lightheartedly.

Toni read on in silence as Jack spun his chair around. "According to this report, the brain stem trauma came postmortem? Did I read that correctly?" Toni asked, trying to cover her smile over him being playful.

"Yea, I read that too." Jack nodded. He again nudged her foot with his.

"Jack?" she widened her eyes at him then returned to the report. "Odd. Maybe it occurred when the body was moved from the murder scene to the secondary scene. According to Brady's report, she suffered a heart attack, which instantly killed her and then she dropped into the coffee table. Why wasn't 911 called? Why take her to the park?" She returned his foot nudge.

"Doesn't make sense, does it? I still say homicide."

"Definitely homicide." Toni returned to reading Brady's report. "But the toxicology reports aren't in this file. Hand me the phone. I want to talk to Brady myself."

Jack put them on speaker.

"Doctor Max Brady, please. This is Special Agent Postell calling—hey, I just read your report on Victoria Taylor."

"Ha, I knew you'd have questions. Remember,

we're still waiting on toxicology."

"How soon do you expect those results back?" Toni asked.

"Another couple of weeks at the most. Anything else you need?" Brady asked.

"There is. The pictures show a large rug directly under the table where Victoria fell."

"Sure, it's in evidence room. Agent Postell, just tell me what I'm looking for."

"Blood amount and if there is something else on the rug other than blood. I want to know what it is. Be sure to type it against the toxicology that'll be coming from Quantico."

"I'm on it."

"Did you ever get that piece of plastic picked up from the park?"

"I went right over, but it was gone."

"Damn. Thanks, anyway." Toni returned the office phone to the cradle. "Who've you interviewed so far, Jack?"

"It's all there in the report. Read."

Toni went through the pages for the second time, noting the mob names were left off. "I see her parents, the mayor and his wife, and a handful of friends. What, no boyfriend?"

"Still in the early stages of discovery."

Toni shifted uncomfortably, adding another secret she's keeping from Jack.

More pages were flipped through. "The mayor said she had a slew of male suitors. How many is in a slew do you suppose?"

Jack shrugged.

"Well at least she worked and didn't freelance on

her parents' money."

"Ms. Taylor made close to a quarter of a million a year."

"Wow, I'm sure in the wrong business. And the city put up paying this extravagant salary for a secretary?"

"An executive assistant, and I bet the taxpayers aren't aware."

"I've a feeling they will by next election." Something in one of the photographs caught her eye and made her queasy. "I'd like to see that purse now."

Jack walked to the file cabinet and pulled out a plastic bag with evidence tape stuck to it. "Signed it out today, waiting for you. You can deliver it to the FBI for me." Toni put on plastic gloves and carefully unwrapped it. She set the purse down on the desk. Other than a change in fabric, it was nearly identical to the one on Mallory's dresser. It measured about 8 by 6 by 3 inches. Had a strong fabric cord handle, and the purse itself was accented in expensive beads, sequins, and antique Czech beads with threads of pink and purple throughout each one. The inside was lined in a lovely shade of satin, In a court of law, she couldn't swear by it but she was nearly one hundred per cent sure those were the beads she sold to her sister months ago. However, what she could swear in court she sold to her sister, was the one-of-a-kind ceramic blueberry croton and the rare antique French Champlevé Enamel APT Cu Paris Guilt Button. And now she was certain the black glass buttons from the 1800s were also from her. The inside label read Roberta Demere surrounded by swirls of golden thread. Could Mallory and Will be involved in her murder? If so, how? Her stomach lurched. Her hands shook. The room seemed stuffy, and she had a hard time breathing. *Careful, remain calm. Eagle eyes is watching your reactions.* The purse she carried on NYE was a gift from Mallory. That particular purse was made from wool. Pearls were hand sewn in floral patterns. She couldn't swear it was made by the same designer as the other bags, the cloth was inferior and the pearls fake. It might be a knock off. She'd check the label when she got home.

"Do you have anything to tell me?" His eyes narrowed.

Toni found herself in a compromising position. Leaning above her, he protectively put his arm around her chair, emotionally and physically trapping her.

"Gorgeous beads and unusual buttons." She slipped her hands down into her coat, where her fingers grabbed a hold of the damp fuzzy wool left there by her mittens. "You mentioned checking out a possible boyfriend lead?"

"I'm sure the name William Thomas is familiar to you."

"Wait? What?" His name was on her list, but she thought it far reaching to suspect him. And this was one of her secrets. Thank goodness he already knew. One less stressor. "I don't believe it. He's engaged to my sister. And believe me, if anyone would know if she was being cheated on, Mallory would."

Jack wryly smiled.

Toni sat up taller and pushed through her emotions to appear in control. "Let's call Will in with his lawyer. I don't want to be in the room because it could be misconstrued later that I zeroed in on him due to our past relationship, as well as how it ended."

"Who do you suggest?"

"How about Susan Hunter? Or is she too tied up with the Frosty case?"

Jack made the phone call. "Hunter is making the call now for Will to come in. I'll inform the examiner."

"Can I watch?"

"It's best you stay completely out it."

"Normally I'd agree, but since this case was plopped in my lap, I think I can watch in another room by camera." Toni moved forward in her seat.

"Okay. Have it your way. Your ex-fiancé is none other than your sister's present fiancé, who had a girlfriend who was recently murdered. Oh yea, she happens to be the niece of the mayor of Chicago."

"Wait, you used the term 'boyfriend'. Will is engaged to Mallory."

"Engaged and yet, still he dates. The new question seems to be how long did they date and where was he the night of the murder?"

"Certainly, you're not asking me." Toni uncrossed her arms and leaned forward.

"It seems to be a family affair. Your family."

"Come on, you can't be serious."

"The honorable congressman dated Victoria before you dated Will, and during the time you dated him. But as far as we can tell, when he met Mallory, he broke up with you, his fiancée, and Victoria, his girlfriend. But they started up again a few months ago."

"Supposition."

"We're going to ask him about it when he comes in. Do you have any questions you'd like for us to ask good ol' William that I can add it to my list?"

"I don't care about him cheating on me, but my

sister might not approve she was cheated on." Toni knew she said too much. Oh god, why did she let that slip? Thanks to her big mouth, Jack probably suspected Mallory, too.

Toni stood and moved toward the door, not wanting to spend another minute in Jack's office. "I'll be back for Will's interview."

"And things are just getting interesting."

Toni dug in her purse for her cell. "I need to take a few pictures of Victoria's purse. Maybe Roberta Demere can give us added information. Since they're numbered and all one of a kind, she might have kept a log."

"You aren't telling me everything. If you have something to say, Postit, say it."

"Give me twenty-four hours; it's all I ask for, please. Then I'll tell you."

Jack set the timer on his watch. Leaning in close to what Toni thought at first was going to be a kiss, he spoke into her ear. "All right. If you're not back here within twenty-four hours, I'll come looking for you."

"Then it's a date. Or is it still an appointment? I'll wear heels either way." Toni kissed his cheek and hurried out of the station to hop a bus.

Chapter 23

The designer's shop was lined with shelves holding unique baguette-shaped purses, with the workroom open to public viewing at the back, separated by a wall of glass. Exposed brick walls gave a unique ambiance to the shop. Antique rugs were nicely spaced on the cement floor. Large sofas with needlepoint covered pillows, and oversized armchairs covered in Edwardian era fabric were arranged in groups. The place was accented with large palms and short ferns. The workers, dressed in white button—down smocks over their clothes were busily working.

Slowly, Toni sauntered the room, looking at purses displayed in glass cabinets. Some were completed while others were a smorgasbord of sorts where one selected the additional materials and enhancements of chatelaines.

A woman about her mother's age, and impeccably dressed in high fashion couture and small heels greeted her. "Hello, I'm Roberta. If you don't see something that pleases you, we can accommodate. Is there something specific you are interested in, such as a color or a fabric?"

Toni presented her badge, introduced herself, and explained the reason for her visit.

Roberta shifted on her feet as her brow took on a crinkled scowl.

"This won't take long. There's a purse I need information about." Toni held up the cell to show a picture of Victoria's purse.

"One of my favorite Baguettes. An individual design I created myself."

"It's simply lovely."

"Thank you." Roberta's nod was more of a bow as if the presentation of her work was worthy of it. "You showed your badge so I assume you are here on business."

"Unfortunately, you're right. Do you keep a record of your customer's purchases?"

"I do. However, my shop policy ensures total confidentiality in these matters. But, since it's the FBI requiring the information, I'll help all I can. Follow me, please."

Toni followed Roberta to the back office where she shuffled through hard copy files. Her perfectly coiffed hair accentuated the beauty of the older woman's face. As she moved, the expensive jade green silk dress showed off her slim figure.

Unable to contain her impatience, Toni took a seat in a large leather smoking chair near the desk.

Roberta chose a file folder and slowly paged through. "Five of these were made and special ordered. Each is a sister to one another. Only the lining and the buttons and beads vary."

"What colors are the linings?"

"Ruby. Cerulean. Misty Rose. Goldenrod. Emerald." She placed the pictures with the individual descriptions on the desk.

"Each purse has a cord handle, a unique sterling silver or gold frame, and as stated, each has a different color lining."

Toni looked carefully at the hand bead work, noting the similarities and differences in the photos. What caught her eye the most were the buttons and Czech beads. Breathtaking and rare. Each purse adorned with as many as twenty in various patterns of floral embroideries.

"This is exactly what I need. May I ask about the buttons?"

"What would you like to know?"

"Were these special ordered? If so, I need to know the source."

Roberta seemed uneasy, sighing heavily and shifting her petite frame.

"Look, I'm not interested in spreading your secrets. I'm just trying to solve a murder," Toni explained.

"A murder? One of my clients was murdered?"

"Not sure if she was your client."

"And you think telling you about my supplier will solve it?"

"Directly speaking, no."

Roberta took a breath. "Very well. The lady who ordered the baguettes brought the buttons and beads with her and she was very particular on how many were used on each baguette. Let me say, they were some of the best and prettiest I've ever seen. Highly desirable. European. The customer selected everything down to the embroidery threads. Of course, I charged her much more than the usual price due to all the extra required work."

Toni's stomach pitched. The trail seemed to lead from her to Mallory to the mayor's dead niece.

"Let me make colored copies of each for you."

"That'd be helpful."

As Roberta ran copies, Toni looked at her own purse. It was black leather. Good size and utilitarian. Boring. But served its purpose.

Roberta ran the copies, slipped them into a folder, and handed it to Toni.

"I have one more question. This looks like your style but there isn't a label. Can you tell me anything about it?" Toni held out the nice, but certainly lower-class baguette that Mallory had given her. "This one was a gift to me."

Roberta looked surprised and snatched it from her hands. "Yes, this is mine, but the quality is only fair due to the request of the buyer. Certainly not up to the others. I do unlabeled baguettes to sell. But I never claim them. This time I will. I'm sorry you were the recipient of it."

"It's all right, really. One other question. Just to be clear; was this purchase made by one person or several?"

"Just one. Mallory Palmer. You can thank her for this baguette as well." She opened the office door. "You must forgive me, but now I need to return to the floor. I must oversee the finishing and give approval of each purse and also personally serve my customers."

Toni got to her feet and followed the woman back into the shop.

"If you have any more questions, please don't hesitate."

"You have been very helpful."

After dropping the hardcopies off in her apartment, Toni changed into her workout clothes and practically flew down the street to the gym. She wore boxing gloves, clubbing the heavy bag with all her weight. Ideas spun inside her head concerning Victoria's murder. Could William have ended her life to shut her up about their nefarious relationship because of Mallory? There certainly was a lot at stake with political ambitions. The Palmer money could back a candidate making an easy win.

What's the big deal over the baguettes, anyway? Roberta Demere could buy any beads and buttons she wanted, and thousands of women purchase her purses and baguettes, just as thousands of women buy other name brand purses. Could this turn out a red herring? Yet, the buttons and beads were puzzling, unless they turned out not to be one of a kind after all. *What a waste of time. And thanks for the basement bargain present, Mallory.* With that, she clobbered the bag in front of her mercilessly. Hitting the bag with all her force, it swung heavily to the left, forcing her to take a giant leap to the right when she stumbled onto someone's foot.

"Oops, sorry!" she said before looking up into the face of Pirelli.

"Hi, Agent Postell—I'd hate to be the person you're mad at." He rubbed his size thirteen feet.

"Pirelli, hi! Sorry about that."

"Jared. Call me, Jared."

"Okay, Jared." She feigned a smile.

"I'll recover. Hey, hope you haven't been running in the park lately."

"Run in the park? I'd love to do just that—no matter the weather. And with the mood I'm in, no one would dare mess with me." Not paying attention, the bag swung bag and knocked her into Jared. At six feet five inches tall, thick curly blonde hair, and a clef in his chin he was pleasant to look at.

"I just finished teaching class. I know you were trained at Quantico, but how about a refresher?"

"I don't know," she demurred, taking a step back.

"Come on over to the big mat."

Facing one another, Toni compared her size to his. Not only was he a good foot taller but also his biceps and triceps were huge. Well-toned. Although in good shape herself, she was a far cry from his condition. "Um, be gentle?" she begged.

"Let me set up a few scenarios for you. In a minute I want you to act like you're walking down the street, so you'll have your back to me. But don't turn around until I say. I'll approach you from behind as a surprise like an attacker would. What I want you to do is to take my fingers, spread them apart, and then bend over and pull me this way."

"That'll make me flip you."

"It's a refresher, remember? Turn around—and here I come."

Toni did as he instructed, and to her delight, she actually flipped him over, landing on his back, sprawled out on the matt. Applause rang from the back of the gym.

"Bravo!" Someone called.

Getting back on his feet, Jared suggested, "Let me show you another move."

For the first time she seriously considered changing gyms. The only reason she remained here so long was its location to her place and its exceptional facilities. It just seemed too creepy to work out with a police officer.

"I better pass. Another time, Jared?"

"Sure." He rubbed the tip of his nose nervously with his index finger.

As soon as Toni arrived home, she called Mallory. The butler picked up and informed her Ms. Mallory Hughes was out of town for a few weeks. Sigh. Toni imagined her in Europe. Was it planned or was it an opportune time to distance herself from William?

Looking out at the gloomy sky, Toni smiled. It wasn't snowing yet but it could start up any time. Hunting season. Come out, come out, wherever you are, Monster. She had spent the last several days working on Taylor's case. Tonight, was all hers, and she'd spend it hunting Frosty. But first hunger started.

Hurrying into the kitchen, she packed herself a light meal of celery sticks with peanut butter smeared into the crevasses, a fourth cup of soy beans she poured into a plastic bag and her favorite, a tomato sandwich on wheat bread. Perp stood on the counter watching every move; realizing this was a sure sign of his mistress leaving for the evening, Perp attacked her knuckles in protest.

"Ouch!" Toni hollered, giving Perp a bit of a shove. "Watch it, bub!"

After steaming her green leaves for tea, she poured the drink into a small thermos and then placed her snacks in a tin box. Wearing jeans, and a heavy cable-knit sweater beneath her down filled coat, Toni checked her gun before holstering it. She slung her purse over one shoulder and a pair of high-powered binoculars over the other. With the tin box under her arm, she locked her apartment.

Chapter 24

Just as she locked the door to her apartment, she heard the dreaded voice from behind.

"Another Friday night and here we single gals are all alone. Again. Well, again for me, but it might not be again for you. Anyhoo, I came over to see if you wanted to go half-zees on ordering a pizza and then watch TV together. There's a girly movie on Lifetime TV tonight. Love them, don't you?" Jo nudged her shoulder. "I'll even bake us some brownies."

"You know, Jo, as much fun as that sounds, I have to work." Toni went for the stairs, but Jo caught her arm.

"Work?" Jo seemed startled. "But this is Saturday night."

"Night shift! And crime doesn't take a holiday. Tonight, I'm just going to drive around to keep the streets of Chicago safe," Toni kidded, shrugged, and finally offered a frown. "Sorry. Maybe next Saturday night."

"Are you a cop?" Jo scooted in front of her, blocking her from the steps. "I thought you were a factory worker?"

"I'm FBI."

"Wow. That's so cool. I don't believe this. I just don't believe this. You live straight across the hall. If I only had known sooner. What case are you working on?

I know! Frosty. It's all my cooking class talks about on Saturday morning. If we had only known that when you came over that time. We would love to have picked your brain about it. We are also crime fighters and try to solve cases the police are having trouble with. We could've been assistance to you." Jo twirled her finger. "If only we had known. Maybe it's not too late."

Toni worried this conversation might go places and Jo right along with her. "Ah, we are doing well in solving this case, but thanks anyway. Actually, I just feel antsy. I might just end up at some corner bar."

"If only I could come along."

"I'll be gone hours. Many long, boring hours. Drinking." Toni looked down the stairwell, hoping to discourage the neighbor.

"You're going on a stakeout. I can tell." Jo tapped her foot.

"Okay. I'm not allowed to take civilians. Sorry. That's a no-go."

"Well, a corner bar would be okay. I'm pretty certain there's no law against us doing that. And I'm game for a stakeout." Jo disappeared into her apartment.

"I think it's best I go alone." Toni raised her voice.

"I can't hear you, you're mumbling," Jo said, somewhere inside her place. "Okay, you've convinced me. I'll come along. I see you have your dinner with you, and it'll take me a quick moment to push my left-over lunch into a paper bag. Be right back! Don't move an inch!"

"Jo, I do these stakeouts alone," Toni hollered.

"By the way, I work in the Lincoln Park area. I'll point it out to you," Jo said from another room.

"It's dangerous—Jo?" Toni inched toward Jo's apartment, afraid a sucking vortex would draw her inside and the door would close, locking.

"Safety is in numbers, as I always say. Now what do they say on those detective TV shows? Oh, I know, 'I've got your back'!" Her giggle was followed by a flushing sound.

"It's usually boring. Jo, it also might be dangerous. I can't be responsible for your well-being." Toni stepped further inside the apartment, keeping her hand against the open door. There was a light scent of snickerdoodles. It was then she noticed Jo's place was cozy with cottage style furniture. It was clean and tidy. Quilts hung over the backs of wicker furniture, and teddy bears sat about on small chairs.

"No one will even find out. And if they do, you can tell them I'm a writer of mysteries and we're collecting ideas for my new book titled "Catch 'Em in the Act," Jo called out, still invisible.

"I don't think that's much of an excuse."

Toni crossed the pink carpet and parted the lace curtains to see the snowflakes coming faster now; thicker. Anxious to hit the street, she turned around. There was a clear shot to the door. Toni made a dash for it.

Reaching the foyer, Jo stepped out in front of her, all bundled up with a huge sack of groceries under one arm and a thick red cookbook under the other.

"It might be boring so I'm bringing my cookbook to read. Okay, ready!" Jo jabbered all the way down the steps, out the door, over the piles of snow and two long blocks to where the Volkswagen bus sat parked. Toni kept trying to think of reasons for Jo not to come, and then she thought of one of why she should come. Toni was officially off the case. She drove her private bus, personally owned. They'd be a neighborhood watch. Afterwards, they could stop by a corner bar and get a drink or two.

Driving side by side along snowy roads, Toni said, "Where's your employment?"

"It's Lincoln Park Elementary."

"You're a teacher?"

"I'm a kindergarten teacher," she said proudly.

"I'm sure you're really good at it too." Toni smiled. The idea never hit her until this moment but somehow Jo as a kindergarten teacher fit.

"Thank you. If you want, we can walk up to the first floor windows of my room and peek in so you can see all the little chairs."

"Maybe another time. Our night is already pretty full."

"You're right. Our grades Open House is this Monday at six in the evening. Mark it on your calendar."

The traffic light snapped from green to yellow then to red. Toni tapped on her brakes and rolled to a dead stop, with crunching snow popping beneath her tires. There was still six blocks east to the location, tempted to ignore the light and keep moving, but hesitated. Cops were all over the place. Three times in defensive driving classes certainly had not been the charm for her and a fourth might cause her to lose her license for a bit; something she couldn't chance. What a hassle to Uber to crime scenes.

"Why do you suppose Frosty started killing in the first place?" Jo asked, her pen poised on her spiral notebook, ready for notes.

"I have no idea." Toni tried to maintain her composure and disregard the incessant chatter, as well as the cheerful songs Jo sang. Jo was good at distraction and Toni needed to remain focused. Finally, up ahead was the park. Toni drove slowly with only headlights and light from the moon to see her way. She didn't want to startle and chase away Frosty. Once settled behind firs, she made sure they were out from the reach of streetlamps, exactly the kind of spot Frosty looked for.

"What are we doing here? I thought it was against the law?" Jo asked.

Toni slowly moved along the parkway at ten miles an hour. "There's blankets in the backseat behind you if you're cold. My heater goes on and off."

"Don't worry about me. I'm just fine. Got my long johns on. Is it time for snacks now? I think so!" Jo dug into her large grocery bag and pulled out a sandwich, offering half to Toni.

"Pass. I have celery sticks."

They sat in silence for a few minutes as smells of pastrami on rye with onions filled the car. Jo nibbled on her sandwich. Toni kept an eye on the area as she pulled out her bag of pine nuts.

"You must be one of those health nuts. That's a pun. Get it?"

"I want to live a long, quality life. Got it."

"Each to his own." After a few minutes of silence, Jo became fidgety. "Are we still looking for Frosty?"

Toni nodded.

"Right now?"

Toni nodded again.

"Oh my gosh. I am so excited!"

"Remember, we are two gals out on the town just driving around the park on our way to a bar."

"Toni, or should I refer to you as Agent Toni?"

"Toni is fine."

"Toni, I don't drink so where else could we go after driving through the park?"

"Ssshhh."

"Now that I've put more thought into it, I'm sure I can get a soda at the bar. Some people go to bars to socialize, ya know." Jo prattled.

"Ssshhh."

"This guy needs to be caught before he gets his next victim. I hope he doesn't get us in the meantime. Do you think that could actually happen? That'd be a twofer." Jo finished her sandwich then pulled out a large candy box wrapped in glorious white shiny paper and opened the lid. With surgical precision, she used her fingers to extract a round chocolate delight from a tiny paper muffin. Gone in one bite. She sneezed.

"What's that?" Toni peered into the box.

"Fanny Mays, the best chocolate in the world! But chocolate makes me sneeze." Jo rubbed her nose.

"Really? Then why eat it?"

"Cause it's really good. Worth the sneeze. And sneezes can be fun."

"But is the candy worth the extra pounds?" Toni asked.

Jo scowled at her.

"What's the name of that candy again?" Toni asked.

"You don't know the name? Oh my gosh! You've never tried Fanny Mays, have you? Let's set wrong things right this moment." Jo held out the shiny white rectangular box to Toni, who tipped the lid and looked inside. "Go ahead, Toni, I know you want to. These are creams. I keep them in the fridge at home. They taste best cold!"

"They're loaded with sugar." She arched a brow.

"So am I. Go ahead, take one." Jo rattled the box.

Toni selected a milk chocolate cream. She bit it in half. Slowly, she rolled the chocolate around in her mouth before chewing and swallowing. The sweet deep taste lasted in her mouth. She banged on the brakes. "Oh, my goodness! This is absolutely delicious!"

"You love it! I knew it, I knew it!"

"May I have another one?" Toni licked her finger.

"Take as many as you like. And they didn't make you sneeze either. That's a good sign. It's meant to be."

Savoring the second piece of candy, Toni noticed a vehicle slowly rolling through the park. It stopped. A man got out holding a long rod and walked around, looking under the cut fir trees. "This could be our man." Breaths came in short spurts. Nervous, Toni thought about using her cell to call the police but decided to wait. Bringing Jo along tonight was certainly a stupid move. Poor judgement. She put a pedestrian in danger. And could be put on restriction.

Finally, the figure walked back to his vehicle and drove toward them. Headlights changed to bright, blinding the women. It pulled alongside of the bus. Toni read the words ANIMAL CONTROL on the side. A jacketed man rolled down his window, so she rolled down hers. "We've had calls about large dogs in the park. Have you seen any tonight?"

"No, not tonight. But they've been around other

nights. They're vicious," Toni told him.

"Hey, are you alone?" He put his arm along the edge of the window trying to peer into her vehicle.

"Hoo-Hah, I'm here too!" Jo chimed, waving at him.

"The park is a dangerous place for women these days," he said.

"We know that, thanks. FBI." Toni introduced herself the same time she held up her badge. After the window was rolled up, she rechecked the doors were locked. Animal Control drove away. Toni knew her cover was blown. If Frosty had been in the park watching, he was long gone by now.

"I bet you cannot guess what my real passion is."

"Tell me."

"Murder."

Toni jolted with surprise. "I would've guessed desserts."

Jo laughed. "My real passion is writing murder mysteries."

"You've got to be kidding me." Toni whelped with surprise.

"Nope. I'm dead serious! Forgive the pun." Jo broke out laughing and nudged Toni for the second time.

"Well, you're certainly a woman of mystery. Here you are a mild-mannered kindergarten teacher. At night, when you should be grading coloring books, you are instead plotting how to kill the principal—by the way, does he know? What's wrong with this picture?" Toni held out her arms as if asking an unseen person.

"That makes me a great undercover agent. You know, I'm not literally killing off anyone. And yes, I always carry around a notepad with a pen to jot down any ideas. I sit up writing about blood evidence long past midnight."

"Carrying around a small recorder with a mini mic is much easier. Any story ideas coming to you tonight?"

"As a matter of fact, yes!" Jo enthused.

"Well, let's hear them."

"Isn't this fun? I knew it! I knew we'd have so much fun once you got to know me. We have *sooo* much in common; I write about murder and you solve them! Being neighbors with you is a co-winkie-dink! Isn't it great? I can use you for research," Jo said, diving for her notepad sticking out of her purse.

"Yes, lots of things in common, like this wonderful candy. May I have another piece of candy?"

"Of course." She held out the box to her. After Toni took her third piece, Jo closed the lid to put it away. Toni made a grab for it then set it on the dashboard in front of her. "Leave it. Okay, go ahead with your story. I'm listening."

Jo pulled out pages from a folder. She cleared her throat. "How odd...the juxtaposition of this brutal murder scene set beneath a cloudless peach with touches of heather, sky. The police found the body among debris of the finest crystal and China laid out on an ivory damask tablecloth on the garden veranda. Obviously, the tea had not ended well. Was it something the hostess had said? The lovely police detective Josephine leaned in for a closer look...yes, this was the work of a fiend she had been following for several months. The deceased was properly attired in trendy clothes, still clutching her sterling silver coffeepot in one hand while her right pinkie finger curled through the handle of her grandmother's teacup. The MO was clearly the same; there, on the feet of the victim, was the killer's signature; her own shoes had been replaced with a pair of Prada heels." Jo smiled at Toni. "What do you think of the story?"

"Sounds like a page turner to me." Toni turned her head so Jo couldn't see her eyes roll.

"Do you really think so?"

"I have a question for you. Why did the killer replace the victim's shoes?"

"Serial killers always leave a souvenir, right?" Jo asked.

"No, not always. They usually take one."

"That calls for a rewrite."

Toni looked out the windows into the dark, turning on the windshield wipers once more, watching for a shadowy figure. One suddenly emerged from the fir trees. Tall and slender and headed straight for the car at a nice clip.

"Toni! Do you see him?" Jo screeched, grabbing a hold of her arm.

"Yes, I do, shit. I knew bringing you was a bad idea. Listen to me, Jo, you've got to calm down." Toni fumbled to unzip her parka and pulled her Glock from the holster. The zipper got caught on the fabric. Frantically, she dug for her gun just as the dark figure reached the bus. Jo held up her cookbook as a shield against possible bullets. Toni finally got her coat unzipped and held the Glock, released the safety lock, keeping it low, out of sight with her finger on the trigger.

"A gun. Bullets will be flying. Oh, my god. I don't like to use bad language but the word I want to use rhymes with luck and starts with an F."

"Remain calm, Jo."

The shadowy figure was only a foot away. An inch of metal separated them from him. A gloved hand reached out, took hold of the door handle and yanked on it hard. It was locked. Jo screamed and grabbed her chest as if having a heart attack while singing Amazing Grace.

Toni's hand slightly shook while readying to raise the gun. The gloved hand reached out once more and cleared the fresh snow from the window. A face peered into the bus.

"Holy shit! Jack! What are you doing here?" Toni yelled, cranking down her window.

"The question is what are *you* doing here?"

Toni un-cocked her gun, put on the safety lock and slipped it back into her holster.

"You two know each other?" Jo lowered her lunchbox.

"He's Chicago PD. Jack, this is Jo, my neighbor. The one I told you about."

"Hi, Jo."

Jo waved her fingers at him and giggled.

"We are having a picnic in the snow." Jo quickly offered him half a sandwich. "We're eating dinner and having girl talk. Next, we're going to a neighborhood bar to get very drunk. Very drunk. Aren't we, Toni?""

"Are you the cookie lady?" Jack wanted to know, accepting the sandwich.

"Yes, she's the one."

"It's too dangerous for a picnic out here. Skip the bar. Go home."

"Sure Jack," Toni started up the bus. "Anything

you say, Jack."

He stepped back to allow them to pull away from the side of the road.

Just out of the park, Jo pointed down the street. "Hey, I see someone else."

"With police all over the place, it's probably one of them. But let's make sure." Toni circled around the block. Sure enough, he crossed over Lake Shore Drive toward apartments. Watching intensely, Toni nearly rear-ended a snowplow.

Jack pulled up in his sedan. "I'm here to see you ladies back home to your front door."

Jo pulled on Toni's coat sleeve, "He's a very take-charge man, isn't he? I think he has his sights set on you. Do you think he'd mind if I wrote him in as a love interest in my book?"

Toni quickly rolled up her window, hoping Jack didn't hear. "He'd totally love it." She chuckled.

True to his word, Jack cruised right behind them for the snowy blocks home. And tonight, of all nights, they had their pick of parking places. Jack parked right behind Toni and saw them into the building.

"Want to come up?" Toni invited Jack.

Jack's eyes lit.

"Isn't it a bit late for a single lady to be entertaining a gentleman friend in her apartment?" Jo asked.

Toni wanted to stuff her mouth with Fannie Mays to shut her up.

"I'll leave you two alone on the stoop." Jo went on inside the building as Jack stuck out his hand and held the door open for Toni.

"You can come in, Jack. It's perfectly all right,"

she coaxed. "We're adults."

"You know Jo is right," Jack said, backing away from Toni, heading in the direction of his car. "It's rather late for a gentleman friend to be paying you a call. And, I do have my sights set on you."

Chapter 25

"She awoke to a peach with touches of heather colored sky." Still in bed, Toni turned sideways to look out the window. "And I awoke to a dreary sky with touches of puffy clouds looking as though they had been pulled from a large bag of ruffles."

Checking her feet, she was pleasantly surprised to find them shoeless. There was not a Prada heel in sight. However, there was a pair of Bass shoes carelessly flung across a bedroom. She looked at her cat still snuggled into the covers. "Time to get up, Perp. Gotta feed you and find the Monster."

Working on her laptop, Toni read through the serial profile and decided to send it into the Trib along with the dates and times of the murders. It might generate new leads that she could work on her own time. Finished, she emailed it to Miranda Styles at the Chicago paper, along with a note that said, "If it's not your birthday, it should be." Within minutes, she received her response. "Wow! Agent Postell, this is great. It'll run all week. I owe ya."

"Yes, you do." Toni smiled, pleased with herself. "By the way, may I have my recorder back? I need it."

"I have no idea what you mean. Have a good day."

Toni leaned toward the screen. Maybe I should do a profile of Frosty's polar opposite. That would be none other than Detective Jack Autry."

Profile
Lead Detective Jack Autry
By Toni Postell
She began to type.

Fortunately, there is a physical description of this person. No woman, young or old, could deny the fact that Jack is a handsome man. As I am about to profile this person let me begin by saying that no list of attributes wanted in a man has landed a boyfriend, fiancé, or husband. Hollywood, in their endeavors to deliver exciting scripts, needs to note this. Their descriptions make it seem easy to catch a man and have him fall in love with the leading lady. However, real life analysis is based on possibility and analytical procedures based on probability. The profiler's work is a blend of methodical evidence gathering and lots of long hours of spending time in his company.

A personality profile on Jack Autry shows that he is a well-educated white male who feels independent and has no immediate need for a special woman in his life. Neither is he a flirt. Jack is comfortable in his own skin and can be charming and helpful without meaning to be.

There are 3 Behavioral Characteristics.

1. A respect for women who are strong and independent.

2. Analytical and sequential.

3. The high standards he holds others to are the same he holds for himself.

Jack is the finest man I have ever known. Unfortunately, I do not know this man as well as I would like. Just when I think I have him figured out, he surprises me. Yet working beside him day in and day out for months I have gotten a sense of this man. He is a man of honor. I trust him with my life, but not with my heart.

Toni printed it and then deleted the information from the computer. She set Jack's profile on top of a folder just as the phone rang. "Hello?"

"So, you think you've pegged me," the voice oozed.

"I never said that." Toni pressed the phone recorder on.

"Your newspaper article quoted you."

Toni walked to the window. The rows of buttons swayed as she moved the curtains to see the street and looked for any man who might be her monster. There was a couple waiting for a bus on the corner of Wellington and Clark Street. She looked up and down the block as far as she could. "You know how newspapers are. They get it wrong sometimes."

"Are you uneasy?"

"Not me. You are." She scanned the room for a hidden listening device, or camera.

He laughed. "Ha, you can't fool me. I like it when women get anxious. It makes them forget how to fight."

"When we meet you'll be the anxious one. Listen well, I'm going to find you, and see you are put away forever. How does that make you feel? Huh?" Toni hung up. She felt more in control ending the conversation herself.

It was finally time to tell Jack about these calls. The Monster wasn't just inside her head; he might be lurking in her apartment. He needed to be exorcised. Not wanting Frosty to listen to her conversation, Toni took her cell out to the street to make the call. Taking a deep breath, she told him about Frosty's calls, playing down their importance, which of course, didn't work, nor had she expected it to. "I've never learned anything new from him. Not yet, or I would have let you know."

"What the hell? I knew you were keeping something from me." Jack hollered. "And you were all over me about holding out on a purse! I should go to your superiors about it."

"You won't do that because now you're as intrigued as I am. Just get someone over here to check my computer and my place, okay?" Toni wished she had thought to put her coat on before coming out. The bright sunlight gave an illusion of warmth. "Wait, bring Agent Hunter. She's also a computer specialist. If there's a Trojan horse in the system, she'll find it."

"We'll be there late afternoon."

Back inside, Toni decided to entertain Frosty with hard rock head banger music, just in case he was listening. It was a great background noise as she went over the mayor's list of names. She picked one to call. Using her cell again, she called without looking at the numbers on the page. She still knew this one by heart.

His private line rang. "Toni?"

Sigh. Of course, he had caller ID just like the rest of the world. "Hi, Will. I just learned my sister is in Europe. What do you hear from her?"

"I was thinking about calling you to ask the same question. I haven't heard from her since she left. Hey, are you free for lunch today?"

Toni looked at the clock; 11 a.m. "Yes, sure."

"My meeting just wrapped. How about I meet you across the street from you?"

"Great. What time?" Not great at all, meeting there

meant she had to put on a dress.

"It's eleven now. How about noon?"

"See you then."

Toni barely had an hour to put together a game plan and needed to dress as femininely as possible since Will liked his women girlie. The blue low-cut clingy dress with hose, dark heels and a pearl necklace with matching earrings would do. Wanting him to open up to her and talk, she needed to play his game. Just as she checked her camel hair coat at the restaurant, Will arrived.

"Hello, Toni." Will greeted with a kiss on the cheek, and then his eyes wandered from her heels to her shoulders. As he took her hand, he commented, "You look great. Blue is your color. Come on, Honey, let's get a table."

She resisted the urge to smack him. Instead, she withdrew her hand from his. It felt natural sitting across from him at the table. They spent many times like this, enjoying a meal together. How many were there, anyway? She lost count. Perhaps the setting would serve as a good backdrop for him to relax and after a few glasses of alcohol start to talk too much.

Toni looked over the menu, deciding she was hungry after all. She ordered a plate of linguini in clam sauce and, against all protests, ordered one for Will. Salads were brought first. Politely Toni dug into the fresh bowl of greens. "When is Mallory getting back?"

"In a few more weeks." Will's words penetrated her thoughts. He knew her so well. And she knew him well enough to know he came with an agenda. But so had she.

"What countries is she visiting?" Toni did her best

to disguise her interrogation.

"The usual France, Italy, Greece, Switzerland, Germany." He seemed bored reciting the names.

"Why didn't you go? There were two tickets."

"I'm about to return to Washington. There's an important crime bill going to the floor championed by the Adam Walsh Foundation. Can't leave the country right now."

"You mean to tell me that my sister is traveling alone?" Toni raised an eyebrow. Mallory never went anywhere alone. She liked an entourage to follow and assist.

"My mother accompanied her."

Quieting a laugh, she shuffled more greens into her mouth. "I find it curious Mallory hasn't kept in touch with you. Don't tell me you two had an argument?"

His gaze reeked of suspicion.

Toni decided to change her tactic. "Perhaps one of you is having second thoughts? Like you had with me. It happens." If she looked into his eyes, what would she see? But she kept them low, not wanting Will to snatch her thoughts.

"Mallory and I are fine; never have been better." He stared across the room, and then slowly worked his eyes back to hers that now were staring at him. "However, sometimes I think I chose the wrong sister."

"Which time?" She leaned her head on her hand and batted her eyes.

"I'm sorry, Toni. You must've been devastated when I hooked up with your sister."

"Hooked up? You mean after I caught Mallory and you rolling among the guest coats on her bed? By the way, my coat was sticky and went into the trash when I got home." She shivered, and not in a good way.

The waiter brought wine. Toni covered her glass with her hand and shook her head no.

"I thought we decided on drinks along with food?"

"I already have my drink." She held up her water glass. "And like old langsyne says 'let old acquaintance be forgot and never brought to mind.' I'm fine; far from devastation. I just don't want the same thing to happen to my sister."

"I had no idea you had such affection for her well-being. Ah good, here's our meal." The waiter set their bowls of linguine in front of them with a basket of fresh rolls, then left. Toni felt brimmed to the gills with food by now, tangling her fork around in the noodles trying to make more look like less. To-go boxes were a wonderful invention. This stuff would taste good reheated about midnight tonight.

"Of course, I care about Mallory. She's a generous, good person especially with her friends." Toni tried to sound nonchalant as she searched for the pill bottle in her purse.

"Yes, I agree."

"Lucky friends who got those Roberta Demere creations this year."

"Right." He shifted in his seat. "She told you about them?"

"Of course, she did. But not who the gifts were for. Other than myself, who were the lucky recipients?"

"Mallory gave them to my three assistants." Will wound noodles about his fork and slid them into his mouth.

"I know she kept one. What did she do with the extra one?"

"She bought it for my mother. How about if we make lunch last into breakfast?"

"Tomorrow morning?" The thought of him touching her skin made her ill. Even though Mallory did what she could to put Will in her bed, she certainly wasn't going into his.

"I thought we might get back together—this time for good." He emptied his second glass of wine.

The thought of being with Will made her choke. She grabbed for her water. "Why would you want me? Mallory's dad has millions." She choked again.

He waited until the choking subsided. "Money means nothing to me. And isn't this lunch about a tête-à-tête?"

"This lunch? No. Sorry." Toni wiped the tears from the corners of her eyes.

"Then what are we doing here?" Will stuck out his lower jaw.

"I'm interested in what sort of a relationship you had with Victoria Taylor. Anything you say, I'll keep from my sister. This is strictly an investigation."

"Victoria Taylor?" Will asked in surprise.

"I hear you two were close friends?"

"Am I being investigated?" He wiped his mouth and set down his fork.

"Right now, everyone is under investigation."

"You've got to be kidding. If you want answers, ask your boyfriend down at the precinct."

"I'm asking you." Toni knew she had just royally insulted him and needed to regain ground but anytime she was even a little nice, he took it as a come-on. "Will, you will always have a place in my heart, but I realize it's been over between us for a very long time.

Right now, I just want to do my job. Perhaps you can help me catch the killer."

"I did care about Victoria deeply. But we just could never get it together as a couple. You see, I love Mallory."

"Didn't you just hit on me a moment ago? Doesn't sound like love to me."

"If you say anything to Mallory, I'll deny it."

"Let's keep that little secret between us by trading information. I want to know if Victoria's death is the reason Mallory went on vacation."

"Of course not."

"How long was your relationship with Victoria?"

"Are you asking as a sister-in-law, or investigator?"

"Take your pick. Whichever you choose, just tell the truth." Toni purposefully made her voice soft. Glancing about the room she wondered if the Monster was nearby watching.

"We go way back. I dated her before you. Then for a while, I dated you both, at once. I broke it off with Vic when you and I got engaged. I didn't hear from her for about a year." Toni mused how Autry had been right about his affairs.

"Go on."

"Vic called two nights before she was murdered. There was something urgent she needed to tell me about the mayor."

"What was it?" Now he had her total attention.

"Since she died before we met, it's only a guess."

"Which is?"

"It might have something to do with his public office since I'm the congressional head of investigations."

Toni leaned forward with great interest. This case suddenly took on a bigger matter. The suspects would be endless. "She didn't tell you anything?"

"No. Never met with her."

"Give me some examples."

"I'm guessing she found proof of kickbacks, mob involvement, drugs, sex, and more corrupt government, if that's possible. Anyway, take your pick of the usual list of crimes that seem to be so popular these days in politics."

"Whoa, aren't you taking a grand jump here? Pretty big leap from needing to tell you something to Congressional investigations."

"Vic made it sound imperative that we meet as soon as possible."

"And you really have no idea what it was about?"

"None. Toni, you cannot let the police know about Victoria's phone call. Everything gets back to the mayor." Will stood and dropped a hundred on the table for lunch and a tip. "He'll think I know something that could implicate him and it's not true. I know nothing."

They walked into the lobby where Will helped Toni back into her coat. "This is what I think; you started seeing Victoria again. She had nothing on the mayor, but she had plenty on you. You didn't want Mallory to find out, so you killed Victoria because she was blackmailing you."

Will wryly smiled. "Now I remember why I threw you over for your sister—you're too rough edged; no refinement and lacking all the elements of social graces. How you ever made it as a profiler god only knows. Oh wait, your uncle got you the job. It all comes together for me now. "

He weighed his words to hit and to hurt.

They did. Maybe she went too far. Did her ego get in the way. "Will?"

"Yes?"

"If it's political as you guess, you might be in danger."

"I told you, I know nothing. We never met."

"But her killer may not know that."

Will walked out without a goodbye.

As Toni crossed in front of her apartment, a snowplow nearly hit her. Toni leaped to the safety of the curb just in time to watch it scrap on down on the street. It was headed in the direction of Lincoln Park. Toni glanced at her wristwatch. Splendid, there was just enough time to run an errand before meeting Autry and Hunter. This one concerned the case she no longer worked.

Chapter 26

The manager at the city facility decided to be accommodating once she flashed her FBI badge at him. "I like smart women." Allen Newman smiled before taking another sip of Kava. "What can I do ya for?"

"I'm working the Lincoln Park murders." Toni explained, having changed into a pair of plain wool slacks and pullover sweater, with a comfortable down-filled jacket.

"Oh, yea, yea, yea. The Frosty case." His lips barely cleared the top of his white coffee mug. Steam fogged his glasses.

"The killer strikes during a snowstorm. While most people stay home, who runs out in the snow?"

"My city workers do." He finished his coffee and set the mug down.

"Exactly." She nodded with enthusiasm.

"Tell me what you need."

"I need the work schedules of your employees, plus the name of anyone who may have called in sick on these nights." Toni slid a paper containing the dates of the murders across the desk. "I'm particularly interested in the people whose territory covers the Lincoln Park area."

"Do you have a search warrant?" Allen didn't take the paper.

"Should I get one?" Toni's back went up.

"Surely you must appreciate my situation in this matter. I can't open my paperwork to just anyone who asks."

Toni hated the sound of his chuckle. It brought her to her feet and she placed the paper on the desk in front of him. "Surely you must appreciate my situation in this matter of finding the killer. I think you've given me enough suspicion to obtain a search warrant for your company's records. Not only am I working alongside the Chicago PD, but also for the Mayor of Chicago. You are acquainted with him?" Toni leaned over Allen's desk, looking him in his horrid little eyes.

"You're not trying to scare me, are you?" His voice was a bit intense for her liking. Her posturing was meant to back him down, not raise his hackles.

"I'm on my way to police headquarters. Next time you see me, I'll have a warrant in my hand. I can't guarantee what all will be listed in it." Toni turned toward the door.

"Hold on, will you, Missy? I was just having some fun. You really should get yourself a sense of humor. Let me get a printout for you of everything you want." Allen's fingers slid over the keyboard, tapping the keys in front of the monitor. Toni walked around the back of his desk watching. Allen wore too much Old Spice and not nearly enough mouthwash.

"Here's my log for this entire year. My drivers must call in their positions every thirty minutes."

"How many workers are in the field at once?"

"On a busy night, can be hundreds. We have to hustle to keep up with the cargo of snow and wind that winters unload on us, and we do a darn good job at it, better than any other city of this size."

"I want to talk to the employees who work in the Lincoln Park area at night."

"There's just one. The fellow you want to talk with is a gal. Erma Jones has had this route around and through Lincoln Park for more than fifteen years."

"Erma Jones," Toni repeated her name.

"She's my married to my step-daughter. Does a good job cleaning up the streets. Climbs up on those big machines and clears the streets for both the mayor and me. By the way, she's on her dinner break across the hall from my office. Go on over." Allen retrieved the paper from the printer and placed it inside a manila folder. He handed it to her before leaving his office.

The city cap covered Erma's short hair, although her jacket had been removed and hung from the back of her chair. It was hard to envision a four foot person managing such a large machine.

Toni took the empty chair across the Formica topped table from her. Introducing herself, she then held up the papers the woman's boss/step-dad had just printed out. "I hear you're a valued employee."

"I guess." Erma slurped her water through a striped straw.

"On any of your runs, have you seen anything out of the ordinary on these particular nights?" Toni showed her the same dates she showed boss man minutes earlier.

"Just the usual stranded motorists."

Stranded motorists. "What happens when there's a stranded motorist?"

"I ask them if they want me to call in their situation to a tow company, but most of them already have done so on their cell phone. Most times, a cop has already arrived to help.

"Do you jot down license plate numbers?"

"Never."

"Is there any particular tow company you use for a stranded motorist?"

"Usually, they have already called. If not, I start calling in alphabetical order and if one place is too busy then I call the next, until I find someone to rescue them."

"Would you mind if I accompany you sometime on one of your routes?"

"I guess it'd be all right."

Toni handed the woman her business card. "If you think of anything else, call me?"

"Why not? Wait, I'm about to make a run through the park. The wind is picking up and some roads are drifting. Want to come? Shouldn't take more than a few hours."

Toni glanced at her watch. There were still a few hours till Jack and Susan were due at her place. "I'd love to."

It was amazing seeing Erma scramble up the side of the huge machine, but she accomplished it with ease. Little arms and pint-sized legs with mountain climber precision easily scampered up the hulking machine. Toni had a harder time grabbing hold and finding her footing. Swinging a leg out to the side, she could barely get the door open, nearly losing her balance and falling off the thing. Inside the cab, special modifications had been made for Erma to successfully drive the plow through the city.

The ride was fun. The perspective, interesting. The wind came soaring straight off the lake and they plowed the streets around the park as grateful motorists waved. Toni waved back. Erma snickered, amused. It was late afternoon by the time they finished.

"I'd like to do this again. Ride with you. Maybe some night during a storm?"

"Would love the company," Erma replied.

Toni hurried back to her apartment where Jack waited outside in his car, only not with Agent Hunter. Pirelli was beside him. Neither looked happy. Jack cranked down his window. "I called you but no answer. That sent alarm bells since I knew how important this was to you and knew for sure you'd be waiting for us. Postit, I used squad lights thinking you might be hurt."

"Sorry, I'm running late."

"You sure are," Jack snapped as Pirelli mouthed a 'Sorry' to her.

"I thought Agent Hunter was coming?" Toni asked, leading the way up the steps and into her place. "Not that I mind Pirelli is here."

"She passed the call to me," Pirelli explained as he sat down at the computer. "I'm even better at this than she is. We both know it." He sat in front of the computer and his fingers glided over the keys. As he punched certain codes different screens came up in jargon, he studied it all.

"No bugs in your phone," Jack announced, putting the landline back together.

"Good. Be sure to check my cell—but I'm sure it's okay."

"Why?"

"He never uses that number to call me." Toni looked back at the screen.

"Ah, here." Pirelli got excited and his voice

dropped an octave. "I found a manmade hole in your firewall. Let me shore that baby up." Again, his fingers went wild over the keys as he downloaded police software.

"I don't understand why your system isn't more secure since you work for the Feds."

"Me either." Toni frowned. "I'll call Agent Palmer about it."

"No need. I can fix it." Pirelli ran his fingers over the keys, typing in codes. "I'd say Frosty has been reading all your correspondence, documents, and website visits for months. But I took care of it, and their window into your cyberspace world is now permanently closed."

"Thanks. But that might make him furious when he goes in and finds out I'm on to him."

"Who cares!" Jack called while examining heating ducts.

"That's what I thought too, Agent Postell," Pirelli said, ignoring Jack. "I put a control window on your computer. Let me show you. When you're working and don't want anyone in, make sure the snitch app on this firewall is on. When you want him to catch what you are doing, just close it off. It'll also isolate him to only seeing what you are doing at that moment and create a file for only the two of you."

"Is there any way he can get into my documents or mess up my computer?" No way could she compromise her files.

"Not anymore."

"Wonderful."

"Is it possible to trace Frosty back to his computer?"

"No, he's a smart one. Uses different IPs each time. The VPN is also encrypted. By the way, did you hear, I'm up for detective?" Pirelli smiled. "Just have to pass the test."

"Congratulations, Officer Pirelli." Toni offered him her hand. "But I thought your dream lay in River Forest."

"I can change my mind. Detective is a great promotion."

"I want him to train alongside me," Jack said.

"Well, he can't have a better person to learn from," Toni said.

"I can take a look at your cell if you'd like? I know Detective Autry already looked, but—"

"It wouldn't hurt." Toni handed him the cell, and asked Jack, "And you found no other device in my apartment?"

"None."

"And you checked the bathroom and my bedroom too?"

"I did, and it's all clear. But I found this." Jack held up the hard copy of her profile about him.

Toni blanched, and tried to snatch it away. Jack held it over her head and read a few lines. "'Jack is the finest man I've ever known. Unfortunately, I do not know this man as well as I would like. Just when I think I have him figured out, he surprises me. Yet working beside him, day in and day out, for months I have gotten a sense of this man. He is a man of honor. I trust him with my life, but not with my heart.'"

It was humiliating, especially with Pirelli there. He looked ill at ease and then busied himself again.

"Jack," Toni pleaded in a whispery voice,

"enough."

He handed it back. Nearly in tears, Toni shoved the paper into the shredder. At this moment, she hated Jack Autry. Hated him.

"You told me you'd have information about the purse in twenty-four hours. It's been over twenty-five hours. What do you have?" Jack had a familiar look in his eye of impatience mixed with embarrassment, perhaps due to his behavior. It was hard to move on from this moment, but it was important for her to remain professional.

"I visited with the designer."

"And?"

She handed him the folder.

Jack sat on the old couch to the moan of tired springs. He slowly went through the pictures. "Interesting."

"One of the pictures is Victoria's baguette."

"I thought a baguette was a long bread loaf."

Toni sat beside him. "Baguette means long piece of bread. See how long these purses are. This one is hers. I collect Czech beads and antique buttons. I string them and they hang in my windows."

"I don't get what you are trying to say."

"Look closely. The beads may or may not be the same ones Mallory bought from me. However, she did buy the antique buttons from me which are very similar." Toni's nerves jumbled.

"Interesting. Buttons from you, to Mallory, to Victoria. Just sounds like regifting."

"Mallory bought five baguettes for Christmas presents—well, six if you count mine, which isn't anywhere near as elegant. Far from it. Mallory kept one for herself. And three went to Will's office help. I suppose the fifth she gave to Victoria. But Will said she had it made for his mother."

"Maybe Schofield can only count to five. Come on, time to go, Pirelli." Jack stood. "When you get time, I'd like a copy of all that. Don't forget."

Toni followed the two men down the stairs. Officer Pirelli went on out to the squad as she and Jack remained in the lobby. Why she even cared about this cranky middle-aged man was beyond her. Perhaps it was the thrill of the chase; once she got him, she would no longer care. That seemed to be her MO with men these last several years.

"I appreciate sharing information."

"Jack, do you think Will killed Victoria?"

"I think it's a stretch, even if he was having an affair. Why not own up and beg forgiveness? Lots easier than spending the rest of his life in jail."

"You don't know my sister, do you? She doesn't forgive. Not ever."

"And you based this all on a purse? There are hundreds of purses out there, so this is a stretch."

"Except for it being tangled in her clothes at the scene of the murder. You really think the baguettes are a misnomer?"

"I do."

"That's a relief."

"How about this; your sister murdered Ms. Taylor out of jealousy. By the way, where is your sister? She wouldn't be using her Christmas present from her daddy to vacation in Europe about now, would she?"

"Yes, she is in Europe, but on the other, you're wrong." Toni felt her stomach pitch. It was a possibility she had already thought of herself. "Is that all you have?"

"No, I have one more thing." Jack followed her inside the apartment where he softened his tone. "The profile you did on me has one glaring error," he whispered in her ear.

"What would that be?" Tears pooled in her eyes. Jack had captured her heart so completely and rendered her speechless when she should rail at him. Standing like this with Jack, she knew she'd always forgive him anything.

"You can trust me with your heart." Jack interrupted her thoughts with a kiss. She tried to pull away. She wanted to give him a shove. She really did. But her willpower melted, and she wrapped her arms around Jack and kissed him with feelings of rage and love until she could no longer breath, or stand, or think. Jack held her tighter, kissing her firmer and longer, deliciously slow, then quicker, harder. He smelled like winter air tasted of peppermint gum. He was so sure of himself. And she did love peppermint.

"We really need to get away from this murder stuff for one day." He squeezed her hand, turned and walked out. She took a deep breath and walked him down to the buildings foyer, watched him leave and get into the sedan. He drove off just as another snowplow moved down the street.

Toni ran up to her apartment and flopped on her bed to catch her thoughts. Jack could be so puzzling. After replaying the kiss a dozen times, she decided to keep her heart closed. And what was that about getting away from the murder for one day? How could that even happen? Was he playing with her heart? Or was he just fickle? After all, he was in his early forties and never married. Perhaps he didn't know how relationships worked. For that matter, did she? Besides, did she really want a relationship with a gnarly cop who's aloof one moment and romantic the next? 'You can trust me with your heart.' Yes, those were his words. If she backed away, would she lose out on someone who just might be the love of her life?

"Time to refocus." She shook away her thoughts of Jack and tapped a pencil on the coffee table. The internet held hundreds of tow truck numbers. Where to start? The top of course; alphabetical order. This was an all-night job for sure.

"Hello, this is Special Agent Postell with the FBI. I'm calling about any tow jobs you may have been called out on between the hours of five p.m. and midnight in Lincoln Park area on any of the following dates." Toni read them off. "None for those dates? And, you're sure? Thanks for your time."

On to the next number. By her tenth inquiry, she hit pay dirt.

The office lady was of tremendous help. "Yes, we were called out to that area on November twenty-eight. Big storm that night. It was for a Marylou Garbe."

"Marylou Garbe?"

"Yes, that's the name on the ticket."

Toni quickly looked over the names of the dead girls again but there was no Marylou among them.

"I can print out this information for you, if you'd like."

Knowing it wasn't a match she had her print the ticket anyway, just in case something later connected to it. "I'll send someone by tomorrow to get it, thanks so much."

Starting to dial the next number on the list, someone beeped in on her line.

His voice was unexpected. "Meet me at 345 Lake Shore Drive."

"Why?" Toni was in no mood for another go round with Will. The creepy crawler just might make another pass and she wasn't in the mood. But the address sounded familiar. It took only a moment to realize it was Victoria Taylor's residence. "Our lunch conversation has bothered me all afternoon. Vic had information for me about her uncle and now I want to find it. Since I don't have it and neither do the police, it might still be in the house. Let's look."

"Don't you think the police have been over every inch of the house?" Toni responded, playing devil's advocate, but the truth was she couldn't wait to get back inside the residence.

"There's a safe they don't know about. The Taylors never would tell them."

"Will, call the police about this information. And if you're worried about any of them possibly being on the mayor's payroll, then talk to Jack." She thumped the pencil against the phone book.

"I want to know what she had before taking it to the police. I still have the key to Vic's house from when we dated."

"Maybe she's had the locks changed."

"Not Vic. Security issues were always the last thing on her mind. Besides, I had an open-ended invitation to return at any time. I don't want to go in alone. I need a witness."

"All right. It's seven o'clock now. I'll meet you

there within the hour. Wait for me outside." Fearing she wouldn't find a parking space, Toni Ubered but got out a block away. Coming up alongside the house, she heard a dog bark in the next yard. The old oak and walnut trees in the yard appeared to have been planted by moonlight in zigzag fashion. Branches were knotted from age and brittle with ice. The wind had blown extra piles of snow in bends of their elbows. The shrubs were round as cupcakes, iced in vanilla. Will sat cozily across the street in his black Lincoln with his driver at the wheel. Toni jogged across to him and knocked at the window. It opened. "I hope you remembered the key."

He got out of the car and told his driver, "I'll call when I want to be picked up."

The limo moved down the street.

Toni walked next to Will in silence. It took him a while as he fumbled for the correct key with his thick fingers at the gate but finally found it, turning it in the lock. Up the stone steps they went and onto the front porch. Lights still lit the corners of the place, with one light on in the front foyer.

"Are you sure no one is home?" Toni glanced about them.

"I'm sure."

Moments later, they were inside the place. Will turned off the alarm system as Toni memorized the numbers. Lemon wax was the first odor she became aware of as they stood in the grand foyer—which wasn't present when she visited the place with Agent Palmer. Victoria was in her grave and yet the mansion was still cared for as if she'd breeze back through the front door at any moment.

"Where to now?"

"The library, of course."

"Lead the way."

Very much at home, Will strutted into the library, filled with floor to ceiling shelves crammed with books and museum quality artifacts of primitive tribes. Carefully, he took down a picture by Picasso from a wall. Nothing was behind it...just more paneling. Pressing on a decorative appliqué in the wood, a large square section slid to the side, revealing a wall safe. But what Toni couldn't take her eyes from was the painting, rich in color and geometric shapes.

"Don't tell me that painting's real."

"It's a real Picasso."

"What do her parents do?"

"You didn't know the Taylor family has owned Lake Michigan's marina for generations? It's old money. Vic's folks are retired and live in Wisconsin now."

"I had no idea of her wealth. I guess I owe you an apology. I thought you were only after Mallory's wealth."

"I told you; I love Mallory." Will recited the combination out loud, "Ten, twenty-four, nineteen." The safe opened.

"Empty. Just like when Geraldo Rivera opened one of Capone's tunnels. Maybe Victoria hid the information somewhere else?" Toni looked around. "I know. Let's check her bedroom."

"I don't want to be caught here." Will shut the safe, closed the panel and put the picture back on the hook, making sure it wasn't crooked.

Toni looked up the cherry wood staircase. "Will,

follow me up." She became suspicious when he stalled.

"It could be in her office downtown."

"Do you mean in the office where she worked alongside the mayor?"

"You weary me with all your questions," he said, hint of anger coloring his tone.

"If the information was in the safe and her parents cleaned it out, then they have it. But it seems to me that lots of people knew that combination; you, her parents, possibly the mayor. So maybe she kept it hidden somewhere else, some place more personal. Up in her room."

"Toni, please, this is the couple's night off, but they could come home at any moment. I don't want to be discovered." Will started to reset the alarm. "Oh no."

"What is it?"

"They're home. The Collins just pulled around to the back of the house. They've returned from the holidays."

Toni followed him out onto the porch. Will locked the door behind them. Slipping the key into his pocket, it caught on the rim and slid down the fabric of his pants, landing on the porch. Toni noticed it, but he didn't. A drop of Uncle Hershey's Christmas mitten was her cover before walking to the gate with him.

"Glad we tried," he whispered, nearly running down the walk.

"Me too. Oh wait, I dropped my mitten somewhere." Stopping short of the gate, she glanced around and then walked slowly back up to the porch.

"Toni, we're going to be caught!"

The dog in the next yard started barking again. Lights went on inside the house. She heard voices on the other side of the door. Where was that mitten and key? "Oh, there." Toni picked up the gold key and pushed it down into the mitten.

By now, Will was safely out on the street walking quickly to the corner. She ran down the salted walkway and pushed through the gate, catching up to him as he used his cell to summon his driver. In another minute they were inside the heated limo, heading toward her place. They rode in silence. Will had no clue that Victoria's house key lay in the palm of her hand. When she got inside her apartment, Toni lifted the lid on her jewelry box and mixed the key in with her jewelry.

Tomorrow, she'd finish her calls to the Chicago area towing companies and turn them over to Agent Hunter.

Anxious to add to her notes of profiling this case, she sat down at the computer and turned it on, making sure the proper firewall was up so the Monster couldn't see what she was doing. It was as if he had a window into her world. How she hated it. After adding to her notes, she stared at the icon that would allow a freak to walk into her place. It was a way to try and catch him. She pressed the icon and now, the speck in the wall was opened to him. What should she write for him? Not wanting to involve or put anyone at risk, she decided to open a file about him that she'd never use. It was her way of taunting him. Frosty is a coward. He hides in snow. He preys on the weak. He can't relate to women, so he hurts them.

The next morning, a short poem flashed on the computer screen.

She has nameless grace with raven tresses that softly frame her face. How pure and undefiled she keeps her secret place until I open, which has been saved for only me. (Byron)

Chapter 27

Lake Mendota, Wisconsin

The structure was three stories high and over a hundred years old. Once an old mansion, it now served to house the mentally ill, strictly for those who could afford the ultimate care. The site was a tranquil eighty-acre area on Lake Mendota in Wisconsin. Toni walked up the front steps and pushed in through the tall front doors. The doctors and nurses greeted her as she sailed past. Toni took the elevator up rather than the stairs, as usual. The floor nurse was just coming out of her mother's room.

"How's she doing?" Toni asked Sophie.

"Your mother is having a better week. She won another Oscar." The buxom African American nurse cheered as though it were true.

"That's a relief. The last time she lost to Sally Field and stopped eating for days."

"Maybe the new cocktail enhancement she's on is doing the trick." Sophie held up her hands as a prayer.

"I don't know how to thank you for taking such good care of my mom." Toni hugged the older woman, who always wore a symbol of faith. She never was without the cross, despite management's requests to remove it.

"Your mother can be a real treat. Twenty years

ago, I remember going to the movies and watching her on the big screen. Mood disorders are devastating."

"Do you think she'll recover?"

"Shifting between reality and make believe, she's lost in time. Delusional Manic Depressives are difficult to control, even on meds. And in all these years, we haven't been able to find the right combination of meds for Lillian Palmer. But with God, all things are possible. Never let go of hope."

"I wish I had your faith."

"You can have it. Anybody can have it. It's free, girl."

A clatter of metal resonated through the corridor. Someone hollered. It drew the nurse's attention. "That's Mr. Channahon. I better go see what he did this time. Yesterday, he threw his breakfast out the window without opening it first."

To make an entrance to catch her mother's attention, Toni turned the doorknob to her room and waltzed inside. "Good morning Ms. Palmer."

Actress Lillian Palmer sat quietly in a chair. The light green carpet was immaculate. The large room was decorated in French provincial. On one side was her traditional queen bed with a satin peach comforter. Cozy padded chairs covered in chintz flanked the large windows, overlooking the gardens. On the other side of the room was a sitting area complete with a defunct fireplace, two blue sofas, a coffee table and several large loungers. The room had its own private bath and an adequate closet, which housed dozens of labeled slacks and blouses and dresses.

Gazing out the window, Lillian sat perfectly still, as if waiting for someone to paint her portrait. Her posture was picture-perfect; her woolen dress still looked stunning on her trim one hundred-five-pound figure. Lillian's strawberry blonde hair held threads of gray and had been freshly washed and styled. No one would argue; even here she remained a starlit.

"Hi, Mama." Toni scooched around the chair and faced her mother.

"Antoinette." She smiled warmly.

"I brought you your favorite hand cream." Toni kissed her cheek and breathed in the sweet scent of lilac water.

As usual, she brushed her daughter's touch away. "Did you hear my acceptance speech? It was aired and televised."

"Sorry, I missed it. I was at Lincoln Park looking for bad guys." Toni and Lillian's worlds existed side by side. One was invisible and the other was impossible.

"Did you find any?" Lillian asked, as if she misplaced her shoes.

"No." Toni set the hand cream bottle on her dresser.

"I remember taking all four of you kids there, to that park, when you were small. We had wonderful times, didn't we? You believed keeping lions and tigers in cases was cruel. You referred to it as jail." Lillian's blue eyes lit with recollections.

"The Lincoln Park Zoo is nicer now. It's more humane, with habitat and environmental thought. This summer, I'll take you. Would you like that? The hot dogs there are so good. Remember how soft and warm the buns are?"

"Why yes, I do. I love those hot dogs! Andre can't get enough of them. We do everything together, don't we? So much fun. We are the perfect family except when you children deny my request to join me at events. It's then I am truly alone. You and Andre and Mallory once loved coming with me to all the award ceremonies. Not one of you would have missed it for the world. What happened? What changed? Last night was a night to remember, why didn't you attend? This morning Mallory didn't even call with congratulations. Neither did Andre. But here you are. At least you are forgiven, the others are not."

"Andre is busy. And Mallory is in Europe." Toni took a chair to the side of her mother.

"Europe? Another extravagant trip from Daniel, I bet. Her father indulges her too much. Always gives in, whatever Mallory wants, Daniel gives to her. That's why I left him. Nothing mattered to him—not even me—only love for our daughter." She swiveled in her chair to face Toni. Joy lit her eyes. "Let me tell you about the awards night. Who was there and where I went afterwards."

"I'm listening." The chair proved to be uncomfortable so Toni moved to sit on the edge of the bed.

Lillian looked disturbed at her daughter's choice of seating. "Antoinette," Lillian cast a displeased look and nod of her head. "You're wearing street clothes on my linens where I sleep. I taught you better."

"Sorry." Toni moved back to the chair.

"The moment I stepped onto the red carpet, I knew the night belonged to me and me alone. As you must've read, I won the Oscar for Blue Heaven. My nerves were rattled beforehand, but when they called my name, and those spotlights shone down on just me, and the

207

applause rose, I stood to my feet and floated to the stage. It was five entire minutes before the audience quieted long enough for me to speak."

"How lovely. Sorry I missed it. What did you wear?"

"I wore my lustrous gold sparkly gown, the one with the puffy skirt and the long shawl. Of course, as always, Tiffany's lent me their best diamonds." Lillian was animated.

"Of course. Was Papa there?" Toni hesitated to ask, needing to know if her father was still anywhere in her mother's mind, even in a place of fiction.

"No, of course not. He has a deadline for that important film he's doing in France. You know that. Time is running out and costs are shooting up. But he called and sent five dozen red roses. At the last minute, Robert Redford stepped in to serve as my escort for the evening. Wasn't that sweet of him? He's breathtakingly handsome, don't you think? I believe he'll have a long future in Hollywood. I'd show you my Oscar, but it's at the engravers. Anyway, I may keep it in storage with the other ones; the help around here likes to steal things."

"I don't think anyone dare steal from you, Mother."

"Servants can't be trusted nowadays." Lillian turned her head to stare out the window again. Her mind seemed lost in the dormant trees, fading like old wallpaper. Toni sat quietly waiting for her mother to regroup. Was she back in Hollywood now on the set of her new movie? Or perhaps she was locked inside a coffin, unable to move. Saying goodbye to her was always very difficult. Toni stood to leave. As if knowing her thoughts, Lillian spoke up again, "Before you leave, will you read to me?"

"Of course, I'd love to." Surprised, Toni selected a book of Robert Frost's poems from the bookcase.

"Robert Frost again?" Lillian heaved sadly.

"I thought you liked him. I can get something else, just tell me what."

Lillian's hand began to shake, and she rubbed her forehead. "If only I could remember the name of it. I can't. It's called…Sam's? Something like that and it's in another book. I wish I remembered."

"Mother, I'm trying to understand. Is the author named Sam? Or is it the name of the poem?"

"It's inside a book. My personal maid Sophie will know. Ask her."

More noise from down the hall accompanied by running feet.

"Mother, I think Sophie has her hands full right now with another star."

"Robert Frost will be fine. I remember him."

Toni opened the small book and read. By the time she finished the second poem, her mother was nearly unresponsive. Placing the book back into the shelf, Toni walked to her. A piece of hair had fallen into her eyes, so she brushed it back. "How I miss you, Mama. I'm glad you had fun last night. I love you so much and wish you'd come back to me. I need you." Her voice crimped as she dabbed at her watering eyes.

On the way out of the room, Toni heard her mother softly articulate, "Antoinette, find your sister."

Toni froze. "I'm looking."

"She's close. Right under our noses. Look there."

The guilt was fresh again. Anxiety shot up her

arms and down her back, propelling her down the stairwell. Banging open the outside door with a vengeance, she got into her car and checked her cell. There were numerous messages from Jack. Right now, she couldn't deal with whatever he needed.

Breathing was labored. She tried anxiety tapping again but this time it didn't settle her. She clutched the steering wheel, sobbing into it. What she needed was to start life again—at the beginning. Tired of being guilt-ridden over constant blame for her sister's kidnapping, Toni couldn't take it any longer. Her mind slipped between the past and the present. Desperate, she needed to get home. After inserting the key into the ignition, she pressed the gas pedal then sped around the circular drive numerous times before exiting. If only she could put a million miles between this place and the rest of her life. A remote cabin in a woods near a quiet lake would do, where she could live out her days in solitude. A car behind her tooted his horn when she swerved out of her lane on curved country road.

Just one time visiting her mother without mentioning Suzette would be lovely. There was nothing more in this world she wanted than to find her sister. No, not Lillian Palmer, who sat in an ivory tower high above them all, trapped inside her own imaginary world as everyone else had reality to deal with.

Uncle Danny always says there's been way too much time passing. Suzette was most likely dead by now. For so long she had held onto optimism. Should she give in and give up? Suzette's bones were most likely in some obscure location, with animals that dragged pieces of her off somewhere. The best she could hope for was that someday the family would give the little elfin-like girl a decent burial.

Tears of anger, sorrow and rage fell from Toni's eyes, blurring her vision. Did anyone in the world feel as devastated? A horn blared as tires squealed. A sports car cut her off and she hadn't even seen it until it was nearly too late. If she died in a car crash, it wouldn't matter. No one would care. Jack would get a new partner. Her mother wouldn't even be aware she was gone. Mallory would most likely be glad. Andre was busy with his wife, kids, and business. Her papa would be too tied up in a new project to come and sort through her things. Maybe Uncle Hershey would care. Only him. But it was someone.

For years, the memory of that day had slipped through her fingers like water. The tragedy of losing Suzette was so horrific, it caused her to bury it deeply and now, years later, no matter how hard she tried, she couldn't recall the truth, although everyone seemed to have their own version.

Just off Lake Shore Drive, Toni decided to check on her mother's empty apartment, where they moved after Suzette was taken. As she often did, she pulled into the parking space along side of the building. Today, church bells rang. That's right, there's a church nearby. *Is it the same church we used to attend as a family?*

Toni walked to the front of the apartment building, surrounded by old stately mansions, and dug for her mother's key inside her purse. The church chimes rang again. She looked into the sky above rooftops and saw a steeple with a cross at the very tip. It was time. Now was the moment. Floodgates opened and poured in a single moment. The bells kicked loose a rush of memories. Just like that, Toni had total recall of what happened on that awful day when she was eight years old—Suzette, almost five. The key turned and the door opened. Memories tumbled out.

****

Church bells rang out into the warm spring air. "Wake up, girls. Do you hear church calling you? The bells are saying, 'come to church, come to church.'" Lillian pulled back the drapes and opened the blinds. "Quick, get ready. I've laid out yours and Suzette's dresses. I'll have breakfast ready for you both by the time you get back from Sunday school."

"Aren't you coming too, Mother?" Suzette asked.

"No, not today."

"But, Mama, you always take us," Toni protested.

"Antoinette, you are eight now and such a big girl. I'm putting you in charge of taking Suzette safely to church and back home with you."

"I'm a big girl too, and don't need Antoinette to take me. I can take myself." Suzette pouted.

"How about you two take each other?" Mother suggested.

"Where's Andre?" Toni pulled off her silk nightgown.

"He's sick. That's why I'm staying home. Mallory is with her dad this weekend, so I'm counting on you."

"We've never gone alone without you, Mama." Toni held up her arms as her mother slid the dress over her head and buttoned it in the back.

"Antoinette, there are no streets to cross. The church is at the end of the block, around the corner. Straight there and right back. I'll be watching the clock, understand? And no talking to strangers. Remember that."

"Yes, Mama." Toni hugged her mother's neck.

Five-year-old Suzette was on the verge of celebrating her sixth birthday. Thinking she was old enough to do as she please, she became defiant and uncooperative.

After she slipped into her light blue organdy dress with the white Peter Pan collar, they picked up their Bibles and walked down the street. Toni reached for Suzette's hand, but she quickly yanked it back again.

"Give me your hand," Toni demanded.

"Ouch, you hold my hand too tight. You're hurting me." She twisted around.

"Come on, Suzette. Mom put me in charge."

"My name is Susanna. Suzette is a stupid baby name. Call me Susanna and I'll come with you."

"Oh, all right, Susanna." Toni pulled on her hand and Suzette pulled back.

"I can walk by myself too!" Suzette folded her arms across her chest and stamped off in her dress shoes toward the church. "I'm a big girl now."

At first, no one noticed the woman in the dark sedan parked by the curb. The side door was open. The woman sat alone on the passenger seat.

"Hi, girls," she called to them.

Suzette stopped. "Hello."

"Suzette, we're supposed to go straight to church," Toni reminded her.

"Suzette," the words purred sweetly from the woman's lips. "I love that name."

"I'm Susanna."

"Even better. Susanna." The woman's voice was melodious.

"This is Antoinette, my big sister. But I call her Toni."

"Hi, Toni."

"Susanna, Toni, won't you pretty girls come with me?" More church bells.

"Do you like candy?" the lady asked.

"Yes. Yes." Suzette clapped.

"No. We need to get to church," Toni protested.

"Do you want some candy, Susanna?"

"Yes." Suzette clapped louder.

"Do you want some now?

"Yes!"

The lady got out of the car and held out her hand. "Come with me. Now. Toni, you come too."

"Okay." The little red-headed girl with curls ran to her.

It was the middle of summer and Toni felt frozen to the strip of grass between the sidewalk and the street. She trembled. All she could seem to do was watch Suzette willingly crawl inside the car, round hinny with lacy underpants showing. Settled in the seat now, Suzette pointed at her and insisted, "Don't forget my sister!"

The candy woman walked up to Toni as though evaluating her. With a leap, she grabbed Toni by the waist. Toni tried to get away by twisting her body and falling to the ground, forcing the woman to carry her. But Toni kicked at the woman and pinched her face. Her short nails to dug into the adult woman's neck. Suzette remained quiet in the sedan with her hands folded nicely in her lap.

Grabbing a handful of Toni's curls, the woman dragged her toward the open car door and pushed her inside, on top of Suzette. Toni ruthlessly kicked and bit the woman until she was released. Toni shoved her aside and landed on the street. The door slammed shut. Locked.

"No. You can't have my sister." Toni sprang to her feet and tried to get the door to open.

Suzette watched silently as her sister pounded on the door. "I'll be back right after candy. I'll give you some too. Don't tell Mama."

The dark car pulled away from the curb and squealed down the street. Suzette stared out the back window. Her eyes were big saucers of blue as she waved goodbye.

"Go right to church and straight home. "Don't talk to strangers," her mother had said.

Toni brushed her tears away and the dust from her dress. She picked up her Bible and Suzette's then went down the block and into church. Afterwards, she tried to clean the dirt off her dress so her mother wouldn't fuss at her for getting dirty. She smoothed her messy hair and then rang the doorbell.

In a moment her mother swung open the door. She laughed. "Toni you didn't have to ring the bell. You girls come on in. Wait. Where's Suzette? Where's your sister?"

"I don't know. Some lady took her to the store for candy."

Mother began shrieking. "Which store?"

"I don't know."

"How could you let Suzette get into a car with a stranger? What did the lady look like?" Mother began shaking Toni violently.

"I don't remember." She dropped the Bibles on the

flowered carpet.

"What color was the car?"

"Black, I think."

We were on our way to church, not the candy store. The lady offered us candy! I remembered it wrong, all wrong. But either way, the results remained the same; Suzette was forever gone. It was almost as if her little sister, covered in freckles from her head to her toe, just simply disappeared into thin air.

Church bells rang again. The sound pulled her down the block. Around the corner, she saw it. Toni gasped at the sight of the large red brick church with wide cement steps; she had forgotten all about it until today. It was the church on Wellington Ave that she and Suzette attended.

Just down the street from the church was the beautiful Tudor house they lived in at the time of the kidnapping. Once upon a time, it was painted the color of cream cheese and trimmed in pink frosting. The fence looked like candles on a cake. The yard was filled with roses of every kind. The family referred to it as The Birthday Cake House. Now the house was repainted a dove gray trimmed with black shutters. Ivy scaled the bricks and was nearly at the roof line. The garden was professionally done so it seemed. *Charming. My house looked charming.* Not able to tear herself away, Toni located a nearby bench and stared at the place until the sky grew dark and snowy.

At home, Toni unlocked the apartment door and dropped onto the couch, exhausted from the day. Relief in the form of tears flooded, knowing what happened to them that Sunday morning. Too tired to undress, Toni curled up in a blanket as Perp found a comfortable spot and wound herself into a ball behind her masters knees. Peace came, which lulled them to sleep. Hours later, the cell rang. Startled, she sat straight up and answered.

"I missed you at the crime scene."

"What crime scene? When?"

"Tonight, we found another girl. I looked across the street, but the proverbial bus was definitely nowhere in sight," Jack said.

"I've been gone most of the day to visit my mother in Wisconsin." She pushed back the hair from her eyes and looked around the room, trying to get her bearings inspite of a numb mind.

"That explains it. Glad you're okay."

"I'm fine. How are you doing?" She didn't want the conversation to end.

"Okay. Parents were contacted. Another hard one. Never easy."

"Well, at least Agent Hunter was with you."

"She was."

"I'm sorry. Hang on, I have something new to show you on my computer."

Toni opened her cell and showed the picture of a poem she found on her computer earlier in the day. "Got this today."

"Looks like Frosty has a crush on you."

"That's all you have to say?"

"He's also into Byron, but paraphrases, making it his own reflection. I think he's referring to you. Time to get you a bodyguard."

"No way." Toni logged off the computer.

"When does your sister get back?"

"I've no idea. Jack, you really don't think Mallory murdered Victoria?"

"There is a definite motive. Oh, how the heart is a jealous mistress. I just need to talk to her. No biggie," he answered. "By the way, do you happen to have any plans for tomorrow evening?"

"Another stake-out?" She hoped.

"I thought we'd go to Hyde Park for some dinner. Like Thai? I promise no business talk. Just a guy and a girl eating some food together."

"As a matter of fact, I do like Thai food," Toni said, and with a smidgeon of playful sarcasm in her voice, asked, "Is this a date, Jack?"

"Yes, it is Toni. Our second date. This time, I'm officially asking you out. Listen, gotta go. The chief just walked into my office with a pile of paperwork. I'll give you a call sometime tomorrow and we'll firm up plans."

"Sounds good…and, Jack?"

"Yes?"

"Get some rest."

"Will do. It's on my to-do list."

"Make sure you do it."

"One more thing," Jack said. "I could drop by and spend the night to guard you myself."

"I said that you need rest. There'll be no rest with you here." She looked down the hall toward her bedroom.

"I'm pretty sure you're right."

"Goodnight."

"Be sure to lock your door."

"I will."

****

Toni picked up her pencil. Inside the spiral notebook, she began writing out a list of names she thought she might pray for. Going to the church reminded her of how important prayer had once been to her. Although she hadn't said a single syllable to God in many years, she figured talking to him to protect people she loved might have a positive ointment on her anxiety. Jack was at the top, then Mallory, Will, Andre, Marie, her mother and Papa, and of course, Uncle Robert Palmer. Wait, one more, Uncle Herschel. There—she'd begin with those names.

Toni leaped from bed. She threw on her jacket and warm hat. Taking the list in hand along with a flashlight, she exited her apartment from the back door. It had stopped snowing but remained brutally cold. Scaling the ice-covered fire escape was a bit of a challenge, but she made it safely onto the roof. Sitting on a long-abandoned piece of cement cylinder, she laid her hands on the list of names and prayed. How wonderful it was shouting the names into the sky.

Chapter 28

Toni yanked open the door to the gym and saw a startling reflection in the glass. Spinning around for a better look, there it was, directly across the street. Fannie Mays storefront entrance. How could she not have noticed the proximity to the heavenly chocolate and unwanted ten pounds before this? "I shall resist the deliciousness of them, if it's the last thing I do," Toni whispered to herself, walking into the gym. She waved at Jared Pirelli, who was teaching a class in self-defense to a group of elderly ladies.

Trying to keep her thoughts at bay, Toni exercised vigorously, but fifteen minutes in, she caved into the call of chocolate. Coat flaps flying, she hurried across the street carrying her gym bag. Glancing through the shelves of assorted candies, she selected dark and light creams. Perfect. The hardest part was deciding on the size of the box. After purchasing the largest box wrapped like a present, she stuffed it into her large purse and went home dreaming about her date with Jack. Perhaps it might be time to order a girdle too.

Standing in front of her closet, trying to figure out what to wear, Toni felt certain it was going to be a great evening. Why wouldn't it be? Jack was the most interesting person she'd ever met; well read, had a sharp mind for criminology, knew how to handle people in all walks of life, had compassion when dealing with the hurting, and yet was so ordinary you'd walk right past him on the street without ever seeing him. But, the tone of his voice when he said her name knocked the wind clear out of her. Toni slipped a white angora sweater off a hanger and pulled a black tweed woolen pair of slacks from the drawer. She brushed her curly dark hair around her shoulders and dabbed on a bit of makeup. Next came out the simple jewelry; hoop earrings, and a Baroque pearl tear drop on a silver chain.

Minutes later, the doorbell rang. Jack was taking her to dinner. Yay for Thai food. Toni pressed the button to open the lobby door, then ran to get her coat from the back of the kitchen chair. "Ready!" she announced, after checking herself in the bedroom mirror again.

"Take your time," he called back.

Toni found him bent over the desk in the front room, scratching Perp's' ears. He was spread out on her desktop. "I think there is a love story in the making here."

"Wow, that's a first," Toni commented.

"What's a first?"

"Perp's soft spot is for no one else but me, up till just now. He must sense your special aura."

Pleased, Jack smiled. "Thanks, Perp, for this honor."

"I'm ready if you are."

Jack's eyes focused on something. A few inches away from the cat was her notebook of names.

"Ah, never mind that," Toni nervously said trying to beat him to the shelf.

Jack was faster.

"What's this?" Jack looked over the list of names in the open spiral. "More profiling? Or is this your list of new suspects? If so, I'm on it. Really?"

Jack appeared irritated. Finally, he allowed Toni to snatch it from him, feeling like a balloon emptying of its air.

"What's my name doing at the top?"

"Never mind."

"What's this list of names for?" he persisted.

"It's my list." Toni hugged it to her chest.

"What kind of list?" He recoiled as though she held a gun on him. "Am I being investigated by the FBI?"

"Of course not. Don't be silly." She laughed. "It's my list of people that I care about."

"Go on."

"I want special happiness for you. For everyone on the list. To be—protected from evil and harm."

"Are you talking about praying?"

"It's important to have faith."

"This is something new? When did this all start?"

"Since...recently, very recently."

"You got religion, Postit?" He narrowed his eyes.

"Not religion. It's more like being loved."

"Do you light candles too?" He furrowed his brow.

"Of course not."

"Want to tell me about it?"

She licked her lips and sat down. "When Suzette was taken, depression enveloped me. I tried shaking it off. Nothing worked. I thought if I ate healthy it would help my mind."

Noticing the half-eaten box of candy, he asked, "Using God as an excuse to eat junk food now?"

"Those are good, or haven't you ever tried one?

Here, try one?" She held out the box.

He pushed it back.

"I've seen therapists. Worked out. Do anti-anxiety exercises. I'm riddled with tension and stress."

"And now?"

"Now I am a bit better. At least for the last few days. Now I sometimes hear the music of life. The joy of living."

"Corny."

"Jack, listen, will you?" She tugged on his sleeve. "I've been put on this earth for a reason. I have a destiny, although I am not sure what that is yet. And if I want to eat a piece of chocolate, by golly, I will!" Toni lifted the lid on the candy box and popped a vanilla cream into her mouth.

"I'm suddenly unsure how to take you." He stared pensively at her.

"Why? I'm still me—but now I have hope. And I shudder to think I could lose any of you I care so much about. Life is fragile." Her mouth went dry.

Jack peered into her face until his eyes were level with hers. "I liked your edge. I thought I could count on you to keep your head."

"I have. It's my heart I gave away. To you."

Without another word, he picked up his coat and walked to the door. It was tempting to run after Jack, but Toni held her place watching him leave. She listened to the heavy beat of his feet going down the stairway, away from her, away from their fun evening together. Toni wondered how she ever lured herself into thinking she could share her thoughts with him. At the window, Toni watched as he got into his double-parked car. Taillights faded into the distance.

Toni sat at the computer staring at the blank screen, replaying the conversation with Jack. She rubbed the back of her neck, where the beginnings of a headache began to ache just as the doorbell buzzer went off. She stumbled across the room to reach the talk button quickly. "Jack!"

"No, not Jack. It's me, Jared Pirelli."

"Jared? What are you doing here? Wait. Never mind, that didn't sound nice. Hold on. I'll let you in." Toni pressed the button to unlock the front door. Within moments he was on her floor, not even breathing hard having loomed the steps three at a time. He acted as if he had taken a leisurely stroll with his breath coming in even beats.

"I was worried about you." Gently, he cuffed her chin.

"Worried about me, why? I don't understand why."

"Frosty has gotten to you."

"He's gotten to us all." Her heart hurt. She didn't want to discuss a case. She didn't want anyone in her apartment, except Jack. She wanted to go after Jack and tell him how she felt. Why did she let Jack out and Jared in?

"While I'm here, why don't I take a look at your computer to see what Frosty has been up to?" Jared didn't wait for Toni's response, instead he seated himself in front of the screen and tapped away for a few minutes. "Ah-ha, you can't escape me."

Toni leaned over his shoulder to see. "What?"

"He's been trying to get into your computer even when it's off."

"Can he really do that?"

"He sure can. Did you know that he can even read

your email and send emails from your system, and you'd never even know it happened?"

"Wow, is that what happened?"

"It looks like he crossed the system just yesterday." Jared looked sympathetic.

"But I thought you fixed it?" Toni was frustrated. "Why is this still happening?"

"He obviously knows more than I do. Sorry."

"Okay, what can I do to get him out forever? Maybe I should call the FBI and have them look."

"I'll talk to my systems analysis member tomorrow and see what he suggests," Jared offered. "Let me do that first. If it doesn't work, then call."

Toni shut down the Wi-Fi connection and unplugged the computer. "Now try to get in!" she hollered at the invisible monster.

"Is there anything else I can do for you?" He glanced about as though hoping to stay.

"Really, I'm just fine." She popped another chocolate into her mouth. Maybe if he left right now, she could take a cab to Jack's and try to restart the evening.

Jared took a seat on the couch. Toni remained planted near the candy, holding out the box to him. "Care for one?"

"I'll pass." He waved them away.

Toni fidgeted, moving her shoulders back and forth, and sat down.

"What's wrong?"

"There's a knot between my shoulders."

"Sounds like stress. It makes you bunch up. Let me help you with that." Jared started to message her shoulders. His hands traveled down the center of her back, then slowly his fingers followed her spine up to her neck, where he lightly pinched the back of it. Gradually, the stroking became harder, and the grip got a bit tighter. It felt good. Toni closed her eyes and lowered her head, feeling herself go into a trance-like quality. A few moments more and she'd surely be asleep. Softly she murmured, "I wanted to go for a run a few minutes ago at the inside track, but now thanks to you I'm too relaxed to move. All tension totally gone. Thanks."

"Let's do it."

"Huh?" Toni sleepily opened her eyes.

"Let's go into the park and run our legs off. Come on!" He stomped his foot at her.

Toni became more alert. "Hey, aren't you on call tonight?"

"Nope. Grab your jacket. Let's go. I'll keep you safe." He slipped his arm around her waist and started to escort her to the door.

"I'm not so sure it'd be a good idea to tempt the situation." Toni stepped back.

"The guy hasn't hit in a week. He's moved on."

"Jared, a week isn't so long. These serials cycle."

"And sometimes they move. Hey, didn't Jack tell you?"

"Tell me what?"

"We just got in a report of the similar thing now happening now in a park in Michigan—started days ago. We're thinking it's our guy, Frosty. A task force is going out there tomorrow to meet with them. Jack is one of them. Susan Hunter from the FBI is another. By the look on your face, I can tell he didn't say anything about this, right?"

For a moment, she couldn't speak as she tried to digest the thought of Jack holding out on her again. "You're right, he didn't." Toni seethed. "But in fairness to Jack, I am supposed to be off the case."

"I know you two are buddies and that you still pass along information." Pirelli watched her. "The report from Michigan came in just as I was getting off work late this afternoon. In fact, I've a copy of it downstairs in my car."

"That is good news for us but bad for those folks in Michigan." Something wasn't jelling. "What part of Michigan?"

"I've forgotten the name of the city, but I'll show it to you on our way to Lincoln Park if you'd like." Jared motioned toward the door.

"It's icy." Toni parted the curtains to look outside.

"A few areas are shoveled and have been salted. Look, it's not even snowing. We're safe. Besides, I'll stick close to you."

The night was still. No fresh snow. Still feeling the sting of Jack's rejection, suddenly the last thing she wanted to do was to sit around the apartment and mope. "I guess it's—okay. Give me a minute to change."

Alone in her room, she slid out of her slacks and into a pair of warm fleece pants. Not suitable for running but the idea was to be in the fresh air and forget about stress. Besides, how long would they be in the park? Thirty minutes? Then home to a hot tub bath and bed. With her hair now wrapped up in a messy ponytail, she donned an old sweater and quilted jacket. "Not meant for running. Maybe a brisk walk," she told Jared as she slipped earmuffs over her head.

Jared followed her down the steps, and just as Toni

opened the outside door, they bumped into Jo Kline.

"What a co-winkie-dink!" Jo beamed with an armload of school paraphernalia. Balancing two book bags, a purse along with her Sponge Bob Squarepants lunch box, she explained, "I forgot my keys at school and hoped you'd be home to let me in and here you are going out so you can let me in. And just where are you off to in such a hurry?"

"For a quick run in the park."

"Toni, that's just not safe." She grabbed at her friend's hand, dropping a book bag. Jared immediately picked it up.

"I'll be safe with Officer Pirelli at my side."

Jo looked up at him. A gaze of confusion crossed her face.

"Let me carry those things up the steps for you." Quickly, Pirelli relieved Jo of her items and headed up the steps.

"Ahh, thank you. I'm at the top floor, the apartment across from Toni's."

"I know," he hollered back.

Jo blinked and then cocked her head quizzically at Toni. "I thought you were going out with Jack tonight."

"Our plans changed at the last moment. He left." Then she gave Jo a squeeze. "I nearly forgot to tell you the Frosty might've moved onto Michigan. Officer Pirelli said a body turned up there."

"Same MO?" Jo asked confused.

"Yes. I'll tell you about it later when I'm back."

Jared plunked back down the steps. "Let's go."

"Toni, wait. I don't have a good feeling about this." Jo pulled at Toni.

"I won't be gone long. See you later." She walked

out to the street with Jared.

On the street, she stopped when she saw the make of his car. "Cool sports car—what a nice Mustang."

"Thanks!" He unlocked the passenger door. Once they were inside buckled up, off they went.

Moving through traffic, he said cheerfully, "I don't know who's more excited about this workout, you or me. We're so much alike."

Hot-dogging it down the city streets, Toni suddenly realized she didn't like his style. Trying to ignore it, she focused where they were headed. "It's too long since I've been able to have a good jog. I can power walk along the streets but that's not the same as an all-out run. I seem to elbow people, knocking them off the curb in my hurry."

"Yea, when bad guys screw up, it disrupts everyone's routine." Jared impatiently laid on his horn for an elderly couple to move out of his way.

Toni scrunched her face in response to his rudeness, feeling her calm dissolve into uncertainty. "Hey, take it easy. You just made an old couple move faster than they have in years. Too much adrenaline at their age can't be good. You're also speeding. How'd it look for an officer to get a ticket?" Toni thought of her tickets, shaking her head.

"We don't get tickets, if you know what I mean."

Suddenly, she wanted Jared to turn the car around and take her back home, yet she hesitated to say anything. It was best to have them run and then have nothing more to do with him—ever. Right along with having nothing to do with Jack, either.

Jared drove around the side of the park and then stopped as though trying to figure out directions.

Finally, he started up again and entered the back way, accessible to the zoo maintenance crew not far from the lake. Fir trees pushed together and crowded the view of the sky as light snowflakes continued. This area of the park was so dark it was hard to see a few feet in front of them. Sounds and smells of the animals were nearly absent since they were housed during the winter months. However, she thought she detected a low, deep moan coming from the direction of the tiger house.

"How'd you know about this entrance? I didn't even know it existed."

"I'm a policeman, remember? I've been over every inch of this place in the past months." His demeanor became arrogant, which was off-putting. Thirty minutes earlier, he was accommodating and engaging. "The jogging trails I'm thinking of are off that way." He pointed to the right. Slowly, Jared continued driving down the narrow tar paths as if he were trying to decide on a location to park the car. He turned up a hill but then turned around choosing another road before pulling to a stop. They were completely enveloped in shadows.

"It's rather dark here." Toni glanced around.

"I know what I'm doing. Stop cross-examining me," he snapped.

"Stop right there. Forgive me if I gave the false impression that we're friends. We are work related acquaintances. I also outrank you. I ask to be treated with respect."

"Okay." His mood darkened.

"I'd like to see that report now." She crossed her arms.

"The report?" His gaze was long and confused.

"You said Frosty may have moved to Michigan. A similar incident took place there. Remember?"

"Duh! That's right!" Hitting his head with the flat of his hand, Jared then leaned over Toni to dig through the glove compartment, deliberately pressing his arm on her leg. To combat his unwanted touch, she tilted away from him until she was smushed up against the door.

"Why did this killer pick Michigan of all places? Do you suppose the guy got a job transfer? Or maybe he's a copycat. I need to read the new police report on this guy."

"Oh, what did I do with it? Maybe I tossed it in the backseat."

Toni turned around to look. Bags of take out with half eaten food littered the floor with a growing pile of newspapers and girly magazines. It was appalling. "You really need to clean out this car, Officer."

"Officer? Now you call me Officer?"

Toni became increasingly uneasy.

Expecting him to rifle through his own jumble, she sat back down. Instead, he didn't move. Beads of sweat welled up on his forehead then rolled down on his face; even though it was thirty-five degrees outside it wasn't much warmer in the car. Toni noted the physiological change.

"You look so beautiful tonight, so enticing." The voice drooled with familiar sexy tones; the same tones she heard on the phone.

"It's getting late, and I'm tired. Let's turn around and do this another time, okay?" A chill skimmed her spine.

"I think you're terrific." He moved closer to her until she felt his breath on her skin.

Toni's inhaling came in short, slow spurts as she tried to quell rising fear. Her hands grew sweaty. "I enjoy working with you, but that's where it ends. I'm not looking for a work related relationship."

"What about Jack?" He slammed his fist into the dashboard. "I bet you're ready for one with him. Oops, sorry, sorry. Didn't mean to get so mad. But I really care about you. I'm worried he'll hurt you."

The rapid change of mood made Toni tremble. She sat quietly, trying to manage her fear. Like Frosty, she had played his game and decided to go along with whatever he wanted to momentarily placate. Right now, he had the advantage over her, here in the park at night, isolated in his car.

"Second thought, maybe you're right. Jack and I were supposed to go out tonight. That was before he got mad at me. He left. You showed up. I guess it was meant to be. I'd enjoy getting to know you better." Her heartbeat got ragged. Breath came in short bits, trying to catch a deep breath was impossible.

He settled back in his seat. "You have no idea what I've done for you."

"Tell me." She sounded open and happy while she shook with fear.

"You were stuck in the park and I helped you get your car started. I drove you home on New Years Eve. I worked on your computer. I kept you in the loop about evidence. I trained you in self defense at the gym."

"Indeed. You did all those things and I am forever grateful."

"I did more." He moved closer.

"Tell me." Her voice was nearly inaudible.

"'A mind at peace with all below, a heart whose love is innocent.' The women…I killed them for you."

Chapter 29

Would tonight be her end? She suspected people would ask—as she had once asked of others—'Didn't she know better than to run in the park with a killer on the loose?'

She glanced at him seated beside her. Toni refused to leave this earth without a fight. She'd make it hard for him. Leave evidence of her struggle. Looking out the window, she tried to get her bearings and strategize an escape.

"Jared, never has anyone done what you have done for me." She tried to smile, but she was shaking so badly that her teeth started to chatter.

"You're cold."

"Chills. I'm so cold. Suddenly I feel quite sick. It might be the flu. Do you mind postponing tonight and drop me home? We can go again once I feel better." Her voice faded into a space of silence. Inconspicuously, she slid her right hand on the door handle, while her fingers arched, ready to pull up on it hard. As if she'd already run a mile, her pulse raced from adrenaline.

Jared pressed a button and heard the locks click. Had he unlocked or locked the doors? It was obvious he hadn't paid attention to her plea.

"Or…perhaps you could take me by a drugstore and pick up some antinausea medicine." Toni did her best to steady her voice. "I'd hate to vomit all over your frontseat."

He reached under the driver's seat and pulled out a small towel to dab at his face, wiping away the sweat, which now had a sickening odor. The towel was stained with something dark, like oil or blood. A shiny metal object slipped from the towel and landed on his lap. They both looked down at the knife and then up into one another's eyes.

"Your skin, so soft. Your face, so elegant." He slowly moved the knife across her face, barely cutting her skin.

Trickles of blood slowly made its way downward. It was bitter tasting on her lips and tongue. The pretense between them dropped. "Hello, Frosty."

"Hello, Special Agent Antoinette Postell."

"Tell me what you want." She quivered; now she was ready to throw up.

"Your smile won my heart. And your eyes, they glow in the night beneath streetlamps. You give me peace and give me your love that's innocent."

"Byron?" Toni had never read him but remembered Jack saying Frosty was quoting him. "You're rewriting Lord Byrons words, making them your own."

"I'm like Lord Bryon because the woman he loved, loved another. Just like you love Jack."

"Me? Love Jack? Ha. I think not." She let out a shaky laugh.

"You were to give to me and only to me the love you have below." He stared between her legs.

"I didn't realize Byron was crude in his writings. I'll have to check that out. Is there a fast food place, close by?" She looked around, feigning innocence. "I'm feeling a bit thirsty. I may have just vomited n my mouth."

Frosty sat as though a pillar of ice, unmoving.

Here sat the Monster. Face to face with him. Alone. Piercing revelations of terror sounded inside her head. Get out now. She pulled up on the door handle, again and again, but the door wouldn't budge.

Tilting her body back, she was able to kick her right leg into his head, hoping to smash it into the window, but missed; instead, she contacted the steering wheel. The leg pain was searing. Immediately striking again, this time she connected with his face and heard her toes crack. More pain.

Blood spattered from his nose. Toni dove across him to unlock the car. Frantically, she pressed all the buttons trying to get out. All four locked clicked at once. Yanking up her door handle again, she pushed out, both feet landing on the pavement, and she was off.

A frigid gust coming straight off the lake penetrated her skin. The only sound she heard was the wind. Avoiding the open space where she'd be seen, Toni ran close to the trees. Unsure of her location, she needed to find the main road leading away from the park. All these little trails squirreled around and interwove with one another, making her circle back. She tried to ignore the pain in her toes, and ankle, but her hip was another matter. She limped.

If she could keep her composure and avoid him until the sun rose, she might have a chance to be spotted and helped. But morning was hours away. She'd freeze to death long before then. With each breath, her chest burned from the cold. Although she was in great shape, Jared was in better. Up ahead was a thicket of bushes.

Sliding behind them, she tried to take in shallow breaths and remain unseen. The icy weather burned her lungs as the searing cold made her shiver in agony.

Where was Jared positioning himself? Think. At the edge of the park? In a line of firs? Out in the open, with the snowfall for cover? Still, there were no signs, nor sounds of his movement. The killer had to find her tonight; he'd never leave her alive.

Her legs ached from the crouching position. She resisted the urge to stretch. Muscles cramped and ice chips formed in her nostrils. Shivering uncontrollably, her teeth chattered. Not having run this winter, she wasn't used to the raw conditions.

"Hey, Toni. Whatcha doing?" The eerie sound of his voice sent electricity through her body. She screamed, then used the maneuver he taught her at the gym. His head hit the icy pavement, leaving him dazed and confused, as she disappeared into the firs.

Moments later, he came again, this time faster, howling and battering his chest. The fear inside made her trip, landing on her knees. He threw himself on top. Straddling her body, he flipped her over to face him, slipping his large hands around her neck. Veins bulged out on his neck and forehead as he squeezed. "You are mine, do you hear me? Mine. All this I've done for you."

She didn't want him to be the last person she saw. Above them, she noticed a small parting in the snowy clouds with a dabble of stars in the night sky. *Suzette, do you see me?* Now, instead of seeing her sister's face in the back window of the car, it was her own face she saw, followed by darkness.

Toni came to minutes later, finding herself beneath

a thicket of firs. These were supposed to be all cut back...she protested silently. Tasting her own blood from biting into her tongue during her hard fall, she ran her tongue along the jagged edge of a front tooth, now broken in half.

"Great move back there. You nearly got away. I teach all the women the right tricks so when I take them to the park, they can try it out. And then I show them how much stronger I am."

"You find them in the gym at your defense class. Then see who is better, you or them. Wow, sparring against women." Toni gasped, needing oxygen—puffs of white air smoked from her lips.

The knife was in view. In another moment, he'd send the knife through the left side of her skull and into her brain, leaving her physically incapacitated—just as he had with the others. Those she was unable to save. *I am so sorry.*

Toni fixed her eyes on a point in the air behind Frosty and murmured, "Jack. You've come for me." It was just enough to distract him, for only a second. And a second was all she needed to lift one leg hard between his legs as the other leg allowed her to hit him square in the nose. He hollered, falling backward and rolled to the side. One hand tucked up in his crotch while the other held his bloody nose.

Back on her feet, she cradled her throbbing rib cage. Each leg felt heavy and stiff as she stumbled forward, looking for cover.

The playground was yards away. Limping there, she squatted beneath the slide, hoping to rest. Something in the darkness stirred. It moved in a confused manner, searching under trees, behind bushes, along trails. Jack? No, not Jack. Frosty. Jared turned in one direction, she went in the other.

If only she could get a sense of the way back to the street, maybe there'd be someone to flag for help. Confused, she was unsure if she was going deeper into the park, or about to come out on the thoroughfare? She slipped and fell hard on her knees. She pushed herself up, noticing her hands were cold from the ice. Ignoring the pain, she hobbled down the trail. Pants soaked to the skin. Shivering violently, she arrived at a fork in the trail and chose the left curl. It was wider, making it impossible to see what was on the other side.

A low growl rumbled. Turning her head, she saw three stray park dogs, just feet away. Picking up snow, she formed them into balls to throw at them but this time they didn't run.

There, up ahead, were lights. Toni followed them to a narrow street which turned out to be the park's side road. The snowplow sat eerily still, inside lights on. Erma? Dogs trailed at her heels and she headed toward the machine.

"Erma. I need help." Toni dragged herself up the side of the plow and knocked on the window. "Erma?" Something was wrong. Snowplows moved. They didn't sit still like this. Toni rubbed the snow from the window and peered inside. There sat Erma, slumped to the side. The door was unlocked. Swinging herself into the cab, she tried getting a response by calling her name and then felt for a pulse. It was weak, but Erma was still alive. All she had to do was turn on the ignition and drive them to safety. The key was gone.

Frosty stood in the open door. He smiled, holding the keys just out of reach.

"Poor wee driver. I followed you the other day. I waited for two women tonight: the city worker Erma and Special Agent Antoinette Postell. I think I can manage two deaths per snow now. Yay me."

"What about Byron's third stanza; 'A mind at peave with all below'?" Toni gave him a hard shove out the door. After climbing over Erma, she escaped through the driver's side and frantically searched for vehicles to flag for help.

"Where, oh where, has my Special Agent gone?"

Weary, Toni hid behind the plow.

"I see you. I see you. Doggone it, woman, you're so much fun. You gave me such a workout. Much more of a challenge than any of the others. Be proud of yourself, but it's time to end our playfulness and get down to business."

Toni turned and ran in the opposite direction; no plan, just get away.

Frosty chased like a wild animal after his prey.

She battled fear. Confused, Toni nearly collided with a low hanging tree limb. For now, it'd be her weapon. She held the icy branch and waited, glancing behind her, she didn't see him. Which direction would Frosty come?

Toni waited. And then here he was. She held the branch, and then swung herself full force into him, striking him squarely in the face. The force landed him on his back and temporarily out.

Seeing her chance, she ran, but slipped, landing on her back. Air rushed from her lungs. In the silence, Toni crawled for several yards, then stopped to rest. She closed her eyes and laid her head down. It was time to give up. Maybe she'd find Suzette in the afterlife.

Then a voice from above called.

"Postit." Jack's face loomed above. He knelt, feeling for her pulse. He tore off his winter coat and wrapped her up in it. "Hey, was it a good workout, sweetie?" There was a tender quality in his voice just when she needed it the most.

"Jack—you came for me." Toni opened her eyes. "Pirelli is Frosty."

"Sshh, lay still, Postit. Help is on the way. An ambulance will be here soon. Just rest. I'm here now. Nothing will harm you."

"Where's Pirelli?" Toni tried sitting up.

"We'll find him." Jack pulled her into him.

"Ah." She cried, holding her side.

"Sorry."

"Jack, I need to get up. My backside is freezing."

"Are you sure?"

"Yes. It's freaking cold on this cement."

Jack helped her to her feet. Her legs felt wobbly as she straightened her back. By now, the ambulance lights filled the air. "Over here." Jack waved at the medics.

In the ambulance, a medic suspected she had broken ribs and temporarily wrapped them.

"Jack, there's a hurt snowplow engineer parked off one of the side roads. She's not far. You've got to find her. Erma, her name is Erma."

Jack radioed to the officers.

"Jack, I had it all wrong, all backward. It's not random attacks. I had Frosty already at the park, lying in wait for his next victim, looming out from the shadows. It never occurred to me that he took them into the park. He chose the girls from his self-defense class.

He sized them up and knew their strengths and weaknesses before he got them into the park. Always a step ahead. What girl wouldn't feel safe running with a strong cop? In his squad car too? No one would ever suspect to look there."

"Hey…" Jack held her hand against his face. "You don't have to talk now. Let's just get you to the hospital."

"Will you come too?"

"Yea, Postit, I'll be with ya."

"How did you know where to find me?"

"I found you because I'm an asshole. The truth is I couldn't stand leaving things between us like that, so I came back to your place. Jo said you were running in the park with some guy. Crazy lady. She also said you were with a police officer who said something about Frosty working out of a park in Michigan."

"Pirelli."

A couple of blue uniforms walked out of the grove of trees.

"We looked all over. He's gone."

"We're looking for Pirelli. Postell identified him. He's Frosty."

"No shit. I never would've guessed," one of the officers said.

"He has to be there." Toni slowly sat up, grimacing in pain.

"Postit, you stay here. I'll look."

"No, wait. Let me look too, Jack. This case is every much mine as yours. Think of how you'd feel if this was reversed," she pleaded, holding out her hand. "But I need your help."

"You've got it." Jack helped her up.

"Sir, she needs to get to the hospital," a medic insisted.

"Are you sure you can do this?" Jack asked Toni.

"Yes."

Together, they went into the trees. Jack handed a loaded revolver to Toni as he drew his own police issue. He signaled for them to go in different directions and then meet in the middle. She nodded and watched Jack disappear into darkness.

Toni skidded over a few frozen gnarled tree roots and bit back her screams of pain. The park was still bathed in shadows. Not a good place to be blindly shooting off a gun. Then she heard the crunch of snow. The sound got closer. Toni stopped walking. A figure came toward her. Slowly, she raised her weapon. "Jack? Is that you?"

"I'm here, Toni."

In a few more steps, she saw his face. Jack.

"He's not here. Ready to go back?"

"Yea, I am," Toni admitted. "Lend me your arm."

He swept his arm around her waist. Jack used the other hand to hold the radio. "Send a couple of squads to Pirelli's apartment."

In response was only white noise and high-pitched screeches. "Strange." Jack shook it and then banged it against his thigh.

A uniform came running up to them. "Everything is scrambled. All the radio's and emergency equipment are blacked out. In the last few seconds someone brought the emergency systems down by scrambling them all over the city."

"Pirelli!" Toni looked up at Jack. "And he's not going back to his apartment."

"Then where?"

"My apartment building. He's going after Jo."

"Why Jo?"

"She's the one who told you where I was. I'm almost certain that's where he'd go. Retribution." Toni hugged herself, willing the pain to stop.

"I'm on the way to your building. I'll see you at the hospital later."

"Okay." She carefully slid back onto the gurney. In the ambulance, she closed her eyes and felt the rock of the vehicle as the door slammed. She was safe. Safe. The medic buckled her in so tightly that it was hard to move. Emergency lights swirled about them in the dark night, lighting up the winter sky. In a few minutes, she'd be at the hospital and hopefully, before dawn, Jack would be with her.

"You look very relaxed."

"I am." Startled, Toni opened her eyes. "Jared?"

He patted her arm. "Pretty cozy back here, don't you agree?"

She began struggling against the constraints. "Driver! Help me!"

"Everything was going so well for us and then you had to play hide and seek." He wiped the hair from her brow and leaned to whisper in her ear, "No worries. I'll be right back." Jared moved to the front. The vehicle jerked to a stop and Toni heard a scuffle. She fought against her restraints, but they held her tightly. A door opened then closed. The ambulance started rolling again but much slower this time and without lights.

"Hello?" she called to the driver. "Are you okay?"

"This is Officer Jared Pirelli and I'm in control of this situation," he said to no one in particular. The vehicle gained speed as they careened around a corner, skidding into another car with a jarring crunch.

"You can do this—you can do this, Jared. I promise you can do this." He spoke low and fast to himself. Turning the vehicle around, he gently pressed down on the accelerator to steer them back toward the park. Pumping the brakes a few times, they slid through gentle curves, coming to a rest near the trees. He got out and popped open the back of the ambulance. "You'll be just fine. I'll take all your pain away. Trust me, Special Agent, I know how to do that." With great care, he removed the straps from her legs and arms. Toni tried sitting up, but by now the pain was so severe she could hardly take even a shallow breath.

"Jared, I really need for you to take me to the hospital. I need help. Please help me."

"Of course, I'll help you." He picked her up in his arms and carried her through the park, as tears ran down his face. "I love you. Don't you know that? I've always loved you. All I wanted was for you to love me back."

"Jared, just turn yourself in, I'll help you. I'll even advocate for you to get the help you need."

"You'll feel better here. And soon all your pain will be gone." Laying her down on the ground, he left her alone for a few minutes as he crawled beneath the cut back firs. "I hate that they did this to some of the trees. It was much nicer, more personal, with the firs nice and full."

Toni bit her lower lip while struggling to her feet. Moving slowly, she tried to get away from him, but he easily caught her. It was now or surrender to death. Her final stand. No way would she die here. Toni made a swift kick to his kneecaps and a fist punch into his throat. He dropped.

So cold now, and in horrendous pain, she stopped to take a breath, followed by another step. This went on for several minutes before hearing far off sirens. Again, she stopped to take a breath, before taking another step. Her head hurt. Her toes were swollen inside of her boots and with each step they throbbed with pain. Headlights appeared. FBI, police and medics rushed the park. More headlights. Doors opened. Doors slammed. Voices shouted. Figures ran toward her in the darkness. Jack.

Chapter 30

Officer Jared Pirelli was arraigned. The charges were assault and battery, along with attempted murder. More serious charges of murder would follow. The district attorney wanted evidence lined up and airtight so Jared wouldn't walk. For now, they had plenty to hold him. Bail was denied. Jared Pirelli was ordered to be examined by a psychiatrist to see if he was mentally fit to stand trial.

Another profiler stepped into the case, and Toni handed over the files. As a courtesy, the profiler made a copy for Toni to read through before submitting it.

'*Raised with three older sisters in a single parent home, his mother looked to him. Instead of being the caretaker of her children, the roles were reversed, and it was thrust upon him to be the man of the home while still in early elementary school. Jared found at a young age that he could manipulate not only his teachers but also his mother and his older female siblings by using his charm. This he tried successfully during his school years. Always butting heads with male teachers, he got along famously with the women; no matter the age or build. Occasionally, he'd see his father. Those times were of great torment for Mr. Pirelli, a New York police officer, berated his son's manhood, fearing he'd become a sissy being raised in a household of women. Yet, he'd never take the responsibility of raising his own son. Jared had several intimate encounters, which resulted in his rejection. Unable to cope emotionally, Jared "put them in their place" by killing them. He hid the bodies under fir trees, which began at the resort in Lake Geneva, Wisconsin. Later, Jared studied psychology in college before entering and putting himself through the police academy.*

He learned how to manipulate the psychological police profile tests when trying out for the force. For a long time, Officer Jared Pirelli would be the focus of many studies.

****

After a few days in the hospital, Jack drove Toni home. "Are you feeling any better?"

"Not much." She winced.

"It takes months for a rib to knit. You've got two that are broken besides a bruised hip and three broken toes."

"Don't forget a bruised liver."

"My pop was a firefighter and fell backward out of a three-story window once, cracking all the ribs on his right side. It was six months before he could go back to work."

"I feel his pain." Toni smiled over at Jack. "This is nice. I like hearing about your family."

"I planned on saying a whole lot more when I picked you up from the hospital, but you've been in and out on those pain killers."

"I'm fully awake now," Toni said. "And ready to listen."

"Bad timing. Here we are at your place. I'll drop you at the door and then park the car. I'll meet you inside. Wait for me and I'll carry you up the steps. By the way, until you're better, you need someone to stay with you. I have days coming, so that will be me. No worries, I'll be a gentleman and sleep on your couch."

Once he parked the car, Jack returned, sweeping Toni into his arms and carried her up the three flights. Gently, he set her on her feet inside the apartment. "Here you go. Inside your home. How does it feel?"

Perp came rushing up and then seeing Jack, abruptly turned to walk away.

"It feels odd. Frosty was here, both literally and figuratively. Perhaps I should move."

"Give it time. Come on, let me help you to your room. Should I carry you again?"

"I can manage. But instead of my bedroom, I'm going to the bathroom for a nice long, hot shower."

"I'll make dinner for us. Call if you need anything."

Toni closed and locked the door. The lock wasn't about keeping Jack out; it was about feeling Jared around her. Toni removed her clothes and stared at her skin in the mirror. She looked painfully thin. There was bruising from her face down her body and legs to her toes, appearing as ink spots.

The hot water soothed her aching muscles. As she reached for the soap, the water from the shower head became snow. Instead of her reflection in the stainless-steel spigot, it was Jared. She drew back in fear against the tile wall. The snow was once again water and the reflection belonged to her. Toni turned off the faucets and reached for a towel.

Hair dripping wet and freshly shampooed, the water cascaded down her body, in between the folds of her small breasts, along her legs, puddling around her feet on the black and white tiled floor. She grabbed loose-fitting sweats then snuggled into a large sweatshirt without a bra.

Barefoot, she padded into the kitchen. It took her breath away seeing Jack there, hunched over the stove cooking for them. Jack was here taking care of her.

"Steak and eggs okay with you?"

"Sounds great. But I wasn't aware I had steak."

"You didn't. You didn't have eggs either. I stocked up when I came over to feed Perp." He held out his arm, inviting her to tuck herself into him, which she gladly did.

"I had no idea you could cook. And thanks for feeding Perp."

"I owe you an apology."

"For what?" Toni asked, wrapping her arms around him.

"For the stupid move I made when I teased you about my profile. I felt flattered and embarrassed both at the same time and didn't handle it well. I wouldn't have blamed you if you never wanted to see me again."

"All is forgiven. But there is something I would like to know." A shot of pain went through her side, and she grabbed for a chair.

"Are you all right? Is it time for a pain pill?" He checked the clock.

"No, I intend on remaining fully awake for several more hours." Toni eased herself into a kitchen chair. "I would like to know why the adverse reaction from you when you read the names of the people I care about."

Jack set the paring knife at the side of the cutting board and stared into the sink. "I was raised to believe that everything good that happens is counteracted by something bad. With your list and cheery explanation, it was like I was a kid again, and if I stayed, something bad would happen. But I left and you nearly died. I'm not so sure about an almighty pushing us around like checkers on the board. I'd like to think I've more control than that over my life."

"Have things straightened out in your head?"

"Somewhat. Didn't take long to remember we had the start of something good. I just don't want anything to get between us."

"We won't let that happen." She held out her hand to him.

Jack took it, then kissed her forehead. He turned back to the stove to scrap the sides of the pan and divided the meal between two plates. "Oops, I forgot about making the potatoes."

"I don't want any. I want—you. I want you, Jack."

"Well, if you change your mind, I have a younger brother who just landed a great job on Wall Street. You'd like him. I can introduce you two," Jack half-teased, setting the plate in front of her.

"Stop that, will you? Don't tease in the middle of me opening my feelings to you," she scolded. "I'm serious."

"I want you too." Jack quickly added.

He set their plates on the table then pulled out the chair and sat across the table from her. "The other night in the park, when I saw how Jared hurt you, I had the same terrible feeling when my dad died."

Toni again reached for him.

"Toni—you don't have to do that." He set his fork on the napkin next to his plate.

"What don't I have to do?"

"Comfort me. I don't like to be comforted. Stop."

She slowly rose and moved to his lap. "We can figure this out." She wrapped her arms around his shoulders and nuzzled her head into him. She was relieved things had normalized between them.

Jack pulled back and eyed her warily. "What are you doing to me?"

"I'm about to kiss you, Jack." Her finger lightly circled his mouth as she hovered an inch away for a tortuous, wondrous second before placing her lips on his. She stood and took his hand in hers. "Come on, bedtime."

"You've been through a lot. Your body is healing. I don't want to hurt you."

"We can figure that out. Come."

Chapter 31

Sisters
Mallory unexpectedly arrived from the airport.

Still wearing flannel pajamas over her midriff wrap, Toni gingerly opened the door. Her sister breezed past her without even so much as a hello and removed her mink to reveal a Sax Fifth Avenue turquoise knit pantsuit. The color made her Tiffany's silver jewelry pop. Then she pulled off her leather gloves, starting with the tip of the fingers. Toni watched the ritual while waiting for her sister to speak. "I had Arthur, my chauffeur, in case you've forgotten, drop me here. I hope that's all right with you?"

"That depends on how long you're staying." Toni couldn't stop her yawn. "Yes, it's fine. But do you know what time it is?"

"Do you mean Chicago time, or Paris? It's good I caught you home."

"Where else would I be?"

"Driving around the city like a hobbit looking for bad guys again."

"Haven't done that since the serial killer was caught."

"Frosty? Are you kidding me? Frosty has been caught?" Mallory dropped like a stone into a chair.

"Nope, not kidding you, and yes, he's actually been

caught, days ago in fact."

"Thank goodness!" She burst into tears of relief.

"You must be exhausted after your long trip. Don't you have jetlag, or something to go home and recover from?" Abruptly, she felt a twinge of shame for being flippant.

"Can't a sister come by for a visit?"

"After midnight?" Toni glanced at the clock.

"Oh no, I wish I had brought along my luggage instead of having Arthur take them home. You've got to see the gorgeous hand knit sweaters I bought for Will and Daddy. They're navy blue with white snowflakes and the buttons are old pewter, with snowflakes etched in black. For Andre and Marie, I bought the most fabulous antique German music box, made from solid cherry wood. It plays five tunes." She began waving her index finger in the air as she picked up her small purse. "I've got something for you too."

"Me? You have a present for me?" Toni felt excited to be included.

A small, ordinary plastic snow globe of the Alps with miniature people skiing inside was pulled from her purse. Switzerland was printed in black on the bottom rim, obviously a cheap tourist offering. She slapped it down into Toni's hand, making it snow again. Placing it on a shelf, Toni tried to hide her disappointment. "Thanks. Can I get you something to eat or drink, Mallory?"

"No, I'm fine." Mallory began pacing the room when she suddenly fixated on Toni's face. "What's wrong? Your face looks bruised."

"Souvenirs from Frosty."

"He beat you up? And you lived? I'm so glad."

Mallory reached her hand out to her sister but withdrew halfway. "What happened? Were you on another stake-out when the killer jumped you?"

"No, I actually went running with him."

"Oh, you've always been a bit bizarre! Why would you do something like that?"

"He's a police officer—or was a police officer."

"Oh my gosh! It was Jack, the guy I met on New Year's Eve! All I can say is shame on you, Toni, for bringing a killer to my home. Wait till Daddy hears about this."

"Dial down, would you? First of all, Jack isn't the murderer. He's the lead detective on the case. Secondly, Frosty was a street cop. Of course, at the time I had no idea what his sideline was. In the struggle, he cracked a couple of my ribs. And a tooth in front. Got it fixed." Toni didn't want to say more.

"How awful."

"Tell me, does Will know you're home yet?" Toni gingerly sat on the rolled arm of the old couch.

"No need to wake him at this hour."

"I take it that's a 'no'. Will said you vacationed with his mother. How'd that go?" Toni didn't hide her amusement.

"God help me. That woman is impossible. I had Arthur take her home right from the airport before coming here." Mallory circled the room. "Wait, you said Will told you—when did you see him?"

"We met for lunch one day."

"And it was only lunch that you had with him?" She looked at her sister suspiciously.

"Of course, it was only lunch." The thought of anything more made her cringe, although she wanted to report that Will wanted a tryst but passed.

"That's right. You've a new boyfriend, Jack Autry." Mallory began shaking. A fresh round of tears exploded from her eyes. "This is going to be hard to believe coming from someone like me, but there's something you should know."

"Mallory, what is it?" Toni was shocked Mallory wanted to confide in her.

"I've killed someone."

It felt as if the earth dropped out beneath Toni's feet. "You can't be serious?"

"I'm the one who killed Victoria Taylor."

Toni inhaled a deep breath. *My sister confessed to killing the mayor's daughter.* How could she handle this? "Oh, God, help us."

"Toni, it was an accident. You've got to help me!"

"Yes, of course." Toni felt overwhelmed with dread as she glanced down the hall, thankful Jack was still asleep in her bed.

"Great!" Immediately, Mallory's tears dried. Her shaky voice became strong and steady. "I want you to fix things so it looks like the Lincoln Park killer did this one too."

"What? Are you nuts? This is unbelievable, even for you. Absolutely not. I suggest you have your 'Daddy' get a very good lawyer instead."

"What's wrong with you? Only a moment ago you said you'd help me!"

"Mallory, keep your voice down. It's late and someone might hear you—like the neighbors. Anyway, I'll help you, but I won't cover for you."

"I'm not talking to anyone about this, do you understand? Can't you imagine how awful this is for me?" Mallory covered her face with her hands. Her French manicure looked fresh.

"Are you sure Will didn't murder Victoria?"

"Will?" Mallory dropped her hand into her lap. "Why in the world would Will murder her? He loved her!"

"Ssh. Your voice. The neighbors. You think Will loved her? I thought that—never mind."

"How many murders did the police officer do?" Mallory asked.

"Four that we know about."

"Make it five. Just slip one more body into the serial murderer's pile. He's getting the death penalty, anyway."

"You've lost your mind." Toni blinked with disbelief.

Mallory stood, walked to the bookcase, took down the plastic snow globe and placed it back into her purse. "I should've known better than to think for one minute that my own sister could be counted on to help. You never did like me."

"Stop it, will you? You can count on me, but I refuse to do anything illegal. Just please tell me what happened."

"Then you will help me?" Mallory swiveled on her heels and held Toni's gaze.

"I said I would, didn't I? But there's no way I'll even consider blaming this on someone else. Besides, the police know this case is much different than the others."

"How so?"

"The other girls were attacked while jogging and— never mind, just take my word for it."

"Maybe we can say the killer was in a killing frenzy and got confused."

"No. We can't."

Mallory started to offer the snow globe back to Toni, who now refused it. "Let's focus on this matter, shall we? Tell me about it."

The gift was placed on the coffee table. Needing a cigarette, Mallory dug around inside her purse. Sliding one from the pack, she stuck it in her mouth. A small flame shot from the neck of the silver monogrammed lighter. Sucking a deep breath into her lungs, she blew out the smoke slowly while reaching next for her compact mirror. Mallory checked her hair. Gazing at herself in it, she finally snapped the compact closed and slipped it back inside her purse. "Okay. Victoria and Will dated. But it was way before he was with me. Maybe he dated you both at the same time?"

Toni knew he had but shrugged.

"Anyway, Victoria just wouldn't stop phoning Will." Mallory blew smoke into the air. "This is all her fault."

Watching three inches of ash hanging at the end of the cigarette, Toni looked about for something to use as an ashtray.

"Why do you think she called Will?"

"To get him back, of course. Duh."

Toni dumped out her pencils and pens from a mug and handed it to her sister, who immediately flicked the ashes inside. Toni opened the window a few inches hoping the smoke would find its way out of the room. The sheers beneath the draperies puffed out from the wind and the antique buttons rattled when they knocked against each other.

"The fact is I saw Will's car in front of Victoria's place. I waited for him at least thirty minutes. When she walked him out, they kissed on the front porch. It was too long for my liking—and for Will's liking it was probably too short. Anyway, I had enough, so I followed Will back to his place, where we had a big argument. I walked out. Then I had Arthur drive me to see that little whore."

Mallory ambled to the windows, where she fiddled with the strings of buttons. "Victoria answered the door in her nightgown and bathrobe. She obviously wasn't expecting me."

"How did Victoria react to you?"

"She just stood there silently when I told her to stop calling Will. He was mine—not hers. She didn't want the neighbors to hear so she invited me in."

"Did you stand in the hallway?"

"No, the living room and she offered me wine. That's where I saw the baguette that Will was supposed to give his mother from me for Christmas. Only he gave it to her instead. What an asshole. I wanted it back. I paid for it. That purse cost me four thousand dollars. Victoria refused to give it to me. I shoved her. She got this strange look on her face, staggered, and dropped onto the coffee table."

"And that's how you killed her?"

"Yes, and you see, it was an accident. Any court of my peers would understand as long as the lawyers stack the jury with rich women who've been cheated on. Anyway, I freaked; my intention was to scare her, not kill her! So, I called Daddy. He said to leave and go right home—he'd take care of it and have the place cleaned."

"Cleaned?"

"Yes, you know, take care of the body."

"And he had her dumped on the sidewalk by the park?"

"Really? That's where he chose to leave her? I guess." Mallory dabbed out the cigarette. "Daddy likes to shield me from such nasty details. He said it was time I went to Europe. But it was hard having a good time wondering what was going on here. It nearly ruined my trip. Well, actually Will's mother pretty well ruined my trip all on her own."

"My suggestion is for you to go home now. Have your 'Daddy' get a high-profile lawyer in the morning and then go to the FBI." Toni walked to the door.

"You said you'd help me. This isn't helping."

"Ssh, again, keep your voice low. This is extremely serious, Mallory. You have important information of an ongoing police and FBI investigation."

"Even if the judge believes it was an accident—which it most certainly was, I still could be charged with manslaughter, right? I could do prison time on that!" she sizzled. "Think of my reputation, would you, please? Besides prison air does terrible things to your complexion; I watch the Discovery channel and I've seen the pallor of those criminals. Tell your boyfriend to look the other way. Cops don't make much. It'll be worth his time."

"I can't believe your blatant disrespect for the law. This is one time your daddy's money can't buy you out of trouble."

"I should've gone to Uncle Charles instead of you." Mallory jerked her coat from the chair, then pulled it on. Picking up her purse, she headed toward the door. "Everyone has a price."

"Well, for once, this is something your daddy can't get you out of, sister dear. This is a mammoth sized case, or have you forgotten that Victoria is related to the mayor of Chicago? That family has way more money and power than your daddy." Toni opened the door. Mallory banged the door shut behind, leaving the snow globe.

Toni needed the toxicology report. If it was clear, then perhaps the argument with Mallory really did give Victoria a heart attack. Mallory could give anyone a heart attack.

First thing in the morning, she'd talk to Uncle Danny about her midnight visit from his very spoiled daughter. Then she'd put in a call to Uncle Charles. Toni double locked the door, turned out all the lights and headed for her bedroom, but first peeked in on Jack, softly snoring, still tucked into bed. And there was Perp, sleeping soundly on her pillow, oblivious to human entanglements.

The moon spilled its light onto the floor of her room. Holding her side, Toni carefully climbed beneath the covers, rolling the facts of the case in her mind. William Schofield lied to her. Only people who had something to hide, lied. With so many voices in the world telling her different things, it was nearly impossible to know the truth. She calmed herself with meditative taps to her face. Finally sleep followed.

The next morning, Toni awoke to the radio. "Good news for the mayor of Chicago's family. This just in, someone of interest is being questioned in the murder of Victoria Taylor."

Chapter 32

Toni looked at the clock. Nine. Damn. Oversleeping was simply not her forte, but today, she felt as though she were in a semi-conscious state. She maneuvered herself upright, and after locating her bathrobe, tried to locate Jack, but he already had left. The note said he was going to the precinct.

It jogged her memory about Mallory's last night's visit. She needed to get to the precinct pronto and chose a pair of loose-fitting slacks to ease into along with a pullover sweater. The socks were difficult because of her taped ribs. Carefully, she drove to the station where a bevy of cameras and reporters crowded the doorway. With such commotion, no one paid much attention as she pushed past.

Jack wasn't in his office but located him in an interview room with wild-eyed looking Mallory.

"There you are, sister dear," she crooned, then attacked. "Why did you tell Jack? I trusted you, Toni! I bet you just couldn't wait for me to leave your place so you could pick up the phone and tattle to Jack Spade over here!" She slammed her fist down on the table.

"Whoa, Mallory, I didn't say a thing to anyone."

Jack gave Toni a puzzled look, that's when she noticed a lawyer and Agent Palmer sitting on either side of her sister.

"You should have told me days ago that Mallory

was a suspect." Toni looked at Jack and Agent Palmer.

Jack stood up and took Toni gently by the arm, steering her back into the hall. "I can't have you in there. Go home. I'll talk to you later."

Toni watched the door close—and wasn't about to go home. There sat Uncle Herschel in a hallway chair, hat in hand, looking confused and anxious. She sat beside him.

"So you've heard, huh?"

"Yes, I heard." He patted her leg and gave a wan smile. "What can you tell me?"

"Nothing, I can tell you nothing. Anything Mallory may have told me is not privy to anyone outside the department and the FBI. Sorry. By the way, thank you for the spring bouquet you sent to the hospital."

"My pleasure. I wish you had let me visit."

"I just needed to rest.

"I understand. But back to Mallory, she's your sister. Though she's a difficult one—you need to help her."

"I wish I could, but she really got herself into a mess this time."

They sat in silence for an hour when the door swung open. Frazzled looking Mallory walked out in a daze, flanked on all sides by FBI agents, Jack, and the city's top lawyer.

"Uncle Herschel, you're here." Mallory threw her arms around him and gave Toni a nasty glare. "Thank you for coming. It means so much to me."

"How are you doing?" he asked, patting Mallory's back in comfort, which upset Toni. Why did she always get the best of everything; trips, money, brilliant lawyers, an apartment with a view, plus sympathy from her beloved uncle.

"Relieved. I just found out that I didn't really kill Victoria, or anyone else."

"Of course you didn't murder anyone." Uncle Herschel's eyes glowed with tears of relief. "Why are you handcuffed? Antoinette, why is your sister handcuffed? Does someone have the key? Find the key, Antoinette."

"Mallory is formally charged with the murder of Victoria Taylor," Agent Palmer answered.

He kissed his daughter's forehead. "I'll be back soon. Be brave."

"There must be some mistake. She just said she didn't kill her." Herschel rubbed his forehead.

"Uncle Hershel. Please, go home. I'll call you later when this is straightened out." Toni kissed his cheek.

He sadly nodded, placed the fedora on his head, buttoned his overcoat, and walked out of the precinct.

Toni went to look for Jack. She found him at the drinking fountain.

"Can we talk, please?" Toni asked Jack.

"In my office."

Jack held the chair for her and then pulled up the second chair to sit close. "I hate to be the one to tell you this, but you're off the case. Be happy. You finally got what you wanted."

"I'm not surprised since the accused is my sister. What can you tell me?"

"The coroner's report came in early this morning. Taylor was poisoned."

"Poisoned?" Toni drew back in surprise.

"A bottle of poisoned wine has Mallory's fingerprints all over it."

"Wait a minute. Are we talking about the wine bottle found on the bar, La Commese?"

"Yes."

"That particular bottle label must be ordered from France. Usually only collectors have it stocked in their cellars. Mallory doesn't collect wine, or even drink wine."

"The mayor has that label in his cellar. Forensics confiscated all the bottles with that label and brought them in for testing. All negative."

"Oh, thats gotta hurt his wallet." Toni gasped then continued. "Mallory also doesn't know a thing about poisons. Jack, we're not talking the sharpest tool in the shed here. Her forte is designer clothes and how to decorate with the color white. The last thing she knows about is a chemical. Chemistry class had to be waved so she could graduate from high school. My sister is innocent."

"How can a high school class be waved?" Jack leaned back in his chair until it creaked.

"When you're a Hughes, you can do just about anything."

"Well, even a Hughes isn't allowed to murder," he snapped. "Look, Toni, I totally understand your concern, but the evidence is strong. Hey, what did she mean when she said you betrayed her?"

"Last night, while you were asleep, Mallory stopped by on her way home from the airport. My advice was to have her dad get a lawyer. I suppose that's what she did."

"Actually, we brought her in about seven this morning." He scratched his head and smiled. "Let's change the topic. Do you like ribs?"

"Huh?"

"Do you like smoked ribs?"

"I like food, any food," Toni answered. "But I'm not hungry."

"Then we'll get coffee. There's a cafe on the corner."

****

Settled on a chair with a coffee in front of him while a green tea latte sat in front of Toni, Jack pulled papers from his breast pocket and read softly as if to himself. "The identified poison is an antihypertensive drug called Methyldopa. It's a white powder. Ingested by mixing in liquid. Tasteless. Side effects immediate; include headache, dizziness, weakness. Sends blood pressure off the charts resulting in stroke or heart attack." Jack took a long sip of his drink then looked up at Toni, speaking louder. "Oh, are you still here? I thought you had left. Just going over this toxicology report on a recent case." Folding it, he put it back into the inside pocket of his overcoat.

"What if Victoria was poisoned before Mallory arrived? The report only proves to me that Mallory is innocent. The scheme is far too sophisticated. When my sister pushed Victoria, she must have literally dropped dead on top of the table."

"Remember, there are her fingerprints on the bottle. Let's go back to my place to finish this discussion. Feel up to it?"

They pulled up in front of a small arts and crafts style house on the west side of the city. Inside, the furnishings were sparse, but actually very nice. A chunky leather couch and an old trunk for a side table was placed strategically in front of a large screen TV.

Along the bookcases on one wall was his college football paraphernalia. She liked the fact he didn't keep his place as neat as a pin like his office. Months old magazines lay scattered next to the recliner. A plate with a hardened sandwich remained on the coffee table. There was a neatly folded Afghan at the back of a chair.

"I've got crackers and beer to offer. Want some?"

"Pass." Toni removed her coat and slipped it over the chair. "What's the reaction time from first ingesting the poison to total effect?"

Jack moved next to her. He kicked both feet up on the coffee table and ran his fingers along her arm. "About thirty minutes to an hour. It also depends on how much was ingested. Mallory gave her the wine, they argued, she pushed her, adding to the intensity of the drug at work. Ms. Taylor collapses because she is dead."

"You think that she slipped poison into the wine bottle, poured her hostess a drink and then pushed her into the coffee table?"

"That sums it up." He leaned in and she leaned back.

"I suppose there's a motive?"

"Jealousy."

"There must be something more. Mallory is jealous if someone's jewels are bigger than hers, but she doesn't go around stealing, or killing for them."

"Maybe not, but her plans for marriage were jeopardized by Victoria's affair with Will." Jack held Toni's hand.

"Will told me he and Victoria were only friends." Toni stared at their fingers intertwined. It felt good.

"I didn't think you believed everything witnesses

had to say. Victoria wore her nightgown when Will was there. Sounds like an affair to me."

"It sounds like circumstantial evidence to me. Do you know what I do as soon as I get home?"

"Please tell me." His eyes twinkled.

"I first remove my bra which I refer to as a torture device, then change into my nightgown. Lots of women do." She squeezed his hand.

Jack squeezed back staring at their hands. "So what?"

"So, that's what Victoria did too. Just stop saying affair."

"Will was there first, then Mallory, who brought the toxic wine. They argued. The poison took effect. Victoria fell into the table. I know I told you that I was taking some days off to be with you, but with this case breaking open, I can't."

"I know. No worries."

"Congressman William Schofield is back in Washington and I'm flying out to see him."

"Shouldn't Will be here in Chicago with his fiancé who has just been arrested?"

"I think he's trying to distance himself."

"Most likely. Bastard. Be sure to ask him about the reason Victoria called him to come to her house that evening."

"What was it?"

"I'll let him tell you. I'm off the case—you told me so, remember?"

"Fair enough."

"By the way, did you find DNA in her bed, or in her panties, or anywhere else?"

"No."

"Doesn't sound like an affair, does it?"

"Your allegiance should be with your sister. It's only normal you defend her. And I must do my job." He looked at her and cupped her face in his hands. "I sure miss my partner."

"I've always been right here, and always will be."

"You've gotten into the middle of my heart." He leaned down and kissed her lightly on the mouth.

Chapter 33

Mallory

Mallory took small steps into the visitor's room. The handcuffs clattered as she sat. Without a doubt, wearing the standardized orange jumpsuit bothered her more than being charged for murder.

"Orange is not my color. I hate this." Her voice filled with bitterness. "These prison garbs need a total redesign. Just because one's in prison doesn't mean you shouldn't feel good about yourself. When you feel good about yourself, you're more apt to be congenial. More congeniality means less crime. Duh! A good beauty shop wouldn't hurt either. I need a trim. My roots are starting to show. And my nails need help."

Toni reached over the table and patted her folded hands. "Didn't your dad have any luck getting you out on bail?"

Mallory withdrew from her touch. "You're right on that one. The mayor is infinitely more connected than my daddy. However, I do have my own private cell, a cell phone, and I get to have the TV room all to myself, and I can take my meals in my cell, catered, including dessert."

"Careful of the starch. Weight gain can be a problem in custody."

"Not when you have a treadmill."

"You're kidding me?" Toni laughed.

"No, I'm not." Mallory laughed now too.

"Has Will gotten in touch?"

"I don't imagine having a jailbird for a fiancé is conducive to his political career. He says he is needed in Washington, but he's just trying to avoid the local press and me. It's all about image."

"You're better off without him."

"Thanks. And I'm sorry about stealing him away from you last year. If I had to do it all over again, I wouldn't. In fact, you can have him back now if you prefer. Didn't you say you two had lunch together? There you go."

"No thanks."

"If only I hadn't come between you two, you'd still be with him, then it'd be you in prison instead of me."

"What are you talking about?" Toni shook her head trying to understand how Mallory always seems to come up with wild conclusions that never make sense.

"If you were still engaged to Will, it'd be you accused of murdering Victoria and sitting here wearing a ghastly orange jumpsuit, and I'd be sitting where you are now, only I wouldn't be wearing what you have on. I'd be wearing something wonderful like Vera Wang or Chanel. Look at this get up I have on. Who knows how many people have had this on their bodies before me?" She shivered. "But unlike me, you'd be placed in with the population. Your dad probably wouldn't even leave France to visit you either."

"What? Can you even hear what you are saying? It makes absolutely no sense."

Mallory smiled knowing she had gotten the better part of her sister.

"At least you're chipper in here. I thought I'd come in to see a very sad person."

"I'm very happy now that I know I didn't kill her. I'm guilty of pushing her, not poisoning her. That can be laid on someone else's doorstep. And I just happen to have a brilliant sister who will prove my innocence."

"If I'm to do that then I need to know exactly what happened—unofficially."

"Weren't you paying attention? I already told you."

"Tell me what happened again."

"Listen closely this time. I hate to keep repeating myself. Will seemed to be spending more time away from me. I knew he was seeing someone else. Gut instinct. I asked him who the woman was. Of course, he assured me there wasn't anyone. Yea, right. I had to find out for myself. Everything came to a head when I had those five purses made: one for me, one for his mom, and three for his office girls. Oh yea, and that other one for you. Up to that point, I thought he was sweet on one of those office girls.

"Anyway, with Will evasive about his whereabouts when not in Washington, and not at his Chicago office and not with me, I decided to follow him. The first few times it was totally boring—cleaners, lunch with men, business meetings, grocery store, oh yea, Tiffany's for me, that wasn't boring at all. But the next time I followed him, he met Victoria for dinner at Olive's Restaurant in Old Town."

"Really? Are you sure?"

"Yes."

"Was that the night of her death?"

"No, it was before then. You have no idea how badly I wanted to walk in and throw a scene, but I knew it'd hit the papers, so I waited for him at his place. I told him I saw him with Victoria. He said they were old friends. Recently, she called him about a family secret, and he agreed to meet her in public."

"Explain to me how your fingerprints got on the wine bottle."

"I'm getting to that. Will promised me he'd never see her again. However, on the night of the murder, he was late picking me up again, so I had Arthur drive me over to Victoria's. Sure enough, his car was parked right in front for the world to see. You'd think he'd at least try to hide it several blocks away or park inside her garage."

"Perhaps it was all innocent and there was no reason to hide the car," Toni suggested.

"Then I saw them on the porch looking all cozy. They kissed and, let me tell you, it was no peck on the cheek either. She had her arms wrapped around my man. It took all my strength not to run right up there and…and…"

"Kill her?"

"I sure felt like it! Can you blame me? But no, I didn't. How many times do I have to tell you? After the kiss, Will looked at his watch, got in his car and drove away. I told Arthur to follow him. I thought maybe there was another lover he needed to see, but he went home. For a few minutes, I sat outside his place, trying to calm down while wondering what my next move should be. Then my cell phone rang. It was Will. I pretended I was at home and asked where he'd been. He told me he had just gotten in from the office. Liar."

"How'd you handle it?"

"I charged up to his condo and confronted him face

to face about Victoria. He assured me it was all business. I could no longer stand the sight of him, so I left and went to Victoria's."

"How long was it between when you followed Will home and returned?"

"Does it really matter?"

"Yes, it does."

Mallory thought for a moment before answering. "About thirty minutes, no more than forty. Traffic wasn't bad."

"How did you get through the front gate? It locks."

"There's a bell. I pushed it."

"What was she wearing when you confronted her?"

"A satin nightgown with a matching robe."

"Was she dressed like that when Will was there?"

"I don't think so. When I got there, Victoria looked as though she had just stepped out of the shower. Her hair was wet and she had a towel in her hand."

"Tell me what happened next."

"Her face was flushed, and she said she felt suddenly very ill and needed to sit down. A wine bottle along with a glass was in front of her."

"How many wine glasses were there that you saw?"

"Just one—she acted drunk. She stumbled a lot. Slurred her words. Once, she even fell onto the couch and nearly tipped over the wine bottle, but I caught it just in time, and set it on the bar. Hey, that must be how my fingerprints got on it. I got out a wine glass, thinking I needed something too, but thought better of it and set the glass down. On the bar, I saw the purse that was supposed to have been given to his mother. I picked it up and asked her about it.

"She yelled at me to put it down. 'No one gives me orders', I told her. Victoria stood up, and came toward me with her hand out, demanding I hand the baguette back to her. She grabbed a hold of the baguette by the handle. She got a far off look on her face and I pushed her away from me, that's when she fell into the table. When she didn't get up, I called Daddy on my cell phone. He told me to go right home, and he'd take care of it. I did exactly as he said. Will came over late that night, but I refused to see him. The next day, Daddy sent me to Europe with Will's mother."

"When you moved the wine bottle, was it full?"

Mallory searched her memory. "Half full. Maybe two glasses had been poured."

"I better go. There's a lot for me to do."

"I hope it has to do with freeing me."

"It does. Just one more thing, do you happen to know what night the Collins have off?"

"Since Victoria's death, they're only there during the day. No one is there at night anymore. Will told me."

"Did Will bring the wine with him, or was it already there?"

"Ask him. But I did notice that it was one of those rare fancy imports. Next time you visit me, bring my skin cream, would you?"

Chapter 34

The next night, Toni slipped into her coat and covered her head with a hood. Taking no identification with her, she only had enough for bus money, and two keys; one to the lock of her apartment door and the other to Victoria's. Precaution when breaking and entering. She rode ten miles on the CTA before exiting. She avoided streetlights as she walked. The night was ethereal, with a clear moon surrounded by thick clouds forming ghostly figures. The snow looked pasty, like globs of stiff oatmeal. Since she didn't have the key for the iron gate, she'd have to either go over the top and chance becoming a kabob or try squeezing between the bars. She chose the latter.

The sharp wind picked up the moment she slid off her heavy coat. It made her feel nearly naked despite her thick woolens. Toni rolled her coat into a ball and pitched it over the top of the fence, but as luck would have it, the corner of a hem caught the tip of a spear. Why hadn't she just slid it through? Dumb. Yanking on it, she heard a rip. Now the coat was really stuck. Never mind; she'd slip between the bars and try to get it down from the other side. She fit her head through. Next a shoulder. Now she inched her trunk in between. Halfway through, she got stuck. An iron bar dug into her back and another one sandwiched into her tummy. There was no going forth or coming back. Blast those

Fanny Mays candy. The wind blew again, this time sounding spooky in the bare limbs of the trees. Toni twisted and turned her body this way and that as the coat flapped down on over her head.

There were now headlights illuminating the yard. The car stopped. Blue and white lights flashed. It was the police. Toni peeped out from under the coat. Thank god, it was Jack. He got out of the car and walked up the drive, chuckling.

"What do you think you are doing, Agent Postell?" Stifling laughter, he shined the flashlight on her.

"Special Agent Postell," she corrected him. Flailing her arms and one leg up in the air, she answered, "Squeezing through a fence isn't as easy as it looks."

Jack crossed his arms. "You look like an octopus in a cage—again I ask, what are you doing here?"

"What does it look like I'm doing?"

"Whatever it is, it's not working."

"I'm trying to get inside the Taylor house."

"Sssh, keep your voice down. Why do you want to get in there?" Jack stepped forward.

"I'm acting on the presumption that Victoria really had something illegal on the mayor by the way of documents that she wanted to pass along to Will. Since he doesn't seem to have them, I'm hoping to find them hidden somewhere in the house. That's motive enough for the mayor to poison his own niece."

"So now you think the mayor poisoned his own niece. Will must be off your list of suspects."

"Don't just stand there looking at me. Aren't you going to help?"

"You're supposed to be off the case, remember?"

"Thus—I'm sneaking into the house to have a look around," Toni explained.

"I don't know what I should do. This looks like a case of breaking and entering to me." He tried angling her shoulders to pull her out.

"I haven't broken a thing and I'm far from entering. Hey, watch where you're putting your hands, will you? Besides, I have a key."

"You have a key?" One hairy eyebrow arched higher than the other. He twisted her position, and she slid out.

"Thanks for helping me." She rubbed her arms while shivering.

"Where's your coat?"

"There." She pointed up to the top of the fence. Jack snickered. Grabbing hold of the cold steel rods, he easily hoisted himself up and yanked the coat down. Letting go of the fence, he landed on a snowdrift. The coat was slit up the back, but she was thankful for it and quickly put it back on. "I'm so cold."

Jack pulled her into him and rubbed his hands up and down her back. "Come on, I'll give you a ride home." They walked toward the unmarked police car. "I'll make us some hot chocolate at your place. I saw some in the cupboard the other evening."

"You can give me a ride home, but I'm turning around and coming right back. This time with a ladder."

"I'll arrest you."

"Arrest away!" She held her wrists together, waiting to be cuffed as her violet eyes filled with determination.

Jack looked at her hard and long, then led the way to the front of the mansion. "Give me the key." He held out his hand.

Thankful it hadn't fallen out of her pocket she handed it to him. "Here, but it's only for the front door. Not for the gate. The gate is the hurdle we must get over first. Maybe you can lift me up and over? Or do you have a file we can use to jimmy the lock?"

Jack reached for the handle.

"I told you, Autry, it's not going to open." She shook her head.

The handle turned. Jack pushed open the gate and stepped back for her to enter first.

"Well, I'll be—Will said it was always locked. I suppose I'll never hear the end of this."

"Never. Not for years and years." His dimples accentuated his smile.

Jack quietly closed the gate behind and walked with Toni up to the front door. She pressed the doorbell and waited for several minutes to be sure the place was empty. When no one answered, they entered. Toni shut off the alarm.

"How'd you know the code? Never mind, I don't want to know."

They stood in the middle of the living room. "I've been all over this room, but I want you to walk me through the crime scene from your perspective, Postit."

This time, there was no wine bottle, no glasses on the bar. Yet the broken coffee table remained. Staring at it, Toni wondered why no one had thought to clean up the mess and toss it out. "I asked my sister how full the bottle of wine was before she moved it to the bar." Toni walked from the couch to the bar and back again, trying to figure out and see what Mallory had the night of Victoria's death.

"What are you talking about?"

"Mallory said that when she first arrived, Victoria claimed she wasn't feeling well and as she sat down, nearly knocked over the bottle of wine, that's when she caught it. Thus her fingerprints." Toni pointed to the couch. Using the vase from the mantle to simulate the wine bottle. "She then was offered a drink, but Mallory turned her down. I asked her how full it was at the time, and she said it appeared to have two glasses missing."

"So?"

"Mallory didn't bring the bottle with her, don't you see? The bottle was already in her house. Someone else put the poison in it."

"That can't be proven."

"It can't be proven Mallory put it in either, even if she did have motive."

"Motive and opportunity."

"But you have to connect the poison to Mallory and there is no way you'll be able to do that. Only moments before she saw Victoria with Will kissing. She didn't have time to get the poison. My sister came here to confront Victoria about Will. There's no way Victoria would've drank anything my sister gave to her—they didn't like one another. They argued, they didn't sit around and have a nice chat over a drink. The wine bottle and glass were both on the coffee table when Mallory arrived, along with the baguette."

"Here we are back at the baguette."

"When the forensic team arrived, the wine bottle and two glasses were on the bar. The murder was done by someone Victoria knew. It took preparation. Something is off. I can't figure it out, though."

"What?"

"I want a look at her bedroom." Toni dashed from the front room, through the foyer, and up the long staircase. Feeling like Goldilocks, opening bedroom doors to peer inside and then closing them again. The master bedroom wasn't easy to find. It was then she discovered a hallway that was nearly hidden. She opened the door. Victoria's room possessed a warm feel. It was not only neat, but obviously she took great care of her belongings. Or was it the Collins did that? Makeup was organized on the vanity along with hairpieces, hairbrush, bobby pins, and hair clips. Shoes were left in their sleeves, and there were floral original paintings hung around the room. Even her purses were organized by color and brand. "Odd her parents haven't come to dispose of her things. Or do they find it was it just too hard to deal with? Does that come much later?"

Jack shrugged looking like a fish out of water. Clearly this was not his element.

The room wasn't the largest bedroom, but it did have the finest view along with a pleasant, enclosed balcony to enjoy. Toni carefully pulled out all the drawers to look through, as well as searching the cabinets in the adjoining private bathroom. What kind of a gal was this Victoria Taylor? Was she really interested in only drawing Will back into a romance, or did she have something that was worth killing for?

Jack leaned on the doorjamb. "Find anything?"

"No. I'm trying to get a sense of who the victim really was."

"What I can see from here, she was high maintenance."

"That doesn't matter. We're trying to solve a murder."

"Just an observance, Postit. Try not to be so defensive, will ya?" With that, he was gone. Jack's footsteps could be heard on the stairs going down. Away from her.

"Jack?" Toni ran to the top of the stairs. Jack stood by the door.

"Come on, Postit, I've gone over this place several times, there's nothing here."

The ride home was awkward. Toni broke the silence. "What did you find out from Will in Washington?"

"It's confidential. But I'll tell you. Keep a tight lid on this."

"Okay."

"Will finally admitted seeing Victoria several times, including the night of the murder. Will also said Victoria never gave him anything on the mayor, although he had a feeling she had found something unlawful about him and wasn't sure how to handle it."

"So says Congressman William Schofield."

"So says the polygraph test. After the interview, we had him hooked up to a machine. He passed with flying colors. We're back to Mallory, and she refuses to take a poly, on the advice of her attorney. Can you reason with her?"

Toni laughed until there were tears rolling down her cheeks.

"I like the sound of that." Jack grabbed her hand. He kissed her fingertips.

"And I like the feel of that." She felt Jack take a giant emotional step in her direction.

Chapter 35

Late winter
Lake Delavan, Wisconsin

Toni stood at the front door of the Taylor Wisconsin lake home and pressed the doorbell. Cute chords. Cheery sounding. Since no solid answers to Victoria's murder were forthcoming in the city, she hoped talking to her parents would provide a fresh lead.

A worried couple opened the door. The resemblance between Mr. Taylor and his brother, the mayor, was amazing, causing Toni to falter at first. Ms. Taylor was a small-boned, short woman with a long nose. Obviously, Victoria received the best of their genes had to offer because she didn't resemble either parent.

"Hello, I'm Special Agent Postell. I'm here about your daughter's murder. May I come in?" Toni held up her credentials along with a small smile, hoping none of the pretzel snack she ate while driving caught in her teeth. Why hadn't she checked the mirror first? Closing her mouth, she used her tongue like a whisk brush.

"You're a little late and out of the loop, my dear. The person who killed our daughter is in custody, isn't she? Andrew, isn't she?" Mrs. Taylor looked at her husband.

"Yes, of course she is," he reassured without

hesitation.

"The one accused of the crime is in jail, that's true. I'm only here on follow up, and make sure we have checked out all leads. We want a solid case. Look, I've driven all the way up here on icy roads from Chicago. Give me only a few minutes of your time. Please. It's cold out here." She looked from one face to the other with hope.

"I dunno. My wife, Joyce, and I've been through so much lately." Mr. Taylor came off as a composed man buckling under a truckload of grief.

"I know this is painful and I don't mean to cause you more."

Ms. Taylor looked forlornly at her husband, who finally nodded his agreement to allow Toni entrance. She followed the older couple into the front part of the house and onto the enclosed, heated porch, where the view of the lake was spectacular. The bluish hue of the ice was spectacular with the wind minimal, creating little movement for the iceboat race taking place.

The couple sat on antique wicker furniture across from Toni who immediately smelled freshly baked pies. Were they apple? No, blueberry.

The young maid appeared. Mrs. Taylor looked up at her. "Oh good, you're here, Ellie. What would you care to drink, Agent Postell? We have iced tea, lemonade, perhaps something from the bar? Or would you like something warm instead?"

"Please, call me Toni."

"All right. And please call us Janet and Andrew."

"Thank you. And lemonade will be fine." Toni nodded.

"Toni and I will have your lemonade, Ellie. What

about you, Andrew?"

"I'm still babying my drink." Andrew held his Bourbon glass up in the air, rattling the ice cubes at them. His bony hands were oddly rounded at the knuckles.

Ellie returned within minutes and set the tray of drinks on the coffee table along with individual little cakes still warm from the oven. Small talk followed: how cold it's been, the amount of snow this year brought, how long they have lived in Wisconsin. Ms. Taylor started the real conversation that Toni had come here to get when she pointed to the hanging picture.

"That's Victoria's graduation picture, Suma Cum Laude from Wheaton College. At the same time, she volunteered nearly twenty hours a week at a woman's shelter in the area. Can you believe our daughter even found time to be a reader for the children's section of the library on Saturday afternoons?" Joyce's pride was evident. "That's before she took a job in Chicago."

Toni stood to look closely at the pictures of the woman whom she had only seen in death. It occurred to her that there hadn't been any pictures in her home. Then again, who bothered to display framed pictures of themselves unless with another person? That's right, Mallory did.

Victoria's eyes seemed to smile; lips were parted just enough in greeting as if she were glad Toni was on this case. Don't give up, she seemed to tell her. Another picture hung beside it, but this one was a man, slightly older. Toni guessed by the tilt of the head and by the expression on his face that he was most likely mentally handicapped.

"And that's our son, Andy. He lives in a private

group home at St. Colletta's. It's the same place where President John F. Kennedy's sister lived for so many years. Anyway, our son is older than Vickie."

"Your daughter certainly favors you, Mr. Taylor, Andrew," Toni corrected. "What a nice-looking family. I'm so sorry for your loss."

Andrew asked, "For which child? Andy with an IQ of 50, or our brilliant daughter who was brutally murdered?"

"Andrew!" Janet was taken aback with embarrassment over her husband's brashness.

"I guess for both. Each is tragic in their way," Toni said, returning to her seat, "Vickie was such a cute girl. I bet she had lots of attention from men as she got older."

"She certainly did." Janet smiled, reflecting. "Our Vickie. It was hard for us to keep up with them all."

"Can you think of any bad break ups, or maybe if there was someone who wanted to be her boyfriend, but wasn't?"

"Like a stalker?"

Toni nodded as she pulled a notebook from her purse. The movement made her back ache, making her wince.

"Vickie never mentioned any stalker to us. And there really wasn't anyone special in her life for the past year. At the time of her death, she was still broken-hearted over a past romance."

"Name?"

"Congressman William Schofield."

"Was she still involved with him at the time of her death?"

"Oh, so you know about him?"

"Of course she would. She's on this case, Janet."

"Vickie told us they loved each other. Later, we learned Will lied to our daughter and was engaged all along to another woman. His fiancée found out about it and in a jealous rage poisoned our girl," Ms. Taylor blurted. Pulling a hankie from her sleeve, she wept.

"Tell me, did Vickie and the mayor get along? Was there anything at work she felt concerned about?" Toni asked.

"Not that I recall." Janet blinked her wet, puffy eyes.

"Think back for a minute."

Taking her literally, the couple watched as the second hand on the clock went around once and then Andrew blurted out, "No idea!"

Janet asked, "Do you think it has something to do with her death?"

"Not really. Just trying to touch all bases."

"We know nothing."

"Or perhaps it was an excuse to be close to Will?" Toni dug.

"We weren't close to our daughter the last year of her life." Janet gazed at the frozen water.

"Nonsense! Our girl was such a joy to us. Loved each moment of the twenty-five years she was with us."

"Twenty-five years? But I thought Victoria was thirty?" Toni wrinkled her nose and looked from face to face questioningly.

"You don't know?"

"Know what?"

"We adopted her when she was about five years old."

"You adopted her at five years old?" Toni repeated,

sitting forward. Suzette was nearly five at the time of her disappearance. Was it possible? Could Victoria be Suzette? Her imagination ran wild with possibilities.

"After having one child with medical problems, we didn't want to try again. When Andy was about eight, we got our Vickie. She was a breath of fresh air and came charging into our life so full of energy."

"Correction, my dear. Victoria wasn't so full of energy when she first got here."

"That's true, I nearly forgot."

"What agency did you work with in her adoption?"

"No agency. It was a private adoption," Janet said.

Toni looked at the wall that was covered in pictures of Victoria. Suzette had red hair, yet, with time, it could have mellowed out to blonde. Or was it dyed?

"We had a go between—the biological parents preferred it to be done that way. But maybe we should think of contacting them now that she is gone to tell them what happened. What do you think, Andrew?"

He didn't answer.

"A go-between?" Toni smiled, trying to understand.

"Yes, a man by the name of Roman Morelli. He's a good friend of my brother-in-law."

Toni's skin pricked with goose bumps since her terrible experience with the mobster a few years ago.

"When we decided to adopt, we visited all kinds of agencies and found out it would take years. The list of people wanting babies is long. Babies were and still are in short supply. Victor contacted Roman for help. He knew a family who no longer could care for their child."

"Actually, we think our Vickie was abused,"

Andrew said.

"Abused? In what way?" Toni asked.

"When she came into our home, she was as a skinny as can be, and such a dirty-looking waif. The doctor diagnosed rickets and malnourishment. Major neglect situation."

"I believe drugs were also involved," Andrew said. "With the parents, that is."

"Vickie's hair was so snarled that we had to have it cut very short and let it grow back out. She used to fight the brush. Why the authorities were never notified, I'll never know." Andrew freshened his drink at the room's portable bar.

"What color was her hair at the time?" Toni asked anxiously. "Do you have a picture?"

"At the time, her hair was blonde with a faint touch of red. As for a picture," —Janet glanced at her husband— "Andrew commanded we were not to take pictures of her in such horrid condition. So, that was that."

"Do you know the name of the biological family?" Toni's hands became clammy.

"We don't."

"You mentioned that Roman Morelli assisted in the adoption."

"Yes.

"He knew the family?"

"Some things are vague. Andrew, can you help with the details?"

"All as I know is he located the child. The parents were willing to give her up."

"Doesn't Roman have affiliations with the mob?" Toni knew he was, but wanted to hear their viewpoint.

"If you're insinuating he's part of the crime family, in a way, yes. But they're legit these days. No more shoot 'em ups or dirty money. Everything's done by the book."

"What book is that?" Toni didn't hide the fact she disagreed.

"The law books. His family was even acquitted a few years back when the state tried to pin a bunch of murders on them."

"Just to prove he's honest, he's Victor's right-hand man," Janet said.

"Oh no, he's not. In fact, they barely speak anymore," Andrew said.

"Do you know why that is?" Toni asked.

"No."

"How long have Mayor Taylor and Roman Morelli known one another?"

"Oh gee, they go way back to boyhood, forty years or more. Our dads were best of friends, so Roman and Victor seemed to team up, and they got just as close if not closer. They had a falling out a while ago and now hardly speak."

"What was the falling out about?"

"A long while back, they started a fishing business together. After it went under, each blamed the other for its demise, resulting in very bad feelings. I thought the situation was ironed out. But the closeness never was the same as when they were boys in the neighborhood."

"Why is that?"

"I was never sure," Andrew answered. "Never asked."

"Would you happen to remember the name of the lawyer who handled the adoption?"

"Yes, it was Dick Honeycutt."

"Perhaps I can interview him. Is he still in practice? Chicago?"

"He passed along years ago from cancer."

"Are any of his records left?"

"No, there was a terrible fire in his office soon after his death. Everything was destroyed."

"A fire?" Toni thought that was too convenient. But the hope of finding the records was another dead end in finding Suzette.

"Electrical. A new system was being put in to replace the old at his offices. A short started it all. Burned to the ground. Good thing it happened at night when no one was there."

"Yes, very good thing. Who was the lawyer that represented Vickie's interests at the adoption?" Toni finished her lemonade.

"We just had one lawyer who handled it for both sides; again Dick Honeycut."

"And Victoria was about five when you adopted her?" Toni reiterated. "What's the date of her birth?"

"August twelfth."

Toni's heart pounded wildly. Suzette's birthday was also in August. August first to be exact. Birthdates could easily be changed. Suzette was the very same age as Vickie when she went to live with the Taylor's. Could they be one and the same? Roman Morelli was a murderer—the least problem he had was lying. Could he have covered up and passed off Suzette as someone else? But Suzette wasn't abused. She was idolized and pampered and lovingly cared for. Toni was trained to exude calmness and control. She needed to hold herself together. Doing her best to control her marauding thoughts, Toni asked, "It must have been hard for Vickie to leave one family and move into yours."

"Yes. For a while. She cried at night, wanting her other daddy. No matter how badly abused they are, children still prefer their biological parents. But soon she accepted us, and after that, all was well."

"Yea, Janet fattened her up till she had a weight problem. But she slimmed down in college," Andrew added.

Toni stood again at the wall of Victoria's pictures, searching for a family resemblance; a nose, slant of the eyes, turn of the lips, shape of the face. It was hard to tell.

"You said you weren't very close the last year of her life. Was there any reason for that?"

"My wife is too sensitive," Andrew answered.

"Well, Andrew, she did drift from us when she went to work for your brother. Maybe we shouldn't have left her alone with that woman right next door."

"What woman?"

"Emily, the mayor's wife."

"I take it you didn't get along with Emily."

"Not at all. Vickie revered Emily for the wrong reasons."

"That must have been tough on the two families."

"Whoa, she felt the same way about me. Emily is high fa-looting. I believe that a simpler life is better. Vickie preferred things as her aunt does, the easy way. My girl was too independent for her own good. I wanted her to come home to visit more often, but she preferred the city life to the country."

"You certainly have a lovely place here, but young women prefer being in the city with other young people."

"When she was little, she begged us time and again to leave the city and make this our home year around. With the lake frozen over in the winter, she could ice skate all she wanted. During the summers, she swam everyday and had her friends out here. They played flashlight tag all the time at night and caught fireflies. Those were the best days. I think what hurt me the most was in the past months Vickie went on a quest to find her biological family. On one level, I understand but on another I couldn't. It was as if she wanted them to replace me. Which parents were better, the old or the new?"

"Do you know if they connected?" Toni's ears perked.

"I'm not sure. Emily Taylor was helping her with that, so you might ask her. Just add it to the list of things Emily purposefully did to hurt me."

"I'm sorry," Toni said, but understood the need for adoptive children during adulthood needing to find their biological family.

"I see your drink is gone. May we freshen that up for you?" Ms. Taylor asked.

"No thanks, it's getting late. I need to get back to the city before dark. The roads will freeze over. I don't want to be stranded." Toni stood and watched the last of the iceboats head for the dock as a blizzard began. Her thoughts returned to Jared and what he did during snowfalls. Would she ever regard snow as a beautiful form of nature again? At least there'd be no murder tonight in Lincoln Park.

"Ah, oh. You better stay the night here. Look at the sky. You'll never make it back on these roads. You can stay in Vickie's room," Janet insisted.

Reluctantly, Toni complied.

After a late dinner of pot roast and carrots, and blueberry pie, everyone turned in. The nightgown Ms. Taylor offered Toni was neatly folded on the slipper chair in the bedroom. No way would she slip on something her daughter wore. It would feel somehow haunted. Instead, she'd sleep in her own clothes on top of the bedspread with her coat pulled over her. She planned on sneaking out at the first light, making it back to the city before rush hour, that is, if the roads were clear.

Toni looked about at the photographs and a small lifetime of souvenirs in Victoria's bedroom. Hanging from her dresser mirror was a sweet little locket. Toni pulled it off and opened it. Nothing was inside. She put it back exactly how she found it.

The house filled with nighttime sounds—the tick of the grandfather clock from the front hallway, creaking floorboards, and the rumbling furnace. Closing her eyes, Toni pulled her coat up around her neck. She curled into a ball and allowed her mind to drift back to Jack. Was he at the office right now? Probably. Did he think about her as much as she thought about him? Probably not. Numb with sleepiness, she luxuriated in the memory of the passionate kiss and fantasized what the next one would be like. Hours later, she was awakened by a noise only feet away from where she slept. Toni propped up on an elbow and saw a flashlight.

"Mr. Taylor?" Toni whispered. "Is that you?"

The figure turned and looked at her.

Toni sat up. "Who are you?"

The figure rushed her, hitting her in the head with a pillowcase filled with hard objects, then ran from the room. Toni cried out and gave chase down the hallway and out the front door, onto the drive, where she saw a car driving away behind a haze of falling snow. Her feet stung with cold. Toni looked down at her sopping wet socks and then bolted back into the house, where the Taylor's, now fully awake, waited.

"What's that all about?" Janet appeared alarmed.

"Call the police." Toni panted, out of breath. She sat on the couch and yanked off her socks. "Someone was just in Victoria's room. I chased them outside where they got into a car. I didn't get a good look at the license plate, and it was too dark to see the make and model."

"We've been robbed?" Ms. Taylor pulled up her robe's collar and glanced around, not moving an inch.

"I'm not sure. I think they left the loot on the bed after they clubbed me with it." Toni touched the goose egg forming along her hairline.

"Oh dear, you're bleeding a bit too. I'll get some ice. Andrew, call the police."

Toni followed Ms. Taylor into the kitchen where the older woman dabbed at the cut and applied a bandage. "You should see a doctor."

"It's just a small cut." Toni tenderly pressed her fingers around the bump.

Andrew returned, holding Toni's purse. "Thank goodness they didn't take this. I just called the police."

Toni grabbed for her purse and shuffled through it. All the cash was gone right along with her magnum. It was infuriating. Was the robbery just a run-of-the-mill break-in, or was it related to Victoria's visit?

Perhaps there was something in Victoria's room that the intruder was after, other than just trinkets. Toni hurried back into the bedroom and closed the door. There wasn't much time to look through all the drawers and closet. After a haphazard search, Toni heard the police.

Janet tapped on the door. Toni opened it and spoke to the chief. Toni observed as Ms. Taylor tried to remember what was in the room in the first place.

After the police report was complete, Toni decided it was a good time to leave.

"If you can think of anything more to help with our daughter's investigation, please call," Janet said, walking Toni to the door then giving her a slight hug.

"Thank you for opening your lovely home to me. I am so sorry about the break-in. Keep me posted on that, will you?"

"Certainly We've been hesitant of new people since Victoria's death."

"I imagine that's a wise decision." Toni paused with her hand on the doorknob. "One more thing. You spoke about Victoria's jewels being in your safe. It's none of my business, but after your daughter's death, did you remove anything from her house?"

"We went one day, but after we arrived, I realized I wasn't up to it. Too painful. We only removed her jewels. Thank goodness they weren't taken this morning."

Toni continued. "Were there anything else left in the safe?"

"Like what?"

"Documents, any kind of papers?"

"Only jewels."

"You're wrong, Janet. There were papers. A large envelope was sealed and addressed to that Schofield."

"Did you open the envelope?" Toni was elated, thinking this could help narrow the field, and perhaps see what Victoria had on her uncle.

"It wasn't addressed to me, so I never opened it."

"Where is it now?"

"Out back in the trash bin. I burned it. Nothing but ash left."

Chapter 36

Toni drove back to the city with one hand on the steering wheel and did a face tapping exercise with the other. What bad intentional luck: an entire building burns down with Victoria's birth record and now possible evidence of the mayor's fraud goes up in smoke.

It was good to be back in the land of WIFI. Her phone was filled with messages from Jack. After checking them, she was pleased to note they all had to do with her personal safety. Not one of them was work related. At least one thing in life was moving in the right direction.

Although she considered returning his calls to discuss Victoria's parents and the break-in, she ultimately decided against it. No way did she want to hear any potential criticism, especially as she was no longer officially assigned to the case. Again. The emerging romantic side of Jack was much more enticing. That's what she wanted to investigate.

The first stop was the Bureau to report her missing gun. Agent Palmer became livid when he heard where she had spent the previous night. "Didn't you hear me when I told you I had taken you off this case?"

"I did."

"I'm going to have to write this up and place it in your file."

"I realize that." Tony remained stoic.

"Aren't you at least going to argue with me about it?"

"No. Write me up. I disobeyed an order. I broke policy. In the process, my weapon was stolen."

"And you compromised this case by your very presence. Any information you might have gleaned is now tainted, as well as our entire case against our suspect. I'm putting you on temporary suspension. This will be a bad mark on your permanent record."

"Yes, sir." Toni stood and placed her credentials and badge on the desk. It was emotionally painful to be turning these pieces of her career over to him, but she had blown it.

Tony drove along the icy streets. She needed another gun. Magnums were by far her favorite. Spying a gun shop, she parked. The man behind the counter brought out several pieces, laying them out one by one. Toni opened the barrels and peered into them. "Nice and clean."

"Mine are the best."

Finally, she settled on the Glock, identical to the one she just lost. After filling out the paperwork, the store owner told her he'd call her when her record came back clean.

It was dark by the time she parked her bus. There, up at the bay window was Perp, perched, looking down at her. It was tempting to hurry out of the cold and into a hot bubbly bath, but the tightness of her jeans had been bothering her for several days. Not only that, but her nerves were on edge. Ready to talk to Jack but not quite ready to go up to her apartment, she decided to walk several blocks.

Crossing Clark Street to Broadway, she got Jack's voicemail. "Hey, I hope you are taking some time for yourself. Call me when you get a chance. I have news."

A navy Mercury drove up within feet of her, and then slowed. Fully aware of its presence, she chose to ignore it. Striding along, she now moved faster. The vehicle kept pace with her. Toni stood at the corner as if waiting for the light to turn. Gauging the car's movement through traffic, at the last minute Toni changed direction, retraced her steps, then crossed midblock, between cars. Stopping amid squealing brakes and blaring horns, the sedan did a fast U turn. Here it came again.

That did it. Now she clearly felt nervous since most of the stores had already closed for the night leaving nowhere to go for help. Even the small neighborhood health food store, Betty and Bob's, was dark with the metal gate pulled down over the door and windows.

At the next corner, she turned east as the car accelerated, stopping in front of her; blinding headlights hurt her vision. Stunned, Toni watched as the driver's window slid down. And there he was. Sooner or later, Roman Morelli always seemed to show back up in her life. The handsome divorced playboy, son of the head of the syndicate, would take over Chicago's Gold Coast as soon as his father succumbed to cancer.

Having questions for him, she preferred asking them down at police headquarters in the light of day, with Jack in the room. Not wanting anything to do with any of the Chicago crime family, Toni walked around the car as fast as she could, but Roman reversed the car again, causing her to walk into the side of it. Traffic whizzed by, honking horns. Even a police car rode on without giving a second look.

"Go away, Roman!" She slammed the hood of his car with her palm.

Jogging the long block, she ducked into an alleyway. Red brick walls from apartment buildings rose on both sides; with a wire mesh fence dead ahead, she had trapped herself. A pair of pit bulls sat ready to attack on the other side in case she decided to come their way.

Turning toward the traffic, her exit was blocked when the Mercury backed in, filling the space. Roman maneuvered the car to pin her between the graffiti wall and a large metal trash bin filled with stinking refuse.

"I give up. What do you want, Roman?"

"You did good with the Lincoln Park murder. I read the case against a bad cop is airtight."

"Is that why you practically ran me over, to congratulate me?"

"I have an invested interest in my rescuer. Thanks to you, I'm free to pursue health and happiness; the American dream. I'm here as your protector in case I need you again to flub a case against me." He chuckled. "No hard feelings."

"Enjoy it."

"I've come in peace." He flashed the peace sign. "Don't make me chase you all over the city. Please, get in."

Toni looked around and finally capitulated. The backseat contained a bevy of pink feathers. She imagined they were from a left-over boa. She sneezed.

"Be sure to buckle your seatbelt," he said. "Don't want to get a ticket." Then he picked up speed down the alley, careening back into the street with a wide right turn into traffic.

"I heard you paid some good friends of mine a visit." Large Italian eyes stared back from the rearview mirror.

"News travels fast. Wisconsin is a lovely state, and I met some nice folks while there, yes indeed. It's too bad about their daughter Victoria though. I never knew your work for the city also covered social services."

"It's all over the papers that your sister has been charged." Roman glanced at the rearview mirror.

"Yes, she's charged, but you and I both know Mallory is a pawn." Feeling more comfortable, Toni slid forward toward the front seat.

"Just like my family was when you helped us." Roman headed straight north.

"Correction." Toni leaned over his right shoulder. "You're guilty for the murder of the owner of the bar which you now own. You were the right guy but with the wrong evidence."

"Whoever did that hit, did a service to mankind and the city owes them a deep sense of gratitude. The previous owner used the bar as a drug drop. Kids got their fixes there. I call his hit recompense."

"Well, here I am. What's so urgent?"

"Your sister. Your older sister. Sorry she's locked up."

Toni noticed the adjective of 'older' to define which sister. "Mallory is innocent. And don't you think Victoria cries out from her grave for justice to be done?"

"That's a touching speech. It gets me right in here." Roman pointed to his heart.

"And since you're the one who brought that lovely,

pitiful waif into the Taylor's lives, I bet you want to see the person who is guilty pay for it as well." Toni saw an opening to ask Roman about the adoption and took it.

"Is this off the record?"

"Yes."

"By telling you what I know it may bring my family into harm's way."

"How so?" Toni hardly believed Roman was foolish enough to divulge one word that could be held against him, or his family. He was much too clever to be caught this easily. Yet a slip of the tongue would serve her just fine.

"Some of our past practices, the law may misconstrue as being less than legal."

"Are you saying the Chicago family had something to do with Victoria's murder?"

"Of course not. Never. "

"Since I inadvertently helped you once. Isn't there anything you can do to help me?"

"Someone can always take her place," Roman suggested.

"Meaning a fall guy?"

"Yes."

"Absolutely not. You sound like Mallory. Listen, Roman, if you know something that can help my sister, say it."

Roman pulled over to the curb and put his arm over the back of the front seat. His face was troubled. "You don't know what you're asking."

"Your conscience must be working these days or we wouldn't be having this conversation. My flub at the trial was to your advantage. Tell your family this is *my* family. Return the favor."

"I'll do what I can."

"Let your conscience be your guide," she said flippantly.

Roman got out of the vehicle and opened her door. Toni was surprised they were already at her building.

"There's one more question." No way could she leave and not ask him about Suzette. Her heart rate picked up. Toni enunciated and spoke half a beat too slowly, the way she did when she felt the world was dropping from under her feet. "My five-year-old younger sister Suzette was kidnapped about the same time Janet and Andrew Taylor adopted a five-year-old girl."

"There's no connection," Roman quickly responded.

"Are you sure?" She narrowed her eyes at him. "Joyce Taylor told me that Victoria cried for her daddy when she first got to their place. Suzette was also a daddy's girl. Roman, I'm begging you, please tell me the truth. I'm asking you one more time—was Victoria my sister Suzette?"

"No."

"Can I believe you?" Toni whispered, stumbling backwards. Torn between wanting to know the truth and fearing the answer, she hardly breathed.

Roman blatantly stared at the spot between her eyes. "Yes. I can give you more information, but you must promise not to turn it over to the authorities. Should you make this promise and then break it, I will not be able to guarantee you or your family's safety. Take time. Think it over."

Toni watched Roman get into the driver's side and leave. Could she really trust the words of a renowned mobster and accused killer? What he said didn't add up. It seemed coincidental that the Taylor's and Morelli's were not only closely connected to one another, but also to Victoria. In this case, there'd be no easy answers.

Perp remained on the top floor's window, this time rubbing up against the glass looking down at the street. Toni waved. It was good to be home. What a long couple of days. Taking the front door key from her purse, she went into the building. Toni sprinted up the steps two at a time. She was shocked to see someone sitting outside of her apartment.

"Uncle Danny, are you all right? You look awful. Come in."

He followed her into the apartment and then sat on the couch with his head in his hands. "You've got to help my girl, Toni. You're the brightest person in Chicago. I want Mallory out of jail and acquitted."

"Uncle Danny, I'm doing everything in my power to make that happen."

"Since you're now suspended from the FBI."

"News travels fast."

"I want to hire you as a private investigator." He pulled his checkbook from his back pocket.

"Don't do that." She held up her hand in protest. "I'm only suspended, not fired. I've already made a mess for myself and should I do anything more, then I'll be permanently terminated and perhaps even charged," Toni explained, knowing full well she'd continue with her investigation privately. "I do have a question, though, to ask you. It's a tough one."

"If it'll help my daughter, ask it."

"When Mallory called you from Victoria's place the night of her murder, did you tell her to leave; that you'd have it cleaned up?"

"Yes, I did." He held her gaze.

"Why did you leave Victoria's body in the park?"

"I didn't. Here's the truth—by the time I got to Victoria's place, the body was gone. I was just as surprised as the cops when her body turned up at the edge of the park."

"Gone?" Toni was surprised. "Any idea who it was that got there before you did?"

"Not a one." Danny wrote a check, tore it from his checkbook, then dropped it on the table. "Consider this living expense money while you are on probation. Despite what happened between your mother and me, I still think of you as my daughter."

Toni smiled, and leaned into him. "Just don't let Mallory hear you say that."

Chapter 37

Chicago, Illinois
Early February

She was on her own. In violation of the law. But it was a chance she was willing to take.

The next day, Toni canvassed Taylor's secluded neighborhood. The fact that the police had already done so didn't matter. With her background in criminology, she was trained in soliciting answers in ways that others weren't, including law enforcement. In her pocket was a brand-new AI Voice Recorder. She was ready.

Toni rang doorbells of elite residences within walking distance of the Taylor's. Mainly live-in maids answered, informing her of the families vacationing in warmer climates during the harsh winter months—of course, no one saw or heard a thing the night of the Taylor woman's murder. Blah. Blah. Blah. They were the type who didn't want to get involved. Two hours later, still undeterred, Toni pressed the doorbell of the last house of the day.

In place of the expected cookie cutter uniformed maid, stood an elderly lady dressed in tones of muted gray, wearing a crocheted shawl held together with an antique cameo brooch. Holding onto a three-legged crutch, the woman leaned a bit to the right. "How may I help you, young lady?"

Since she was required to turn in her FBI badge, Toni flashed her driver's license. "Hello, I'm Special Agent Postell."

The woman's eyes lit up. "Come in, come in!" A small thick woman who walked bent at the waist, Toni gratefully followed her into the front parlor that was decorated in tons of soft gray. Offered a seat, Toni took it. "I'm sorry, I didn't get your name."

"I'm Eva Shuler. What can I do for you?" Eva held onto her steel crutch with both hands and peered over it.

"I'm investigating the murder of Victoria Taylor."

"Oh my, the mayor's relative."

"Yes, the mayor's niece."

"That's right. The children around here seem to grow up so quickly and they all clutter my mind when trying to keep track of who's who. I remember when they once cluttered my lawn with their bats and balls, and their bikes, which was surely easier to tend to than a faltering memory."

Toni sensed it bothered her greatly. "You're doing just fine, Mrs. Shuler. Did Victoria grow up in this neighborhood?"

"Yes, right next door to the mayor's, only he wasn't the mayor back then. It was his father who held that title at that time."

"When did the Andrew Taylor family move to Wisconsin?"

"They summered up there on a Wisconsin lake for years. The wife wanted to get away from the hubbub of the city and her husband's family. When Andrew retired, they couldn't leave Chicago fast enough. That's when Vickie took over the city residence. After all, the mayor owned it all these years so the choice was his of who could stay there. I hope you don't want something to drink. It's the maid's day off. I suppose I could get you something."

"No, I'm fine."

With a mischievous laugh, she replied, "Actually, I no longer have a maid. It's just something I say so I can fit in with the other snooty people who live around here. I wouldn't have someone hovering over me if you paid me! Now, where were we? Oh yes. Both are very nice families, although I do remember a bit of jealousy between the two women. What are their names? Don't tell me, I'll think of it in a minute. Joyce, no Janet, and Emily. No, wait, that's wrong; Janet married Andrew Taylor and Emily married Victor Taylor. It's a good thing you came. You're stirring up my memory, keeping the streams flowing in my brain."

"What caused the jealousy?"

Ms. Shuler leaned toward Toni and whispered as if there was someone close by listening. "I don't like to gossip but I believe it was over spoiling the girl. Emily couldn't have children and Janet didn't want to be pregnant again due to her boy who wasn't quite right."

"You mean the young man who is mentally handicapped?"

"Mentally handicapped?" she asked with surprise. "It was a bit more than that. Quite a bit more. When Andy was a boy, he would do despicable things. There was a time that he burned a cat. Really awful, *awful*. Another time, he fed the mayor's wife's little six-week-old terrier to his boa constrictor. Why his parents ever gave a child with his mental capacity and disposition something like that I shall never know. Bad judgment is what I call it." She shuddered. "It's too bad Victor didn't keep his love child."

"His what?"

"Love child. You see, Victor had an indiscretion many years ago with his maid. The maid turned up pregnant, so when she told him about the baby, he said to get rid of it. The maid refused, left his employ and had her baby in some charity hospital."

"Do you remember her name, or happen to know where she is now?"

"In the grave, my dear, she died during childbirth."

"What did Emily say when she found out about this child?"

"To my knowledge, she never did find out."

"Then how do you know this?"

Ms. Shuler looked confused. "Right, good question, how do I know this? Let me think for a moment." She rubbed her forehead.

Toni remained silent.

"Now I remember! All the neighborhood housemaids gossiped up and down the block. I did have a maid back then and she told me."

"And the child? What happened to the child?"

"I'm sorry, my dear. I don't know any more than that."

"Do you know what year the maid had her baby, the month, or remember her name?"

"Oh, now you are really asking a lot of an old woman." She giggled. Eva looked up to the right, trying to remember. "Let's see, that summer my son started college when the baby was born, and that was about twenty-five, or thirty years ago. Let me write it all down for you." Eva got to her feet and limped to her desk. She plopped down and pulled the front of the cabinet down. Taking a small sized piece of monogrammed stationery from a box, she scribbled. She stood to her feet and handed the paper to Toni.

"I don't remember the name of the Taylor maid, but my former maid might remember. Her name, phone number and address are written down. We still exchange cards at Christmas, so she'll be easy for you to find since she still lives in the city."

"You've been of so much help, Ms. Shuler." Toni got up. "Do you happen to remember if the baby was a girl, or a boy?"

"I don't believe I ever heard. Why are you so interested in the mayor's child?"

"I'm trying to learn as much as I can about events surrounding the family. Helps me in putting together the entire picture."

They walked to the door.

"If you think of anything else, would you give me a call? Here's my card. I bet you've lived here for a long time." She smiled at the sweet woman.

"Oh, my dear, yes. My late husband and I lived here for the better part of fifty years, and my father before that. He tried buying the mayor's mansion and the one next door to it; the one that Vickie's parents lived in, for my Herbert and me when we first married. We wanted our kids to be able to visit through the underground tunnel. Legend is that plenty of good homemade brews were made there during prohibition for speakeasies." Ms. Shuler seemed delighted to give out this historic information.

"Underground tunnel?"

"Yes. I wonder what secrets it holds."

"I wonder about that too. I live right across the

street from a restaurant which once was a speakeasy. More secrets there, do you suppose?"

"Chicago is just full of history. I love it here. But sadly, neighbors aren't as friendly as they once were. With the mayor so close, it's like a lockdown here. Now with the murder, it's a busy place but rather entertaining too. Constant police patrol up and down the street, thrill seekers driving past. Why, the other night, I even saw someone hanging on the front garden gate." Her eyes grew wide with fright. "It was rather horrifying."

"Really? I can only imagine." Toni crossed her fingers that Eva suddenly didn't realize it was she who was out there that night.

"Yes, I was going to call the police, but then I saw a squad car stop. I hope that person's posterior was hauled off to jail. Oh, pardon my language, dear."

"You're such an interesting person, Ms. Schuler, and filled with so much history. I just may come back and visit sometime again soon, if it's okay with you?"

"You must. My Herbert was a professor of Chicago history at Northwestern, and he has passed on so much information to me. And next time, I'll be sure to have cookies and something warm to drink."

"I'll look forward to it."

"Bye for now." Ms. Shuler closed the heavy door behind her.

Halfway down the stone steps, Toni turned and caught the elderly lady peeping at her through the curtains. They waved to one another.

Out on the street, Toni yelled, "Thank you!" High-fiving a tree limb, it answered by dumping snow on top of her head. Shivering, Toni hurried to her vehicle, then sat waiting for the heater to kick in while searching through her purse for something to dry off with. A folded tissue was all she found. She sat wondering what to do next when her cell rang. "Hey there, Jack." Talking to him set her heart racing. Just thinking about him made her smile too.

"I heard about your suspension."

"There's a good reason for it. I'll tell you about it in person."

"I was just wondering what a profiler does when she is taken off a case and has endless amounts of time on her hands," he said a bit too curiously.

"And you called to find out? Are you checking up on me, Jack?"

"Just making sure you aren't taking anymore house tours."

"Don't worry about me."

"Toni, I just drove by your place. I noticed your bus wasn't parked in its usual spot. That worries me. Are you doing something you shouldn't be? Tell me you're taking it easy or having lunch with Jo, please."

"Ask me no questions, I will tell you no lies," Toni said. "You came by my place? You have news on the case?"

"No, I came by your place to call on you such as people do when one person is interested in seeing more of another person."

"Sounds to me like a social call. Want to meet somewhere?"

"Let's meet at Starbucks on Congress. But first, I must make a stop. See you in thirty minutes?"

"I'll see you then. Can't wait."

"Me either."

Humming again, Toni drove down the block past Victoria's house, trying to figure out the exact location of the tunnel below street level. The two houses were enormous. When you have two magnificent homes right next to one another, how would one decide which one to live in and which one to allow family members to use? There was no telling.

Both were prestigious and unique in their own individual ways, including the gardens that spread about the mansions as a ballet dancer's tutu. Toni noticed movement on the front porch. Someone was sweeping snow away—Mrs. Collins? In a flash, Toni slid the bus into a parking space, whittling back and forth from reverse to drive until she was snug between two cars, up against the curb.

"Excuse me!" She waved, coming up the walk.

Ms. Collins looked up. "Yes? What is it?"

Toni showed her driver's license again. "I'm Special Agent Postell, investigating the murder of Victoria Taylor. I was given recent information about an existing tunnel running between the two houses here. I was wondering if it's still open?"

Silence.

"May I have a look?"

Mrs. Collins shook her head firmly. "Not without a warrant, or the mayor's permission."

"I imagine the police know about it, right?"

"Why don't you read their report, Special Agent."

Toni realized this lady was a tough nut. "I can be back with a warrant in an hour, or I could also go next door and personally talk to Victor." Purposefully using his first name, it would allude to the possibility of her being a personal friend of the mayor. "He personally assigned me to the case of his niece's murder. Yes, the day after in fact. I sat right in front of him in his office."

Ms. Collins suddenly nodded yes and opened the door, granting the FBI woman entrance. As she stepped over the threshold, Toni smelled fresh paint. In the living room, she noticed the rug had been replaced. The broken table had been hauled away. There was nothing in its place. "How do I get to this secret tunnel?" Toni turned about to see the mayor. "Hello, sir." Holding her hand out in greeting, he gamely shook it.

"I hear your sister is being held for the murder of my niece. Any truth to that?"

"My investigation is far from over," Toni added.

"Give her full access to the basement, Beulah, but nowhere else."

"I'll be done in thirty minutes," Toni promised, guessing he hadn't yet been informed of her removal from the case.

"There's nothing worth seeing longer than ten minutes." Mayor Taylor held her gaze.

Beulah Collins led the way. She was not a talkative woman. Good pick for employment to keep gossip in-house and not blabbed all over the neighborhood like his previous help. By the sour look on the maid's face, Toni knew she was unwelcome. She glanced at her wristwatch and hoped Jack would be late to Starbucks because she sure would be.

"Right this way." The stout woman led her through the house and into the kitchen where she began twisting the double locks and single bolt on the door leading down the steps. Toni thought that much security on an inside door was just plain weird. It was as if something terrible was being kept below there. Did it want in?

Finally, Beulah jerked opened the door in need of oiling. Pointing down the steps, she flicked on the light. For a moment, Toni thought the woman was going to dog her steps. Not wanting that to happen, she quickly came up with a plan.

"Ouch! What an awful door squeak. The sound of it is still ringing in my ears." The noise was enough to set anyone's teeth on edge. Toni shook her head, which sent the maid into the pantry in search of WD-40.

With Beulah now out of sight, Toni went for the steps. With her penlight in her hand, she felt thankful for the long railing which guided her down about fifteen feet to the cement floor. The area gave her the willies. It was just the kind of place that witches used in the scary flicks she watched as a kid. Shaking off the memories, she touched the crumpling plastered walls, finding them damp. No mold was present but there was a scent of Clorox. Interesting. Clorox could not only be used to brighten dingy whites but came in handy when obliterating blood evidence.

Above her head hung a single bulb of 40 watts that cast a low light creating long shadows in the murky environment. Taking a step, something crunched under the weight of her foot. It turned out to be a miniscule piece of broken glass. She slipped it into her coin purse to check it out later. The basement of such a huge mansion was surprisingly small and bare. Toni walked the perimeter and found U-Haul moving boxes stacked in the corner. One had toppled over. Inside each box were packing materials, except for the box that was on its side. That was empty. Toni remembered seeing a large plastic sheet caught in a tree the night of Victoria's murder. Had her body been wrapped in that piece of plastic from this box and then transported to the park?

Toni drew in a deep breath and expected cords from an organ to ooze from the walls. careful of her footing, Toni walked to the tunnel's entrance. Yes, indeed, it had been kept open. Very cool. It looked as though she were entering a cave. Slowly, she walked forward, hoping not to trip over anything, while keeping watch for Al Capone's ghostly silhouette. She felt energy in the walls. The tunnel meandered a bit, connecting the basements of the two houses. It had to be a good twenty yards from Vickie's house to the mayor's with poor lighting. With Vickie, having traversed the tunnel perhaps thousands of times, coupled with subzero temps outside, it was the obvious choice for her to walk that fateful night.

A minute later, she walked into the mayor's cellar. With her penlight she located the light switch. Flipping it on, the room flooded with bright lights. It took a minute for her eyes to adjust. The difference between Vickie's side of the basement and the other side didn't escape her. It was extremely clean, too. There was a floor to the ceiling wine rack that covered an entire wall. Each bottle was carefully categorized for inventory dating back to the start of the century. None were younger than ten years old. Most of them weren't domestic. And none of them were dusty, showing this area of the house was as important as the upper residence. Ah, the bottles were even in alphabetical order. All the twisted paths of the crime led back to Mayor Taylor.

Now she saw it. A dried spot on the floor no more than a tablespoon's worth. Leaning down to examine it, she felt a hand squeeze her shoulder. Leaping back, it was impossible to stifle the scream that careened from her belly. Staring into the face of the mayor, she could tell her reaction startled him. "Oh, it's you. Sorry, I think I caused us both to lose our vitamin C for the day." She panted, patting her chest.

"Have you found anything of importance?" His eyes seemed to drill through her skull and into her thoughts.

"Still looking. Do you have any idea of what this dark red spot is?"

He cast his eyes down, then not seeing it well, got down on all fours. "Never noticed it before. Could this be from....Victoria?" Struggling to get back to his feet, he crawled to the wine rack to help pull himself up to his feet again. Then whipping a monogrammed handkerchief from his pocket slapped the dirt from his pant legs.

"Has a crime lab been through here?"

"The crime lab has been all over the place," he grumbled.

Toni kept looking at that spot on the floor. Was it paint, blood, a stain? "Mind if I take a scraping?"

"Help yourself."

On her knees, she exchanged the penlight for the pocketknife from her purse, and began scraping at the stain until she had loose shavings. It wasn't a lot. She hoped it'd be enough. She smelled it before depositing the possible evidence into one of the new baggies she always had a stash of inside her large purse. Samples for analysis were tantamount to all her investigations. This one had no odor she could detect.

"Has it been there for a long time or is it new?"

"I don't know. Tests need to be run. It certainly isn't fresh. Blood turns brown on the surface soon after it dries. And it's a reddish brown."

"Then you're certain it's blood."

"Lab analysis will tell."

Feeling his impatient eyes on her, she quickly scanned the freshly painted white walls of the cellar. "What's this?" She pointed to a black metal door on the outside stonewall. Without waiting for an answer, she tugged at the handle. It easily opened, revealing a tunnel. Six feet on the other end was another door that appeared to open to the outside.

"It's how boot leggers got their product out of this basement during prohibition."

"So illegal liquor once was made here?"

"On the very spot we stand."

"But how does this prevent anyone from entering your residence from the outside?" Toni thought it could've been the point of entry the night of the murder.

"Don't worry; the mayor of Chicago's house is secure. That door has been sealed shut from the inside and the outside."

"Have you tried it lately just to be sure?"

"I didn't, but the police did. And if you're thinking the murderer entered in through here, then you're wrong."

She bit her tongue not liking to admit when people figured out her thoughts.

"There's another door to the outside just like this one but on the other side of the basement," he told her.

"I didn't notice. It's so dimly lit over there. Why is that?"

"Janet preferred it that way when her daughter was little. It discouraged Victoria from using the tunnel to visit us so much. Being an only child, Victoria had no sibling rivalry, but our two families seemed to have plenty when it came to her."

"Victoria wasn't little anymore. Why wasn't the lighting improved?"

"It just wasn't," he answered with a shrug of his shoulders.

"Did Victoria use this passageway often?"

"All the time. As an adult, she wasn't one to be afraid of the dark. Are you finished here yet?"

"Yes, for now. I may need to come back." Toni wanted to reserve the right to examine the space again if something new came up. The crime scene kept drawing her back to it. The answers she needed were right here.

After saying their goodbyes, the mayor went up the stairs and cut the lights, sending the room back into darkness. Toni bristled over his blatant rudeness. The tunnel was pitch black at worst, murky at best. This time she kept the penlight off while focusing walking toward the single bulb's light on Victoria's side of the cellar. Counting, it was exactly thirty steps from basement to basement. Just then, something small and cylindrical caught her eye. It was lying where the wall and floor met as if it had been dropped and accidentally kicked there. Stooping down, she discovered it was a souvenir pen. Digging through her purse she grabbed an unused hankie to pick it up with. Holding it to the penlight, she rolled it to read what it said, Navy Pier, with a tiny ship which moved side to side in water. How long had this advertising pen been down here? A bit of dust had collected on it but it wasn't grimy. Not cracked or faded either. The picture on it seemed to depict how the pier looked years ago. Maybe it was vintage? Carefully, she wrapped it snuggly then put it into another baggie. Did this belong to Victoria? The mayor? The killer? She wanted prints but doubted the possibility due to the curve of the instrument.

Now back where she had started this journey, Toni searched for the other tunnel. At last, she found the same square opening identical to the one on the other side. Only this one was in a slightly different location. Pulling on the door, it creaked open. The antiquated latch pinched the side of her hand, making her drop her purse. "Ouch!"

She sucked on the small cut, trying to stop the prickles of blood. Then Toni leaned in for a good look at the tunnel, again using her little penlight. It was hard to see but looked to be of the same dimensions as the mayor's.

"What are you doing?"

The unexpected visitor made her heart hammer. Toni jumped back to see Beulah Collins standing right behind her. "That's the house's old coal bin."

"I thought it was used to transport liquor crates to cars parked in the alley?"

"That happened on the mayor's side since it's right on the alleyway. This one held the coal for both old furnaces that are no longer in use."

"You must have your own suspicions of who murdered Victoria."

Beulah stood as stone. There was no way she was about to say anything that would land her on the street without references. "The cellar door has been oiled, ma'am."

At the top of the stairs, the mayor waited. He held the phone. "Agent Palmer is on the line. Imagine how upset he was to learn you are here. Imagine how upset I am to learn you are suspended from the Bureau."

"I think it's time to leave." Toni picked up her purse from the floor and moved past them both out the front.

Chapter 38

Toni checked the time again. No way could she make it across town traffic in three minutes but what the heck, she'd give it a whirl. She got in the bus and searched for her keys inside her purse but couldn't find them. Then she checked her pocket. Had they fallen out of her purse when she dropped it? Gazing back up at the house, Toni hated the thought of returning and facing either one of those dismal people, but there was no choice unless she wanted to take public transportation forever. She gave Jack a call to say she'd be late, but it went to voicemail.

Back at the front door, she rang the bell. No answer. That's when she saw Ms. Collins backing out of the driveway in a Lincoln. Toni waved and called but the woman didn't hear or notice. Toni started down the steps to walk over to the mayor's house when she noticed the housekeeper stop in front of his house. Toni ducked down behind a snow-covered bush to have a better look. After a couple of honks, he came hurrying out, buttoning his winter coat. He got in on the passenger side, slammed the door, and the couple drove away. Curious. But she still needed her keys.

Toni returned to the porch and tried the door. It was securely locked and she didn't possess the house key, although she recalled Will mentioning that Victoria had only installed alarms on the doors because she preferred to keep the windows open during the summer months. It was winter, but perhaps one of them would be unlocked. One was all it would take to get inside the place. Toni walked along the stone walls of the house and tried each window. Nothing.

Next, she tried the mayor's house, hoping someone there could let her in to find her keys. "Doorbell rang and no one came," Toni sung out. Undeterred, she walked around the house to the back and found someone had left the back fence unlocked. The coal tunnel caught her eye. It was too high, and she couldn't reach the latch. At the side of the house, she found a cinder block. It gave her enough height to reach the handle. According to the mayor, it was sealed. If he was correct, then this would be another dead end. She pulled on it and just like that, it opened.

With great effort, she pulled herself up and then wedged a toe of her shoe into a chip in the stones and scooted inside the tunnel, leaving the door open for light. She crawled along on her belly, feeling like a TV dinner. When she reached the end, she found the door that led to the mayor's basement. Toni unfurled her body as she stepped out and then snapped on the light switch. Once her eyes adjusted to the light, she searched for her keys. No luck. She walked through the tunnel to Victoria's side of the basement. As she reached for the light switch, she was hit on the head, dropping face first onto the cement floor.

When she opened her eyes again, it was in the pitch of black. Her skull felt like it had broken into a hundred pieces. There was a musty odor mixed with a horrid tasting powder in her mouth. More collected inside her nose. When she tried to sit up, her head hit against metal tube. She reached out her arms, but they also hit metal. She was in a tomb. The coal tunnel tomb.

There was no time. She had to get out of this metal grave. Terror set in. She wriggled toward one end until her head bumped into the tunnel wall.

"Hello? Help!" she hollered. The sound of her voice reverberated about the inside of the cylinder. She jammed both hands over her ears until the echoing stopped. Claustrophobia brought on hyperventilation, but she worked her way back down the tunnel until her feet hit the other end. There, she hit a latch with the bottom of her feet and with the toe of her shoe tried to knock open the latch. The handle was stuck, the space confining; the air, toxic. Toni hit the iron door with her feet and covered her ears.

The door popped open. Hands latched on to her ankles and pulled. Toni covered her head with her arms, fearing she was about to hit her head on the ground, but arms went around her waist and she was gently placed on the ground. Coughing from the dusty bin, she sat up, sputtering chunks of black powder onto the white snow. Thick layers of coal dust covered her from head to toe. She looked up. There was Jack.

"What are you doing here?"

"I'll explain but first I need to catch my breath. Bound to take a while." She pounded her chest as dust wafted off her clothing.

"I was on the way to Starbucks when the call came in that someone broke into the Taylor's home. I had a feeling it was you, so I took the call myself."

"Was it Ms. Schuler who called it in? All I can say is thank goodness for nosy neighbors. I could've died in that thing." Toni kept inhaling the cold, fresh air into her lungs.

"Answer my question. What are you doing here? Why did you break in?" He held out his hand and helped her up. Jack took off his coat and wrapped it around her. "Come on, let me drive you home."

"What? No matcha green tea for me? I had my heart set on that."

Toni wobbled, about to lose her balance. Jack put both arms around her. By the look on his face, he didn't mind this at all. She sure wouldn't complain.

"I didn't break in. I had a nice talk with the mayor about speakeasies and he showed me his wine cellar. By the time I got back to my car, I realized my keys were gone at the same moment he drove off with Ms. Collins. I found a point of entry to retrieve what I needed but was hit on the head before I could find them."

"What knocked you on the head?" Jack asked, examining the bump on her head.

"A person is what knocked me on the head."

"Maybe we should go to the emergency room and have that checked."

"I'm fine.

Jack helped Toni to his car and turned the heater on high. "How did you get in there, anyway? The place is locked tighter than Fort Knox."

"The coal bin. There's a door to the outside, but it wasn't sealed like he said it was. Why?"

"Maybe he thought it was."

"Maybe. It was an easy open. If I hadn't lost my keys, I never would have discovered that."

"I'll give you a ride home."

"What about my bus? I can't just leave it here."

"I can hot wire it to get you started, but you may have to call your brother to get a new ignition key. Do you happen to have a screwdriver?"

"What girl doesn't? In my glove compartment."

Jack sat in the bus's driver's seat ready to pop open the glove compartment when something caught his eye. He walked back to his squad and dangled car keys in Toni's face. "They were still in the ignition."

"Well, I'll be! They were there all the time. Ha. Thanks, Jack."

"Anytime."

"Hey, what about going for coffee now?" she asked, rubbing dirt from her cheek.

"It's too late for coffee. And you need a bath." Jack waited for Toni to pull away and head down the street before he took off in the opposite direction.

Climbing the staircase to her apartment, she saw a large brown envelope addressed to her without return address stuck in the doorjamb. No postage either. *Hmmm, hand delivered. Strange.*

Toni sat at her computer. It was a copy of legal adoption papers made out by the late lawyer Dick Honeycutt; written five years after Victoria's and Suzette's birth. What happened to the first five years? That all depended on who Victoria really was. Roman Morelli knew.

Chapter 39

Late February

The thermometer read thirty-five degrees when Toni entered the Bureau through the side door, wondering if she was also banned from the forensic lab. Her knee jerk reaction was 'most likely', but when the techs didn't pay her an ounce of attention she figured they hadn't been informed. Not yet. Toni took full advantage of the situation and found the updated file on the Taylor case. There was something new this time— the results of the rug stain. The rug contained cast off blood spatter from Victoria, wine, and dirt. The dirt was analyzed but it didn't have the calcite that was on her slippers. Toni quickly made copies of the report then handed the scrapings from Taylor's wine cellar to a lab tech along with the Navy Pier pen to have it checked for prints.

Toni stopped by Brady's office to show him the glass fragment from the basement. He held it up to the light. "Interesting." Taking a similar size chard of glass from the cup, he compared the two under a high-powered microscope. "Hot dog, it's a match. Where'd you find it?"

"Victoria's basement."

"Basement? Figure her body was carried out that way?" Brady asked.

"I think it was pushed out through an old speakeasy tunnel left over from prohibition."

"Any glass in it?"

"None. It may have been swept."

"I'd love to get a look but there wasn't any coal dust found on her body and once coal is in a bin like that, it's nearly impossible to get it all out. Still, I'd like to look."

"Agent Palmer can get you in. Just don't mention I was here, okay?"

Outside, Toni placed a call to Olivia Hemming, the name Mrs. Schuler had given her the other day when she canvased the neighborhood. Olivia's husband explained his wife was at the park, near the pond, feeding pigeons. Toni motored around the park until she found a parking spot. She found the aging former maid of the Taylor household seated on a city bench. Shoulders stooped, she appeared heavy in a black coat, tossing bits of bird feed to pigeons. The ducks from the half-frozen pond waddled over, wanting their share.

"Excuse me, Olivia Hemming?" Toni asked.

"Yes, I am. And you must be the FBI profiler, Ms. Postell."

"You've been in touch with Ms. Schuler." Toni sat.

Olivia held up her cell phone. "My husband called. My friends here and I have been watching for you. Haven't we?" She sweet-talked her birds. The woman seemed to be in her early sixties but didn't allow gray in her hair. Her hair was colored brunette, and her face was smeared with makeup. Since her smile was easy, Toni suspected she also loved to talk.

"Nice spot to spend the day when it's not too cold. Pretty birds."

She pointed to the pigeons. "See the one with the white spots across her throat?"

"Yes."

"That's Lady Bird. That other one that is all gray is named Gray—and the white with the brown is Mort. My favorite. I named nearly all of them. Oh, and the ducks can have some food too. Here you go." She flung them some seeds. From another pocket, she pulled a hard roll. Tearing it into pieces, she tossed only the largest section. A flurry of wings and Lady Bird won.

"I'm here to ask you about something that happened a long time ago. I've heard rumors about a maid who became pregnant with Victor Taylor's child."

"It's true. The woman was my best friend."

"I'm sorry about her death."

"Yea, you and me and everyone is sorry except for Victor Taylor, the ever grand, popular mayor of Chicago. To him, she was just another conquest. But to me, she was a gem, a good person who believed his lies and was taken advantage of."

"Again, I'm very sorry."

Olivia stopped staring at the birds and turned to attention to Toni. "It's been a lot of years. Why are you suddenly interested in this now?"

"I'm working on a case and this information is important to it. I need to know your friend's name and the date of the baby's birth."

"My friend's name was Sally Harp. Her baby girl was born August twelfth. Sally died in childbirth."

"How tragic. And her little girl survived?"

She nodded.

"And you're sure of that date?" The birth date matched Victoria's.

"Positive. I was there with Sally when her baby was born. And when she passed."

"Can you tell me what happened to the child?"

"I wanted to raise her as my own. I begged Victor Taylor to allow me that pleasure and promised to keep the secret. He thought I'd eventually blackmail him, but I'd never do that, especially not to Sally's memory. I only wanted her child."

"Do you know what became of the baby?" Toni asked.

"He disposed of the baby."

"Disposed?" Toni suddenly felt sick.

"And years later found out his own wife couldn't have children." She gave a chuckle with a lift of her shoulders. "Karma."

"Are you sure he killed his own baby?"

"I believe so. How else would he be assured of never being blackmailed?"

Toni thanked her and then walked away. Olivia went back to feeding the pigeons. "Come here, Mort. I have a special treat for you. See my nice apple?"

Chapter 40

Roman Morelli

He sat smoking a Cuban cigar at the back of the lounge on the Gold Coast section of Chicago. Reams of smoke swirled around his head. Roman Morelli smiled when he saw her walk toward him. Getting to his feet, he motioned Toni to sit at the private table with him.

"Thanks for your gift." She held up the large brown envelope she found stuck in her door. Toni took a chair, then stared into his face. Under the lights, it was easier to see him clearly than it had in the dark backseat of his car. He had aged since the last time in court a few years back. Still, he was a very handsome man who hadn't lost his swagger.

"Gift?" Trading his half-smoked cigarette for a long drink of his Manhattan, he set the butt on the edge of the glass ashtray. His pretense was obvious.

"Let me refresh your memory." She pulled out papers and a few pictures from the envelope. "As you know, I visited with Stephen and Janet Taylor. I see they adopted Victoria at age of five, about the time Suzette was kidnapped. Guess what I thought?"

"That Victoria was Suzette." Roman purposely used his words to arrow her heart.

"The timeframe fits. Birth dates too." Toni suck air. "I now know she's not, but I did at first."

"It's a natual assumption." Roman calmly agreed. "Sorry, it wasn't what you wanted."

"I can deal with the truth, nothing else matters. Just another dead end. Eventually I'll find out."

"Good attitude."

Toni watched Roman's expression as she laid out the legal adoption papers signed in family court by a judge. Next, she removed a five by seven picture taken of Victoria the day she went to live with the Stephens along with a head shot taken recently.

Roman started shaking his right leg nervously under the table. It was more than the liquor that he consumed that had him on edge. Toni knew he witheld information she needed. How was she going to make him release it? Roman lived at the edge of personal destruction.

Without looking at them, he shoved it all back into the envelope, resulting in a nasty papercut. He wrapped a paper napkin around his bleeding finger. "I don't know where you got these, but they didn't come from me. Besides its all legal so what's the big deal?"

Toni ignored his protest. She wasn't about to get into a debate. "When I first got this case, I thought I'd be falling all over the Morelli family. But I haven't seen any of you except for that one time when you nearly ran me down."

"Picking on the Morelli's again?"

"Nice change of attitude you suddenly developed. You've been known to hang with the Mayor. With a family member murdered, I thought you might have a lead for me."

"No lead. But I'll let you know if I hear anything."

"I'd love to take you at your word—yet there's

things that niggle me." Toni looked perplexed.

"Such as?"

"Adopted at the age of five, there's no prior history of where she was. No court documents. I've researched for foster homes and social agencies, but nothing. Maybe you can tell me. Where did Victoria spend the first five years of her life?"

"We put our trust in the law and wait for justice to be served," Roman said stoically. "We're law abiding citizens these days."

"Maybe." Toni folded her hands on top of the envelope.

"What are you trying to pin on me this time?" He glared at her.

"She was born at Memorial hospital. Adopted at age five. Explain to me please."

Roman looked over at the bar where a six-foot muscled blonde was tending. "Hey, Princess, more drinks."

"Does your girlfriend want anything?" she called back.

"Water would be nice. Thanks," Toni answered. Turning back to Roman, she continued, "According to the hospital records her given name at the time was Patty. Father: Unknown. Mother: Sally Harper. I find it odd that Patty's name was changed to Victoria, Isnt that odd that it's so close to the mayors first name?"

"Sounds to me as though they named her after the man who they admired."

"Or the birth father, Victor Taylor."

"I could be in a lot of trouble here." Roman hissed glancing around.

"I'm not here to create trouble for anyone. Just

solve a murder." Toni remained silent as Princess dropped off their drinks. "Thanks, Princess."

The woman smiled. "Anything else?"

"No. Thanks." Roman watched her return to the bar.

"Roman, please, tell me what you know about Victoria's first five years. It could be relevant to the case."

"What makes you think I know anything?"

Toni unfolded her hands and leaned into the chair. "Years back when you were brought up on charges of racketeering, I knew the prosecution had an airtight case. Yet, your attorney brought in evidence—"

"That proved my innocence."

"I'm not here to discuss that case."

"Then why are you here and discussing it?"

"Because the two cases are somehow linked. As I was saying, your attorney—the same attorney the mayor uses—brought in evidence that made my case look, well, lacking. I even thought I had messed up, until lately."

"Should I be worried you have new drummed-up evidence?"

"No. Hear me out. Here's what I figured so far: Sally Harp was a maid who worked for the mayor. They had an affair and Sally ended up dead."

"How do you know this?" His face wrinkled in surprise.

"At the time there was a pipeline of gossip that ran up and down the alleyway between the household maids."

Roman looked angry enough to have a stroke.

"Sally died in childbirth. What happened to that

baby?" Toni pushed again.

"I think this conversation is over," Roman stood.

Toni hunkered down, unmoving. She kept the information flowing. "The mayor didn't know what to do with a baby and a dead lover. He turned to you. You helped him."

"Why would I do that?" Roman stood.

"That's what I was wondering. There's got to be a quid pro quo somewhere here." Toni remained seated.

"Princess, Special Agent Postell is ready to leave. Would you mind showing her the door?"

"It's my pleasure." She bolted from the bar area, heading directly at her. Toni cringed knowing she was about to get hurt.

"Come on, play this game with me. Patty turned up and Suzette disappeared." Toni sat up straight, doing her best to maintain her composure she gripped the tabletop with both hands. Suddenly she felt herself being lifted up under her armpits, feet off the ground, and before she knew it, was shuffled out the front door of the establishment.

"Just one more question." Toni hollered as the door slammed closed in her face. She turned around and saw traffic. At least she was alive.

****

At home, she changed out of her smoky clothes into something more comfortable and went to work on her files, noting there were gaps. She needed holes filled. After a bowl of soup, she grabbed a towel for a hot shower just when the phone rang.

"I'm sitting outside your place," Jack said.

"You are? Right now?" She hurried to the mirror to see if she was presentable. No, she was not. It wasn't a pretty sight. She was an apparition in her kitty pajama bottoms, an oversized sweatshirt, and a striped band in her hair that needed a good scrub. Plus, she reeked of smoke.

"Look out your window."

Toni parted the curtains. Jack blinked his brights at her, and she waved. "It's late. I'm dressed for bed."

"In sexy clothes?"

"Definitely if you're into old t-sweatshirts and fleece pants."

"Get dressed or stay the way you are because it doesn't matter to me. I'm coming up just as soon as I find a parking space. Fair warning."

Toni figured she probably had thirty minutes until Jack found a parking space at this time of night. But just in case, she dashed to her bedroom and pulled on a pair of jeans, pulled off her sweatshirt, buttoned up a blouse, brushed her teeth in eight seconds flat, tore out the ponytail, powdered her hair, and then ran a brush through it just as the downstairs buzzer sounded. *Man, you found a parking spot fast. You're good Jack, you're good.* She pressed the button to unlock the downstairs door, then quickly spritzed a bit of cologne.

Jack was already running up the stairs when she opened her door.

He spun her about and kissed her with longing and passion. "Hello, gorgeous."

"I like the way you say 'hello'."

Toni moved her files from the couch so Jack could sit. It seemed natural with him here with her, stroking Perp's head.

"When this case is over, we need to take a long look at us."

"And what kind of long look would that be?" she asked, easing down next to him. "Listen, Jack, I know I shouldn't have gone into the mayor's house, but suspension or not, it's hard to sit back and do nothing while my sister is accused of murder. I have skills and contacts available to me that can be accessed to clear her. It's not that I don't trust your handling of the case. I do. We're in a difficult situation. Do you want to know what I did to be suspended?"

"I'm sure you had a good reason, and we can talk about it later. Tonight is about us, but I need you quiet for just a minute. Can you do that?" He kissed her lips to silence her.

"Us? There's an 'us' in this situation?" What an impact a two-letter word had on her hopes. She locked her lips with an invisible key.

He grinned. "It's gotten personal for you and personal for me. I keep thinking about the first time I saw you standing in the middle of that bridge, and then you walked into the middle of my life."

"Correction. You walked into the middle of my life. Don't forget the canopy of stars."

Jack set the cat aside and stood.

Toni got to her feet.

"You're a snazzy dresser." He tugged her shirt.

"I dressed like this just for you."

"Thanks." He took her by the hand and pulled her toward the bedroom.

"Hey, Jack, I really think I should shower first."

Chapter 41

The next day, a box was delivered with Toni's name scrolled in gold letters. Without a return address, and no stamps decorating the top right corner, it had to be hand delivered. A bit skeptical, she carefully carried it into her place, setting it on the coffee table.

She stared out the windows. It was snowing again, and the wind kicked up. Frosty. Even though he was in jail waiting for trial, she thought about him whenever it snowed. Frosty cold air seeped through the sashes. It was as if he returned as an invisible vapor. Would thoughts of him arise each time it snowed?

The mysterious package remained untouched on the coffee table. Trying to figure out why someone would send her an unmarked package was definitely cause for trepidation. It might be a bomb? They were constantly going off somewhere in the world—maybe this time it'd be in her apartment? Her visit with Roman turned out badly, leaving her to wonder if this was from him. His group had a reputation for guns and bombings.

Normally she'd call her Uncle Palmer, or Jack, or someone at the Bureau to come for it, but since her reputation had recently been sullied, she'd handle this herself. Toni held the pretty box at arm's length and walked to the bathroom. With great care, she set it on the toilet seat and started the bathwater which rumbled down into the cast iron tub. When filled, Toni set the box on top of the water and watched as it slowly sunk. The phone rang. Toni shut the door behind.

"Hello?" she whispered.

"Hi, Toni!" Mallory chirped.

"Mallory!" Toni looked back down the hallway toward the bathroom. "How are you doing?"

"I called to see if you've solved the case yet because I'm ready to get out of here. My birthday is next month, you know."

"Yes, I know. It's time for the big birthday countdown. I suppose you want me to pick up the party invitations?" Toni joked.

"How sweet of you to offer, but actually Daddy is having them printed as we speak." Mallory sounded self assured.

"You're sure optimistic about getting out of jail by then." Toni heard the water dripping from the faucet into the tub. She needed to get back to deal with her little parcel or the overflow might be problematic for the downstairs tennants.

"I only called to tell you I'm having color swatches delivered to you from the top designer of couture, Lorenzo Coberto. Per my request, he's driving to your apartment this morning in fact, so you'll have them there at your disposal. Be careful with them because they need to be returned in pristine condition. He didn't want to deliver them, rather have you come into his showroom so you could look at them there. But that would do me no good because I'm the one that must select the material. Bring them along with you on your next visit. Make that visit tomorrow." Then she whispered the next part as if he might hear, "He doesn't know I'm in prison. Ssh!"

"What in the world are you talking about?"

"Listen up, he's making me a gown to wear to my party and I'm choosing the fabric. That man is so distrustful of letting anything out of his showroom, so naturally I couldn't tell him to bring it to me in jail. I finally convinced him that of all the people in the United States of America you are the most reliable and he has nothing on earth to be worried about because you carry a gun and will guard them with your life. Daddy faxed him your resume for good measure. By the way, we tweaked your resume a teensy bit and it now also includes you being the president's bodyguard, so just play along."

"I never was the president's—swatches?" Toni blanched as her voice took a high pitch. "Did you say swatches?"

"Yes, for my birthday dress. He has my measurements so it's just a matter of me deciding. You should get one made for yourself. I'll pay. Whatever you do, stay out of Mom's closet this time, okay?"

"Uh, I think your package might've already arrived—a few minutes ago."

"Wonderful! What do you think?" She squealed.

"Ohm. I haven't had a chance to look at them but will do that right now."

"When?"

"Now."

"Don't eat your dinner while looking at them, Toni. You know you always drip something on you. All your blouses have stains on them."

"Not all of them." Toni checked the bodice of her blouse.

"Now get out there on the streets of Chicago and

find my killer, pronto! Right after you bring me the swatches."

Dropping the phone back into the cradle, Toni ran to the bathroom and snatched the water-soaked package from its watery grave. "Now what'll I do?" The brown wrappings from about the box nearly dropped off of its own accord. "Not such pretty a package anymore, are you?" The cardboard box nearly disintegrated in her hand as water poured out the sides.

Sure enough, there, along with the waterlogged swatches, was Lorenzo's card. It looked like it might have been a fancy one too. One by one she wrung out the swatches and then laid them flat on tables and on the wooden floors, putting books on them to keep the material from curling. Within an hour, they were dry, but the fabric seemed to have shrunk a bit and they still formed little waves. They needed ironing.

Carefully, she ironed each piece but by now they'd lost their shape and shrinkage was involved. After sliding the dry swatches into a freezer bag, she set them by the front door to remind herself they need to be delivered to Mallory who was behind bars for murder and only had partying on her mind. "Well, at least this is better than a bomb."

Toni returned to what was her priority, and spread out all her notes, tapes, and evidence on her bed to go over each one by one. It was past midnight when she logged her handwritten notes and stacked her tapes together. Her eyes blurred and could no longer focus. Her mind turned to sludge. She needed to talk the case over with Jack.

****

The next morning when she arrived at the station,

Jack was already at work. Without a word, she set down the files and tapes on the desk. Jack looked suspiciously at them. He picked up the paper and first looked at the column of names on it. "Another list of people for wishing good thoughts?"

"Not this time. This time it's a list of suspects. Relax, your name isn't on it. By the way, I think Ms. Emily Taylor may have murdered Victoria."

"What happened to your suspicion about Will?"

"My investigation is leading me in other directions." She sat in a chair then swung one leg over the othere. Curious as to what he was working on, she leaned on the table with her chin in her hand.

"Correction. You no longer have an investigation." He raised his brows.

"Or much of a career due to the fact that I had a wonderful conversation with Victoria's adopted parents in Wisconsin."

"Victoria Taylor was adopted?" He frowned, obviously not liking the fact he missed something. Jack shut his office door. "If you insist on investigating, at least keep me in the loop."

"If I do that then you could lose your badge. I'll pass things along when there's something that helps the case. Now back to Victoria's biology. Her adoptive parents told me they adopted their daughter when she was five. I haven't been able to find out who fostered her before then. As far as I'm concerned, it wasn't done legally and she wasn't cared for. I think charges should be made against these people once we find out who they were."

"And you know this because…?"

"It's a hunch."

"You have a hunch," Jack repeated, letting the air out his lungs.

"Yes, but it doesn't sound quite right when you say it."

"However it sounds, let's call Emily Taylor down here for a nice visit—alone. No husband in tow."

"Great. By the way, let's find out where their 'sonny boy' Andy was on the night of her death."

"Isn't he in some home? For what?"

"I believe he's institutionalized. Low IQ and borders on being psychotic. However, he might've been home on a pass. I'll find out. By the way, I found possible blood in the mayor's basement. I'm still waiting for the results to come back from the lab."

"Doggone it. You're still delivering evidence to the lab? Okay. Don't answer." He dropped his pencil and held up his hand. "When it's in, I want that information."

"Of course. You'll have to get it for me, due to my little situation."

"When Ms. Taylor is here, don't say one word. I want you to concentrate on body language. Let me do the talking. Remember, you're suspended, so stay out of the room and just keep behind the two-way glass."

"Of course, Jack. Anything you say." She plunked a kiss on his forehead before leaving his office.

Chapter 42

Emily sat at the green table in the green room acting as though she were surrounded by germs. Her attitude was more of distaste than fear.

"Your husband and Roman Morelli are good friends."

"You think so? Years and years ago yes, they were close, before the fishing business venture went belly up."

"There's still bad blood between them then?" Jack asked.

"Roman tried to clear the rift. Looking back on it now, I think he was hoping for another business venture; one that would prove to be lucrative this time. But he didn't have any money to invest and Victor would need to finance the whole thing again."

"If he was broke where did Roman get the money to start the bar?"

"No idea. If something doesn't directly concern me, I don't concern myself with it."

"There's been talk about his mob connections." Jack mused.

"That's another reason he didn't want Roman around. He didn't want the mob in his circle. Yet, when Stephen and Janet adopted Victoria, Roman started hanging around a lot again. Of course he did it on the sly without Victor knowing."

"Why do you suppose that was?" Jack asked.

"Would you want a gangster hanging around your child? I certainly didn't."

"What about her biological parents?" Jack asked.

"I don't know a thing about them other than they're both dead. Victoria was curious about finding out about them like anyone would. I told Vickie I'd help. It caused strain on the family since Janet was totally against it. She felt it was a betrayal to her motherhood. But as I told her 'You've got to let her find her roots so she knows where she came from'. It did no good. Janet had very little to do with her daughter after that. It's only natural a person would want to know their history. From then on, they hardly spoke. That's about the same time they left the house Victor bought for them and returned to Wisconsin to live."

"Any result in locating Victoria's parents?" Jack asked.

"The records we needed had been destroyed. We did what we could through other means. We came up with nothing."

"And Roman wasn't helpful?"

"No. Why would he be? He had nothing to do with anything."

"Could Victoria have continued searching on her own without you knowing?"

"Maybe,e she could have, but I doubt it. We were so close; she surely would've said something."

"Could Roman have given Victoria the information?"

Emily thought for a while. "Again, why would Roman even care?"

"You were close to your niece."

"What can I say other than she's a doll—was a doll. I loved her." Emily's eyes misted. "I would've given my life for her. In fact, I was furious at Victor for allowing Stephen and Janet to adopt her when I wanted her for my child."

"Do you know anything about the foster family?" Jack fished to see if she had information that spooked her husband.

"No, I don't. And Vickie had few memories of that time."

"What can you tell us about the night of the murder?" Jack asked.

"I already told you this, Detective." She huffed. Twisted her body and eyed the door obviously hoping to leave.

"Do you mind going over it again?"

Emily thinks for a minute. "Victor and I went out for a late-night dinner and when we came home, there was Roman walking down the steps from our house to his car."

"Maybe he'd first been to see Victoria at her place?"

"No, he had been at ours. I could tell by where he parked the car—centered in front of our place, not hers."

"Did he have anything with him?"

"No, nothing," Emily answered.

"Okay, what happened when you saw Roman that night."

"We hadn't seen Roman for a while, which was fine with me. But Victor invited Roman to come in. He did. The guys had a drink, a martini, while I whipped up dessert. Want to know what dessert, in case it helps you solve this case, Detective?" she arrogantly asked.

"Sure, tell me." Jack laughed and nodded his head.

"Strawberry short cake. Got all the ingredients from the grocery store. Would you like to know which one?"

"Pass," he spoke calmly.

"That night, Victor and Roman got along. No arguing. No wild schemes to make money at Victor's expense."

"Any wine served that night?"

"If you're referring to my husband's private wine, then the answer is no. He never shares it—he keeps it all for himself. We had martinis served in crystal I bought recently at an estate sale."

"There's a tunnel that runs between the two houses; did Roman know about it?" Jack asked.

"Of course, why?"

"Did Victoria use the tunnel very often?"

"All the time. When we bought the two houses, the tunnel had been sealed for years but we had it opened. We found all kinds of fun antique brewery items that are now displayed in our bar area."

"The night of the murder, did Victoria use the tunnel?"

"Yes, she did. She always came through the tunnel and up the steps into the kitchen to see us. That night I was fixing more drinks and the dessert for Roman and my husband. Victoria said that Will Schofield was at her house, and she wanted a bottle of wine to go with her French bread and spaghetti for their dinner—hoping he would agree to stay longer. To make it special, I suggested she take a bottle of her uncle's favorite wine that Roman had just brought." Emily paused. "I think she said, 'Will is in a hurry to leave but hopefully wine might slow him down.' My husband enjoys this one kind that's nearly impossible to buy for its only sold in France and it has to be flown over to the States. It's so expensive we never offer it to guests, not even on special occasions. Will knew that, so this was a really big deal."

"Name?"

"La Commese."

Jack glanced toward the window that Toni stood behind, half expecting her to dash into the interrogation room at any moment.

"There was an open bottle on the kitchen counter and then there was the uncorked bottle of La Commese. Before Vickie got there, I offered the open bottle to the men. They wanted something stronger. When Vickie arrived she said hello to everyone and then reached for the opened bottle of La Commese to take back with her but I stopped her. I handed her the uncorked bottle because I was hoping they'd spend a nice long evening together."

"I'm sorry to ask this next question: Ms. Taylor, did you or your husband want to kill your niece, Victoria Taylor?"

"How dare you even ask me that. No, of course not." Her eyes dripped tears as her hand slapped the table. "Why would I want to do that? Both my husband and I loved her. I'll swear to this in a court of law or on a stack of Bibles."

Emily's face displayed genuine disbelief over the allegation. As she spoke, she reached into her bag and pulled out hand sanitizer. "Neither of us would ever harm her. I would've given my life for her. She was like a daughter to me. I wish we had adopted her. Janet never really appreciated her. Vickie always came to me with all her problems. Vickie and Janet had terrible arguments."

"What did they argue about?" Jack asked.

"Janet wanted Vickie to return to Wisconsin to live. She even had someone in mind for Vickie to meet. But Vickie wasn't about to let her mother run her life. She loved the city. She loved Will."

"Did the women argue about anything else?"

"They always argued about something. In her younger years, Vickie wanted to wear in a certain style that Janet didn't approve. Or, she couldn't watch certain shows or listen to certain music growing up."

"Did it ever come to blows?" Jack asked.

"Never. Detective, it's hot in here." She glanced around. "When can I leave?"

"Just one more question. Do you remember what Vickie wore that night you saw her?"

Taking a deep breath, she thought a moment before answering, "It was a lovely black pantsuit with an organdy shell top. There were diamond studs in her ears and a small silver cross about her neck. Her hair was combed down about her shoulders, looking like spun gold. How gorgeous she was that evening; the vision of her was so angelic that it shall forever stick with me."

"Ms. Taylor, you've been helpful. We may want to talk to you again, so please don't leave the city without telling someone where you're going."

"I'm always available to you."

Once she left, Toni walked into the interrogation room and sat. "What do you think, Jack?"

"She admittedly handed the victim the poisoned

bottle. And it so happens the victim turns out to be her husband's love child. In all their digging to find Victoria's biological parents, surely Ms. Taylor uncovered the truth. There's your motive. 'I loved her like a daughter' hogwash."

"I disagree," Toni started. "Her emotions seem genuine. They were raw and at the surface. Believe me, she didn't have any idea. Again, I keep going back to what Will said about Victoria having information about the mayor. The bottle came from his place. If only we could figure out what she needed to talk to Will about."

"Together we agree it's either Emily or Victor."

"Or someone in power that held something over Victor's head."

"Which takes us to suspect three. Mallory, who discovered the affair."

Toni glanced at her watch. "Have you heard from the lab yet about possible prints on the pen and scrapings from the basement?"

"Prints are too smudged to get a clear read, and the blood scrapping off the floor is nothing but wood stain."

"Another dead end. Thanks. Jack, I need to go. There's something I need to check out."

"Like what? May I remind you're off the case."

"Fair enough. Right now, I'm on my way to get my clothes from the cleaners. I need to be sure they got the stains out. I also need to grocery shop. Want to see my list?" She pulled it from her pocket and held it out.

"Let's go for dinner instead."

Chapter 43

By early evening, Toni was in panic mode, getting ready. Then Jack called to say his car battery was dead. That meant she'd drive. It gave her less than an hour to pick him up. The thought of him weakened her knees, and she could think of nothing else but sitting across the table looking into his eyes, listening to his voice. She had to look her best. Toni showered, shaved, powdered, perfumed, brushed, curled and primped until she thought she was turning into Mallory.

Jack was already waiting curbside by the time she arrived. It was obvious by the look on his face that he wasn't too keen to be riding in her VW Bus. "What a relic," he said, shaking his head.

"That's not the name. This is Watson and he prefers that name, not relic."

"You actually named your bus?"

"Yep."

"How long will it be before Watson warms up?"

"No idea. Whenever he feels like it. Where to?" She shook her head, her long, dark hair falling over her shoulders and down her back in tendrils.

"You're driving. You choose." Jack held his hands to the heater. "Still blowing cold."

"Then we're going to church—there's a revival." She pressed on the accelerator.

"What?" He gasped.

"It'll be good for your soul." She patted his knee.

"My soul is just fine," he muttered, looking around as though he might open the car door and leap out.

"Relax, I'm kidding." She laughed.

"Good. By the way, you look great, Toni. Agonizingly beautiful."

His words made her lose her train of thought, causing her to miss her turn. It suddenly became so quiet between them that all she could hear was the sound of him breathing. Butterflies kicked in. "Thanks, Jack. It took a lot of work to look like this tonight."

"You always look beautiful. There's not a prettier sight than seeing you at a crime scene, cheeks all rosy red, your voice filled with excitement."

"My mouth filled with vomit. Let's mix pleasure with a bit of business, shall we?" She glanced at him.

"You sure know how to win my heart." A smile slid up the side of his face.

"That's good to know." Driving with one hand, her gaze was fixed on the snowy streets. Toni fished in her pocket, pulled out a paper and waved it in his face.

"A second grocery list, per chance?"

"I found out that there are a few restaurants in Chicago that do carry La Commese. Surprise. Here are the restaurants with the addresses. Since the wine has to be purchased in person and hand carried back to the United States, it sells in the neighborhood of five hundred dollars a glass, and two thousand a bottle."

"And how many bottles are we drinking tonight?" Jack read the list. "Only two places? Well, at least that'll make our job so much easier. And the first is River Blu on Navy Pier. Great food and ambience. Take the Outer Drive, it's faster this time of night."

Toni turned in that direction. "I spent hours on the phone between the manufacturer and ferreting out restaurants."

"You called France?"

"Yes, I did. I also called my papa." She smiled.

"Was it a good call?"

Toni's eyes watered over. "Yes. It was a very good call. I miss him."

"You should go for a visit."

"Perhaps. Maybe you'll come too?"

Jack ignored the question to read the road signs and pointed. "Take the Illinois exit."

Toni snapped on her turn signal. She watched for changing lights, and ignored horns as she darted in and out between cars, pushing the speed limit. "The highways are filled with slow drivers tonight."

"It has something to do with the snow and ice," he said wryly. "Be careful, Toni."

Ten minutes later, they were on Kinzie Street.

"River Blu is the best nightclub in the city and has a great view of Lake Michigan right on the pier beneath the shadow of that huge Ferris wheel. Now where is it I turn in for parking? I think it should be just down this street. Ah, there it is! They're certainly busier than I suspected. What in the world are all the fireworks about?"

"It's Mardi Gras tonight," Jack said.

"What fun! "You think so? Years and years ago yes, they were close, before the fishing business venture went belly up."

"Wanna go for a ride on the Ferris wheel?"

"No thanks, think I'll wait for warm summer breezes."

"I love fireworks!" Even in the bus with the heater at full tilt, she heard them detonate then explode in the night air above them. It seemed a paint factory had caught on fire and spewed its colors onto the dark soil of the sky. Toni parked near the lake's edge. "What a perfect view. Look at the distorted reflection on the ice."

Jack held Toni's hand as they walked into the restaurant. They sat at a table with a remarkable panoramic view of the water. "When we were kids, Mallory and I used to watch the Fourth of July fireworks and pretend we were picking out diamond rings. We always said we'd marry men who'd give us diamonds and pearls."

"Supercilious goals."

"I grew up. Mallory—is still growing. Didn't you like watching fireworks when you were young?"

"I liked the sound they made. Reminded me of gunfire."

Toni laughed. "Have you ever been in love?"

"Wow, getting kind of personal there, aren't you, Toni?" he chided.

"I guess I'm feeling nostalgic about things, and it made me wonder about you." She stared at him wistfully.

"Just once and it didn't work out. Not enough money." Jack cleared his throat and shuffled his feet under the table, appearing as though he was interested in his napkin.

"Was it, Susan Hunter?" Toni pressed feeling just a tad jealous if he said 'yes.'.

"Nah." He chuckled. "I had a crush on a 1968 Harley Davidson. It turned out to be unrequited though, for I never ended up with her."

"It's always about the money." She brightly smiled and under the table, touched his shoe with the tip of her's.

"I guess your personal life is a closed subject."

"I do have something to share with you. It's a decision I made."

"Can't wait to hear."

The maître d' arrived at their table. "What wine may I serve you this evening along with your meal?"

"What's your finest wine in the house?" Jack asked.

"We have a delicious new wine from Italy."

"Not interested. Do you happen to have La Commese from France?" Jack asked.

Acting pleased with this question, he answered, "We have a bottle, or two in our wine room but only are selling by the glass. Would you care for a glass?"

Toni stepped hard on Jack shoe beneath the table, signaling him to say 'no'. But she needn't have worried. His answer was perfect. "Not tonight. However, I may want to order a bottle or two for my private stock sometime."

"It takes months for those orders to be filled, and there is a waiting list."

"Hey, I was wondering if this man ordered any from this restaurant?" From her purse, she pulled a picture of Roman. "He promised he'd buy us a bottle if we gave him the money first, which we did, but now, he's say it never arrived."

"Our customers are kept confidential."

Jack pulled out his wallet and flipped to his PD badge with his picture.

The maître d' looked closely and replied, "No order was taken by me from this man. We also don't accept payment for the wine until it's here. If the buyer doesn't come through, or changes his mind, then it goes into our private stock. However, we do have private orders taken quite frequently and this one may have been placed with a different wine manager. May I show the picture to the other buyer? He's here tonight and I can get an answer right away for you."

"Wonderful! Thanks so much."

"Okay, Postit, tell me about your decision."

"As you know, I abhor bloody crime scenes. I'm interested in only psychological aspects—nothing in the field like I've been doing."

Jack sat back. "You're taking the show biz job."

"How did you find out about that?"

"Your references and fingerprints were checked out by the network at the precinct. Imagine my surprise."

"It's not show biz. It's analyzing the actions and childhoods of past serial killers. But, I have come to a decision, and I turned down their offer weeks ago."

"Really?"

"You look pleased."

"I feel pleased to the point I just might order us a glass of that fancy French wine."

"Don't you dare." She gasped.

"Turning down the offer is the right choice for you. Does that mean you are staying with the FBI once you're reinstated?"

"Not in my present position."

The white-jacketed waiter arrived, introduced himself, and took their order for steak and fresh lobster.

After he left, Toni gushed. "This is fun, Jack. I love being here with you. We're not only on a date but also working a case."

"I figured I owed you since pizza was the fanciest meal I've taken you to."

There was that great smile of his traveling across his face. It warmed her down to her toes. She didn't have to drink wine to feel dizzy. Jack was in the room.

"Excuse me." An elderly man dressed in a suit stood at their table, holding the picture of Roman.

"Hello." Jack nodded.

"You asked if this man, Roman Morelli, put in an order for La Commese?"

"Yes, did he?" Jack asked.

"The man in this picture picked up the bottle, but it's not the name he used."

"What name did he use?"

Looking down on the order form, he read aloud two words. "Victor Taylor."

Jack dropped his salad fork, clanking against the plate, which had several patrons turning their heads. Toni bit back a smile.

"Do you have the order number and the signature?" He wiped his mouth on a cloth napkin.

"Yes, I do."

"I'll need a copy of it."

"Right away, Detective. Our records are impeccable." Leaving the picture on the table, he hurried away, returning with a copy of the signed order within minutes. On it was the restaurants crest, the bottle number, the restaurant stamp and the number in the series. There, scrolled on the bottom was this name, along with a copy of the credit card purchase and signature of Victor Taylor.

"And you will testify that this was the man who ordered the bottle and picked it up?"

"Yes. If I can help you any further, please let me know." He bowed at the waist before leaving.

The waiter arrived with their meal.

"This could mean credit card fraud."

By now, Jack was nutty with excitement. His hands shook as he cut into his meat. "I'm calling the mayor back in for more questioning."

"Hold on. I've an idea first."

"I'm listening."

"Let's enjoy this evening. "Now that we have actually made it to having dinner together, let's try not to wolf it down," Toni suggested. "Until we reach the car, no more work-related talk. Our subject is us."

"I totally agree."

Minutes passed without speaking.

Jack watched Toni as she stabbed and sliced her meat. "Are you all right?"

"Of course," she repeated, delivering a small piece into her mouth.

"I never figured you for a surf and turf gal."

"There's much about me you don't know. I'm a woman of mystery."

"I'm trying hard not to disappoint you."

"You never disappoint me, Jack." Toni's feet danced under the table.

When dinner was done, Jack paid the bill. A complimentary Navy Pier pen was given to them. But it was different than the one from the tunnel. She asked the front desk manager about it, describing her pen. He told her that it sounded like one from when the Pier was first put up in 1995.

They squeezed through the growing Mardi Gras crowd on the boardwalk. Many dressed in costumes, while others wore everyday duds with heavy coats buttoned over on top. Face paint and glitter seemed to be popular; it was on everyone. The partiers blasted horns. One woman, dressed as a joker, kissed Jack on his lips and then blew in his ear before taking off.

"Doesn't she know I carry a big gun?" he asked, twisting his earlobe.

"You sure do." Toni laughed as she placed her hand between his legs and gave it a squeeze.

Jack jumped with surprise. "Whoa. You're pretty frisky tonight."

"Just you wait."

Within minutes, they climbed back into Toni's vehicle.

"Since the meal is officially over, may we discuss the case now?" Jack asked.

"Go right ahead." Toni started up the engine and pulled out of the lot, turning right onto the street. "Sorry it's so cold in here. The heater needs time to warm up. This weather is pushing Watson a bit."

"I'm thinking, Taylor may have ordered the wine and sent Roman down with his credit card to pick it up for him."

"Emily said they hadn't spoken in years up until the night of the murder," Toni said.

"Emily might not know all of his dealings. It seems so strange that Roman suddenly visits after years of staying away, on the night of the murder. Emily said she was surprised to see Roman. Maybe he brought the wine Victor ordered over that night. It'd be his purpose for being there."

"We already know he hasn't told his wife everything. It's ten p.m. Do you think right now is a good time to talk to them?"

"I do. Let's get him out of bed."

****

Mayor Taylor answered the door in his bathrobe. His hair was rumbled. "It's late. What's this about?"

"We need to ask a few questions. Would you like to call your lawyer first?"

"I don't need my lawyer present. I've nothing to hide."

"Good."

"Let's talk privately." He led them into his study and closed the door.

"What we've learned so far is that Victoria was adamant about getting a hold of Will Schofield. He visited her the night of her death. Do you know why she needed to see him?" Toni folded one arm over the other.

"No, but I can guess." Taylor went to his desk and unlocked the drawers with a key. He pulled papers from the bottom drawer and handed them to Jack. Toni read over his shoulder. It was Patty's original baby's birth certificate with the mayor named as the father. "I kept the original then had a bogus one created to keep it from my wife and the public. Recently, Victoria found out that I'm not her uncle. I'm her biological father. One of my maids from years back, was her mother. She died giving birth to Patty. Emily was never told—until a few months ago. She didn't take it well.

"Tell me specifically how she reacted. It's important." Being a profiler, Toni was trained in people's reactions to bad news, what made them lie, if they were prone to kill or harm, and a textbook filled with information.

"The two bonded in ways I think they couldn't have had she known about Vickie. I think my greatest fear wasn't her finding out about the affair, nor that it produced a love child, but that I didn't give Emily a chance to raise my daughter as hers. And now she knows and I'm not sure my wife will ever forgive me."

"How did Victoria find out?"

"I kept the authentic birth certificate locked up at my office. Vickie stayed late one night and needed to get into the cabinet for a report she was working on. She called, asking where the key was. I had forgotten the birth certificate was also kept in that drawer. After telling her where to find the key, she naturally located it among my legal matter documents."

"What was her reaction?"

"She took it hard. The last time I saw her, she still didn't want to speak to me. I imagine that's why she wanted to see Will."

"Why him?"

"I don't know. Past love to be consoled by?"

****

Walking down the sidewalk toward the VW, Toni said, "We've been looking at this all wrong. The intended murder target wasn't Victoria Taylor."

"Now you've totally lost me." Jack opened the driver's door for her.

Toni got into her seat and waited for Jack to get in. Slowly, she expelled a deep breath. "The intended was—the mayor".

"I'm confused," Jack said.

362

Toni turned to look back at the house. "Roman bought the wine and slipped in the poison, most likely with a hypodermic needle through the cork at the top. Then resealed it carefully to make it look like a fresh bottle. Roman brought the bottle to the mayor's, but they drank liquor instead. Meanwhile, Vickie walked through the adjoining tunnel to get something special for her and Will to drink. Emily unknowingly handed her the tampered bottle."

"Good supposition but shouldn't Will be dead too?" Jack asked.

"Obviously he didn't drink any."

"How do you know. There were two glasses," Jack interrupted.

"Simply because Will is still alive. All we know is Victoria may or may not have drunk the wine when Will was there. We do know she walked him out to the porch where they kissed goodnight. Mallory watched from her car. After Will left, Mallory left too, stewed a bit and later returned to Victoria's. Meanwhile Victoria took a shower and got ready for bed. The doorbell rang. Victoria thought Will had returned, She opened the door and it was Mallory."

"Do you realize the case you are building is against your sister?"

"Hear me out, Jack. Remember the wine came from Roman's hand to the mayor's house to Vickie's place. Will came and left. Mallory pushed her way into Vickie's when the door opened. Neither Mallory nor Victoria had any idea the wine was poisoned. My sister is darn lucky she didn't drink anything or there'd be two corpses. Between the two, I imagine there were lots of accusations. Vickie needed to steady her nerves so she opened the bottle and drank a glass or two. Offered Mallory a glass but she refused. Obviously, because only one glass was used. The extra glass had been for Will but he didn't drink it either.

"With the wine quickly taking effect, Vickie stumbled with the bottle in her hand. Mallory grabbed it and set it on the bar. That's where her fingerprints came from. Within seconds, Vickie's heart stopped and she fell onto the coffee table. Dead. Once Mallory saw the blood and couldn't wake Vickie, she called her dad, who said to leave and he'd take care of it."

"Makes sense but now we have to identify the drug. And link it to Roman." Toni pulled into the front of her building.

"After the birth of Victoria, her mother dies. Victor wanted news of his love child kept from his wife, and out of the public arena. Most importantly, he didn't want to lose his bid for city mayor. People were less understanding in those days than they are now. Following in his dad's footsteps into politics was a must. He had too much to lose with a pending race and a wife."

"Do you think people really care about affairs?"

"Of course, people did care, especially if he's running in a dead heat. He couldn't gauge his wife's or the public's reaction and didn't want to take a chance of taking big political hits. Victor Taylor certainly didn't want to make his daughter a ward of the state either for whatever molecule of feelings he had for her. It was Roman who kept the baby for the five years."

"How do you figure?"

"Roman wasn't forthcoming at all about a foster family because he had Victoria. With monthly money coming in, it was a nice padding to the business he lost. Also, the child could be used later as a pawn to blackmail."

"But doesn't Roman already have a treasure trove of finances? His family is wealthy."

"Roman's family owns much of Chicago's Gold Coast area, but not him—at least not at first. Since his dad wanted him to learn the business from the ground up, it included little pay. Roman Sr. wanted to make men of his sons, starting with having them earn their income."

"How do you know all this?"

"When the Morelli family went to trial, I did in-depth research. And since that time, I've learned a lot more. Roman lost his pants when the fishing business with Victor went belly up. It didn't hurt Victor one iota, but back then it sure crushed Roman since he'd invested all he had. Wiped him completely out. At the time, he was newly married to a woman who was under the mistaken impression she had married into Chicago's wealth and power. Reality set in and now he had to do something. The extra finances helped smooth things over. So now he has Victoria as a future pawn and also a monthly flow of cash from his odious ex-business partner."

"And you learned this all from your investigation?" Jack was skeptical.

"I also heard it from Roman. Only Roman tried to pin the care of Victoria for five years on another family. There wasn't another family. He took care of Victoria himself. His wife left him by then," Toni explained.

"This sounds farfetched."

"Five years after the baby's birth, Victor's brother

and his wife wanted another child but not a biological one due to fear of having another handicapped child. They decided to adopt. Victor saw this as an opportunity to be near his daughter—and bought out the house right next door. He asked for his daughter back. This time though, they hired a lawyer who would keep the secret of her birthright and do the paperwork legally. Then all records are burned in a fire. Pretty neat how all that fell into place for the mayor."

Jack nodded. "And since Victoria wasn't the target of the poison, and the mayor was, I better call Saverino. If you're right, the threat on the mayor's life remains. He needs more security. By the way, there's still something I can't figure out. Why Roman never told Emily about who Vickie really was. It would've been perfect revenge."

"I think murdering the mayor is the perfect revenge. Where do we go from here?"

"I walk you to your front door and call Saverino. If he's not still up, this is important enough to get him up."

"Hold on. There's only one problem. Victoria's adoptive parents said she came to them dirty, sick and malnourished. That doesn't make sense. Roman's family would have treated her well."

"We can't figure it all out. Let's just go with what we have."

"Something is off about this."

Toni parked in The Ivanhoe's parking lot. Jack walked her to the door. "You should've let me drop you off, Jack. I've driven home all alone at night before."

"Not tonight. Tonight, I take you home to your door. Tonight was special. We had a date, we worked the case, and got the mayor out of bed to question him. Dates don't get much better than that."

"I can think of how this perfect night can get even better." Toni took his hand and lead him inside, up the steps, into her apartment.

Chapter 44

District Attorney Ari Reynolds peered at them over his horn-rimmed glasses. He looked none too pleased that Agent Postell was again in his chambers; the woman who single-handedly almost shot down his entire career over the Morelli debacle. The revelation of faulty evidence coupled with newspaper reports of innocent men sitting on death row made for a dicey couple of years. With the election recently over, Ari maintained his seat by a hair-splitting margin.

"Hello, Detective Autry. What do you have for me this time, Agent Postell?"

Reynolds resembled every bit of the tyrant she knew him to be. He touched his fingers tips together, playing the role of all knowing judge and jury. Perhaps this was his way to begin to even the score. With so much at stake, she'd let him make his power stand.

Jack and Toni sat opposite of him. She'd be darned if she let this man catch her shaking in her skin. Smartly, Toni drew up her chin in Reynolds' direction and answered, "We want to bring Roman Morelli to you on a silver platter. Our evidence will be correct and airtight."

"I seem to remember you making the same assertion last time I spoke with you in my chambers, Special Agent Postell, or should I say Miz Postell."

"It's your preference."

"I'm not so eager to jump back into court with you." This man was all about payback.

"My information was correct, just as it was the last time," she pointed out.

"I disagree but I'm not anxious to rehash old times. You also should be aware that I'm not inclined to listen to what you have to say." Slowly, he slid his pen across the papers on his desk.

"Then you'll be letting the killer of the mayor's niece and the attempted murderer of the mayor roam the city streets freely."

"An attempt was made on the mayor's life?"

"We think the real target was the mayor." Toni crossed her arms.

"I need more proof." Reynolds pushed aside his ashtray.

"Dropping the charges against the Morelli family was an honorable thing at the time. However, a new warrant for his arrest on this evidence will be your redemption, sir." Jack's gaze tapered.

"I've gone over all the facts of the case before you got here." Reynolds laid his large hand on a thick folder. "Will the mayor's wife testify to Roman being at their residence the night of the murder? I've already spoken to the mayor. He's reluctant about testifying himself. Doesn't want his name associated with the mob. Pictures of him going to and from court isn't his thing."

"Subpoena him." The room became deadly quiet after Toni's flip comment. Clearing her throat, she added, "The Mayor of Chicago should be treated like any other citizen. Call him in."

Reynolds burst out laughing. "And will you deliver

the subpoena to his doorstep?"

"It'd be my pleasure to do so, but I'll let Detective Autry have the honor."

"You heard her. Does Agent Postell keep her promises?" Reynolds was the kind of man who loved to play with people's emotions.

"Yes, sir." He looked into Toni's eyes. "Special Agent Postell keeps all her promises."

Reynolds flipped through the folder again. Finally closing it, he gave his answer. "I'll sign a warrant for Roman Morelli's car to be impounded. But before I do, connect the poison used in the wine to him and I'll swear out the warrant for his arrest myself. Without that, you get nothing."

"But Roman has lots of cronies on the street. Anyone of them could have given him the drug."

"All you have to do is find the right blooming person among the thorns and have them admit it. Until then, there's no case. I'm not about to get my career trashed again. Believe me, after Special Agent Postell's little act in court the last time; there'll be plenty of scrutiny this time around. I want it so airtight that Roman won't see daylight for the rest of his life." The judge stood to his feet and stared at the door. "You've made lots of important enemies on both sides of the law, Special Agent Postell. Good luck."

Just outside his office, Jack said, "Any ideas on where we start to find out who passed the drug to Roman?"

"We start with the Princess."

"Who?"

"Roman has a female bodyguard slash bartender. You should see her. Big gal. Strong too."

"Princess." He hummed.

"Get her to talk about Roman. Maybe she knows about the drug," Toni said.

"Since you seem to know her, why can't you get this information?"

"I don't think she likes me. Didn't I tell you? Roman wanted me kicked out of his place. Princess made it happen."

"Tell you what. Let's sit out on the street in my car across from his place for a few hours and see what happens. Not a good idea to walk in on his territory and start asking questions. Don't want to raise suspicions. Right now, Roman is edgy enough. If Princess comes out of the place, we'll both have a talk with her. Let's see if we can think of a reason to take her down to the station for it. Then she'll be on my home territory."

Chapter 45

Princess

People hustled in and out of Roman's place all afternoon. Mainly men. Occasionally, a hardened looking braless woman sauntered through the door. They looked helpless to do anything but to destroy themselves.

The afternoon sun coming through the car windows made Toni sleepy. To keep awake, she needed to keep talking. "Roman has insulated himself so well that linking this drug to him is going to be difficult. And I have the feeling Reynolds is using this excuse as a way of getting back at me."

"I think he doesn't want to make the same mistake twice. We know Roman bought a bottle of wine using the mayor's name and credit card. But he's got a point; unless we can link the drug to him, all we have are credit card fraud and a lot of circumstantial evidence. And all that's happened to Roman is a slap on the wrist for impersonating the mayor."

"I agree," Toni admitted. "We may have to settle for credit card fraud, just like the city once had to do with Dillinger and tax evasion."

"No good. I want Roman on murder charges."

Two men got into a brawl on the street, cursing while smashing bottles on each other's heads. Within seconds, a blue and white with flashing lights pulled up and hauled the brawlers away. In the meantime, Princess, dressed in a pink leotard bodysuit and a matching jacket with her trademark boa, ran out of the lounge and headed toward their car.

Toni was shocked when the woman opened the rear door and slid into the backseat.

"Hi, guys." Princess waved with two-inch pink glittery fingernails.

"That's Princess?" Jack asked.

"That's Princess."

"Sorry if I was too rough on you last week," Princess said.

"I bruise easily. What's up?" Miniscule boa feathers flew, making Toni sneeze again.

"I'll say in a sec. First, who's the cutie?" Princess pointed at Jack.

"The cutie is none-other-than Homicide Detective Jack Autry."

"Drum role, please," Jack said turning a bit red from embarrassment.

"Ah, I've heard of you. Hey, let's ride around for a bit, okay?" She glanced about nervously while sliding down in the seat. "I can't be seen talking to you."

"Sure." Jack put the car in gear and pulled into traffic.

"Let me see your purse," Toni insisted.

Without hesitation, Princess tossed it into the front seat.

Jack drove, glancing in the rearview mirror. Toni turned enough to keep an eye on her as she went through the purse. Make up, brush, false eyelashes, and a couple of dollars. Toni passed it back to her. A suspect in the backseat was always a cause for concern.

"I'm not carrying heat on me. Jack can frisk me if he'd like," Princess offered, holding open her arms.

"What do we owe your unexpected visit?" Jack asked.

"I used to be employed in the prosecutor's office, Jack. But your girl here with her good efforts got the Morelli family acquitted. Trouble upon trouble occurred. The office was downsized. There was no place to go for work but Roman."

"Ironic." Toni rolled her eyes.

"Isn't it," Princess agreed.

"There are no other jobs in the city for a highly educated woman but with the crime family?" Toni retorted with sharp sarcasm.

"Not if you want evidence on him. I was upfront with Roman when I told him I had worked in the prosecutor's office. I flashed him my muscles and told him I'd be a dynamite bodyguard for him. Jared Pirelli, AKA Frosty, helped me build my frame, isn't that ironic too? Since I couldn't jail Roman, I thought I might as well join him. He agreed. Here I am!" Pink Princess flailed her arms about. More boa feathers ornamented the air. "But actually, I put myself undercover to get the bastard."

"I don't understand," Jack said.

"I'm here to take him down. But only the three of us know that plus Reynolds."

"And here you are with us, why?"

"Reynolds called me this morning. Said the only thing between Roman and a warrant for his arrest is the drug that was poured into some fancy bottle of wine. I did a search through his medicine cabinet. Not too smart, what you need was front and center. I got it for you with Roman's prints all over it. I love to get my man."

"Princess, I love you!" Jack crooned.

"You don't happen to be married, are you?" Princess asked, being very flirty.

From her back waistband, she took a small bottle with liquid inside, wrapped in plastic, then tossed it to them. It hit the dashboard and broke.

"I don't suppose there's another bottle with his fingerprints all over it in there?" Jack sighed.

Chapter 46

At the forensics lab, carpet yarns from Roman's trunk were pulled from their tubes and then put into the polarized light optical machine. "I see calcite on these. Now let's see how these fibers compare." Brady was animated. "They overlap nicely."

"Then it's a match?" Toni asked.

"So far, but we have to be sure it's the same material, which I'll do now." Brady spent several minutes looking through the microscope. "Yup, they're both the identical wool blend. I'd call it a match."

"We got him!" Jack said.

"We have the car she was transported in. But we still don't have his fingerprints or the murder weapon," Toni pointed out. "I have a nice story all planned for Roman."

"Does this story mean you're seeing him again?" Jack asked.

"It does."

"Then you wear a wire."

"What's this talk about a wire, and why are you even here, Agent Postell?" Palmer inquired, as he walked into the room.

"Got a minute?"

After discussing the recent events in the case, Palmer officially reinstated her as she wired up. Reynolds' name went a long way with Palmer.

Just as they were leaving, Brady stopped them. "I just got the DNA results on Victor Taylor and Victoria Taylor. It's not a match. She isn't his blood daughter. No relation."

"What? That's impossible," Jack said.

"Are you sure?"

"We ran it many times."

"Then where did this baby named Victoria come from? Where is the mayor's biological daughter?"

"Does the mayor know she wasn't his child?"

"One problem at a time to solve. Come on." Jack pulled her toward the car.

****

Agent Postell pushed through the front door of the lounge. "I need to speak with Roman Morelli."

"He's in the backroom," the bartender said.

"Good."

"Stop right there!" he hollered, now wielding a bat.

She held up a folded paper. "I have a warrant for his arrest."

He blasted a belly laugh. "You're going to need more than that piece of paper to arrest Roman if you've come alone to get him."

"I'm not alone." Toni pulled her Magnum from her purse and held it up. "I brought my friend." Toni continued through the back double doors. "Roman Morelli! FBI. I'm here to arrest you!"

She caught him going out the back window of the bathroom. "Stop there, I have a gun aimed at your backside."

Roman looked around. "Where's everyone else?"

"I've come alone."

He smiled and sat on the toilet seat. "So, this might

not really be an arrest?"

"We'll see. I have this warrant for your arrest, but when I left the DA, I noticed the date is missing. My bad. However, I have a pen in my purse. I can jot in the date. Or—"

"What do you want from me?"

"Princess stole something from you."

"Oh, you heard about that?" He acted more at ease, which pleased Toni because his cockiness would throw him off balance.

"We picked her up. She's in jail."

"Good, that's just where she belongs. You want me to press charges?"

"You can press charges only if what she stole from you is yours."

"Of course, it was mine. Send her away."

"So, the little vial she took was yours?" Toni wanted to make sure they were discussing the same poison and not have it tossed out later.

"Yes. I am certain."

"What was in the vial? Name the drug."

He turned pale. "Now I get your game." He stood to his feet.

"What was in the vial?"

"I have no idea." He shrugged.

"You just said Princess stole something from you."

"I never said that; Princess has nothing of mine." He was calm again.

Toni noticed his medicine cabinet was open. As she stepped toward it for a closer look, Roman rushed toward her, toppling her over the sink and then headed straight out into the lounge where Special Agent Palmer and a dozen FBI agents waited.

Two officers grabbed him as Jack searched Roman, finding the vial in his hand. "Roman Morelli, you're charged for the murder of Victoria Taylor and the attempted murder of the Mayor of Chicago, Victor Taylor," Agent Palmer said.

"Are you nuts or what?" He shouted as two officers cuffed his wrists.

"You bought the wine the mayor drinks. Then you laced it with poison," Toni said. "Then you carried it to his home."

"You can't prove any of this!"

"One of the restaurant buyers clearly remembers you only by a different name—Victor Taylor," Toni said.

"It sounds to me like you should be arresting the mayor and not me. Victor asked I buy the bottle for him."

"Your face stuck in the buyer's head because you kept calling, bugging him for the wine for weeks on end. Not realizing he may be dealing with the Mayor of Chicago, he thought he was dealing with just another impatient customer and couldn't wait to see what you looked like. When you came in and signed the credit card for the purchase, your face stuck in his memory. He's confident in picking you out of the lineup we have waiting back at the precinct." Jack jerked him toward the front.

"You can't prove it's the same bottle."

"But we can, and we already did. The bottom of the bottle is stamped with a special number indicative only to that brand in a series, unique to the store. The bottle has it, the owner will testify. Plus, it does have your fingerprints."

"Emily Taylor is ready to testify that the bottle you gave to the Taylors is the bottle Victoria took."

"I'd never hurt her."

"That I believe. But you would murder the mayor."

"On the night of the murder, you went to the mayor's house to leave the poisoned wine—only it wasn't being brought as a gift by you, because you would've been identified as the gift bearer. The mayor had mentioned that day he was taking his wife out for dinner. You used that opportunity to leave it in their house. Just as you were getting into your car, the mayor and his wife arrived home. They called you, inviting you inside and you had to accept or it would have been too suspicious. Inside, you and the mayor chatted a bit while Emily Taylor went into the kitchen to make dessert. Meanwhile, Victoria comes over looking for something special to drink and unwittingly is given your poisoned wine bottle. When she gets back to her place through the tunnel, the congressman soon leaves. Victoria takes a shower. Now alone and in her nightgown and bathrobe, she drinks about sixteen ounces.

"About that time, Emily mentions to her husband that Vickie came over and took a bottle of his favorite wine back to her place—the bottle you gave to them. Not wanting Vickie to be harmed, you excused yourself to use the restroom and went through the tunnel, but it was too late. Victoria was dead. You put a coat around her, wrapped her body in plastic that you found in a moving box from the basement and placed her in the nonfunctioning coal bin on her side of the basement along with her baguette and identification.

"You visited a few minutes more with the mayor

and his wife before leaving. When they went to bed, you drove to the back of Victoria's house and put her body in the trunk of your car. You didn't know what to do. Then you remembered about the park murders so you took her there. But while depositing the body, you saw another murder taking place. The Lincoln Park serial killer. You ran. You returned to the mayor's and sealed the outside door," Toni finished.

"Is your warrant for the murder of Victoria Taylor?" Roman asked.

"Yes, it is," Jack answered.

"Then it's not any good. It's not Victoria Taylor who died." Roman seemed sure.

"What are you talking about?" Jack called his bluff.

"Someone else drank the poison, but it wasn't the one you all call Victoria Taylor. The warrant is written wrong, and you can't hold me. You'll see."

"This is just more of his feeble excuses. Let's go," Palmer instructed as the agents put Roman into the back of a police sedan. At rush hour, it took an hour to get to the downtown Bureau. Toni and Jack were in the room with Roman when he was questioned.

"Tell us, Roman. What happened to the mayor's child? We know the person who died at the park wasn't his biological child," Toni said.

Roman seemed anxious to tell his story. "Victor gave three-day-old Vickie to me with instructions to find her a home, and my intention was to do just that. But when I brought her home, my wife and I fell head over heels in love with her. It sounds goofy but we did. My wife had just lost a baby, so this seemed like a gift. He even offered us money each month for her care. Of course, I never told Victor that the family I found for his daughter was mine. Then five years later, Victor wants her back, just like that. By that time, she was ours—our daughter—although not legally, but every way that really mattered. I just couldn't let her go. And I didn't. I never gave Victor's daughter back to him. Not ever."

"If you didn't give his daughter back, who is Victoria?"

We renamed Victoria Taylor, Dovie Morelli, the name of the baby we just lost. It was easy to get birth papers on her. Why not? Her own father Victor rejected her once, and we loved her. He couldn't snap his fingers and get her back. Do you know he even stopped us on the street once to talk to us when she was three years old, and he didn't even know that she was his daughter?"

"We need to check your story. Where is Dovie?"

"I don't know."

"Roman!"

"I'm telling the truth. Soon after her eighteenth birthday, she left—ran off with some low life. Never came back. Never called. Although I've tried along with my family members, we never found her. It broke up our marriage."

"If what you say is true, then who is the girl in Victoria Taylor's grave?"

"Her name is Patty. Patty lies in Victoria Taylor's grave."

"Who?" Jack asked, not sure he was biting.

"A girl no one has ever searched for. When the mayor said he wanted Dovie back, my wife and I had no other choice but to leave the country forever. My father began making the arrangements. The day before we left, I decided to take Dovie one last time to her favorite place in the world, Lincoln Park Zoo. We wanted to see the animals and say goodbye to her favorite, the giraffes. We were eating cotton candy when Dovie pointed out a bony, filthy girl in a torn dress looking through garbage for food. Anyway, I didn't think any kid should go hungry, so I bought the girl a couple of hot dogs. Boy, she sure gobbled those down fast. Then this wretched looking street woman walked up to us. It turned out it was her mother. She thanked me for buying her daughter food. Then she actually offered her daughter to me for one hundred dollars' cash.

"Victor needed a daughter, and she needed a real family. I looked at this unwanted street girl and then back at my sweet girl. They were about the same age, so why not? Victor hadn't seen his daughter since she was a baby. He'd never know. In one moment, all our problems were solved, the mayor would be given Patty. Patty would get a good home. I handed her mother the hundred, and just like that, Patty was mine and all my problems were over."

"You bought a little girl?" Jack was livid.

"Yes, I did. If I didn't someone else would have and let me tell you they might not have been so nice to her. This street child was given a family, a home, and a fine education," Roman defended himself. "Victoria was loved, and given opportunities, growing into a successful woman who worked in the office of a powerful successful man."

"And a poisoned bottle of wine," Jack added.

"And you have no case."

"How about attempted murder of the mayor? How about buying a child?" Jack asked.

Chapter 47

Spring
Lake Mendota, Wisconsin

All the roads of her life in some form seemed to lead back to her mother; through thought, splashes of memories, old photographs, and cloned mannerisms. And now without more excuses to keep her away, Toni drove the long winding road through the familiar Wisconsin countryside to see the woman who gave her life, the woman who sang her to sleep, the one who took her to movie premiers, until that fateful bright sunny morning when they lost more than Suzette. That was the day they also lost one another and a part of themselves.

Arriving at the asylum, Toni inquired of the ebony buxom nurse, "How's my mom today, Sophie?"

She smiled and clapped her hands. "Each day I see a little bit more improvement while at other times I think she regresses. But then suddenly she becomes perfectly clear for short spurts at a time."

"Clear?"

"Yes, cobwebs dissolve from her mind and then Lillian Palmer re-emerges. But then the webs suddenly return unexpectedly again. But she's improving."

"You are a gem. She's so lucky to have you."

"My goodness sakes, girl, she's a joy to care for.

I've seen all her movies too. Don't let me take up anymore of your time. Go see your Mama."

Toni found her mother seated in the same chair as the last time. The small cliff of snow on the outside sill was melting in the sunlight.

"Hi, Mama." Toni gave her a kiss on the cheek. Her mother was unaware of her presence until the physical touch, and then she jumped.

"Oh, Antoinette. You just missed your father. Maybe you saw him in the hallway?"

"Papa? Papa was here?" Toni looked from the doorway to her mother.

"Yes, only moments ago."

How wonderful it would be to see her papa. Turning about she spotted Sophie standing in the doorway shaking her head no. No, Papa hadn't come.

Toni sucked back her obvious disappointment. "I brought a gift for you, Mama."

"Is this a celebration of just wrapping up my latest movie?"

"Your latest movie?" Toni glanced back toward the doorway where Sophie had stood only a second ago but now her spot was empty. For privacy, Toni pushed the door closed. "What movie was that?"

"China Town."

"Wasn't Jack Nicholson in that?"

"Little Jack is my co-star. Some say it's my finest movie performance ever. I'm a shoo-in for another Oscar. I want you children to attend with me this time."

"Here's your gift." Toni handed her a small box wrapped in white tissue paper.

Tearing off the paper, she opened the lid and took out a picture of the family before Suzette was taken.

She let go a whimper and covered her mouth. "Oh, look at this beautiful family. I once had a family that looked like this one."

Her mother fell silent holding the frame to her chest, gazing out the window. How beautiful she remained despite all her mental battles. Watching her mother nod off, Toni picked up a shawl and wrapped it around the woman's narrow shoulders. "Mama, I need to leave now, but I'm going to find our Suzette for you. I'll bring her home."

Without opening an eyelid, her mother spoke. "Daniel Hughes."

"Uncle Danny?"

She snapped her head up, jerking forward. Eyes opened.

"Mama, what's wrong? Tell me."

"He knows about Suzette. He knows." Lillian seethed.

"Mama, yes, that's right. Uncle Danny knows."

"Yes-s-s-s," she hissed with glazed eyes. "He knows because he is the one who took her." Looking into her mother's hazel eyes she saw hatred. The room suddenly became smaller and stuffy.

"Mama, you're wrong. It was a woman who took Suzette."

"He hates Franco. He hates you," Lillian pointed her finger up into her daughter's face, "and he hates Andre as well. But most of all he hates Suzette!"

"You're confused. It's simply not true."

Now her mother turned to face Toni. "He had someone come for you children to take you all away from me, to get even with me for leaving him. Daniel knew all three of you would be on your way to Sunday school. You all were supposed to disappear. But his plans were ruined when Andre got sick and stayed home. You were strong. You fought off your attacker. Only Suzette was taken. But it was enough. It was too much of a loss. Daniel Hughes is a brutal man. I had to escape him. Your father helped me get away from the evil, evil man." Lillian wept hysterically.

Dropping to her knees, Toni cried out, "Mama, Mama, calm down. Please calm down. I can't take it when you get like this." She brushed Lillian's hair back from her face. Her mother's eyes grew glassy, her spirit unreachable. Lillian finally spit out one more sentence, "He uses money as a tool for his evil ways. Remember, Antoinette, remember." Suddenly, she stopped talking and moving.

"Mama, come back to me. I miss you so much—I miss you even more than Suzette. Can you hear me at all?"

Leaving her for a moment, Toni raced down the corridor to the nurse's station. "Where's Sophie? I need Sophie now."

"Calm down, here I am." Sophie came down the hall pushing a rattling cart filled with afternoon snacks.

"Thank God! Sophie, something's happened to my mother."

"I'm coming to have a look at our Ms. Lillian." Sophie hurried back to the room. Seeing the state of the patient, Sophie ran back out again and quickly returned with a hypodermic. "Here, sweet Angel, just hold on for a minute more and things will be fine, just fine. Don't you fret." The long needle easily slipped into the soft tissue. The liquid in the tube slowly disappeared into her arm. Her mother's eyes fluttered to the back of her head.

"Ohhh-h," Lillian murmured.

"There, there."

Toni and Sophie helped Lillian to her bed.

"What is going on with her? She seems crazy—she's saying crazy things! I thought you said she's getting better?" Toni burst into tears.

"Sometimes, I said 'sometimes'. The more lucid she becomes on the drugs the more the past reveals itself to her and that's when she breaks down."

"Could she be remembering things which aren't true?"

"Of course. Things get all somersaulted inside that brain of hers. Go on home now and let me care for Ms. Lillian. I'll call you in the morning. She'll be better by then."

Chapter 48

Summer
Chicago, Illinois

On the busy street beneath the shadow of the El, Toni admired the new sign, hanging tandem beneath Uncle Herschel's shoe repair sign. Shaped like a lamb, the words LOST LAMBS INVESTIGATIONS were hand painted.

"Good sign, Postit." Jack strolled up the street. "Yup, I like it. You'll do well. Now that you've resigned from the FBI and have your own private eye business, do you mind if I swing some business your way?"

"I insist that you do. Mind if I use some of your police resources?"

"I insist that you do," he parroted back with a beguiling smile. There were those dimples again.

And here came her heart racing after him again.

"Great, then we're still partners." Toni cupped her hand over her eyes, shading them from the dazzling summer sun.

"Okay, here are the conditions."

"More conditions? You know I don't make deals."

"Your days are your own, Postit, but when murder hits this city, be sure to save the night for me. I'll be looking up from the crime scene for that relic bus of yours."

"Watson. Its name is Watson."

Jack laughed.

"Just look around at this wonderful city of ours. Tell me what you see?" Toni asked.

"I see lots of people who appear to be in bad frame of mind."

"Yes, and someone knows their name."

"Even mine," Jack said.

"Especially yours."

"I've been thinking about what your mother told you. Do you believe Mallory's dad had Suzette kidnapped?"

"Absolutely not. That man has been there for Andre and me our whole lives. Uncle Danny even saw to it I went to college. He helped Andre with his loan when he first bought his business years back. My mother's reality and illusion run neck in neck in her mind. Her baseless accusations are only the ranting of an insane woman triggered by her desire to find her youngest daughter."

"Spoken as a true profiler with a degree in behavioral science. I bet I know what your primary case will be."

"Suzette and Victoria, or should I say 'Dovey'?"

"For help, you can count on me, Postit."

"I know I can." Toni cupped her hand to Jack's face. "Meanwhile, I already have my first official paying case."

"Would that be to find the mayor's biological daughter?"

"Yes."

"You certainly have your work cut out for you.

You've got big dreams, Postit."

"You gotta dream, Autry."

"Hold fast to dreams
For if dreams die
is a broken-winged bird
That cannot fly,'" Jack quoted.

Toni continued, "'Hold fast to dreams
For when dreams go
Life is a barren field
Frozen with snow.' Langston Hughes."

Jack grinned and Toni loved it.

"I have something for you." He pulled a small box from his pocket.

Toni snatched it. "Thanks, I love gifts."

She lifted the lid to a gold dress clip adorned with Czech glass, resting on a white cotton puff. It was in the shape a large crane with seed pearls. "This is beautiful! Thank you." Then she noticed a long black narrow cord attached to it. Puzzled she looked up at Jack.

"It's a camera. The bird's eye is the lens. Now you'll get not only what others are saying from fifty feet away and will be able to see what they're doing when you get home."

"Now I *really* love it!" She stood on her tiptoes and kissed his lips.

"Tell me, how does it make you feel that your profile on the Lincoln Park Murders was spot on about the killer?"

"It's rewarding in the sense that I might be of help in catching the next one. Unfortunately, there'll always be the next one. The D.A. called last night with the news that Jared Pirelli's trial is in a few months."

"Will you be spending time in court on that one?"

"If course. Won't you?"

"Sitting right beside you—but prepared for a possible plea bargain."

"Pirelli won't go for it. He wants to appear misunderstood and woo the female jurors. And more news. Along with my new business, I was recently asked to teach a class to new profilers."

"You're amazing."

The bell over the door jangled. Princess walked out the shoe shop barefoot in a Daisy Duke outfit.

Jack's jaw slacked. "Princess?"

"Princess."

"I'm surprised to see you here," Jack said.

"Didn't Toni tell you? We're in business together. I'm her new assistant. And by the way, my real name is Zoe Witherspoon."

"Zoe needs a job and I need a law expert."

"This'll suit me fine and sooner or later, I'll pass that bar exam. I believe in me."

"She's your law expert?" Jack turned back toward Toni, who smiled at him in a new way. "There's a certain fragrance about you, Toni."

Uncle Hershel appeared in the doorway. "Hey, what are all you doing out here on the street talking when there's bobka and turkey and hard rolls and many other Kosher delights are inside to be eaten? Come, come!"

"I'm coming right now, Uncle Hershel." Princess sashayed back inside.

"You go ahead, Jack. I'll be there in a minute."

"Do me one favor?"

"Sure."

"Keep your heart open for love this year."

"I'm not sure I'm any good at love."

"I'll catch you if you fall." He stared at her intensely.

"Jack?" Her heart caught and in that moment, she felt the beginnings of love.

"I'm going in for some bobka now. Don't be long." He tucked her into his side and kissed her lightly on the lips. It made her feel safe, cared for—that somehow things would be alright not only between them, but also in finding her sister. Jack would be there with her if she tripped up or needed his shoulder.

Toni watched him enter the shop and the door closed. She looked up into the bright blue sky, thankful for this extraordinary time in her life.

"Hey there, Toni! Your sign looks great!" Erma hollered, waving her small arm out of the window of the street sweeper. A few drops of water from the sprayer hit her arms. The sound from the bristles was nearly deafening.

"Hi yourself! How are you?"

"Great! I'm on Allen's radar so I better keep rolling. We'll talk later!"

A car horn drew her attention from the firmament back to the sooty city street where a limo pulled up at the curb. A man stepped out onto the sidewalk.

"What are you doing here, Uncle Danny?" Toni asked with a joyful lilt to her voice. "It's so good to see you."

"I hear you're opening a new business. 'Lost Lambs', huh? With your uncle's shoe business, I guess this makes you a real gumshoe now. Here, I've come to contribute." He handed her a folded check.

Toni opened it and the amount nearly bowled her

over. "Wow, I think this'll support the business and me for an entire year while I get on my feet. You're wonderful, thanks." She threw her arms around him and hugged him, but then remembered her mother's words and quickly drew back. 'He hates you…hates Franco, hates Pierre, and he hates Suzette most of all. He uses his money as a tool for evil'.

Without missing a beat, he added, "After helping Mallory, it's the least I can do. Now go out and save all those missing children."

"That's the plan." She rocked back on her heels, feeling incredibly thankful.

"By the way, leave sleeping dogs lie with Suzette," he cautioned. "I hired plenty of private eyes over the years and they came up empty-handed. We need to accept the fact she's gone forever. Let's look to the future. See you later, my dear." Quickly, he climbed back into the limo.

Toni watched the back of his vehicle drive away. Something was wrong. Toni stared down at the check. It didn't feel right, this money. It felt dirty.

"I'm coming, Suzette," she whispered in determination. With sharp, quick movements, Toni tore it into tiny pieces and threw it into the gutter. "You betcha—I'm coming, Suzette."

A word about the author…

I grew up in the Lincoln Park area of Chicago, Illinois. The mob was a part of supplying my dad's nightclub, a speakeasy at the time, with alcohol. The Ivanhoe Restaurant still stands in its original form as a castle on Clark St. and Wellington Ave. According to family history, Mob boss Bugsy Malone supplied boot legged alcohol which was stored by Grandpa Jansen in large quantities at his Iowa farm in a deep hole on the property. To conceal it, he parked his car over the deep hole where the alcohol was kept. In the 1930's Al Capone and Bugsy had an ongoing street war over my dad's establishment. These days, the place is a legit alcohol and cigar flagship store (my hard liquor drinking, cigar smoking dad, Harold Jansen, would be proud).

Fun Fact: As a teen, I dated the son of a mob boss, who later went on to run a Chicago transportation company.

A bit about me. I have two adult children, two teenage grandsons, and two rescue dogs. I'm a retired teacher and live near Dallas, Texas.

Thank you for purchasing
this publication of The Wild Rose Press, Inc.

For questions or more information
contact us at
info@thewildrosepress.com.

The Wild Rose Press, Inc.
www.thewildrosepress.com